Just Getting Started

Timber Falls, Volume 5

Fiona West

Published by Fiona West, 2021.

This is a work of fiction. Similarities to real people, places, or events are entirely coincidental.

JUST GETTING STARTED

First edition. May 18, 2021.

Copyright © 2021 Fiona West.

Written by Fiona West.

This book is dedicated to my friends, family, acquaintances, and book buddies bravely pursuing recovery. I see you. You can do this.

Author's Note

THANK YOU FOR READING Just Getting Started! I hope you'll enjoy it. Please be advised that Chase's recovery from opioids is a central plot line in this book, including an opening scene where he nearly overdoses and is arrested. There is no other drug use depicted in the book, but recovery is a common topic of conversation for the characters.

I realize many people may not have read the first four books (or have just forgotten!), so here's a list of essential characters. Don't be intimidated: it's probably excessive, but this book has more characters than most since Lizzie spends so much time in the community. This list is just a failsafe in case you get overwhelmed.

Enjoy, book buddies!

CAST OF CHARACTERS

- **Chase Robert Carpenter**: Son of Harrison and Carmen Carpenter, stepson of Willow Carpenter. Twin brother of Christopher, older brother of Carter. Works in marketing at Timber Falls Paper Products. Recovering from opioid addiction. Falling in love with Lizzie.

- **Elizabeth (Lizzie) Louise Painter**: Granddaughter of Tansy Draper. Daughter of Penelope and Barry Painter (deceased). Sister to Charlotte (Lottie). Deputy with the Linn County Sherriff's Department, focusing on Timber Falls. Shy. Falling in love with Chase.

- **Tansy Draper**: Lizzie's grandmother, who moved up from California when Lizzie was twelve to care for her after her parents died. Real estate agent.

- **Charlotte Painter**: Lizzie's sister. Dating Jeremy, whom she met on an app. Pharmacist.

- **Jeremy**: Lottie's boyfriend. Clueless and spineless.

- **Captain Hansen**: Lizzie's boss. Checked up on Lizzie and Lottie after their parents died. Retiring this year so he can take his wife on trips before they're too old to enjoy them.

- **Mark Wright**: Lizzie's new boss. Originally from Silverton, Oregon.
- **Sergeant Hillerman**: Lizzie's desk buddy at work and sometimes partner.
- **Pancake**: Lizzie's yellow lab. Also her best friend. His best friend is a tennis ball.
- **Harrison Carpenter**: Grade-A jerk. Also Chase's dad. CEO of Timber Falls Paper Products.
- **Willow Carpenter**: Chase's stepmother. Recently diagnosed with early-onset Alzheimer's. Her story is told in *Right Back Where We Started*.
- **Carmen Carpenter**: Chase's biological mom. Left when he was young.
- **Christopher Carpenter**: Chase's twin. Lives in New York and works for a subsidiary of Timber Fall Paper Products called Albany Paper. Does not come home for holidays. Does not have girlfriends.
- **Carter Carpenter**: Chase's younger brother. Works as an actuary in Salem. Engaged to Martina Lopez, who is also his stepmother's nurse. His story is told is *Right Back Where We Started*.
- **Martina Lopez**: Engaged to Chase's brother, Carter. Works as a nurse practitioner for the Carpenter family in caring for Willow, Chase's stepmom. Her story is told in *Right Back Where We Started*.
- **Mrs. Sánchez:** Works for the Carpenters. Very close to Willow and the boys. Tolerates Harrison (barely).

- **Harriet (Hattie) Meyer-Bagsby:** the unofficial mayor of Timber Falls and the owner of Timber Falls Paper Products. Long-time friend to both families. Part of Tansy Draper's book club, The Mind Readers.
- **Kyle Durand:** Son of Evan and Farrah Durand, brother to Daniel, Philip and Maggie. ER Doctor. Engaged to Ainsley Buchanan. Autistic. His story is told in *Must Be a Mistake*.
- **Ainsley Buchanan:** Daughter of Gary and Nancy Buchanan. Engaged to Kyle Durand. Elementary school teacher. Nosy and overcommitted. Her story is told in *Must Be a Mistake*.
- **Maggie Durand:** daughter of Evan and Farrah Durand, sister to Daniel, Kyle, and Philip. High school senior. Quiet rebel.
- **RJ Horowitz:** EMT. Helped when Chase was overdosing.

PROLOGUE:
Chase

TWO YEARS EARLIER

Cold. He was so cold; the shakes and sweats made his sweatshirt feel thin even though it was June. Chase needed a fix; it had been twelve hours since his last one, and there was no way he was going to sleep tonight without a few pills. He'd already called around to friends, but they either didn't answer or had none to spare. Everything hurt; even the mid-morning sun was too much. An injury had gotten him into this mess, and now he was in worse pain than before. He paced around his townhouse, spinning his phone between his hands, unable to sit, unable to rest. He'd worked all night, and now he just needed a hit, and then he could sleep. Finally, Benji called him back.

"Hey, man." He could hear people noise in the background, the muted rumblings of a large crowd framing Benji's voice.

"Hey. You got anything for me?" Chase cringed at his own abruptness, but he was too desperate for pleasantries. His stomach lurched, but he swallowed it down.

"Yeah, I got something. But I can't get away. Girlfriend wanted to go to the centennial thing . . ." Oh, right; Chase remembered kicking in some money at Timber Falls Paper Products for the event when they'd passed the hat.

He grimaced. Downtown Timber Falls was going to be full of people who knew him; things like this were better done elsewhere, but . . . but he couldn't say no. He literally needed it.

"Okay. Where are you?"

"East side of downtown. By Past Presents, that antique place . . ."

"Okay."

"See you."

Once he hung up, Chase threw up, wiped his mouth on the back of his hand, then got into the car. The heat wasn't helping his nausea. Once downtown, parking wasn't easy to find. The town had been planning this party for a year; couldn't they have figured that there would be too many people? Oh. There was a shuttle, bringing people over from the high school parking lot so maybe they had. Man, he needed a hit. Just a little one. He jostled his way through the crowds of families; the smell of food and sunscreen was not helping. He finally found Benji near the dunk tank.

"Hey, man."

"You got it?"

"Not even a hello?" his friend teased. Though Chase wasn't sure Benji really counted as a friend; this was a business transaction.

Chase stared down at the lollipop Benji held out, disbelief making his headache throb harder. "What the hell is that?"

"It's good stuff."

"Those aren't Vikes. I need my pills, I'm in *pain*."

"Trust me, man, you'll be feeling no pain. It's good stuff. Just take it already."

"What is it?" Chase pressed, even as he got out his wallet and fished out some cash. He didn't know why he was asking; he was going to take it no matter what. It was all he had.

Benji's girlfriend Jenna came up and threaded her arm through his. "I want cotton candy."

"Course, baby." He pushed the drugs at Chase with a grin, then turned and moved toward the concessions stand. Chase stared down at the berry lollipop in his hand. "Don't eat the whole thing," Benji called over his shoulder, laughing as Jenna dragged him away.

Chase ripped off the wrapper and stuck it in his mouth; it was berry-flavored. Relief flooded his system almost immediately, and he grinned as he tucked the lollipop into his cheek.

"Hello, darling!" His mother waved at him from a booth, and he strolled over to her, hands in his pockets. She air-kissed his cheek. "What a nice surprise."

"Hey, Mom. What are you raising money for this time?" Her booth was intricately floral, almost like a parade float.

"In fact," she sniffed, "as it so happens, I'm not raising money for anything; Councilman Foster asked me to staff the ice cream booth."

He took a good look at her outfit for the first time and started laughing; she was wearing an asymmetrical white linen dress.

"And this outfit said, 'Let's scoop chocolate?' Why?"

Willow scowled lightly. "Just for that, you can't have any. I was lead to believe I'd be supervising, not doing the scooping myself. That turned out to be a misunderstanding..." she said, wiping her hands on a towel, even though she was wearing disposable gloves.

"I don't have any tickets anyway." He looked around. "Is Dad here?"

"I believe so..." After a quick scan of the crowd, her gaze settled back on Chase, eyes narrowing in clear concern. "Are you feeling all right? You're all sweaty."

"Yeah, it's *hot*," he smirked.

"And your eyes..." she started, but he slid away from the booth just as he spotted his brother.

"I see Carter; I'll see you later, Mom." She'd been making more comments lately about his health. He thought he was hiding things well; he had them under control, for the most part. He needed Vicodin to manage his knee, but it also made him ultra-productive at work. He'd gotten caught up on weeks of marketing copy and ads and emails that he'd left undone for too long. And now, he just wanted to have fun. Lightness and joy were his... he felt he'd float away if given the chance. He pulled out the lollipop; there was still quite a bit left.

Might as well finish it.

"Hey." His brother was hanging out with some of his Salem friends, a pretty black-haired woman was hanging off him; damn, one of them might've had Vikes for him.

"Hey. What're you doing here?"

"Just came to hang out."

"Really?" Carter raised an eyebrow. "You don't like crowds . . ."

"I don't mind them so much sometimes . . . like today." He laughed, and several people near them turned to look at him. Couldn't they see? Didn't get they feel it too, the color and sugar and sunshine? They were all invading his mind at once, it was impossible to push out the glory of them. The goodness, the goodness. He couldn't help being loud; he was just *so happy*. There was a live band outside the fire station . . . he loved this song. He charged through the crowd, trying to get closer to them, ignoring people's shouts and grumbles that he'd jostled them. One or two of them might've fallen, he didn't look back to find out. He started dancing with a cute blonde, who quickly pushed him away. He turned to another, who also rebuffed him. *What was their deal?* No, he didn't smell great, but whatever. There had been no time for cologne when he was throwing up. Was that today? He couldn't remember. He didn't feel like throwing up now.

He started belting out the chorus, spinning around under the bright summer sunshine. He couldn't get enough room around him; all those other people were too close, that's why they were getting whacked by his outstretched hands as he spun and spun and spun. Oops, maybe he did still feel like throwing up. That was enough spinning. Now all he wanted was to jam with the band; he'd played a little in college. It would come back to him, as soon as this dumb guitarist let go of the instrument and let him have a try. Why was everyone so against him today? Was he going to have to yank it out of his hands?

"Mr. Carpenter?" A high firm voice had him letting go of the guitar. "Sir, we've had some complaints about your behavior."

"Oh, yeah?" He laughed. "They don't want to have a good time?" He opened his eyes; it was a woman a little younger than he, dressed in a khaki-colored uniform, her straight red hair touching her shoulders. Her name tag said "Painter" in block letters. She didn't look like a house painter . . . Carter was suddenly at his side; where did he come from?

"Sorry, he's just an exuberant guy sometimes," Carter said, giving the woman a sheepish grin. "Come on, Chase, I'll buy you an ice cream."

Her gaze was traveling over him, but it caught on the candy . . . he still had some sense of self-preservation, inside of this euphoria. Chase broke into a run, darting past her, knocking several people into her way, but she was quick. She caught up to him within ten steps; she swept his feet out from under him, and his face was suddenly pressed against the hot asphalt. His arms were hauled behind his back and held, and a bright light flashed in his eyes.

"No pupil reaction; they're tiny. Should we give him the Narcan?"

"I guess so," said another voice, whose owner was also khaki-clad. "We're running low, though."

She pulled the lollipop from his mouth. "What is this?" she asked, and he winced at her volume. Bright sunlight behind her made her hair shimmer and glow . . . she was a red-headed angel.

"You're so pretty," he sighed, and the woman who was probably not a house painter rolled her eyes at him.

"Bag that and we'll test it. I'd bet anything it's fentanyl. Come on, Mr. Carpenter." She yanked him up by his shoulders and marched him toward the cruiser. "You are under arrest for disorderly conduct. You have the right to remain silent. Anything you say can and will be held against you in a court of law . . ." She was still talking, but Chase wasn't listening. He felt good now, he felt better. That was all that mattered. *Fentanyl?* He'd never had anything this strong before. The pain was just a memory now . . . *Benji was right*, he thought, as he flopped over onto the back seat of the sheriff's department cruiser. *That was good stuff.* A moment later, his red-headed angel was shoving an applicator up his nostril and spraying something up into his sinuses. The deputy rolled him onto his side, and he watched the gold chain around her neck sway in front of his face; there was a diamond ring on it.

"Go get RJ, would you? He really should be checked out by a paramedic. I think he's giving little kids a tour of the ambulance."

"Right. On it."

"I wasn't that disorderly, was I?" Chase asked, sleepy now.

"Yes, Mr. Carpenter."

"It's Chase." He didn't want his angel to be so formal. This car seat was more comfortable than he'd thought.

"The noise qualifies. I deemed it unreasonable. Pretty sure everyone else did, too."

"But Angel, I was just singing."

"It's Deputy Painter. Not to mention spinning around, impeding pedestrian traffic, attempted theft, smacking the good people of Timber Falls. You knocked down some kids."

"Did I?" he asked through a yawn. He was antsy. His stomach lurched. "What did you give me, Angel?"

"Stay calm, Mr. Carpenter. I want the paramedic to check you out."

"Chase," he said, looking around frantically, feeling like he needed out of this tiny car now.

"Fine," she said, her tone softening. "Stay calm, Chase. Please."

He moved his shaking hands to pillow his face against the vinyl. He could see his mother through the window, her mouth covered with one still-gloved hand in that foolish white dress, tears in her eyes. Carter was next to her, his face red, hands on his hips, on the phone, shaking his head. He was probably calling their lawyer. He'd have this handled soon enough.

"What's your name?" She tapped her name tag, but he shook his head. "Your first name."

"Lizzie."

"Nice to meet you, Lizzie." He couldn't help but grin at the way the name felt on his tongue. Like it was meant to be there.

Then she was gone, replaced by urgent voices and lights shone forcefully in his eyes.

CHAPTER ONE:
Lizzie

NOVEMBER

"Fan mail, Lizzie," Captain Hansen said, tossing a white, letter-size envelope onto her desk. She rolled her eyes; he always said that, no matter what it was. Not that she got much mail at work. It was probably more junk mail for life insurance policies she didn't need. Being a single woman with only two living relatives, one of whom was pushing ninety, life insurance just didn't make sense. Besides, law enforcement was actually fairly far down the list as far as dangerous jobs: the loggers working for Timber Falls Paper Products, the big employer in town, were in far more danger than she was. Farmers and construction workers, too. Fishermen. Airline pilots. Folks like that. Captain Hansen had been doing this job for thirty years, and he'd never had a major injury. Timberites were, by and large, a good community . . . her thoughts trailed off as she noticed the return address on her mystery envelope: Carpenter, 55 Tumalo Springs, Redmond, OR . . . *Carpenter?* She knew several Carpenters, but her interactions with one in particular stood out. She'd thrown him to the ground and arrested him in front of the entire town. And that being the case, she'd sort of wondered how he'd been since then. Glancing around to make sure no one was paying attention to her, she slid a finger under the flap and opened the letter.

Dear Officer Painter,

I don't know if you'll remember, but you arrested me at the town's centennial celebration. I just wanted to thank you for that. I've been to rehab several times since then, but the program I'm in now is different, and I've been taking a hard look at my life. That moment was a real wake-up call. I know it's maybe an odd thing to write, "thank you for arresting me," but I bet your job is pretty thankless, especially when it involves people like me. I think I knew I had a drug problem before then, but it didn't really occur to me how bad it was. That I was threatening my own life with those painkillers. And I never meant to hurt anyone else.

Anyway, I hope this letter finds you well, and keep up the good work.

Sincerely,

Chase Carpenter

It was written on yellow legal paper in blue pen, which she found unremarkable, but his penmanship . . . it was perfect. He'd printed it, but it was still curved and sloped in such a graceful way, almost playfully, even though it was all impressively uniform. Her own handwriting reminded her of a serial killer; if she were prone to profiling, she would definitely look into her background and known associates. Carefully, she re-folded the letter the way it had come, and tucked it into her backpack; she shared this desk with Sergeant Hillerman. He was close to retirement and probably would take no notice of a random letter in a drawer, but still. She didn't need the whole division knowing she'd gotten *actual fan mail.*

She sensed her approaching visitor before she saw him; Lieutenant Mark Wright didn't seem to think there was a thing as too much cologne. She disagreed.

"Big plans for the weekend, Elizabeth?"

"No." *Do I ever?* Sometimes, she was tempted to lie to him, just to have something to report. What would she even say? *Oh yes, I just remembered, I'm interesting after all. I've got a group of friends that magically materialized overnight, and we're all going out to Annie's. Silly me. Would you like to join us?*

"I was thinking of going downtown . . ." he said, straightening the pile of papers on the corner of her desk subtly.

"Downtown Timber Falls?"

Mark laughed. "No, downtown Portland."

"Oh." She scrunched her freckled nose as a reflex. *Why?*

"Don't you think it's more fun to drink too much when you don't have to worry about anyone you've arrested judging you?"

"I don't really drink." The last time she drank was last Thanksgiving when she'd had half a glass of white wine. It just didn't appeal to her. Besides, if they called her into work, she wanted to be ready. Public service in a small town wasn't without its perils, and apparently, drinking was one of them.

"Why don't you come with me? I think you'd have a great time. You said you didn't have any plans . . ."

"Oh, thank you for the invitation, Lieutenant, but—"

"Elizabeth, I keep telling you to call me Mark."

She squirmed a little in her seat; he was her superior, she should probably do what he wanted.

"Not this weekend, Mark. Thank you, though."

"All right. I'm gonna keep asking, though." He winked at her as he started back across the open office, toward the captain's office.

Great. Something to look forward to . . . Mark wasn't a bad person, but they weren't on the same page. She knew already how it would go with him: they'd drink, talk— though she expected the conversation would be a struggle since they had no common interests beyond law enforcement—then dance maybe. Then kiss goodnight. Then she'd just be alone again. Her grandma would say that it was good to give things a try, but since she hadn't dated since 1967 and never in the age of Tinder, Lizzie didn't think she was a reliable source of information.

"Staff meeting in the conference room," Captain Hansen bellowed from the doorway of his office, and Lizzie wondered briefly if it would be about sexual harassment. She felt like they often scheduled those during a lull, and everyone was around this morning. But she hoped not. She should probably just tell Mark that she didn't want him to continue to ask her out. It wasn't polite. But Lizzie's conflict resolution methods tended toward hinting at what was bothering her until people got tired of her anyway or figured out what she was trying to say. That didn't seem to be working in this case. Well, that was her style unless someone was breaking the law in her town. In which case, her method usually had a lot more to do with knocking on their door and firmly requesting that they come down to the station with her. Pursuing in the rare instance that they ran. Honestly, there wasn't much crime in their town. She didn't credit herself or her colleagues with that. Yes, people were people everywhere, and they did stupid things and needed to be reminded why the rules existed, but it usually wasn't malicious.

Lizzie gravitated with her co-workers toward the conference room, sharing some surprised looks with a few of her fellow officers. Staff meetings usually happened Monday mornings at 8:00 a.m. sharp. This was a Friday, which told Lizzie that he wasn't inviting comment on whatever this was until after the weekend. Either that or Captain Hansen didn't mind if people were blowing up his phone and knocking on his door during the Seahawks game. She sat down and found Mark next to her. She did not stifle her eye roll, but she also didn't let him see it. She had better manners than that. Sue sat down on her other side and patted her knee.

"How are you, sweetheart?"

Lizzie smiled. No one else called her anything like that. They didn't see her as sweet. Sue was their dispatcher and the only other woman at the station. She seemed to feel a kinship with Lizzie over their shared gender that Lizzie didn't reciprocate, but she still appreciated her attempts to chat with her, even if she couldn't keep up. She reminded her of an aunt or something. Most people would probably say a grandmother, but Lizzie's grandmother had destroyed the cuddly grandma image many years ago. Not that she was cold; nothing like it. But she also wouldn't be caught dead baking cookies or doing any kind of needlework. She was much more likely to be found out in the garage, sanding and re-painting something or up on a ladder or hanging off the edge of the roof hanging Christmas lights.

Captain Hansen cleared his throat at the front of the room. "Thank you all for pausing your work to attend what I hope will be a brief meeting."

Since Lizzie had no idea what he was referring to, his message was not reassuring her so far.

"As several of you know, my wife has been having some health problems lately. I promised her years ago that I would take her to Hawaii, but we've never gotten around to it. Then we started adding up all the things we've never gotten around to . . . the trips, the hobbies we haven't made time for, the friendships with people we hardly ever get to see . . . and well, we're both retiring."

Lizzie couldn't have been more surprised if he'd pushed her out of a moving vehicle; she sat perfectly still, even though the stress made her want to fidget. She wasn't the only one; Sue shared a shocked glance with her, and low murmurs rippled through the room. Captain Hansen wasn't old. Not at all. Despite his salt-and-pepper mustache, he was only in his mid-fifties.

"Lieutenant Mark Wright will be taking over, following his promotion to captain, and I know he'll do a fantastic job. Please make him feel welcome in his new role."

Lizzie watched as Mark walked to the front of the room. This was a serious problem. She felt her hands curling into fists and had to consciously relax them as Mark started into some kind of canned speech about how he hoped they could all work together. *I guess that's why he's been hanging around the station more often.* At least it hadn't been related to his crush on her; that was a relief. Besides, he'd probably be too busy to talk to her much once he was in charge. A twinge of jealousy had her lips twisting to one side. He wasn't that much older than she was, but he'd risen through the ranks so quickly. It probably didn't hurt that his uncle was the county commissioner. Lizzie's only living relatives were both slightly batty and politically unimpressive, and she was fine with that.

That night, Lizzie took her dog for a long run to tucker him out and took a quick shower. Then she got out a sheet of linen paper and a ballpoint pen from her grandmother's desk. Gram was out, of course. She knew Gram didn't mean to rub it in, but sometimes, it hurt that someone fifty years older than her had a more active social life than she did. Small-town socialization could be a little clique-y, to say the least. Ainsley and Starla were nice, but Lizzie didn't know their friends very well. Ainsley had invited her out a few times, but it just grated to be tagging along on someone else's night out. She had Third Wheel Syndrome . . . she hated being on the periphery. It wasn't personal, she just enjoyed her own company enough to make it not worth it. But tonight, she thought, sitting down on her bed, it would be nice to spend a little time with someone, even if he was sort of removed from her situation. The day's events weighed on her mind; she'd been working up the nerve to ask Captain Hansen for a promotion. She'd only been on the job three years now, but she felt she'd proved her mettle. Not that it was all about her, but she couldn't help but feel disappointed. Now she *definitely* needed to accelerate her ten-year plan; she was not going to beg Mark for a promotion. It would seem like pandering. It would be improper. She sketched out some thoughts on the back of a life insurance policy offer (more? Sigh.) she'd pulled out of the recycling, and then she was ready to compose a response.

> *Dear Mr. Carpenter,*
>
> *Thank you for your letter; I appreciate you taking the time to let me know how my work in law enforcement has affected you. You're right in thinking that not many people thank me for arresting them. In fact, I am fairly sure you're the first. Don't be so hard on yourself with phrases like "people like me." You seem like a perfectly nice person, now that I'm not forced to put a knee in your back, smash your face into the pavement and read you your Miranda rights in front of the whole town. I hope I won't be forced to do so again.*
>
> *I am seeing more repeat offenders recently for drug use, especially young people, and I worry that some of these places aren't really helping them. I'd like to know more about this rehab; if you don't mind, would you send me a brochure?*

Sincerely,

Deputy Elizabeth Painter

Was that too formal? Better to err that way than the other. *And*, her brain prompted smugly, *this gives him a reason to write back.* It wasn't very professional to have a little crush on someone she'd arrested so publicly, but ultimately, she felt it was harmless. It wasn't like anything could come of it. But on a Friday night, sipping a glass of whole milk, watching reruns of *The Office*, it felt nice to pretend. She was still on the couch when her grandma came home.

Tansy hung her purse by the front door; the dog lifted his head but didn't get up.

"You have a good night?"

"I guess so. How are the Mind Readers?" Her grandmother's book club was much more than just a book club; tonight, they'd been to Portland to see a new Chihuly exhibit, on loan from a museum in Seattle. Her grandmother sat down heavily on the sofa and toed off her sensible flats.

"Good, good. Well, not Barb; she pulled a ligament training for that marathon walk she's doing, so all the standing in the museum was tough for her. But we got her a wheelchair, and everyone treated us like feeble old people after that." Tansy chuckled. "Poor Barb. She tried to get me to sit down and play the invalid for a while, but I said 'no way, not me.' Hattie and I took turns pushing her, though. How was *Jeopardy!*?"

"Not bad. I missed the Daily Double, though."

"What was it?"

She'd been repeating the details of their favorite game shows for years. "'The subject of the documentary Tiger King, this man's legal name is on the register at FMC Fort Worth.' The category is 'Not-So-Average Joes.'"

Tansy scrunched her nose. "I don't think Joe Exotic is his legal name, but I'm not sure . . ."

"It wasn't. You're one step closer than I was; I've never heard of the man. I did better with Joe DiMaggio and Joseph Smith, Jr. I wish they'd stick to real history."

"It is real history," her grandmother assured her, "just not the sanitized, academic bit."

"Mmm," Lizzie said, and Tansy bent forward to kiss her on the forehead.

"My little hummingbird," she said, smoothing her red hair down. "Still so light on words. You going to bed soon?"

"Maybe." It was only ten-thirty. She often stayed up until one when she had the next day off; she didn't need a reason. The quiet called to her, the darkness felt soothing. Tonight, it was almost a full moon, so she'd probably be up a while longer. Sometimes she just stared at the moon; she couldn't explain it, but she'd always loved looking at the moon. It always gave her the impression that unbelievable things were possible; its pure beauty just evoked a sense of awe that she couldn't explain. Her mother had made her move her bed away from the window as a child because she wasn't getting enough sleep . . . thoughts of her mother felt like a hug tonight, and she reached subconsciously for the ring on the chain around her neck.

"All right, well, I'm gonna hit the hay."

"Okay."

"Oh, I remember what I was going to ask you: did you hear that Daniel Durand is getting married in January?"

"Old news, Gram."

Her grandmother chuckled a little. "Well, with your lack of social acumen, I never know. Anyway, isn't your friend Ainsley his fiancé's roommate?"

She thought for a minute. "I think so."

"So won't Ainsley have a vacancy once she moves out?"

"A vacancy? Is she running a hotel?"

Tansy huffed a little impatiently. "You know what I mean. Maybe she'll be looking for a new roommate."

"And?"

She sat down on the couch. "And maybe you should talk to her about it. You don't need to be living with old Gram still."

That ruffled her feathers a bit. "I *like* living with you."

"I know you do," she soothed, "but don't you think it would be fun to live with someone your own age? Go out, do young people stuff?"

"I'm happy with how things are, thanks."

Her grandmother's shoulders drooped a little. "Okay. Don't forget to turn off the lights when you head up," she called. Lizzie just smiled after her.

CHAPTER TWO:
Letters

Dear Deputy Painter,

Your last letter had me laughing . . . I hope you won't be forced to do that again, either. It was unpleasant; I had some serious bruises afterward. Not to mention a bruised ego from making an ass of myself in front of the entire town and bruised eardrums from my dad yelling at me.

No, I wouldn't mind at all sending you a brochure. I can also put you in touch with the director if you want. This program has been very unique, and it's having a big impact on my life. It would make me happy to know that more people are getting help. I'm sure you see a lot of people who have problems with opioids come through the station, even in a small town like ours.

Kind of ironic, isn't it? I started taking them for pain, and they just ended up causing a lot more pain in my life. There are a lot of things I wish I could do differently, including how we met. But as Gretta reminds me, you can only live life forward.

Sincerely,

Chase

❧

Dear Chase,

You had bruises? I'm so sorry. I didn't mean to do that. Well, I did mean to arrest you, but I didn't mean to injure you in the process. You should've told someone in the sheriff's department, I'm sure we would've paid for your medical bills. I have to admit, that was the first time I'd taken down anyone as big as you, and it made quite an impression on the town; I now have a reputation as a total badass, not to be messed with, so maybe I should be thanking you.

Actually, we had met before the day I arrested you. You took my sister Lottie to the winter formal when you were home from Duke on a break. We met when you came to pick her up from my grandmother's house.

Who's Gretta?

Sincerely,

Lizzie Painter

Dear Lizzie,

Gretta runs my rehab program, and she is 72 with long white hair, wears long, bohemian skirts pretty much exclusively. She used to have a substance use disorder way back in the day, got caught up in the seventies. But she's been in recovery for a long time now, a few decades I think. A stellar lady who I have all the respect in the world for.

I had totally forgotten about that date with your sister. How's she doing these days? If I remember right, she wanted to study engineering? I don't even know if she got into the college she wanted . . .? Totally lost touch. I'm not good at the social media thing.

And thankfully, I don't need anyone to pay my medical bills; I'm Timber Falls royalty, remember? Trust fund and everything. So please don't worry about it. I deserved what you dished out, especially since I ruined everyone's celebration.

Sincerely,

Chase

Dear Chase,

There you go again, being hard on yourself. I don't think anyone's day was ruined, except maybe the Fishers' kid, whose snow cone I knocked to the ground. I gave his mom some cash for another one after I put you into the cruiser.

I'm not good at the social media thing, either. It makes me feel better that I'm not the only one; it feels like I am sometimes. I tried it for a few months, but it seemed like people were mostly posturing. I just don't need to compare myself to everyone else. Anyone who wants to know how I'm doing knows where to find me; I rarely leave Timber Falls. I've had the same phone number since 1997. So being available to them 24/7 seems very unnecessary and is a huge waste of time anyway. I'll go to the reunion if I want to know how everyone's doing, and that'll take one day out of my life instead of hours every day. I mean, I already know who's in jail, right?

Charlotte is doing well. She did get into the school she wanted (U of O), but then she changed her major. She's a pharmacist now, lives in Eugene. She comes home a lot, so I still see her a couple of times a month. She's dating someone, Jeremy. Not sure how to describe him . . . smarmy, maybe? One of those people who's always trying to sell you something even when he's just talking to you over dinner, you know?

I guess I'm not Germy's biggest fan. Not that my opinion matters.

Sincerely,

Lizzie

CHAPTER THREE: Lizzie

APRIL

It had become her Saturday morning ritual: a coffee for Gram, a tea for her, a cinnamon roll for each of them, and Chase. His latest letter was in her back pocket as she walked to Riverside in downtown Timber Falls. The way the water dripped off the lavender crocuses and bicolor daffodils more than made up for the gray, troubled sky. Who needed sunshine when she had the fresh smell of rain all around her? She could take his letters up to her bedroom—Gram wouldn't bother her up there—but still, this felt like a treat. She didn't mind getting out of the house once on the weekend. Her yellow lab Pancake trotted along next to her on his leash, nosing into people's shrubbery and getting all wet in the process. He wagged his tail slowly, head up and alert, as if to say, "you're coming back with my treat, right?" as she tied him up to the bike rack.

"Stay," she said, knowing he could probably pull her knot out if he wanted to. He sat down obediently, tail still moving steadily against the cement. Maybe there was hope for him as a police dog yet; she'd bought him with that intention, but there'd been no time to train him.

Lizzie pushed back her hood as she entered the coffee shop; it was bustling as usual this time of day, local people getting their caffeine before starting their weekend projects, a few tourists trying to wake up after playing too hard. She pulled out the letter with a glance over her shoulder; she didn't know the man behind her in line, so he wasn't a Timberite. He was safe.

Lizzie,

Okay, so I don't know how you did it, but you had me up half the night thinking about whether this crime thriller I'm reading is accurate as far as police procedure. Even since you mentioned your dislike of cop shows, now I can't help but wonder if I've been lied to all my life. So thanks for that. I'm in marketing, lady. I never had this problem before you.

That article you enclosed about hurricanes in your last letter was fascinating, too. I wish I got to be the guy who names hurricanes, but no parent is going to name their kid after the storm that destroyed their house, so you'd basically get to put some names out of commission. There'd be immense power in that. No one would name their kid Fernando again for years.

Happy birthday, by the way, in case we don't get another round of letters in before your big day. What are you going to do to celebrate? And don't say nothing, because even an introvert can have celebration plans. You should do something, even if you just stuff yourself with cupcakes. I was going to get you a present, but I had no idea what you'd want. Content people are hard to buy for.

"What'll it be?" Paige asked, giving Lizzie a wide smile as she shuffled forward.

"Medium roast black coffee, a raspberry iced tea, and two cinnamon rolls. Oh, and a cup of whipped cream."

"Coming right up," the woman smiled. "And happy birthday, Deputy."

Lizzie stiffened. Had she seen Chase's letter? Was she going to sing? Paige had a beautiful voice and sometimes played the coffee shop's tiny stage on the weekends. The cute blonde barista looked taken aback by her response or lack thereof.

"Did I get the day wrong? I thought for sure . . ."

"No, it is. I just . . ." she lowered her voice conspiratorially. "I don't really love it when people sing to me."

Paige stared at her for a long moment, then threw back her head and laughed. "Don't worry, Deputy; I won't torture you. Sawyer doesn't like it, either. I won't take offense."

"Thank you," she said, passing over some cash, grateful for the reprieve from public attention. "How are things?"

"Oh, you know," Paige said, waving a hand. "Same old same old around here. Nothing ever changes."

Lizzie nodded in agreement. She thought Timber Falls had a nice, comfortable way about it, like a broken-in sweatshirt, but she wasn't sure that was how Paige meant it.

When she got back outside, the rain had stopped, and she bent down and gave Pancake his whipped cream, which he greedily lapped up as she finished the letter just as greedi-ly.

What's the best birthday you ever had? Mine was in fifth grade. I got two skateboards—the long kind and the trick kind—and my brothers were so jealous. My parents let us watch movies in the bonus room all night, and we ate all the junk food we could want. It wasn't the most elaborate party I had by a long shot, but somehow, it just fit. Looking back, my parents pressured me the next year to have a big party, so I caved. I never got my laid-back birthdays back after that. I wonder how my life would've been different if I'd known I had anxiety back then. Would they still have pushed me? Would I still have given in?

Anyway, sorry it's a short one this time, but I've got an appointment with Gretta. I'll make it up to you next time. Hope you have a great day.

Chase

THE NEXT DAY, SUNDAY, Lizzie was mowing the lawn when her grandmother's friends started showing up. Hattie was first. In a large-brimmed hat, she just gave Lizzie a wave as she went up the walk. Lizzie was no detective, but even she could tell a present in the backseat of someone's car when she saw one. She groaned and let the kill switch up.

"What are you doing here?"

"Now, Deputy, that's hardly a polite way to greet one of your oldest friends."

Lizzie felt a smile pecking at her lips. "Oldest like known the longest, or . . .?"

Hattie gave her a mocking laugh and Lizzie grinned. "Hello, Mrs. Meyer-Bagsby. What time are the rest of them coming?"

"You've got about half an hour," Hattie said, foregoing all pretenses. "Plenty of time to finish up here and get in the shower."

"I told her I didn't want a party," Lizzie grumbled, wiping her sweaty brow with the back of her wrist. "Le sigh." All of Gram's constant language practice must be rubbing off on her.

"I guess she didn't listen to you this year. Or last year, come to think of it. Or the year before . . ."

"Yeah, we get it," Tansy called from the porch as she carefully descended the steps. "I'm a bad listener. It's just a little family get-together, Lizzie, go get cleaned up. I can finish this."

"I got it, Gram," Lizzie replied, reaching down to pull the ripcord on the lawn mower again. "I'll do it."

Tansy shrugged and smiled at her, but she seemed somewhat dismayed at Lizzie's response. What had she expected? *Oh, Lizzie, I know you said you didn't want a party or anything, but I invited all my friends over to celebrate you anyway.*

So please re-arrange your evening to accommodate a surprise party that you were absolutely clear about not wanting. She did the last two lines of the front yard, then emptied the grass catcher onto her compost pile in the backyard, where the old fence sagged toward the alley. Pancake jumped against the screen door, his big paws stretching the material to its limit. Lizzie scowled at him, and he got down and sat, looking at his leash. She didn't feel bad when she dashed his hopes and locked him in the laundry room; the last thing she needed was him bumping into the back of everyone's knees all night as he wove through the circles of conversation, trying to find someone to play with him. She tried to reason with herself, telling herself that it was only one evening of her life . . . but when she looked into the bathroom mirror, her face was just as sour as it was when she'd first spotted that present in the back of Hattie's car. She pulled her straight red hair out of her hat. She wasn't dressing up.

Lizzie showered, dressed in jean shorts and a green cotton tank top that matched her eyes, and went downstairs to help her grandmother pour lemonade. When the Mind Readers showed up, they didn't pinch her cheeks; they never had. They did quiz her about work and give her huge hugs and push cards at her, supplying reasons for why she probably wouldn't like what they'd selected. She didn't have a favorite of the bunch. They were all too different.

Anne Foster had just joined the book club recently, so Lizzie knew her the least. She was a recent widow, unlike the rest of them. Except for Jean Helsing, whose husband Perry was awesome, their partners had all passed away long ago. The women were disinterested in changing their marital status but were willing to date around. Hattie had been a widow the longest of any of them; her husband Davis had died of a brain tumor more than twenty years ago. It was only three months from the time he was diagnosed to the time he died. He didn't even try any treatments, from what she'd heard. Lizzie had been young—only five or six. So of course, Gram had never met him, since she didn't come to Timber Falls until Lizzie and Lottie's parents died.

Her big sister engulfed her in a hug.

"Twenty-eight! How is my baby sister twenty-eight?" Lottie gave Lizzie a big smacking kiss on the cheek followed by a tight squeeze which Lizzie gladly returned. Then, over her shoulder, she saw Jeremy. Of course. God forbid they be apart for one weekend.

"Hi, Jeremy." *Ooh. Too flat.* She should've tried harder to sound friendly. Maybe on someone else's birthday.

"Got you a little something," he said, handing her a card with an oily smile. It felt like they were watching her, so she opened it. Cash. How . . . interesting. She must have been telegraphing her thoughts because Lottie hurried to explain.

"I told him you love cash. Then you can get more space stuff or whatever."

"Astronomy stuff," she clarified, but she made herself smile. "Thanks, Jeremy."

"Sure." He wandered toward the alcoholic drinks, a clear indicator that they were staying the night. Hopefully, they'd be quieter than last time; this was an old house. The walls were thin. Last time, she'd ended up sleeping on the couch.

"This gonna be the year you finally nab a boyfriend?" Lottie teased, and Lizzie raised an eyebrow.

"I don't think I have much control over that," she said, munching a cucumber slice with hummus. At least Gram had nailed the food. "And I already have a man in my life."

"Pancake doesn't count, Lizzie Lou. Did you ever install that app I told you about?" She tried to remember what it had even been called. She couldn't.

"Probably not," Lizzie admitted. "I don't think dating apps are for me."

"That's how Jeremy and I met," she reminded her, shooting her boyfriend a smile over her shoulder, which he returned. *Blech.* She couldn't put her finger on why she just didn't like him. She and Gram both had their reservations about him, but when Gram tried to talk to Lottie, her sister just nodded politely and went right on dating him. Three was not a good number for family members; two were always ganging up on the other one. Usually, it was the other two against her. Maybe she should be glad Jeremy came along. If he wanted her approval, maybe she could get him to side with her once in a while.

"Are you at least going to get your own place?" Lottie asked, sipping a hard lemonade.

"Why would I?" Lizzie said, sitting down on the couch with one leg tucked under her. "I hardly pay any rent here. And I can keep an eye on Gram."

Lottie squinted at her skeptically as she sat next to her. "Does she need you to keep an eye on her?"

"Someone to hold the ladder, then." She snapped off a carrot between her teeth. "Someone to mow the lawn."

"We could hire someone to mow the lawn," her sister pointed out, but the conversation died when Barb Jameson sat down with them, and they both angled to include her in their conversation.

"Hi Barb," Lottie greeted. "How's your marathon training going?"

Barb gave a big sigh. "Postponed, I think. This ligament just isn't healing, and I don't want to be hobbling around in Paris."

"Ooh, that's right, the big trip is coming up!"

"Only sixty days away now. Got my passport just in time. I can't believe I'm actually going to Europe. Your grandmother is so wonderful to organize all this. She's such a special lady."

Both her granddaughters nodded, and Lizzie's gaze flitted around the room. Gram was finally taking a trip to France; Lizzie was très fatiguée of listening to their weekly French conversation Zoom class through Alliance Française in Portland. They hadn't wanted to drive to the community college every week. It was annoying, but it was good to see them excited. All the Mind Readers were going: Hattie, Anne, Barb, Mildred, Jean. France wasn't going to know what hit it. Even though Tansy wasn't leaving for eight more weeks, she'd already started packing. And why shouldn't she? After an extra decade of parenthood, she deserved something wonderful for herself.

They were all very special, really, she thought as she refilled her lemonade and snagged a handful of M&M'S. She was thankful to have these women in her life, even if they did force her to socialize. And their taste in gifts was fairly appropriate, actually; after a salmon dinner and vanilla cupcakes, she opened the giant box that had been in Hattie's back seat: a telescope. Not just any telescope: it was the Orion StarSeeker IV 130, the one she'd been coveting for months now. It was cherry red, but to Lizzie, it gleamed like gold; she held her breath for fear she'd damage it somehow.

"Do you like it?" Gram asked. "This is the one you wanted, right?" All Lizzie could do was nod mutely, overcome with emotion. She ran her fingers over it gently, leaving oily marks that she quickly wiped away with the edge of her shirt. "It's supposed to sync with your phone so you can aim it precisely." Lizzie looked around the circle, dumbfounded, hardly able to believe what she clutched to her chest.

"She's speechless!" Jeremy announced.

"That's nothing new," Lottie quipped, and the two of them shared a private chuckle. For once, Lizzie couldn't care less. Let them tease her; she was holding the birthday present of her dreams. She pulled out the instruction manual and started to read, and the women began to clear the table. They each came over and kissed the top of her head or squeezed her shoulders before they left, and even though her deepest wish was to break in her new favorite possession as soon as possible, she paused her reading each time to say goodbye. Soon it was just her family. Well, and Jeremy, who looked like he wanted to go to bed despite it being only 9:30 p.m.

Apparently, Lottie didn't mind if he went without her, because she grabbed another piece of cake and sat down at the table next to Lizzie, one leg tucked under her.

"Excited about your toy?"

"It's not a toy," Lizzie murmured, still reading. She glanced around; Gram was still outside saying goodbye to her friends. "How's work?"

"Pretty good. We just got a new aide. She seems pretty cool."

"That's good."

"We're thinking about buying a house . . ."

"That's a good idea." She'd read that the market was good right now. And Eugene had a very competitive market.

"And getting married."

Lizzie put down the booklet. Jeremy, who had been lingering at the bottom of the stairs, took one look at Lizzie's face and fled up the wooden steps like a mountain goat. *Coward.*

"Why?"

Lottie's smile was gentle. "Because we're in love, hon."

Lizzie just barely stopped herself from rolling her eyes. "If you say so."

"I do, Lizzie," Charlotte said firmly. "We are in love. This is happening. I'm not asking your permission, just giving you time to get used to the idea."

Lizzie had been in this position before with Lottie. Her uber-dramatic way to making declarations like she didn't care what Lizzie thought was ridiculous. The safest thing to do was to wait for her to change her mind. This was a big decision and hopefully not one she'd made lightly. . . but Lizzie was not going to be baited into fighting with her. If Lottie wanted to spend her life with Germy, it was inconvenient for Lizzie and probably a mistake, but it wasn't Lizzie's problem. Well, except for holidays and the odd weekend.

"Okay." She picked the instruction manual back up.

"Okay? That's all you have to say?" *Don't bite, don't bite...*

She set the book down again. "What do you want me to say, Lottie? You said you didn't want my approval, which is good, because you don't have it. You can do better." Well, at least she hadn't yelled it.

Her face flushed with anger. "I can't believe you. You're so jealous you can't even congratulate me?"

Lizzie snorted and glanced down at her left hand. "No ring?"

Lottie made a fist like she was trying to hide the emptiness of her fourth finger. "We're saving up for it."

Lizzie gave her a perfunctory nod. "Cool. I'll save my congratulations as well, then. Thanks for making my birthday all about you. I'm not jealous, I just think you're making a mistake." She gathered up her telescope and started toward the stairs. "Oh, and if you're going to have loud sex, would you please do it downstairs? I don't want to sleep on the couch tonight. I have to work tomorrow." And with that, she marched upstairs and slammed her bedroom door.

CHAPTER
FOUR: Letters

Dear Lizzie,

Yes, I know what you mean by smarmy. My twin is like that sometimes. He thinks he's being charming, and sometimes he is, but sometimes, it's obvious he just wants something. It's a weird thing to think about the person who used to be my best friend. Do you have a best friend? I feel uncomfortable now, thinking about how I might've contributed to his manipulation. There's nothing like a six-month timeout to make you think about who you want to be when it's done. 'Smarmy' is now at the top of the list for adjectives I hope won't be used to describe me.

I'm still so embarrassed that I don't remember meeting you. I guess you're a little younger than I am, but not by much. I always was pretty self-involved. I once spent an hour getting ready for a date, only to dump her twenty minutes in when she complained about my cologne. Had a pretty good temper back then. You're a redhead, you get it.

Yours in embarrassment,

Chase

Dear Chase,

For your information, I may be a redhead, but I do not have a nasty temper. I'm probably the only redhead in the world who doesn't, but I honestly don't. That's not to say that I don't react if something truly upsets me, but it takes a lot. My sister once filled my Crocs with tuna fish as a joke, but I just hosed them off and kept wearing them. I think it was the best revenge I ever got. She couldn't even complain about it. Gram did, though. I can't blame her, looking back. Did you and your brothers pull any epic pranks on each other? Or other people, taking advantage of the twin thing?

My dog is probably the closest thing I have to a best friend. I intended to train him as a police dog, but I haven't ever gotten around to it. I realize that's weird. I should probably make some real friends. Like, human friends. I had them in high school, but then people moved away and went to college, and when they came back (the small percentage who did), I felt like they'd all had this big bonding experience that I couldn't begin to grasp. Law enforcement is what I'm best suited for, so it didn't make sense for me to do college. And honestly? I just didn't want to. Living in a dorm sounds like one of Dante's lower circles.

Sincerely,

L

CHAPTER FIVE:
Chase

MAY

Chase sat on his twin bed, his bags between his feet, staring out the window, waiting for his younger brother Carter to pick him up.

"I'm gonna miss you, man," Jesse said, rolling on his side to face Chase. He smiled at his roommate, remembering when Gretta had introduced them on his first day: "I'm Jesse. I'm Black, I'm gay, and neither of those things will be a problem for you because you're not my type." Before Chase could answer, Jesse had pivoted toward the bathroom to show him where he could put his clothes and get toiletries. Their worst conflict had been keeping the room picked up and enduring each other's snoring.

"We're not gonna lose touch, are we?" Chase asked.

"Nah, of course not," Jesse grinned. "Just can't believe you're leaving before me."

"It's been nine months. That's too short?"

"For some people."

"Makes you wonder why anybody tries those 28-day programs . . ." Chase played with the strap on his duffle bag and checked his watch involuntarily. Carter was late. Maybe he wasn't coming. *Of course he's coming. It's just a long drive.*

"I don't know," Jesse said, grinning even wider. "I spent a lot of time on beaches in Miami. Hot guys. Lots of sunshine. You could do worse."

"But did it help your addiction?" Chase pressed, raising an eyebrow at his friend. They'd laid it all out in counseling and long talks on the back porch at night, smoking, watching the sun paint Smith Rock in gold. Jesse had been battling a heroin addiction for a decade, in and out of rehab. This was the longest he'd been sober in years.

"No," he admitted. "But I kept going back. I didn't know what else to do. I knew I'd die if I kept using."

Carter's black SUV turned into the long driveway, and Chase stood up. He was ready to get going, but he couldn't leave the conversation on that note. Carter was the one who was late; he could wait a minute. Chase put down his bags.

"Stand up, man."

"Aww, am I gonna get a goodbye hug?" Jesse snarked, but he rolled to his feet. Everyone in the house teased Chase about his bear hugs; even for the recovery community, which was generally big on hugs, he gave out a lot. Chase honestly didn't care. He just kept giving them out, and they all just kept taking them, some even started asking for them. But Jesse had been the most resistant, so he didn't want to make him if he didn't want to.

"I see you overthinking it. I'm just messing with you, man. Relax, all right?" Jesse opened his arms and Chase pulled him in for a tight hug, complete with back slap.

"You take care, all right? You need anything, you call me. I'm there." He'd made all the residents the same promise, and he meant it. These people, they were like family to him. They were going through the same thing. No one else could understand him the way they did.

"All right, all right. Go. Get out of here. Go eat something that's never touched dirt." He pushed Chase toward the bedroom door, then picked up his bags for him.

Chase threw back his head and laughed. "I happen to like healthy food now . . ." he said as he led the way down the wide staircase.

"Leave it to a white dude to waste this opportunity." He cast his gaze toward the ceiling. "Forgive him, Lord, he doesn't know. Doesn't know what he's doing."

"God invented vegetables, so He's on my side," Chase shot back. Truth be told, he had been jonesing for a big, messy burger, but he wasn't going to admit that. When they reached the foyer, Gretta was chatting with Carter, his mom and Carter's fiancée, Martina.

"And you wouldn't believe how naughty they both were," Willow was telling Gretta. "They used to switch shirts to try to trick me, but I knew." She noticed him and her face lit up like a Christmas tree. "Christopher!" she said, calling him by his twin's name. "How are you, darling?" He didn't know how long his mom had had Alzheimer's, but he was still trying to get used to it. He wasn't sure if he was supposed to correct her, and he hoped the pain of hearing his twin brother's name wasn't obvious. He was still texting him a few times a week, but he hadn't heard anything back in over a month.

"Actually, Willow, that's Chase, not Christopher," Martina said quietly, touching her arm, and there was no judgment in her tone. He felt a surge of gratitude to her for taking the job caring for his mom.

"Oh," Willow blushed. "How funny, after what I just said."

"Nevermind," Chase said, grinning at her. "Thanks for coming to pick me up, Mom." He started the hugs with her, pressing a gentle kiss to her temple. She was technically his step-mom, but he barely remembered his biological mom, and as far as he was concerned, she was his parent. Period. "You didn't all have to come, though," he said, turning to Martina for her hug. He hadn't even gotten to congratulate them in person on their engagement yet.

"What kind of employee would I be if I didn't pick you up?" Martina teased, her big brown eyes sparkling as she tossed her dark hair. Chase rolled his eyes at the joke: she and his brother had been high school sweethearts, and ever since Carter had started dating Martina again, Chase had taken over paying her for his mother's care, just to keep things clear.

"Oh, of course we did," his brother agreed, running a hand through his blond hair, the same shade as Chase's. "We wanted to celebrate. This is big, man."

"It's very big," Gretta agreed. "Recovery is a big deal. He's made a wonderful start. We're very proud of him, and I'm glad you are, too."

Chase blushed at his mentor's frank praise. "Still have a long way to go, though," he mumbled. He stared out the open front door. He'd never been more terrified to walk through it.

"But you're going to chase recovery now the way you used to chase a high. You'll surround yourself with supportive people, like these. You'll take the tools you learned here to manage your anxiety and start using them." Gretta was looking at him, waiting for an answer, and he just nodded, his voice knotted in his throat. "Oh, I almost forgot." She turned and hurried down the hall, and Chase turned to his family. Carter just shrugged. The white-haired lady soon came back, a travel mug in her hand. "For you."

He smiled. He knew what was in it already: the scent of chamomile wafting from the small hole in the top confirmed it, but he took a sip anyway.

"Thanks, Gretta." It did calm him down in a weird way; he needed to add it to his grocery list. Oh dang, he was going to need a grocery list again. "I'll mail the mug back to you."

"No, you'll bring it back when you come visit. Now you've got an excuse, not that you needed one. Come any time to any session. I trust you know the schedule by now. It's good for us to see you, even if you're struggling. Yes?"

"Yes, Gretta."

She reached up and hugged him. He realized a line was forming behind her, and he hugged them each in turn: Jim, the judge from Grant County; Drew, who played baseball for the Hillsboro Hops; Sarah Beth, who'd gone to Julliard on a violin scholarship; Laquelle, the college professor; Thom, who owned a chain of gourmet grocery stores. If he'd seen them lined up, he'd have never guessed they were like him. Based on his education from after-school TV and

DARE presentations in school, drug addicts were homeless, impoverished, skinny, and missing a lot of teeth. He'd been struck over and over by how "normal" these people were. Middle-class, anyway. Opioids were weird like that.

"Would you all like to stay for lunch?" Gretta asked his family, but Chase blurted out, "No." Now that the hard goodbyes were over, he just wanted to leave. On his way to the car, Chase dropped one last letter in the mailbox. It would make more sense to mail it from Timber Falls, but every minute he held onto it, he felt his confidence evaporating more and more. He didn't need to see the paper to remember what he'd written.

> *Dear Lizzie,*
>
> *I'm coming home today. I'll be staying at my condo in Salem for a while: I've enclosed my new address. I hope you'll let me see you. I know we're only friends on paper, but your friendship has been really important to me. Just putting that out there.*
>
> *Sincerely,*
>
> *Chase*

He'd agonized over that letter; on the one hand, there was no reason anything should change. He was simply changing locations. But on the other hand, he now had a friend—a real, drug-unrelated friend—and he didn't want to lose her over a misunderstanding. Yes, it was fair to assume she'd keep writing to him, but they hadn't exactly defined things between them. Shit. Maybe he shouldn't have said 'friendship'? He didn't want her thinking she was being friend-zoned, but he didn't want her to think he didn't care, either. Maybe he shouldn't have asked to hang out in person; she could've come to Redmond to hang out with him, right? She'd never asked. Of course, he hadn't invited her, either.

Stop. Drink your tea. She'll probably write back. Just chill.

Chill was evasive at the moment. So much so, he'd left his luggage sitting in the foyer when he went outside; Carter appeared to have it covered. He slipped into the front seat, throwing on his sunglasses. His mom and Martina climbed into the back without a word . . . he probably should've let one of them have the front. He'd forgotten how to be a gentleman.

"Do one of you want to sit up here?"

"Oh, no," Martina said, grinning. "We're good back here, aren't we, Willow?"

"This one takes good care of me," she said, patting Martina's tawny hand. "Can you hand me my bag?"

He looked down; a bag with a magazine, a stuffed cat, and some snacks were at his feet. *So you totally took her spot. Great work, Chase.* He passed it back with a smile.

"I'm so glad you said no to lunch," Carter said. "I've been craving restaurant food. Lunch is on me; where do you want to go? Steak? Teriyaki?"

"Tempeh?" Martina asked from the back hopefully, and Chase pivoted to shake his head at her slowly. He made a circle with his hands.

"One of those places where you can get a burger as big as your face." Healthy food was all well and good, and he hadn't really been missing restaurant food. But he had missed the atmosphere of being out with his family. That had him thinking of his whole family. Including the two that were barely speaking to him.

"Perfect," Carter said, then put the car in drive. "I've got just the place."

"Dad working today?" He hadn't really thought his dad would show for the pick-up, but now he had to know.

Carter shook his head a little. "Haven't seen him in a while. Must be on another trip. You know how he is."

"Yep." He'd just have to see him at work . . . if he still had a job. The HR guy, Victor, had assured him months ago that his job would still be waiting for him when he got back, but he never knew what to expect with his dad. At least Carter knew not to paint over the cracks when it came to their dad; they'd made an unspoken pact years ago not to bother covering for him anymore. His brother knew he wouldn't want any comforting words about how Harrison wanted to be here.

He pulled out his phone.

Chase: Getting out of rehab today.

Christopher: Good.

Chase: No congratulations?

Christopher: For what? Being stupid enough to get caught?

Chase: Nice, Chris.

Christopher: Fine. Congrats on successfully wasting your trust on more rehab!

Chase: Sorry I said anything. How are you?

Christopher: I'm rich, single, and I live in a city full of beautiful women.

Christopher: So I'm far better than you.

Chase: Okay then. Have a good weekend.

Christopher: Enjoy your freedom.

"Christopher being a jerk again?" Carter asked, breaking Chase's focus on his phone.

"How'd you know?"

"You make this little grunting sound when you text with him." He glanced at him, then back at the road. "Kind of an angry chipmunk noise, like someone took your sunflower seeds."

Chase couldn't push Carter even jokingly since he was driving, so he just glared at him, which made Carter laugh.

"I'm just saying. It always seems to put you in a foul mood. I don't know why you're still trying with him."

"Because he's my brother. Just like you."

"Not like me," Carter corrected. "I mean, not really. You guys were always . . . closer."

It wasn't surprising with twins. They had, after all, shared a room by choice up until high school when they wanted to bring girls home. And even after they'd gotten their own rooms, they'd left their connecting door open most nights. Roomed together at Duke. It wasn't until Christopher had moved to New York that they'd spent more than a night or two apart. Not that it mattered, but . . . it kind of mattered. Christopher seemed permanently hacked off at him, and he didn't know why. There had to be a deeper reason, something past the drugs and the rehab. He couldn't figure it out.

"Yeah, I know what you mean," Chase said, as they pulled into the restaurant parking lot. He'd think about that later; right now, he had a burger to demolish.

CHAPTER SIX:
Lizzie

I HOPE YOU'LL LET ME see you. She should've seen this coming. Lizzie's fingers gripped the steering wheel of her truck tighter as she drove to work, her knuckles turning white. It wasn't that she didn't want to hang out with Chase, but there was no point. She had the urge to bang her head against the dashboard. Maybe she could let him down easy . . . she'd have to spend some time tonight trying to figure out how to write back. How to give an excuse that didn't make her sound so . . . so pathetic.

The moment she walked into the station, Captain Hansen called her over.

"Good, you're here. Lizzie, you know Mark."

"Of course. How are you, Lieutenant?"

"Fine, thanks. I was hoping I could ride along with you today."

Lizzie felt her forehead wrinkle, and she pressed a hand to it briefly to try to smooth it back. "With me? Why?" They rarely gave her anything interesting to do. She certainly didn't want him thinking that parking tickets and trespassing charges were the extent of her abilities.

"He's trying to get to know Timber Falls a little better before he's stuck behind a desk doing my job," Captain Hansen explained jokingly, "and you're the expert on Timberites." Being from Silverton, Mark didn't know Timber Falls all that well. It was going to be different having a captain who wasn't so embedded in their community.

He held up a yellow slip of paper. "Sue says Shane and Darby are at it again."

Lizzie grimaced. "All right. Thank you, sir, I'll take care of it."

"I know you will," he said, clapping her on the shoulder in a fatherly way. "Have a nice day, you two." Lizzie dumped her stuff on her desk and grabbed the keys to the cruiser. A glance over her shoulder told her that Mark was indeed following her. *Yippee.* Usually a call was a chance to get away from the noise of the station, which was pretty much the last place she wanted to be right now, given her state of mind over Chase's perplexing letter. She would've preferred to be alone, but it was good for Mark to be informed.

"You have a good weekend?" Mark asked as they got into the car.

It was like every other weekend. "It was fine. How was yours?"

"Great. I went to the range."

"Oh. That sounds fun." It did, actually. She hadn't been shooting in a long time.

"Yeah, it was. I took my brother."

"Mmm."

They fell into not-so-comfortable silence as she drove; at least he hadn't insisted on driving. She knew where Darby's place was all too well. Lizzie pulled into the driveway and the reason they'd been called became very apparent. A white man about six feet tall with dark hair stood on the roof of the single-level house, arms crossed. A white woman with blonde hair tipped in purple wearing a black apron with several creative variations on the f-word glowered up at him.

"This doesn't look good," murmured Mark, leaning forward to see better through the windshield.

"Oh, this is nothing," Lizzie said. "Last time, I found him naked and her burning all his clothes. They're why I always keep several blankets in the back."

Mark turned to her, his eyes wide. "How often do you get called about them?"

"Couple times a month," she said, throwing the cruiser into park. "I just hope we can get away before they start making up. Come on." Lizzie looked away before she could see Mark's reaction to her statement; could he have picked a worse day to come along? Despite feeling a sense of urgency to move this along, she got out of the car slowly, as if sudden movements might spook them. "Darby. Shane. What seems to be the problem?"

They both started yelling at once, punctuating their thoughts with very emphatic pointing in each other's direction. Lizzie held up her hands, and they both stopped abruptly, the tension still hanging in the air like condensation.

"First of all, where's Bailey?" Ensuring that their little girl was not being ignored in all this was always her first instinct. Although, it seemed like they were able to hold things together when Bailey was around . . . she was like a cute little brunette buffer between them. They both adored her . . . but once she was out of earshot, that's when all hell seemed to break loose.

"She's at my aunt's," Darby said, and Lizzie could've sworn they both went a bit softer thinking about their little girl.

"Darby, you went first last time, so Shane, let's hear it."

Darby huffed, crossing her arms, but didn't say anything.

Shane smirked. "Thank you, Deputy, I appreciate that courtesy. I'm glad you're here to witness this; this is spousal abuse. I just came up here to fix the satellite *like she asked me to*, and the next thing I know, she's moved the ladder so I can't get down!"

"I told him, we can't keep paying for fancy TV. I told him to *take it down*, not fix it. He doesn't listen to anything I say." Lizzie wanted to point out that it was fine for the dish to stay up even if they stopped paying for the service, but her gut told her it wasn't the time and that wasn't the point.

"I do too listen! There's no point in taking it down until the subscription runs out!" He shot back.

"Are you actually going to cancel it this time? Or just conveniently forget again?"

"You were the one who wanted to watch *Hamilton*!"

Darby rolled her eyes. "That was streaming, doofus. We don't need satellite for that."

"So what I hear," Lizzie said gently, "is that Shane was trying to be considerate and economical, but he got the facts wrong. Is that right, Shane?"

He nodded so ardently, Lizzie worried that he'd lose his balance and fall off the undoubtedly slippery roof.

"And Darby, it sounds like you're worried about money. Is that right?"

The young woman rubbed her arms. "We've been in the hole four months running now. We can't keep this up."

Lizzie nodded, hoping her sympathy was coming through. "You might consider applying for WIC; it would help with the groceries. I can also point you to some budgeting resources."

Shane pushed up his hat to scratch his head, then sat down hard on the edge of the roof, his long legs hanging off. "We're in debt?"

Darby said nothing, but her silence was apparently all the confirmation he needed. Shane gave a meaningful head jerk toward the ladder, and Lizzie quickly stood it up and put it back where he could dismount the roof. He climbed down, going straight to Darby and wrapping his arms around her from behind.

"Why didn't you tell me?" he murmured, and Lizzie looked away. Such a moment deserved privacy. Not that she knew how it felt to share an emotionally intimate experience with someone like that. Heck, she'd never even been kissed.

"I tried," Darby said, and the sniffle in her voice told Lizzie that she wasn't pushing him away. "I told you to go easy on the snacks. I told you to use a coupon when you got your hair cut. I told you to hold off on those concert tickets."

"Babe," he said slowly, "why didn't you just say, *we can't afford that*. I'm not smart like you. I don't notice stuff. You've gotta just say things, all right? Just hit me over the head with it."

Lizzie glanced at them to see how Darby was taking this, ardently hoping his invitation would be restricted to information. She was smirking as she wiped away a tear that she tried to play off as an eyelash.

"You're not the brightest bulb in the box, huh?" Darby teased gently.

"Totally not. Definitely not an LED like you. I'm one of those big old white ones, the kind that gives you cancer when you drop 'em, the kind that cost a bunch to run. The kind we apparently can't afford." Darby snorted at that, and Shane grinned at her.

She gave a little sigh, a relief signal if Lizzie had ever heard one. "I just didn't want you to regret getting married. I wanted you to have the same stuff, the stuff you like. I didn't want us to cramp your style."

"Cramp my . . ." Shane shook his head slowly. "D, you and Bailey are everything to me, okay? I can go down to Annie's to watch the game. I can bum free snacks at work. But I can't ever replace my girls. You're worth giving up anything, all right? Any kind of luxury or bonus or whatever. We're a team now, and I don't expect you to take care of all this alone. Even an idiot like me knows a good thing when he sees it, and you two? You're the best thing."

"So are we good?" Lizzie asked, and they both nodded, then turned and gave each other a tender peck, like they'd planned it.

"Glad to hear it." She turned to her temporary partner. "Time to go." Lizzie was already power walking back to the cruiser, leaving Mark scrambling to catch up with her.

"Wait—are you sure?"

"Yes, I've learned the hard way. As soon as there's kissing, you've gotta take off unless you want to see more. A lot more."

"Really?" Like Lot's wife, Mark glanced over his shoulder. "Wow. Oh wow. My bad. You're right, let's go."

Violet waved them down as they came back to the main road. "All better now?"

"Yes, ma'am," Lizzie assured her. "Back to business as usual."

"Thank you, Deputy. The neighborhood appreciates you; I thought he was going to fall and break his neck on that roof."

"So did I," Mark admitted, then he stuck his hand out. "I'm Captain Mark Wright," he rumbled, giving her a dazzling smile.

Not yet, you're not.

"Pleasure to meet you, Captain. I'm Violet Garrison." As she shook his hand, she gave Lizzie a side-eye that said, *isn't he a charmer?* But Lizzie just adjusted the fan speed in the cruiser. "Are you patrolling Timber Falls now?"

"No, ma'am, just riding along with Lizzie, getting the lay of the land. I'll be the new captain in this area when Captain Hansen retires this summer." *Lizzie. Not the deputy.* This did not bode well for her promotion; did he see her as a woman or an officer of the law? Or both?

"Oh, I see. I wasn't aware he was retiring. Is he ill?"

Violet was well-known in Timber Falls for being the reason that mothers weren't home from the town meeting in time to help put the kids to bed. She was the reason PTA meetings were now planned for before school so that they couldn't run over. She was why they didn't have an open mic poetry night at Riverside anymore. Mark, of course, did not know this.

For the next twenty minutes, Lizzie smiled perfunctorily, nodding at key moments, pretending to listen as Violet sucked more gossip out of Mark. Privately, Chase's letter was still giving her plenty to think about. She tried to compose several openings in her head. *I don't think meeting is such a great idea . . . My schedule's pretty full, but would you like to keep writing? . . . So glad to hear that you're moving on with your life, I'm sure I'll see you around.* That was a lie; hardly anyone 'saw her around' unless she was working, and the thought of having to arrest him again made her feel heavy and sad.

"Great to see you, Violet," Lizzie said, letting the car roll forward slowly. "We've got to get back. Thanks for the call."

"Oh, of course. Nice to meet you, Captain."

"Nice to meet you, Victoria."

"Violet," Lizzie mumbled.

"Violet," Mark corrected louder with a smile, giving her a wave as they drove away. "Wow, I thought she'd never stop."

"She never would have. She's one you have to be firm with if you're on a schedule."

When he said nothing, she glanced over at him: he was taking notes. In a spiral notebook.

"Would she make a good confidential informant?"

Lizzie tipped her head back and forth, considering. "Timberites don't seem to have much of a problem tattling on each other. If anything, it's the opposite problem."

Mark nodded and did more scribbling. "Who's she related to?"

"Her aunt Mildred is in my grandmother's book club. Her husband Dan is the principal at the high school. Her son Teddy was in my grade. His sisters Grace and Jamie were younger and older than us, respectively. All of them are now married and live elsewhere."

"Slow down, this is good stuff." He was drawing some sort of diagram. "Grace, Trevor, Jamie . . ."

"Are you charting the genealogy of Timber Falls?"

"Yep. I think it'll help me get a handle on all these names."

"Interesting." She left him to his writing for the remainder of the trip, her brain still working. *I regret to inform you . . .* she sighed. Why did Chase have to go and make things awkward? No matter what she did now, it was going to get more awkward. A lot more.

When they got back to the station, they went their separate ways, Mark muttering something about letting him know if she was going out again. No sooner had she started on the paperwork describing the morning's events than she was interrupted again.

"There you are," Martina said, as if it was perfectly logical for her to come waltzing into the station with Willow looking for Lizzie in the middle of the workday. As if Lizzie had been hiding. *Haven't you been?* She hated that condemnatory voice.

"Good morning, Mrs. Carpenter," Lizzie greeted.

"Good morning," Willow echoed with a gracious smile. Martina smiled too, conveying silent gratitude to Lizzie for acknowledging her future mother-in-law.

"I have a proposal for you," Martina said, leaning forward.

"Shoot," Lizzie said, glancing back down at her work. She felt like things were a little awkward ever since she'd had to pull Martina over last year. Harrison Carpenter, Chase's dad, had put her in a terrible position, and Lizzie still hadn't forgiven him.

"We're all going to Annie's next Wednesday . . ."

Lizzie held up a hand. "That's enough information. I'll pass."

Martina stomped one platform sandal on the tile. "You didn't let me finish."

"I don't like drinking, Martina."

"I know you don't drink, but this isn't about that. Seriously. There's no alcohol being served, to let the high school kids play, too. Besides, we've gotta stay sharp, if we're going to win."

That last word had Lizzie lifting her head. "Win?"

Martina nodded slowly. "Trivia night. Cash prize. I'll bring the sports knowledge, Carter's got business smarts, Kyle's got the medical stuff, and Ainsley's our kid expert . . ."

"Who else?" She couldn't just come out and ask if Chase was invited, too. Martina was nosy when it came to rumors and romance.

"Starla's going to come if she can work out her childcare." She'd make a good addition; librarians knew all sorts of things.

"And me?" Lizzie asked, eyebrow cocked.

"You're my ringer," Martina said, her dark eyes gleaming. "You soak up random facts like a roll of paper towels in a kiddie pool. More random facts than anyone I know."

"I just do a lot of crosswords," she demurred, but it was kind of true. And then there was *Jeopardy!*. And Trivial Pursuit.

"I think it's more than that," Martina said with an easy smile. She leaned forward onto the desk. "I need you, Lizzie. Be on my team. Bigger teams do better. Just give it a try; one night. If you hate it, you can always quit, right?"

Gram and Charlotte would both be thrilled if she did give it a try. She could probably get them off her back for months this way. Lizzie chewed on the end of her pen, thinking. Maybe she could say yes now and then back out at the last minute. But it did kind of sound like fun, especially if no one expected her to drink. Maybe this was a form of social interaction she could actually be good at.

"All right."

"Oh, Lizzie, thank you, thank you!" Martina cried, giving her a big hug. Lizzie patted her back awkwardly until she let go. "You have no idea what this means to me. Thank you so much."

"Well, I'll give it a try," she said, feeling the need to distance herself from that kind of enthusiasm toward her participation. That was setting Martina up for disappointment. She needed to temper that hype.

"I'll pick you up at 6:45 next Wednesday the first. I've got your address. You're the best!" Martina said over her shoulder as she rushed off, arm-in-arm with Willow. She was already out the front doors when Lizzie's brain caught up to what she'd said.

Wait. Pick me up? No, I can't cancel if she . . . Lizzie retrieved her phone from her belt and scrolled through her contacts until she got to the M's. She didn't even have Martina's number. How was she supposed to call and cancel if she didn't have her number? She certainly wasn't going to start a social media account just to cancel a social engagement . . . that would definitely lead to more problems than it could possibly solve. *Rats.*

CHAPTER SEVEN: Chase

THE TALL, DARK-HAIRED man sitting at a table for two at Riverside was reading a Bible, and Chase figured this was probably the pastor he was supposed to meet. The sleeve tattoos down both arms were the only thing that made him hesitate.

"Hey, are you Kellan?"

"I am." He offered his hand, then gestured for Chase to sit down. "This is just a brief meeting. I find people are more inclined to meet here than at my office at the church."

Chase gestured to his chamomile tea. "It's working for me."

"Glad to hear it. I just wanted to go over sponsorship a little bit and let you know what to expect. I'm not going to keep tabs on you all the time; if you need my help and support, just reach out to me and let me know. I do run the meetings here in town, and I'd expect you'd want to attend."

Chase pulled out his phone and opened up his calendar. "When are they?"

"Monday, Wednesday, and Friday afternoon at the Methodist church, in the basement. It's technically Alcoholics Anonymous, but we welcome all flavors of addiction."

"Great," said Chase. "I'll plan to come Mondays at least." Were the people around them listening? It wasn't a secret, really, but he might've been more comfortable in the church office, only because it would preserve the anonymity piece of Narcotics Anonymous better. But everyone knew about his struggles anyway.

"Tell me your story," Kellan prompted, and Chase's anxiety caused him to suck in a harsh breath. He hadn't thought to form a cogent story before this meeting . . . and that was a mistake.

"Okay," Kellan chuckled, "so I see your 'deer in the headlights' look; that's okay. Just think about how you'd describe your journey, and we'll talk about it next time."

Chase nodded, trying not to feel embarrassed. He looked around the café in an effort to ground himself; they'd decorated for spring. Paige had a daffodil in her black apron. He counted the couples. He smelled the scent of coffee and whipped cream. Then he could breathe a little more again.

"You married?" Kellan asked.

Chase shook his head. "But there is . . . someone. Kind of."

Kellan raised an eyebrow. "I trust you're not thirteenth stepping?"

"Oh, no! She's not in recovery. She's just a friend." He couldn't blame him for asking, though.

"You should really wait a year before you start dating . . ."

"It's almost been a year," Chase said. "I spent nine months with Gretta and two months on my own before that. Although, in the early days of my sobriety, I was kind of holding on by my fingernails."

The pastor let out a big sigh. "Yeah, I remember those days."

It was a good meeting; they talked for a long time, then the pastor checked his watch a few times before Chase suggested that he walk him back to the church, and the man smiled gratefully.

"Sorry, I'm supposed to be doing some pre-marital counseling for a couple . . ."

"Oh, that's my brother and his fiancée."

"Carter and Martina? Really?"

"Yeah!"

"I'm going to perform their wedding in August."

"Oh, wow. Small world."

"No," Kellan smirked as he took a sip of his coffee, "small *town*."

IT WAS A FRIDAY NIGHT. Bored of organizing and re-organizing his belongings in his condo, Chase had come over to the estate at Carter's invitation for pizza, beer, and, of course, Scrabble. It was a very welcome distraction from thinking about starting work again the next week. Chase put down "qadi."

"That's not a word," Carter glowered, and Chase held back a smile. Carter should know better than to challenge him by now. Some little brothers never learned.

He raised an eyebrow. "Is this an official challenge?"

Carter looked torn. He glanced from the board to Chase, then back down to the board. "What happens if I lose, again?"

What a punk. He knows what happens, he just wants me to be a nice guy and bend the rules.

"You lose your turn. Do you want to challenge?" This was one arena where he didn't mind being a little ruthless. Carter appeared to be thinking.

"Yes, I call bull—"

"Cookies!" Mrs. Sánchez sang out as she entered the room. It was his favorite, oatmeal chocolate chip. She beamed as her gaze bounced between the two of them, and Chase couldn't help but smile back as he thanked her. It had him wondering if he should've moved into the old estate after all, but then again . . .

Right on cue, the front door slammed downstairs, the signal that his father was home. That wiped the smile from his face real quick. Dad was the reason he'd stayed away; it was bad enough working together, especially when his father apparently wanted him gone. No, that was unfair; if he wanted him gone, he'd be gone. TFPP was his company now, except for Hattie's influence. But his father found him embarrassing. He'd made that perfectly clear.

Chase got out the dictionary and cleared his throat: "Qadi. A Muslim judge who interprets and administers the religious law of Islam. Eat it."

"Don't mind if I do," Carter said, shoving a cookie into his mouth before choking on how hot it was.

"Got milk?" Chase quipped. Carter laughed as he tried to get his breath back. Chase leaned over and whacked him on the back until he pushed him away. Then Chase laid down "quetzal" on the 'q' he'd already put down, and this time, his brother didn't say a word about it.

"Why aren't you hanging out with Martina tonight?"

Carter scowled. "How often does my brother come back to town after being gone for months and months?"

"She was busy?"

"Well, she did have a thing she'd already planned with some girlfriends. But even if she didn't, I would've wanted to hang out with you. The timing just worked out, that's all."

"Uh-huh. Your move."

"Wolves," Carter said proudly. "That's fourteen points."

"Yes, I can do math, actually." He paused, rearranging his tiles.

"Just pointing it out. I'm getting better." Chase glanced at the board . . . he could play 'female' off the 'e' in 'same' . . . that had his mind drifting back to Lizzie.

"This thing with her girlfriends . . . who's going to be there?"

"Martina's thing?" Carter asked, pursing his lips as he considered his hand. "I don't know, probably just her usual friends. Winnie, Ainsley, etc."

"Mmm." It was a noncommittal noise. Casual. Hey, it could even be in response to the cookie he was eating . . .

Carter's gaze narrowed, and Chase knew he was caught. "Why? Who do you want to see?"

"Who, me? Nobody." *Lizzie. I want to see Lizzie. I want to find out if those letters meant anything. If they meant as much to her as they did to me. I want to talk to her in real time. I want to stare at her until her pretty red hair is imprinted on my brain. Lizzie.* He felt the most innocent of longings, just to see her and soak her in. At the very least, read her most recent meandering thoughts in her chicken scratch scrawl.

"Uh-huh," Carter said, clearly skeptical. "I wouldn't mention anyone to Martina unless you're serious about them. She means well, but she's pretty pushy where romance is concerned."

"I said nobody."

"Your mouth said *nobody*. Your eyes said *somebody*. Who is it?"

"I'm not telling you."

"So," Carter said, leaning back as he put his hands behind his head smugly, "there is someone. Somebody from high school?"

"No."

"How did you even meet her when you were two hours away?"

"We've only met once." He didn't know why he was uncomfortable talking about Lizzie; having a pen pal was a relatively normal thing. *Yeah, if you're nine and your pen pal lives in Japan, maybe.* He just didn't know where they stood exactly. And he should've gotten a letter from her by now; it had been a week. A full week. The longest week he'd had in years. Chase told his anxiety to shove it and cast a glance back to his brother.

Carter had his head cocked like he was doing long division in his head. "Just once?"

"Here's more," Mrs. Sánchez called as she swept back into the room with another full plate of cookies, which she set in front of Chase.

"Why don't you dote on me like this?" Carter asked, throwing an accusatory hand at the plate. "I'm here every night. But I can't remember the last time you made my favorites."

"Yeah," Chase said, piling on, "can't you see how much weight I've gained already?"

The older woman cocked her head, squinting at him. "All I see is a prodigal son come home, handsome as ever."

Chase smiled at her; her words eased something inside him. He hadn't realized he cared so much about how he looked now. He'd quit playing sports in college, but he hadn't started to get rounder until he started treating his addiction. In some ways, he felt it suited him better; he didn't have the same hard edges he'd had back then, in terms of his personality. So if his abs weren't toned and well-defined, well, that was okay. Running again might be fun, but he was kind of enjoying not being driven for a while. At least, he had in rehab. Now? Who knew. He felt like he didn't know about anything now . . . he hadn't ever really been a sober adult. He'd gained some new tools, but he felt like he was staring at a kit he'd bought to build a life, turning the directions over and over, trying to figure out how to start. And the biggest step, restarting work, was hanging over his head.

"Thanks, Mrs. S." He grabbed a cookie and pointedly ate it as she glowed. "These are amazing." His phone buzzed, and he smiled apologetically as he glanced at the screen.

Martina: Hey.

Chase: Hey. What's up? How's your night going?

Martina: Good. I was thinking of getting together a trivia team. You in?

Trivia? That wasn't exactly his forte, but hey, it was something to do.

Chase: Yeah, sure, count me in.

Martina: Awesome! Don't tell Carter; I'm going to recruit him, too, but I need to warm him up to the idea first.

Chase turned to his brother. "Martina wants you on her trivia team."

He groaned. "This again? I told her, we don't have enough people. Only the big teams win."

"Well, since I'm just an amazing brother, I'll help you out." Carter shoved at his shoulder, and he pushed him back. "Now quit stalling and play, Mr. Wolves is Fourteen Points and I'm Getting Better."

On the stairs, his father was coming up, his slow, tired footfalls each like a drumbeat. He closed his eyes for just a minute and tried to reframe his thinking. Cookies were good. Scrabble was good. Family time was good. Now he just needed to keep these good vibes rolling when it came time to go to work on Monday . . . and maybe even find a subtle way to track down his MIA pen pal.

CHAPTER EIGHT: Lizzie

"I'M NOT FEELING GREAT." Lizzie still hadn't showered when her smiling friend showed up on Wednesday night. "I don't think I should go," Lizzie sniffled, touching her disheveled hair self-consciously. She didn't like to lie, but Martina was leaving her no other option.

"Are you sick?" Martina whipped a digital thermometer out of her purse, and Lizzie's mouth dropped open in shock. She stood there like she'd been frozen in time, letting Martina scan her forehead. "Hmm, no fever. What hurts?"

"Pardon?" She hadn't forgotten that Martina was a nurse, but it was still strange to be ushered into a distinctly clinical situation on her own front porch. "Nothing. I mean, I'm not in pain or anything, I'm just . . ." She sniffled again for emphasis. "I think I might be coming down with something."

"Well, if you can't determine what's bothering you, why don't you change your clothes and get into my car and we'll go have some fun?" Martina's face was impassive, but her eyes twinkled like the jig was up. That's right; she worked with Willow, Carter's mom. She was probably used to uncooperative patients. She'd worked with children before that, too.

Even she had to admit that she was maybe being a little bit childish right now, making excuses instead of just facing the music. She just wished the music didn't sound so much like death metal to her ears. Social situations so often did.

"Fine." She trudged upstairs and found a pair of jeans and a clean T-shirt without too much effort; the shirt was gray with a design of the space shuttle in blue and white with "NASA" written across the top. She'd had it since middle school, and all its crumply softness and faded designs were her own doing. She'd made the mistake of telling someone once how old the garment was, and it did not inspire bonding with the other woman. Quite the opposite; now she told people it was vintage instead.

Martina was chatting with her grandmother about how Sawyer Devereaux had recently had a seizure in the public library when she came downstairs.

"Ready." Both women gave her a look that said they disagreed, but Lizzie ignored them. They could make her feel guilty about trying to break her word. They could make her change her clothes. But they couldn't make her like it. "Bye, Gram. Love you."

"Get into some trouble, for heaven's sake," Tansy called after her, and Lizzie just shook her head as she got into Martina's little black car.

"Your grandma is a hoot," Martina commented as they backed out.

"Yeah." Lizzie genuinely enjoyed living with her grandmother; she could find her own place, but she had no interest. Living at home was cheap and had built-in companionship from someone who understood her.

"How long have you lived with her?"

"Since I was twelve."

"Oh, right," Martina said softly. "I'm sorry, I didn't mean to bring up your parents."

"It's fine." She was over their accident now. It had only taken her a decade. "How's work?"

"Oh, it's good. It's nice to see Carter every day. Willow's a good patient, for the most part."

"For the most part?" Was it okay to ask that? She wanted to show interest but didn't want to be nosy. People's privacy should be respected.

Martina sighed. "I tried to take her to a meeting of the women she used to plan charity events with. It didn't go well. She couldn't remember their names, and she saw the looks they were giving her. I should've prepared them more. It was my fault."

"Well, you have all my respect. I don't think I could do your job."

"Why not?" Martina asked, turning on the radio.

Lizzie hedged. "Well, just nursing in general. I mean, I've seen my fair share of injuries and such, but . . ." *But they don't usually send me out to those since I always throw up.* "I don't know. It'd be hard to bond with someone, knowing they're going to die."

Martina tipped her head from side to side. "Yes and no. It's easier with Willow, since she's going to be my mother-in-law, and we were already friends. Her loss would've hurt whether I was involved or not. But I get what you mean. It's emotionally risky business, I guess." She glanced at her.

"But surely your work involves some kind of emotional investment."

"We had to remove two children from their home the other day. Safety issue." She could still hear the kids crying when she got into the cruiser sometimes.

"Oh, that'd kill me," Martina groaned. "How heartbreaking." She paused. "Who was it?"

Lizzie rolled her eyes. People were always asking for gossip.

"You know I can't tell you that . . ."

"Come on. I can always read the police blotter."

"Then read it. It's not professional for me to spread people's private business around."

Martina huffed discontentedly as she pulled into the parking lot of the restaurant. "All right, that's fair. But we're going to do our best to take your mind off all that heavy stuff tonight. You deserve a fun night out. And I deserve a win."

Lizzie smirked. "You do?"

"Absolutely. I love big trophies. I love them even more when they're mine." She winked at Lizzie, and they got out of the car. The food smelled good . . . she realized she'd never eaten dinner. In all her worry, she'd forgotten. Maybe there were peanuts. Lured into the building by the delicious smells wafting out the front door, she moved forward like a woman under a spell. That spell, however, was broken the moment she spotted their table. Lizzie stared at the back of Chase Carpenter's blond head for a long beat, then yanked Martina off-course by her elbow, leading her back into the dark hallway toward the bathrooms.

"What is he doing here?"

"Who?"

"Chase!"

She'd never responded to his last letter, the one where he said he wanted to meet. She'd folded it up, feeling like her throat was closing up at the same time. She didn't know what she'd been thinking, encouraging him with letter after letter. One date, and he'd know that she was just quiet, boring Lizzie, not the interesting conversationalist from her letters. When she wrote, it was easy to sound put-together, to answer his questions eloquently after she'd had a chance to think about them all day. In person, her mind went blank. When she had to look into someone's eyes, baring her soul became intolerable. Even small talk was a challenge. Somehow, he'd snuck past those roadblocks with his careful script and self-deprecating humor. But now he was here, and he was going to know. When Martina cocked her head in confusion, Lizzie changed tactics.

"You really think bringing someone in recovery to a bar is a wise idea?" she hissed.

"He said it was okay. He never had a problem with alcohol, and they're not serving tonight. I don't think anyone's going to slip him fentanyl here . . . I mean, I'll kill them if they do."

Lizzie peeked around the corner at his blond head. "You just didn't tell me Chase was going to be here!"

"Oh, I didn't?" Martina had zero poker face; she probably thought she looked innocent right now. Nothing could be further from the truth. And Martina knew about the letters because Lizzie had been dumb enough to mention it during her stressful traffic stop . . . she cursed herself inwardly for being so open-handed. Look where it'd gotten her. "Starla couldn't make it after all, so Chase was a last-minute addition. We can have up to six, so I figured we should fill up our roster, you know? Give ourselves the best chance."

Lizzie crossed her arms, not buying a word of it. "Uh-huh." *Convenient that the rest of the team is already coupled up.*

"He just got out of rehab, you know. I just wanted him to go somewhere fun . . . he's been a little mopey since he got home."

Because you didn't write back. She pushed the thought away; it was assuredly unrelated. He was probably just adjusting to being back in his normal life. Still, she felt guilty; she should've been more supportive. What had she thought, anyway? That they'd never run into each other? This was Timber Falls, for heaven's sake; you couldn't spit on the sidewalk without someone at your elbow, commenting on the rain. She smoothed down her T-shirt. She really felt more comfortable in her uniform . . . street clothes just felt weird sometimes. At home, she mostly wore pajamas. Why hadn't she at least worn a skirt?

"Don't worry about it, you look great," Martina said, taking her by the wrist and dragging her out into the restaurant again before she could protest. All she had time to do was pull the elastic out of her hair and let it tumble down around her shoulders before they reached the table. "Hey everyone," Martina chirped. "Look who's here!"

When Chase turned, it was obvious he hadn't expected to see her, either. His smile faltered momentarily, then he jumped to his feet and pulled out the chair next to him. "Deputy Painter. Have a seat."

Well, that's better than I deserve. His courteous response after she'd ghosted him drove the shame of her decision even deeper.

"Thanks, Chase." Her voice was too soft for the boisterous crowd, but he smiled at her nonetheless. She quickly glanced around the table: Kyle, Ainsley, and Carter were smiling at her, too. "Hi everyone."

"Would you like to sit over here between Ainsley and Martina?" Kyle asked, starting to stand, but Ainsley put a hand on his shoulder and pushed him back down.

"Nice try," she said, patting his shoulder. "You'll go sit over there, then you'll make some excuse and slip away before I can talk you out of it. Besides, there's room by Chase."

Kyle's expression went a little stormy. "For your information, I was not planning to leave, and I'm insulted by the insinuation. I was just trying to be polite."

"This is my skeptical face," Ainsley replied, but she squeezed his hand, and his ire seemed to fade a little at her touch.

"Hello everyone!" A man in his early twenties stood on an overturned plastic milk crate, wearing jeans and an Oregon State T-shirt, holding a microphone, his dark hair damp with sweat. She recognized him as one of the Kovalenko boys. "I'm James," he hollered, holding up his hands for quiet over the boisterous crowd, "and I'll be your MC for tonight." Lizzie frowned. She could've sworn his name started with a V. "So quiet down, and let's get started. The first thing . . ." He dropped the microphone momentarily when it appeared no one was listening. Lizzie wanted to stand up and make them listen—she excelled at crowd control—but she was supposed to be having fun. She settled for shushing her own table, who quieted down immediately. The quiet spread, and as he gained their attention, James lifted the microphone to his lips again. *The man should be a teacher or something.* "The first thing I need from each team is a roster of your members and a name."

"Fellowship of the Quiz," Ainsley said. "Too easy."

"No," the men chorused, and Lizzie hid a smile behind her fist.

"We need a name that inspires fear," Carter said. "What about Quiz Kings?"

"Too basic," Martina said. As they argued, Lizzie looked around at the other teams . . . their team was distinctively nerdier than most of the rest of them. Maybe they could do something with that . . .

"What do you think, Lizzie?" Martina asked. "Trivia Busters or Question Heirs?"

"What about Geek Tragedy?"

"I love that," said Chase. "Even though I'm the least geeky person here." She didn't turn to look at him; she was already surprised he'd supported her idea so quickly.

"That's classy," agreed Kyle. "All in favor of Geek Tragedy?"

Everyone's hand went up, and Lizzie added hers, too, even though it was her suggestion. It felt nice to agree, to at least appear to be part of a team.

"Great, someone go tell Vassili," said Carter, sipping what appeared to be a Coke.

"Vassili, that's what it was," said Martina, snapping her fingers. "I knew James didn't sound right."

"I think it's his middle name. He started using it when he went to college. He got constant teasing in high school due to the *Princess Bride* connection," Ainsley added.

"That's *Vizzini*, not Vassili," said Kyle, frowning.

"Yeah, try telling that to a bunch of sixteen-year-olds."

Was no one going to go take the team name up? They should do as the man asked. Was she the only one who cared about order around here?

"I'll go talk to him," said Lizzie, pushing back from the table at the exact moment that Chase said, "I'll put our name in." They stared at each other for a moment until Martina cleared her throat.

"Maybe you should both go," she suggested.

"Sure," Lizzie agreed, just to have something to say. She facepalmed internally a moment later. *Yeah, because that's not awkward or anything.* Chase gestured for her to go first, and she led the way to the front of the bar. Another team was in front of them, and apparently, they'd decided to all come up front and get in line while they decided. Maybe she wasn't as big of a goof as she felt. They queued up behind the other team, and Lizzie felt the awkwardness setting in like a cold.

"How are you?" she asked. "I mean, how've you been since you got back?"

"Good. Fine." He paused. "I was supposed to start work again two days ago, but I decided to take a little more time, try to kind of . . . get my feet under me . . . first. It's not my strong suit. But I start back tomorrow."

She stared at him. She'd assumed that his forthrightness was a product of distance and the relative anonymity of a letter. She would never have believed he just wore his insecurities on his sleeve like that. It was a breath of fresh air in a stale bar to hear him admit a weakness so readily. "That sounds challenging."

He ran a hand through his hair. "It is, I guess. My condo is feeling kind of worn out right now. Not really like me."

"So sell it." They shuffled forward in unison.

"Just like that?" Chase's eyebrows went high, and Lizzie blushed a little in the darkened room. She felt she knew him, in a way. It made her a bit bold. *This is going to end in ruin.*

"Yes. Just like that. Start over somewhere fresh. A new start, new digs, no old memories lingering around. Gram would probably do it for you if you need a realtor." It had been a relief to her when Gram had sold their family house after her parents died. She'd felt she was living with their ghosts. She couldn't be the only one. Plus, the new house was closer to the river, and it was this grand old rambling thing that no one else wanted. Gram had fixed it up with countless orders from Restoration Hardware. She'd been a real estate agent for years, so they didn't lack for money, and Gram knew houses like the back of her hand. Lizzie loved that house, its weird balconies and random outdoor sleeping porches that didn't seem to match the rest of the neighborhood or Oregon in general. But when she slept in one of the hammocks, she could stare at the stars as much as she wanted and let the river rub away her worries with its soothing song. It was no wonder she didn't want to leave, now that she thought about it.

"Hmm. Maybe I will."

Lizzie bit her lip. "About your last letter . . ."

He perked up and seemed to stand a little taller, his bright eyes meeting hers. "Yes?"

"I—"

"Next!" James/Vassili called, and they found themselves compelled to move forward and interact with him. They told him their names, Lizzie supplied spellings for everyone's last names, and she followed Chase back to their table, wishing she could leave behind the uncomfortable conversation she was about to have with him. And to her surprise, they did. There really wasn't a way to continue it. Not when James clapped his hands behind them as they turned to leave, trying to get everyone's attention.

"All right, let's get this party started!" The crowd whooped and trilled and whistled in a way Lizzie found overly exuberant. And yet, the whole event had an excitement to it that she did find attractive. And there was some kind of cash prize. She'd never won anything before. This could be a fun first. Plus, then she could afford a new lens for her telescope and maybe a second premium streaming service. There was always more TV to watch. Nights were long.

"Here's the first question," he said, pausing for quiet as people shushed their teammates. "For whom is Victoria Falls named?"

"Too easy. Queen Victoria," Kyle said, and everyone agreed. It must have been fairly obvious because only one team missed it: the laughing teenager team. Kyle and Martina both seemed distracted by whatever was happening over there, but it seemed perfectly innocuous to the deputy in her.

"Next question: Which racer holds the record for the most Grand Prix wins?"

"Michael Schumacher," Martina and Carter said in unison, and then grinned at each other. Lizzie hadn't spent much time with Martina this past year, and it was genuinely nice to see her in love again. Kyle keyed it into the app on his phone, and another point went up on the scoreboard for them.

"How many presidents have been impeached?"

"Three." The answer was out of Lizzie's mouth before she could even think about it. "None were removed from office, though."

"Correct!" Kyle announced when the answer turned green, and even he looked impressed.

"Which Avenger other than Thor was able to pick up his hammer in the Marvel movies?"

Ainsley nearly jumped out of her seat. "Oh! Oh! Wait, I know this one because Daniel and Winnie wouldn't shut up about it when we watched *Age of Ultron*. It's Vision!" Lizzie found herself chuckling with the rest of the table. She learned most things she knew from TV and magazines and books, but Ainsley seemed to glean most of hers off others.

"How many future presidents signed the Declaration of Independence?"

The others appeared to be thinking . . . was the answer not as obvious as it seemed? Of the fifty-six signers, only two delegates would go on to the presidency.

"Did Washington sign the Declaration? I can't remember . . ." Ainsley said.

Time was ticking down, and her heart rate shot up. She didn't want to seem like a know-it-all, but this was kind of why Martina had invited her . . .

"It's two."

"You sure?" Carter asked, and there was a slight edge in his voice Lizzie didn't like.

"Positive." She felt her attention drawn to Chase, who was staring at her. Kyle keyed it in quickly, just before time expired.

"That's my ringer," Martina grinned, and Lizzie smiled back, just a little bit. Based on the groans and boisterous shouts, all the other teams had gotten it wrong. Chase held up his hand for a high five, and Lizzie shyly slapped his hand. Her hand tingled for a long while afterward, and not just from the sharp contact. Martina had gotten a few orders of fries for the table, and Lizzie's stomach rumbled, impolitely reasserting itself. She leaned forward and dunked one in the garlic aioli . . . Levi Zane really was a good cook. They were lucky to have him in their little town.

She sat back a little in her chair to watch the group chatting and teasing each other. Next to her, Chase was laughing, repeating something his brother had said, laughing so hard that his lemonade came out of his nose when Carter answered him. Chase hadn't answered any questions correctly yet, but he seemed happy to put forth answers, even when he was wrong. She wished she had that kind of self-assurance.

Lizzie reached toward the middle of the table for another fry, distracted by Carter, who was trying to convince Martina that Sacajawea was the second woman to appear on U.S. currency, not the first. Her hand met someone else's in the basket, and she pulled back like she'd been burned. Chase was smiling at her, and she felt her cheeks heat.

"Did you want the last one?" He held out the basket, daring her with his eyes to take it.

"No, no. You take it."

"Please, I insist." Those sparkling blue eyes paired with his laissez-faire beard—she just couldn't look away from him.

"Hello?" Martina sounded exasperated. "Earth to Lizzie—who was the first U.S. billionaire?"

"Henry Ford," she said, not tearing her gaze away from him, and his smile just got wider. Chase shook the basket a little, tempting her again, and she gave in and took the last fry.

"Thanks," she murmured, and he nodded at her, his gaze still warm, teasing. Maybe there were advantages to being with someone in person. But it would be different if it were just the two of them, having to make actual conversation, not just spew out random facts. The minute he looked away, she felt like a cool breeze had swept over her, and Lizzie shook herself. She should stay focused on the other people at the table, too, but she was starting to fade. The lack of real dinner and the combination of excessive socializing with the noise of the other teams was sapping her energy. She glanced at the scoreboard; they were about half done. She could stick it out. Hopefully, Martina would want to leave as soon as they were done. Next week, she'd just drive herself. *Next week?* Was she really considering coming back? Chase knocked his shoulder into hers as he laughed with Carter about something she hadn't heard. Yeah, she was considering it.

CHAPTER NINE:
Chase

CHASE HAD BEEN HOLDING his feelings in all night, and his emotional grip was getting slick and sweaty. Seeing Lizzie like that had a hundred things tumbling around inside him; she'd started to say something about the letter, but then they'd gotten interrupted, and there'd been no private opportunity to follow up with her. So when the doors of Carter's SUV slammed at 9:30, he turned to his brother.

"Did you know Lizzie was going to be there?"

"No," Carter said, his voice low. "And my fiancée and I will be having a conversation about it tomorrow morning . . . I can't *believe* she'd invite the woman who arrested you." He inched the car forward as they waited their turn to merge onto the highway.

"Well . . ." Chase hesitated. He wasn't sure he wanted to spill the whole story to Carter . . . but he also didn't want him thinking Martina had been inconsiderate. "It's a bit more complicated than that."

"Oh?" Carter raised an eyebrow.

"Yes. We've sort of been . . ." He searched for the right word. "Corresponding?"

His brother's glance was pure surprise. "Corresponding . . . how?"

"We kind of wrote letters back and forth, while I was in Redmond." Why was he sweating? He hadn't done anything wrong . . . but he couldn't help but feel a little uncomfortable telling his little brother about his failed friendship. A friendship he'd hoped might be something more now that he was back.

"I see. And who initiated this . . . correspondence?"

"I did."

"But she wrote back?"

He nodded. "A bunch of times. I thought we were cool, I thought we were even kind of friends . . . and then, when I told her I was coming home, the letters just . . . stopped."

"Huh." Carter tapped his thumbs against the steering wheel, a habit their father also had. He hated that it bugged him, but he wouldn't mind going a whole day without thinking about his father. "So she was your mystery woman, then?"

"Yeah."

"Maybe she thought you were still in Redmond?"

"Maybe," he shrugged, trying to play it off like he didn't care. Chase looked out the window; what was he doing? Sliding back into old emotional hang-ups was too easy . . . that's not who he was now. He sat up straighter, turning more toward his brother. "But I don't think that's what happened. I think it freaked her out when she knew she was going to have to talk to me face to face. She probably doesn't want to be associated with someone in recovery."

His brother's glance was sharp. "And why would you assume that?"

"I don't know. It just seems possible for an officer of the law."

Carter glanced at Chase. "I didn't get that vibe from her. Tini says she invites her to stuff all the time, but she never comes."

A thought dawned on him. "Do you think she came *because* I was coming?"

"Maybe. Maybe she feels too shy to be alone with you, but in a group, she can handle it? I don't know. Just brainstorming."

Chase rubbed at his beard, trying to slow the thoughts tumbling around in his head. "No, this is good, it's good to talk it out. I just don't get why she didn't keep writing. I know she got it; she started to say something about it, but we got interrupted."

"Maybe hers got lost." Carter glanced over at him again. "You both wrote *actual letters*? Not emails?"

Chase cocked his head. "What's so hard to understand about this?"

"I don't know, I just . . ." Carter chuckled a little, like it had slipped out. "You're just full of surprises. If you'd written emails, you wouldn't have to wonder if she'd gotten them."

"Emails aren't . . ." *Romantic. Say it. Emails aren't romantic.* No, that was too much. He had no right to claim a romance with Lizzie. Not yet, anyway.

"Aren't what?"

"Never mind."

"What, technology is too convenient for you? It's too easy to get a message to someone?"

"I just think," Chase said firmly, "that there's something nice about letters. There's something nice about seeing that someone took the time to find a pen and a paper and send you something that you can hold in your hands. It's a sign of respect."

"Respect. Interesting," Carter said, sounding like he thought it was more than just interesting, but wasn't going to pursue it right now. "So why did you start writing to her?"

"Gretta had us all write letters, thanking people who'd had a hand in our recovery. I never imagined she'd write back, honestly."

"But she did. And what did she say?"

"Nothing at first. Polite stuff, thanking me for validating her work, asking for more info about Gretta's program. But then they became . . ." They were pulling into his condo's driveway; the garage was the bottom level. "I don't know," he said, picking the dirt out from under his thumbnail. "I don't know. It just became something more. Or so I thought."

"I saw that something more. I don't think you were wrong."

"Yeah?"

"Yeah."

They sat in the parked car, silent. "I just wish she'd written back."

"Maybe she'll write back to your next one."

"My next one?"

"Yeah. It's not a game of tennis, Chase. So she didn't write back; we don't know why, but there could be a hundred explanations. Write another letter if you've got something to say. She was open to that, once. Maybe she still is. Just go back to what was working for you."

Chase nodded slowly, not feeling at all sure, but letting the words sink in. It wasn't a bad idea. Carter was right; he didn't have to wait for a response. He didn't even have to acknowledge the gap or how much it had hurt him if he didn't want to. "Don't yell at Martina, okay? I mentioned the letter thing once, and I think maybe she blew it out of proportion."

"She shouldn't be playing matchmaker without your permission, though. She tends to meddle. I'll still talk to her about it. But I don't yell at her."

"Yeah, I guess I knew that. It's nice."

Carter's crooked smile made him smile, too. "I'm really glad you came with us tonight. It's really fun having you around again."

"Me too," he agreed.

That night, Chase dug through his desk until he found a yellow legal pad. He made a pro/con list about selling his condo, which came out with way more pros than cons, and then he wrote a letter.

Dear Lizzie,

I don't know if I can still call you Lizzie instead of Deputy Painter, but I do feel like we were on a first-name basis up until a few weeks ago. I'm not sure if you didn't want to continue writing letters or if you didn't get my last one, notifying you of my address change. I guess if I don't hear from you, I've got my answer. My brother thinks it's dumb that we're not emailing or texting . . . but that just doesn't feel as right as letters. Everything in my mailbox is always so boring: bills and ads and coupons (which are really just more ads). But your letters were never boring; they were the highlight of my day. Maybe even my week. Maybe it's weird now that we live in the same town, but I have more to say, and I thought maybe you do, too.

Recovery feels really different back in my old life, especially in my old condo. Like I said before, I'm not sure I like living here . . . there's too many bad memories. Too many things I can't remember. Carter went through everything and had it cleaned professionally, so there's no drug paraphernalia . . . but some things just don't scrub away. I remember pacing this floor the day you arrested me, calling everyone I could think of for a fix. A really clean slate is just what I need. I think I might go live with my mom for a while, just until I can find a new place. I don't suppose you know anyone in Timber Falls who's renting? The problem with living with my mom is that she only sometimes knows who I am and she also lives with my dad, and I'm not his favorite person right now. Actually, I'm not sure he's ever had a favorite person.

Can you put me in touch with your grandma? I think I would like to talk to someone about selling the condo. Here's my phone number: 509-555-1005. How in the world do you know so much about presidential history?

Hope to hear from you soon.

Seriously, though.

Very sincerely,

Chase

P.S. Here's my address again.

On his way to work the next morning, he drove by her house and stuck it in her mailbox. Chase needed to know she'd gotten it, for sure this time. He couldn't wait for the postal service to do their thing. Not about this. His anxiety felt like a drumline in his chest; he wasn't going to be able to concentrate worth a burnt brownie today at work.

CHAPTER TEN:
Lizzie

LIZZIE WAS EATING FROSTED Flakes in the kitchen nook when she saw a car pull up in front of the house. Someone was opening her mailbox . . . *if that's Dean Yoder again, I'm going to arrest him so thoroughly . . .* She separated the front window's sheer curtains just a sliver, just enough to see. It was Chase. Her mind went blank for a second before she realized what he was doing. She took the stairs two at a time to grab her robe, but he was gone by the time she came back. Lizzie ran out the front door, flinging the gate open, fingers shaking as she opened the mailbox and then the envelope. She scanned it quickly, the gravel pricking her bare feet, feeling more and more disheartened with every line. *They were the highlight of my day.* She'd hurt him. Of course she had; she should've written back, said *something.* The silence had clearly been deafening. It had communicated much more than she meant it to. She could skip a shower today; this needed to be dealt with—and now. She hurried inside.

Dear Chase,

Lizzie paused. She didn't want to lie to Chase, and she definitely didn't want him thinking he'd done something wrong. But the truth was embarrassing. Could she just leave it at that? Not explain herself, just . . . go back to how things were? That didn't seem fair. She owed him some kind of explanation.

I'm fascinated by presidential history, in part because of my dad. He was a trivia nut like me, and he used to read to me from his favorite books. I'd fall asleep listening to him going on about William Howard Taft didn't really get stuck in his bathtub, but he did take it with him to Panama in 1909 aboard the USS North Carolina. *And how Benjamin and Caroline Harrison were afraid to touch the electric light switches in the White House and made the staff turn the lights on and off for them. Little things like that, things that made me feel better about my own insecurities and oddities.*

But your latest letter made a few show through. I'm sorry for that.

She paused again. Lizzie let her forehead rest in her palms for a moment, trying to formulate her thoughts.

I do have more to say. I regret not writing you back; I just couldn't find the right words. It wasn't about you, it was about me. Wow, that sounds so cliché, but it's true. It had nothing to do with your recovery or your personality or anything. I'm glad you're back and I think what you're doing is both brave and admirable. I hope you'll believe me. I hope you'll keep writing, too. Or maybe we could try hanging out, but just . . . just lower your expectations, maybe. I'm not usually very good company in real life.

She looked over her last few sentences; she'd written them so quickly, they were hardly readable. As if writing them faster would make it easier, as if getting them down quickly meant thinking about them less, the way she squeezed her eyes shut and said the alphabet backward when she had to get her flu shot.

Regarding your housing options, I know of a few people renting rooms, but I'm guessing that's not what you're after. I'll keep my ears open. I think living with your mom sounds like a good thing; you said it was a little uncomfortable around her, didn't you? Maybe it would help her to remember you if you were around more. Maybe it would help you to learn what she needs now, too. I'll talk to Gram and see what she knows.

"What I know about what?" Gram asked, startling Lizzie enough to make her jump.

She scowled at her. "Do not read over my shoulder, please! We've talked about this."

Gram chuckled as she lifted her coffee cup to her lips. "It's not every day my granddaughter goes running outside half-dressed to get the mail long before Mr. Graves comes around. I just thought I should check on you. Everything okay?"

She turned the paper over in case Gram was still curious. "Chase Carpenter is thinking about selling his condo in Salem and moving closer to home. He's looking for a rental, but he may want to buy, I don't know. Will you give him a call?"

"I didn't realize he was back in town . . ." Her gaze drifted to Chase's open letter. "Is he the one you've been exchanging all those letters with?"

Lizzie lifted her chin. "It's not a crime."

"Of course it's not," Gram murmured, her face soft and sympathetic. "I'm just surprised, that's all. I thought you had a strict policy against fraternizing with people you've arrested."

"I do. I did." She wasn't avoiding them, exactly, but she didn't want to appear to be biased. It felt tricky to her; it wasn't like she didn't think people could change, but . . . well, Chase's problem was an illness, wasn't it? That's what he'd said in his letters, anyway. It's not like he'd been stalking people or breaking into their cars or driving recklessly. She wasn't even sure it made sense to arrest people for using drugs, based on what she'd been reading.

"Hmm," Gram said, tapping the side of her coffee cup with a long fingernail. "Well, I'd be happy to talk to him. Go ahead and give him my number."

"Here," Lizzie said, pulling over his letter to copy down his number, but Gram shook her head.

"Lizzie Lou. You text him my number, and if he wants to call me, he will."

"Okay." Her belly flopped down as hard as Pancake, who threw himself at the ground like he was afraid he'd miss it otherwise. She didn't really want to move to texting with Chase, but it appeared she had no choice if she was going to keep her word.

"Don't chicken out."

"I'm not going to," she said, trying not to let her feathers get ruffled by the comment. Lizzie hurried upstairs and was changing into her uniform when her phone rang. The caller ID said Barb Jameson.

"Hello?"

"Oh, good, I got you. I need an officer out at my place. I'll see you in twenty."

"Mrs. Jameson, is there an emergency?"

"Not exactly," she hedged, "but you're needed. It's a matter of *importance*."

Lizzie grimaced. In her experience, she and the Mind Readers defined the word 'importance' very differently. She was tired of being asked to shoo away stray dogs (he was right here a minute ago ...) or change front porch lightbulbs (I can't see if it's a robber with the light out, now can I?).

She sighed. "I'm on my way."

Twenty minutes later, she stood on the south end of Barb Jameson's property.

Lizzie stared up at the tall pines on the edge of the shallow, burbling river. Boughs bent under their weight, six bald eagles sat, regally ignoring the two women.

"Someone's been feeding them," Mrs. Jameson said, arms crossed, staring up into the trees.

"I . . ." Lizzie didn't want to insult the woman, and she searched her mind for a polite way to rebuff the claim. "Who do you think is feeding them?"

"Frank Fellows, that's who. You know he's a birdwatching fiend."

She had to admit that she'd often seen Frank birding in the woods around the Falls. He often called the sheriff's office to request that they set up a barrier to prevent people from trampling a nest of a rare species . . . those requests were usually denied, much to his dismay.

"You've *seen* Frank feeding the eagles?"

Mrs. Jameson flattened her lips into a displeased line before sputtering her answer. "Well, no, but he's my prime suspect."

"I think eagles—as well as other birds—are just sociable creatures . . . I think they're prone to group behavior," she said, letting her voice trail off meaningfully. Lizzie would pull out her phone later, probably over an apple with peanut butter, and investigate the truth of the statement. But she knew that the good people of Timber Falls—especially the older set—did not look kindly on the sheriff's office blowing off their concerns.

"Maybe you could drop in on Frank. You know, unannounced. See if he's got unnatural quantities of meat lying about."

Lizzie pulled her lips to one side. "I think I'd need a search warrant for that, and I don't have enough to go on right now . . . and anyway, feeding the eagles isn't a crime."

"They're a public nuisance!" Mrs. Jameson cried insistently, throwing out one hand toward the riverbank.

"Well, be that as it may . . . it's just not my jurisdiction. Would you like the number for Fish and Wildlife? I'm sure they could tell you more than I could about bird habits."

Mrs. Jameson deflated. "That won't be necessary. Well, thank you for coming by." She patted Lizzie affectionately on the back. "It's not your fault the laws of this town are so backward."

"Laws that prevent me from searching Frank's property needlessly are good ones, Mrs. Jameson. I wouldn't want anyone just barging into my house without permission." *Except maybe Chase.* For a split second that morning, she'd thought he might park in front of the house and come sauntering up the front walk in that way of his . . . it was a welcome thought.

"Barbara Jameson! I hear you talking smack about me!" Since that was an unusual choice of words for a man in his seventies, Frank must have been picking things up from his grandchildren again.

"Then don't give me a reason to, Frank! Quit feeding the eagles!"

His sigh was so big, it carried across the chain-link fence between their properties. "For the last time, woman, this is just what eagles do!"

"Then why are you down at the river every morning?"

"To take their picture!" he yelled, storming around the end of the fence toward them, so exasperated that his silver mustache was quivering. "I told you, I'm entering that National Geographic contest!"

"A likely cover!"

"No, it's not a cover story, it's just a contest," he said. "Lord, woman. Try listening."

"That's uncalled for," Barb sniffed.

"I think my work here is done," Lizzie said, trying to slide toward her cruiser as subtly as she could.

"Very well. Would you like to come in for a sherry?" Why couldn't her grandmother's friends be normal and offer, like, cookies? It was ten o'clock on a Thursday morning, for crying out loud.

"No, thank you. I have some other stops to make this morning." And she felt no need to go back to the station smelling like alcohol. Besides, sherry with Mrs. Jameson had a way of spinning out of control. She'd already had to reprimand the Mind Readers for noise complaints after the last time they'd met at her house.

"Tell your grandma I said hi," Mrs. Jameson added, giving Frank and the eagles one final glare before she climbed the porch steps to go back inside. Then, at the top, she paused. "Oh dear, my porch light is out. Deputy, while you're here . . ."

CHAPTER ELEVEN: Chase

CHASE OFFERED A FRIENDLY nod to several people as they filed into the big conference room, smoothing down his tie nervously. There still hadn't been any public acknowledgment that he was back; today would be the day. His father's chair at the head of the long table was empty; Chase's place had been right next to him. Today, there was a legal pad on one side of him and a pink sweater on the other. It made the ceiling feel lower . . . or maybe that was just his stomach. Well, it wasn't reasonable to expect that nothing had changed since he'd been gone. Chase slid into a spot farther down the table, very near the foot of it, and listened to the low chatter of the room. There was some big announcement being made, but no one knew what it was.

One minute before the meeting was set to start, Chase got a text.

Unknown number: Thank you for your letter; I wrote one back. I sent it to your house.

Lizzie. This was better than he'd projected.

He fumbled to text back quickly just as his father swept into the room, dead on time as usual. He wore a dark blue suit, his silver hair swept back off his forehead. He met Chase's gaze for a moment, then looked away. Was that guilt in his dad's eyes? A sense of dread swept through Chase.

"Good morning, everyone. I'm pleased to be able to make an announcement many of you have been waiting for. As you may remember, a few years ago, we acquired a partial interest in Albany Paper in New York. Like our company, it's a small operation that's grown over the years. Unlike our company, it hasn't had good leadership." Chase resisted the urge to roll his eyes at his dad's backdoor compliment to himself. "So I sent my son Christopher to work with them. I won't bore you with all the details, but when we purchased our half, we locked in a rate in case we wanted to buy out the original owner, Bill Swanson." Chase hadn't known that. He wondered if anyone had told him or if he'd just been too out of it to know what was going on. "He has worked tirelessly to improve the company, weeding out the dead weight, con-solidating departments, boosting their marketing and sales departments. I'm pleased to finally be able to announce that we have finalized all the details with Albany, and we bought it for a fraction of what it's now worth. Christopher will be coming back to help us handle the merger. Let's welcome him home." Everyone began to applaud, and Chase's head snapped to the back of the room where Chris was leaning against the wall.

No text. No call. No 'hey, I'm gonna be in town.' Just shows up, casual as you please. Chase tried to swallow down the hurt of that as Christopher took his place at their father's side.

His twin picked up the yellow legal pad. Oh, it was double hurt now. Because Dad hadn't even mentioned to the team that Chase was back, and here he was, introducing Christopher like a conquering prince come back from a foreign land, the head of their enemy in his fist.

Christopher gave them his signature smile, empty but somehow knowing. "Nice to see some familiar faces around this table." He avoided Chase's pointed gaze, and Chase wondered if he realized the deep irony of that. "My role will be to help facilitate TFPP taking over Albany's west coast clients and Albany taking over our east coast clients, in order to streamline our operations. This is a fantastic opportunity for both companies, and we're looking forward to sharing the vision of our operations with all of you. I'll be working closely with marketing to help them understand both companies and come up with a plan to unveil the merger in a way our clients will appreciate, as well as rebranding the companies as a single entity." Marketing. Great. He'd be spending extra time with the golden boy, undoubtedly being upstaged by him at every turn. Chase chided himself inwardly for the bitter thought, but this galled. He hadn't even gotten a "welcome back" back slap, and here was Christopher being hailed as a hero. And yet, he knew it wasn't really Chris's fault. His dad was really the one to blame, not his twin. He was just doing as he was told. "I'll be splitting my time between New York and this office for the next few months, so if you need something, please arrange it through my secretary. I will send you her information by email. I'm excited to be back, and ready to help TFPP into this new phase of our success."

More applause. Chase looked around as they beamed at his twin. Their hero. The successful Carpenter son. On one hand, Chase couldn't blame them: Christopher was good at his job. Always had been. On the other hand, he hated that no one could see his potential now. He was just as smart as Christopher. Just as capable, despite his anxiety. He sat up straighter and put his phone down on the shiny conference table. He'd just have to show them. Show them that he'd changed, that he could be dependable, too. The weight of that made him sink an inch deeper into his chair. Wasn't it that drive, that competition, that had gotten him into trouble in the first place?

"Can you tell me about what happened?" Dr. Archer had asked. "This doesn't look good." That wasn't news to Chase or his father; they'd come here to Salem to see an orthopedic specialist after Dr. Durand recommended him.

"He took a bad fall in the playoffs," Harrison had explained. "The other guy just came down right on his knee, twisted it."

"Mmm," the doctor had grimaced, gently probing Chase's injury with his fingers. "It looks like you've got a combination of issues here. I'm guessing you've got tendon tears with possible posterior cruciate ligament damage, based on how your knee is falling back like that. We'll do some x-rays and an MRI . . ." Chase had stopped listening there. There was no time for this; he was trying to get his team to State. They were depending on him.

"Can you give me something for it, so I can keep playing?"

Dr. Archer nodded, pulling out his prescription pad. "But you have to promise you'll do your physical therapy . . ."

"I promise." He would promise anything to get back on the field. To make his dad proud.

"Hey." Christopher stood at his elbow, and Chase forced himself back to the present. Almost everyone had cleared out of the room, except for a few lingering conversations.

"Hey." Chase stood up and went to hug Christopher. His twin looked like he was expecting something else—a punch in the nose, perhaps?—but when he squeezed him right, he patted Chase's back in reluctant reciprocity. "Why didn't you tell me you were coming to town?"

"It's a short trip. I don't have time to socialize."

"I didn't realize having a meal together would be such a burden . . ."

"Give me a break, Chase."

"What?" Chase asked innocently.

"You sound just like Mom. Before . . ." he trailed off meaningfully. *Before she starting losing her memories?* Chase didn't think that was much of an insult.

"Oh, she still sounds like that," Chase chuckled. "Are you staying at the estate?" *And why didn't you tell me you were coming? You knew we'd run into each other. You knew I'd find out.* He kept those uncomfortable questions to himself. If he could just talk to his brother, maybe he could figure what had gone wrong between them and fix it. Twin love ran deep . . . at least from his side of things. Deeper than promotions or any of this work BS.

"Yeah."

"Okay if I come by for dinner?"

"Not tonight. I have an engagement."

Chase rolled his eyes so hard they hurt, and the overhead fluorescents didn't help. "No time to socialize? Right, Mr. Booty Call in Every Town."

His twin scowled a little, his smooth façade dropping momentarily. "It's not a booty call," Christopher muttered. "Dinner. Tomorrow. Don't be late." Hope, like an antacid, bubbled a little before it ran out. This was a start. It was something. Christopher hadn't turned down his offer; he hadn't been aware of how much he was afraid of that until he knew it wasn't going to happen. He wanted to joke with him. He wanted the good stuff back.

"Why does everyone assume I'm going to be late?"

"Mr. Carpenter," Nicole called from the doorway, her gaze bouncing between the two of them when they both turned. "Uh, Mr. *Chase* Carpenter. They're waiting for you on your conference call."

Christopher smirked as he walked out, leaving Chase scrambling to gather up his stuff. He checked his phone for the time and saw Lizzie's message again.

"I'll be right there," he told Nicole, focused on the phone, finishing the text he should've sent twenty minutes ago. When the object of his affections texted him for the first time, it would not do to keep her waiting, whoever else he had to keep waiting instead.

Chase: Awesome. Fantastic. Marvelous.
Lizzie: And here's Gram's number. She said she'd love to meet with you.
Chase: Great. I'll give her a call. Thanks, Lizzie.

At least something was going right today; his eyes lingered longer than they should have as he stared at her name and number, now programmed into his phone. Even on such a bad day, he could find a little sunshine, a little something to be grateful for. And that was Lizzie.

CHAPTER TWELVE: Lizzie

THE NEXT FEW DAYS WERE busy as the station started preparing for Captain Hansen's departure. Both times Lizzie had tried to talk to him about her promotion, they'd been interrupted and the talk was delayed. Both times, Mark had needed something, and it had taken precedence over her concerns. He'd ridden along with her in the cruiser both days, too; she'd always politely refused the offers to send her out with a partner in the past, and now she knew why. By 6:30 p.m., Lizzie was already unbuttoning her uniform shirt with one hand when she closed the back door, ready to shed this day.

"Gram, I'm home," she called. The kitchen smelled like apples, thyme, and pork, and she suspected that something amazing was in the oven . . . but it felt quiet? Too quiet? Where was Pancake?

"We're in here," her grandmother called back, and her heart rate went down momentarily before she realized what she'd said. *We? The strange car on the street.* She'd assumed it belonged to one of the neighbors. Now her heart rate was back up. Lizzie held her shirt together at her neck, even though she hadn't gotten far enough to show anything. She contemplated going up the back stairs . . . they were right there, so convenient. She felt they were beckoning her, inviting her to escape from whatever social nightmare this was going to be. But then her grandmother's visitor laughed, and she paused with her foot on the bottom step.

Chase. What is he doing here? Quickly re-buttoning her shirt, Lizzie ambled into the living room like that had been her plan all along.

"Oh, there you are," Gram grinned. "How was work?"

How was work? Really? No mention of Chase, currently rubbing my traitorous dog's belly? Lizzie glanced among the three of them, waiting for an explanation that was apparently not coming. At least Pancake had an excuse.

"Fine. Nothing to report. Hello, Chase."

"Hello, Lizzie." He was looking at her like she'd just stepped out dressed for prom, not dusty and wrinkled from a long day of work, strands of hair escaping its bun.

"How was your day?" she asked, her gaze bouncing between them.

"Just fine." Her grandmother went on, "I asked Chase to come to dinner after we were done seeing houses. His condo should fetch a good price, and—"

"That's great."

Gram gave her a look that said she didn't care for being interrupted but didn't comment on it.

"Yeah, we thought it'd be fun," Chase said with an easy smile. "Do you mind, Lizzie?"

My kingdom for a time machine. She would go back and slap herself silly for encouraging him to use her first name so casually, so off-handedly, as if it didn't make her heart squeeze whenever he uttered it.

"Of course not." She couldn't be rude. *Say more. Say something so he won't expect to spend the whole evening together.* "I have plans, though."

Gram chuckled knowingly. "You can record your shows for one night."

Lizzie scowled. "My plans might not include TV, you know. I could've meant something else."

Her grandmother cocked her head at her, then motioned her to come closer. When she did, she pressed her cool hand to Lizzie's forehead.

"What are you doing?"

"I'm trying to figure out what's got your panties in a twist." Chase chuckled, trying to hide it behind his fist and a cough.

"Gram!"

"You don't feel feverish," Gram muttered, ignoring Lizzie's resentful tone and the hot blush working its way up her chest toward her cheeks. She couldn't bear to see Chase's reaction to this humiliation.

"I'm going to go change." She darted out of the living room at top speed, only to slow her feet on the narrow back steps for fear of falling. The whole time she was upstairs, she tried to figure out if she should be hurrying to be polite or stalling to avoid small talk. She ended up sitting on the edge of her bed for a few minutes, staring at herself in her vanity mirror. His laughter drifting up from the kitchen finally drew her back down. *He laughs a lot*, she thought as she crept down the stairs, trying to eavesdrop. *I like that.*

"Oh good, you're just in time," Gram called, rudely ruining her attempt to listen in, and Lizzie changed her gait to walk normally by the time she reached the bottom. "Can you take this to the table?" she asked, holding out a basket of rolls, and Lizzie obeyed, ignoring Chase's lingering gaze. What was he even looking at? It was an old basketball T-shirt and a pair of jeans. The fact that she wasn't in her pajamas—that's what people should be noticing.

She jumped when Chase was right behind her, looking concerned. "Is this not okay?" he asked in a low voice, too low to be heard in the kitchen over Gram's pot and pan clanging.

"No, it's fine. It's good. You're fine."

"Because if it's not, I can go. Just say the word. I can make up some excuse."

"No, it's okay."

"I thought maybe you'd mentioned dinner to your grandma when she invited me because your letter said . . ."

She blinked at him. "How do you know that?"

He ran a hand through his hair. "After I got your text, I drove here on my lunch break and stole it out of your mailbox before Mr. Graves got to it."

"That's a federal offense, you know," she sniffed, but he smiled at her like she was something wonderful. It made her heart feel like fondue: melty and disgusting. It was too soon for gooey feelings toward the man. "Expectations, Chase," she muttered. "Manage them."

"Which ones?"

"All of them," she replied quietly, forcing a smile as Gram started toward them.

"Too late," he grinned. He turned to Gram. "Anything I can do to help, Mrs. Draper?"

"Oh, please, call me Tansy. Can you bring in the pork? The potholders are hanging on the fridge . . ."

Chase slipped out of the room, and Gram turned to her.

"Be polite," she hissed. "Seriously, Lizzie. It's one dinner."

"I didn't say anything!" Lizzie hissed back. "I'm being nice."

"He's a client. This is business." Lizzie didn't bother pointing out that she'd never had a client over for dinner before they'd signed the final paperwork and rarely after. Chase came back, and they all sat down.

"So . . ." Lizzie said, hating the silence, and they both turned to look at her. She probably should've planned what she was going to say before she said "so." She cleared her throat uncomfortably. "Did you see anything you liked today?"

"I don't know," Chase sighed. "I don't exactly know what I want. Your grandma was very patient with me. She's going to be sick of my indecision long before I actually buy something."

"Nonsense," said Gram, waving her fork emphatically. "What's truly annoying are the people who think they know what they want, but don't. At least you're honest."

He is that, Lizzie thought, *in spades*.

"I mean, should I get a house? Another condo? Do I go for a bungalow, since it's just me? Or do I try to plan for the future and get something bigger, something with a yard for kids or whatever?" He sighed again. "I have no idea the right thing to do."

"That's because there isn't one," Lizzie said, serving herself some salad. Chase glanced up at her from carving himself some pork, and she suddenly realized she'd spoken without thinking about it. Or rather, without overthinking about it. Apparently, even outside his letters, he had that effect on her.

"Why do you say that?" he asked, popping a bite of roasted apple into his mouth.

"Every decision is going to have upsides and downsides. Nothing is irreversible. That's all."

He nodded slowly. "That's a good way to look at it."

That was enough attention for a while. She kept quiet through the rest of most of the meal, only interjecting when she had something really important to add. Lizzie was just starting to relax when Chase wiped his mouth with his napkin.

"This was so good, Tansy. Thank you for inviting me. I should get going, let you two get on with your evening." He gave Lizzie a look that said *I know you're ready for me to leave*, and she hid a smile behind her napkin, wiping it off with the crumbs at the corners of her mouth.

"Are you sure? We usually just watch *Jeopardy!*."

"No wonder Lizzie was so good at Trivia Night," he said, giving her a little wink, and she felt her brain cells fry just a little bit at that tiny flirtation.

"Oh," Gram said, sitting forward, "were you there, too?"

"Are you kidding? Geek Tragedy would be nothing without me!" They laughed and Gram walked him to the front door. Pancake, who'd been lying at Lizzie's feet, mostly because she was dropping morsels of pork for him, jumped up and ran over to him.

"Are you going with him?" Lizzie asked, glancing between their guest and her dog. Chase bent down, cooing to the dog.

"You're a good boy. Good boy. You stay here and guard these ladies. I'll see you soon?" Chase glanced up at her when he said this, the question lingering in his gaze. This had been okay. A little painful, but not too bad. She'd do it again. Lizzie gave him a little nod, and he grinned as he straightened up.

"Thanks so much for dinner. You two have a nice evening."

Pancake sat at the front door, staring longingly out the screen door well after the first column was cleared in the *Jeopardy!* round 'Colleges and Universities'.

"So," her grandmother said, when a commercial interrupted the show, "Chase was at Trivia?"

"Yeah." Lizzie stuffed some popcorn into her mouth.

"How was he?"

"Terrible." *And yet, I think he had more fun than I did.*

"Mmm. Who invited him?"

"Martina."

"Martina? Isn't she marrying his brother?"

"Yup."

Gram sat back, looking dissatisfied with the one-word answers. *What else is new?*

"He's pretty good-looking."

Lizzie shook her head slowly. "Gram."

She held up hands innocently. "I'm just saying. He's handsome, he's got money, he's got a sense of humor. Your grandfather had two of those things, and we made a pretty great life together. He's kind of a catch."

Lizzie turned toward her. "You remember why he got arrested, right?"

"Sure," Gram nodded, "but that's not who he is now, is it?"

"I don't know." She squirmed a little in her seat because she *did* think she knew: it wasn't.

"So maybe just give it a chance. See where it goes."

Lizzie rolled her eyes. "There's nothing to go anywhere. We're friends, sort of. That's all." She turned her attention back to the TV. "What is the Nile?"

Gram muttered something under her breath, but Lizzie ignored her. Her phone vibrated.

Chase: Sorry I dropped in like that. I'll try to warn you next time. Hope I didn't screw up your evening plans too badly.

Lizzie: No, it's fine.

Chase: It's not fine. I don't like surprises, either.

She blinked. That was true. She hated surprises . . . it was one thing at work, where she'd learned to expect the unexpected, but she didn't want to feel that way at home. That was what had stung about the surprise birthday party Gram had thrown, him showing up for dinner, all of it. But it surprised her that Chase had picked up on that just from her letters.

Lizzie: It's really fine.
Chase: I wanted to stay. I love Jeopardy.
Lizzie: You could've. Maybe next time.

Maybe next time? Way to be presumptuous, Painter. Although all signs did point toward Chase wanting a second . . . whatever this was. Dinner. Not a date. It didn't count as a date if your grandmother mentioned your panties in the course of the evening.

Chase: Yeah. That sounds nice.
Chase: And thanks for your letter. It was a good one.
Lizzie: You're welcome.

"This young man makes Elizabeth grin," Gram said, affecting a game show host's careful enunciation. "Who is Chase Carpenter?"

Lizzie wiped the treacherous smile from her face and jammed her phone in her back pocket, crossing her arms. "What is nonsense?"

"That's not the right question," her grandmother replied, smirking.

"It most definitely is," Lizzie returned as she stared at the screen.

CHAPTER THIRTEEN:
Letters

DEAR LIZZIE,

Your dad sounds awesome. I remember him a little, actually. He came to our Cub Scouts meeting once and talked about fire safety. Wasn't he our chief for a while, or am I imagining that? It was always weird watching them put on all the pieces of their outfit, slowly turning from a human to some sort of outer space alien. I'd never really worried about fire before he came, but his talk gave me nightmares for weeks. Not that it was his fault or anything . . . I've never exactly slept well. For comparison, the only time my dad ever came to Cub Scouts, he gave out samples of Timber Falls facial tissues and talked about why they should come work at the mill when they were older.

You were right about living with my mom; I'm enjoying it. Kind of weird being back in my old bedroom, but it's good, too. Lots of routines around here, and I thrive on routine. I've started having a cup of tea with my mom in the morning before work; we don't really talk about anything, but it's nice just to sit with her. I've missed her. And even though she doesn't know who I am all the time, I think she knows what we mean to each other, if that makes sense.

Will I see you at Trivia this week?

Sincerely,

Chase

P.S. I'm so glad we started this up again. I missed it.

DEAR CHASE,

No, he wasn't the chief, just a regular volunteer. But he liked giving talks in the community. My uncle Ed was burned badly as a kid when one of their fireworks went off too close to him, so it's something he really cared about. Uncle Ed's always been kind of a daredevil; he likes skydiving, goes every year. He used to tell me these wild pirate stories when I came over to his house, set on Tortuga or Hispaniola or other places I'd never heard of. He was teaching me how to stand on my bike seat until my dad made me stop. Sometimes I wonder how Uncle Ed is still alive.

Sleep is overrated as far as I'm concerned. I've never been one of those people who gets eight hours a night. When I try, I wake up at 4 a.m. and can't get back to sleep. That's worse than being up late, especially since I'm not a coffee drinker. Sunrises just obscure the stars.

I don't know if I can make it to Trivia. Maybe.

L

CHAPTER FOURTEEN:
Chase

IT WAS LASAGNA NIGHT at the Carpenter house, but the atmosphere at the dining room table did not remind Chase of Italy whatsoever. Christopher, Carter, Martina, Willow, and Harrison sat around the long oak table with him; no one spoke. His father and his twin were on their phones, apparently still working. In his mind, he couldn't help but compare it to meals at Gretta's, which were usually laughing and loud and just made him feel like he belonged. The only thing warm here was his entrée, and it just wasn't cutting it. Chase wiped his mouth.

"How was your day?"

Martina looked up. "Who?"

"Anyone. Everyone. You start."

"Um, it was good," she answered. "Willow and I went shopping."

"Yes, we went to the outlets," his mom added. "It was lovely. I found a pair of navy pumps."

"Is that right?" Chase asked, trying to make it sound like a rhetorical question, even as he glanced at Martina for confirmation. She gave him a wink. He did not know how to interpret that, but at least people were talking now.

"And you, Carter? How's the mathematical world of actuary work?"

"Predictable as ever," he smiled. "How was your day?"

He had not thought this through. Both his father and his twin were paying attention now, their phones still glowing up at them like faithful hunting dogs, waiting for their next command. Today, he'd met with Christopher about the merger. They didn't agree whatsoever on how to approach it, and his marketing team had spent the rest of the day throwing a giant hissy fit. Albany wanted to hyphenate the name with theirs first, and Christopher had already agreed. The logo would resemble TFPP's more than Albany's, but still. Their faithful clientele up and down the west coast were not going to like this; the main draw of their business was that it was local. Sustainable. Putting the east coast name first was going to take some serious spin.

"Thank you for asking," Chase said slowly. Stalling wasn't going to work, and he knew it. But he didn't have to look at them when he told the truth. "My day was a challenge."

"Oh?" Harrison said, leaning forward. "Why's that?"

"Because my department wasn't consulted on a huge decision, and they were upset. I felt caught in the middle." Gretta was big on expressing your feelings in a healthy way, and Chase had had plenty of practice in an environment where everyone valued that ethos.

As previously established, however, this was not Gretta's.

Harrison snorted. Christopher just stared at him, unreadable. Martina's gaze was sympathetic, Carter's was curious, watching to see their family members' response.

"So sorry to injure your feelings," Harrison drawled, "but this is business, not counseling." He was used to his father's sarcasm; he was fluent in it. But it still felt like a dig at his rehab experience, and Chase couldn't help but resent it.

"I'm not criticizing you, just stating a fact," Chase returned, and he shoved another bite of pasta into his mouth so he wouldn't say any more.

Christopher muttered something aside to Harrison, and their father laughed. Chase felt his temper spike like he'd just been slapped. There had always been a bond between his dad and his brother that he couldn't touch, but they'd never flaunted it like this. Privately, it had been him and Chris against the world. But Chris seemed to be making it clear whose side he was on now.

"My navy pumps are really pretty," Willow said, spearing some salad on her fork.

"They are," Martina agreed. "What do you say we go upstairs? You can bring your plate if you want." Maybe she sensed the brewing family storm or maybe it really was time for Willow to start winding down; Chase didn't know. But he hated the feeling that he'd driven them off, just because he couldn't stand the silence. Uncomfortably, the silence came back as the ladies left, their voices echoing in the foyer as they climbed the front staircase.

"She can't remember to turn off the sink when she's done washing her hands, but she can't stop talking about those shoes," Carter chuckled once they'd gone. Even his father and brother seemed amused by the comment. But then Harrison and Christopher went back to their phones, now that the entertainment was over. *Just as well.*

"Hey, you wanna get some air?" Chase said, elbowing Carter. "I was thinking about a walk."

"Sure," Carter said. "Let me just text Martina and let her know."

Christopher made the sound of a whip cracking without looking up, and Carter's face went cold.

"That's funny coming from the guy who literally never stops working. At least what I love loves me back." He pushed back from the table and stalked out of the room and into the back hallway and Chase followed, throwing a glance over his shoulder just long enough to take in Christopher's stunned gaze. He chuckled a little; he had to admit, he was a little stunned himself, since Carter was usually the peacemaker these days. His younger brother was standing by the back door, texting his fiancée with one and hand massaging his temple with the other.

"I shouldn't have said that," Carter muttered.

Chase toed into his tennis shoes. "It's not untrue," he said, leading the way outside.

"But it didn't need to be said." He paused as they descended the stairs. "Did he tell you he was coming to town?"

"Nope. And he didn't tell me he was coming back to work at TFPP. He barely responds to my texts, and when he does, it's so scathing, I want to sue him for libel."

Carter laughed, but it was obvious by the crinkles on his forehead that it also concerned him.

"Don't worry about it," Chase said. "Not in our control. Doesn't need to be. If Christopher wants to be our brother again, he knows I'm here for it."

Carter shook his head. "Old Chase would not have been so cool about this."

"Old Chase was an insecure donkey who tried to control other people because his world felt out of control."

"Donkey," Carter snorted. "You swear like an old man."

Chase wasn't ready to let the other conversation go that easily. "Don't you feel that? The need for control?"

"It's an easy trap to fall into, I guess. Even with Martina, I find myself wanting to tell her how to do things, even though she doesn't need me to. I just want her to need me."

"I'm pretty sure she does," Chase said. He did not mention that he'd seen Martina through the kitchen door the other night, leaving the house just after midnight, her hair messy, her smile betraying some kind of private joy.

"Speaking of lady loves," Carter said, bouncing his eyebrows, "how are things going with your pen pal?"

"Um . . ." Chase wasn't sure where to start. "Complicated?"

"Why can't you just ask her out?"

"Because I'm ninety-nine percent sure that she'd say no."

"Wait. But didn't she write back?"

"Yeah, she did . . ." He let out a sigh. "She's kind of a mystery."

"Is she just shy or what?"

"Yeah. She's, like, shy to the extreme, I think."

"Hmm. So the challenge is letting her get comfortable with you?"

"I guess so, yeah." He gave his brother the side-eye. "I'm surprised you're backing this. Christopher would tell me she wasn't worth my time."

"I'm not Christopher. And it seems like she's important to you, so . . ." He shrugged. "I can let bygones be bygones. It was her job to arrest you, after all."

"Yeah, I can't hold that against her."

"You're braver than I would be. She kind of intimidates me."

Chase laughed. "Why?"

"I don't know," Carter shrugged. "I just always feel like she's watching. Waiting for me to do something illegal."

"Oh, she definitely is," Chase joked, nodding sagely. "But she knows a heck of a lot about dead presidents."

"Oh, that reminds me—I don't think Martina's available to pick her up this week for trivia, and you know she'll bag on it if no one makes her show up."

Chase squinted at his brother in the waning evening light. "Is she 'not available,' or is she actually not available? I don't want her to meddle."

His brother grimaced. "I'm telling you, the meddling was inevitable the minute Lizzie mentioned those letters during her traffic stop . . ."

Chase felt his eyes go wide. "She did?"

"Yup," Carter said. "If anything, we should be praising Martina's restraint in not sending out wedding invites on your behalf. I have endured endless speculation about you two. *Are they still writing, do you think? What do they talk about? How did it start?* I assumed it was just nonsense until you started asking questions about her friends."

"Way too early for wedding planning," Chase said, but he had to laugh. His new sister-in-law was awesome. It was nice to have someone in his corner who wanted him to be happy. "But tell her I'd look at fonts if she has some picked out."

CHAPTER FIFTEEN: Lizzie

IT HAD BEEN A HECK of a hump day at the station; most of them had been called out to a multi-car pileup on I-5, leaving Lizzie to hold down the fort by herself. Thankfully, there were no fatalities, and no one from town had been involved. Her coworkers had just gotten back when they got a call late in the day, so she offered to go even though it involved two of her least favorite people. Mark, of course, invited himself along. He made small talk in the cruiser, which she responded to with as few words as possible, so as not to encourage him. He eventually got the message and shut up.

"Gentlemen," Lizzie greeted, hoping it would inspire the men toward civility. It was never fun getting in the middle of an argument between two giant jerks, especially in the parking lot of Annie's.

"I want this man arrested," James Miller said, stabbing a finger in Levi Zane's direction. "He *poisoned* me." How this man could be related to sweet Jason Miller was unfathomable to her. His resemblance to his son Charlie was more obvious.

"If I'd poisoned you, you'd be dead," Levi retorted. "And you don't look dead."

"Can you tell me how this started, Mr. Miller?"

"I picked up pizza on Tuesday night for me and my family. He knows I always get a personal size supreme pizza for me because everyone else likes mushrooms."

"Mushrooms are gross," Lizzie sympathized.

"Right? She gets it," James said, calming a little. "So everything's fine and we take the pizzas home, and that night, I'm a sick as a dog, up until two a.m., barfing my guts out. No one else, just me."

Lizzie clicked her pen. "Can you tell me what was on the pizza?"

Levi shrugged. "If he ordered a supreme, it's just sausage, black olives, pepperoni, onions, and green peppers."

"Peppers?" Mr. Miller was frowning. "Has it always had peppers?"

"Yes," Levi bit out. "Unless you ask for them to be left off."

"Oh." Mr. Miller shifted his weight like a boxer. "My wife usually calls in the order, but she was busy, so I did it. But you should know what we order by now! It never changes."

Levi huffed out a humorless laugh. "You can't expect me to remember your food preferences, man. I make about a million pizzas a week, and I'm not the one taking your order. If you have a problem with that, go talk to Annie. I'm done here." He turned and stalked back into the brick building, slamming the heavy door behind him. James Miller stood still, staring after him, his face red.

"I still maintain he knew what he was doing. It's well-known that I have an intolerance to green peppers."

"I think you'd be hard-pressed to prove that, sir . . ." Especially because Lizzie hadn't known it, though she would make a note of it when she got back to her desk. She kept files on everyone. *Harriet the Spy* had been a favorite book of hers as a child, and in her opinion, Harriet's only mistake had been leaving her diary where someone else could read it. Lizzie's files were under lock and key. It was nothing unflattering . . . well, mostly nothing unflattering. Nothing illegal, anyway. But it didn't hurt to keep her finger on the pulse of the town, for reasons just such as these. If she'd known James couldn't eat peppers, she could've figured out what happened in less time and been back on the road by now. In her mind, conflict management mostly came down to knowing your audience; she'd seen moms practicing the same strategies for years.

"Do you really want to get banned by the only pizza place in town, because you sued them over a misunderstanding?" Mark asked.

James was stalking off now, too, grumbling under his breath, seeing that he was going to get no justice from either of them. She checked her phone; no messages from the captain. She'd drop Mark off at the station, run in to get her backpack, and then, finally, go home.

A gray minivan pulled into the parking, and Ainsley waved at her through the window. "You're here early," she sang out, then Lizzie saw her confusion as her gaze traveled down her uniformed body. "Wait, are you still working?"

Early? Oh crap. It's Trivia Night. There would be no escape for her. *Great.*

"I just finished . . ." She glanced at her new boss. "But I'll have to take Mark back to the station first." *Then maybe I'll just forget to come back.* But if she did that, she wouldn't get to see Chase tonight. They'd exchanged another letter, and it was feeling . . . comfortable? He hadn't pushed to see her again, much to her relief. But she'd been thinking about it. About him.

"Actually, I'd like to stay," said Mark.

Five words. Just that. Five words could completely incapacitate Lizzie, apparently. She imagined herself sitting at a table between Mark and Chase, and she already felt frozen. It was bad enough trying to socialize with people she was actually friends with, but with Mark there, who was she supposed to be? Was she still the go-getting deputy who wanted a promotion or was she "one step up from pajamas" relaxed Lizzie? It didn't really feel possible to be either . . . not without upsetting someone. This was a bad idea. Maybe she could just tell him there wasn't room on the team . . .

"Oh, how nice," Ainsley said with a smile, covering for Lizzie's silence, and she winced inside. "Kyle had to duck out tonight, so we're one short. We'd love for you to join us."

"Great! I'm Mark Wright, by the way," he said, holding out a hand, which Ainsley shook. "I'll be taking over for Captain Hansen at the station."

"You're from Silverton, right?"

"Yes, ma'am. I believe we met at a town meeting when we worked on our districtwide gun safety initiative a few years ago."

Ainsley continued to make small talk, but Lizzie, now in a full panic, had tuned out. Right now, he was still in professional mode. It was obvious that Mark wanted to be sheriff someday, and this job was his stepping stone. But was he staying because he was working, getting to know Timber Falls better like he'd said, or was he staying because she kept turning down his invitations to socialize? Did he think this was some kind of *date*? What was Chase going to think if they showed up together? *You're not dating Chase. You're just writing letters, like a chicken.*

Lizzie stalked into the building abruptly, noting the brief pause in conversation behind her.

"Is she okay?" Ainsley asked, but Lizzie didn't hear Mark's answer. She weaved through the half-empty tables, past James setting up, past Annie at the bar, straight to the bathroom. Lizzie splashed cold water on her face, then pressed a paper towel to her skin as she tried to think. What was she going to do? How was this going to work? If she pretended to be sick, would Martina take her temperature again? If she left now, would Chase think she was blowing him off? Also, was it her imagination, or was she hyperventilating a little bit? Home, home, she wanted to go home.

"Lizzie?" Ainsley's voice behind her was quiet. "Everything all right in here?"

She nodded but didn't uncover her face.

"Is there anything I can do for you?"

"Can you get rid of Mark?" she asked timidly, her voice muffed through her hands.

"Why?" Ainsley sounded alarmed. "Is he bothering you?"

"No. Well, kind of, but I doubt it's intentional."

"Why do we need to get rid of him, then? Is he unsafe?"

"No, no, nothing like that. I just don't know how to be around him like"—she gestured to the room around them—"like this. In this kind of place. He's a work person, not a friend person."

There was a long pause. "I see. So you want me to knock him off? Because you'd know it was me, and I don't think Kyle would be cool with me getting arrested . . . he's really looking forward to getting married, and all that entails."

Lizzie chuckled and let the paper towel drop. At least she never wore mascara, so there was nothing to run. She carefully wiped her slightly teary eyes.

"I would totally arrest you."

"I know you would. You're great at your job. But it's okay to let us all see a side of you that's not job-related, too. Even if Mark is here." Ainsley had slid closer as she spoke, and she rubbed her back in a way that was calming, even if it was a little patronizing. Lizzie let out a shaky breath.

"Okay."

"Okay, you'll stay?"

She nodded.

"Oh good, I didn't want to have to listen to Martina complain if I let two team members leave before she even got here," Ainsley chuckled as she wrapped an arm around Lizzie's shoulders and gave her a tight squeeze. "And you tell me if I can do anything to help."

"No, I'll be okay."

"Okay." Ainsley held the door open for her, and they went out to the table where Mark had struck up a conversation with Martina and Carter.

"And through our partnership with local businesses, we've managed to bring that number down significantly." They were nodding politely when he turned to her. "Oh, there you are. Everything okay?"

"Of course," she said, debating which chair to sit in. Probably better if she sat between Chase and Mark, then she wasn't playing favorites. But Chase wasn't here yet. "No Chase tonight?"

"Oh, no, he's coming. I sent him to your house to pick you up, but that turned out to be pointless. I should've communicated better."

Lizzie felt horrible. Not only was she sort of here with someone else, but she'd also sort of stood him up, and now she *really* couldn't pick a chair. This was a disaster, this was horrible, she could not handle it if Chase was upset . . .

"Hey, everybody," Chase greeted with a smile. "Hey, Lizzie."

She brushed lightly at his dress shirt, which had two long smudges down the front of it. A blue dress shirt, the perfect shade to bring out his eyes. If she was writing about them, she'd describe them as a dazzling shade of aquamarine. But here, face to face, she couldn't say such things aloud.

"Hello. You're all dirty," she noted, blushing at how unintentionally familiar she'd been, putting her hands on his chest like that without asking first.

"Oh, it's no big deal," he said, also attempting in vain to wipe off the stains. "Pancake was just saying hi." Of course he had. Of course he'd gotten out of the car and opened the gate to pet her giant, ill-behaved dog. Based on the amount of hair on his trousers, he had spent considerable time with him. From anyone else, she'd think it was a dirty, rotten trick to win her affections. But not from Chase. He looked past her momentarily, squinting a little.

"Oh, hi. Sorry, from the back, you looked like Kyle, so I thought . . . I'm Chase Carpenter," he said, rising and reaching in front of her to offer his hand to Mark.

"Two Carpenters in one day?" Mark grinned. "Man, I'm a lucky guy. Mark Wright. I'm a friend of Lizzie's."

She tried not to make a face. Was he a friend? No. She might be able to put up with the term as it had been applied to internet relationships, but face to face? No. And he was her superior. Why had he suddenly gone from Work Mark to Casual Mark? Weird. She really wished he'd just pick a persona. She really wished he was not here. *Stay calm. You can do this.* She should've banked up more comfort from that nice back rubbing in the bathroom.

Chase was glancing between them, and she couldn't read his expression. She expected his usual exuberant greeting and good nature, but he offered a quiet reply instead. "Oh, really? Nice to meet you, man."

James was up front again, trying to get everyone's attention. The high school team was shouting—*shouting*— and the adult teams were no better, still milling around and paying James absolutely no mind. This time, her nerves brittle and failing, Lizzie put two fingers in her mouth and let out a whistle that had the whole room falling silent.

"Thanks, Team Geek Tragedy, you've gotta . . . teach me how to do that," James said, his amusement obvious. Lizzie gave him a nod and sat down, feeling the gaze of too many people on her. Awesome. This night was getting better and better.

CHAPTER SIXTEEN: Chase

ONE GINGER ALE, TWO baskets of fries, and one burger with bacon and cheese later, they'd only answered five questions. His anxiety was performing well; it had decided to make him a champion eater. It was better than drugs or violence, definitely, but it wasn't helping the anxiety at all. Maybe he'd get a mudslide next . . . the whole thing. Just for him. And anyone who tried to share with him was going to get their hand slapped. *Even Lizzie?* his heart prompted, and Chase ignored it.

No. I know better than this. When they took a five-minute break, he slipped outside behind the building. He'd just smoke one. Just half of one. Just enough to calm his nerves. Sitting outside her empty house had been frustrating, but petting Pancake had been a nice reset. However, walking in to find her sitting next to Mark Wright, "Lizzie's friend," was a whole new level of frustration. He pulled out the package, but out of the corner of his eye, he saw that teenage team, talking and laughing as they leaned on a vintage yellow sports car. He didn't want to set a bad example: Kyle and Martina both had siblings in that group. It wasn't too likely that seeing him light up would encourage them to start, but on the off chance . . . he tucked the package back into his coat pocket and patted it. He opted instead to take some deep breaths, visualizing himself in a hot air balloon, floating over Timber Falls. He blew all his fears, all his doubts and worries into that balloon and let it lift him high in the pleasant blueness of his mind.

"Chase?" Lizzie's voice was small, and it made his eyes snap open.

"Yeah?"

She was watching him with deep concern. "Are you all right?"

"Sure," he said, giving her a smile to reassure her. "You brought a friend, huh? That's nice." She should have friends. Lots of them. As many as she wanted.

"Yeah . . ." Lizzie drew out the word, and her arms were tight across her middle. Still in her uniform, she looked formidable. It was giving him flashbacks to his arrest . . . he had vague impressions of the sunlight tangling in her straight red hair. It was pulled back in a severe bun now, but then, it had been loose, swinging. He'd wanted to touch it, wanted to feel it against his face. He swallowed down the thought.

"I mean, no. He's not exactly a friend."

Chase's heart felt pricked with a hundred pins. "Oh. Are you guys . . . dating?" He held up his hands. "Sorry, I shouldn't have asked that. Not my business." *Yes, it is*, his anxiety insisted. *She's ours. We saw her first.* He mentally gave himself a shove away from that line of possessive thinking. That's not who he was now, and it was her right to date whomever she wanted.

Lizzie's eyes widened comically. "No! Absolutely not. He's my superior. I don't know why he said we were friends. I don't even know why he's here."

Chase felt his eyebrows go crinkly. "You didn't invite him?"

She shook her head ardently. "He invited himself." Behind her, the teenage team was shuffling toward the back door.

"Oh. Okay, well, good to know. I think they're starting again," Chase said, but Lizzie put a hand on his chest, stopping him.

"I want you to come over." She was using her cop voice. Firm, authoritative, but kind. It was hot. But he could see why Carter was kind of intimidated by her. He wouldn't want to be on the wrong side of it.

"To your house?"

"Yes." She gave one curt nod. "Just to hang out. But I can't talk to you the whole night. There will be some silence. Possibly a lot of silence."

"Well," he said slowly, his hopes blooming like one of those time-lapse videos of a rose, "I'd be concerned if there wasn't *some* silence."

"I'm just saying. You need . . ." she looked around, frustrated, her hand still planted in the middle of his chest, warming his skin through his thin shirt. Those mossy green eyes finally came back to him. "You need to lower your expectations," she said finally.

"Maybe what I want to do doesn't require talking," Chase murmured, pressing into her hand as he edged closer to her, and her eyes widened again, so much so that he could see himself reflected in them. *Oops. Too strong, backpedal. Backpedal, you fool!*

He cleared his throat. "Sorry. I would love to hang out with you, no matter what we do. Does tonight work?"

"I'll be t-tired tonight," she stuttered. "Tomorrow?"

"Tomorrow," he agreed, wrapping his hand around her fingers and giving them a squeeze.

"Where in the world are—oh, there you are! Quick, Lizzie, how many versions of the American flag have there been?" Martina was anxiously gripping the phone with the trivia app, finger poised to answer.

"It's in the upper twenties, I know that," Lizzie replied, her tone perplexed.

"27?"

"Probably."

Martina keyed it in and grinned. "Yes! Now get in here, you two, we're getting killed." And with that, she disappeared inside, letting the metal door slam shut, having made no mention of the fact that her teammates were holding hands in the smoking area like weirdos. Lizzie must have had the same thought because she pulled away from him gently and held the door open for him to come back inside. As they settled back in their seats, he looked over at her. Just past her, Mark was giving him a dark look, and Chase just smiled. Leaning back, he slung a friendly arm over the back of Lizzie's chair and ignored the man. He wasn't touching her; in fact, she didn't even seem to notice, as she was once again monopolizing the group's french fries. *Alpha move, too possessive,* his mind chided, and he removed it again. But it didn't dampen his mood much; Chase had plans to spend time with his favorite woman in the world tomorrow night, and that guy didn't. Well, he was fairly sure he didn't. The thought made him frown. He'd just have to make their night amazing, unforgettable . . . in a way that somehow also communicated that his expectations weren't too high.

Yeah. Right.

CHAPTER SEVENTEEN:
Lizzie

SHE WAS PACING IN THE living room, peeking through the curtains at embarrassingly close intervals. Pancake kept bringing her his favorite toy—a twisted hunk of rope with enough of his saliva integrated into it that it was always wet . . . it smelled accordingly. She kicked it for him, sending them both sliding across the hardwood. She wiped her sweaty hands on her jeans; she hadn't gone straight for PJs, and it had therefore taken her approximately 5,000 years to pick an outfit for the evening. If she dressed up, it would negate her whole "lower your expectations" speech. If she didn't dress up, it would seem like she didn't care. She'd finally settled on jeans and a plain green T-shirt . . . they were just hanging out, right? As friends? Her gaze fell on a family photo of her with Gram and Charlotte, and immediately, she thought WWLD: what would Lottie do? She ran back upstairs and Pancake loped after her, tail high and wagging. She put on some loopy silver earrings that she'd gotten a few Christmases ago and never found an occasion to wear. She grimaced at her reflection, considering her other options.

The doorbell rang, and Pancake took off barking, his toenails scratching against the wood steps. Lizzie hurried down after him, raking a hand through her hair. Should she have put it up? She was more comfortable with it down, but dates weren't really about comfort, were they? First impressions were lasting impressions, after all. Did it count as a first impression if you'd already sort of met a bunch of times? If you'd already told too many stories in letters, stories you'd never bothered to tell anyone else? Her hair tangled in the earrings as she tried to pull it up, so that solved that question, and she let it flop back down. Lizzie rolled her shoulders as she passed through the kitchen, the sound of Chase's laughter drawing her forward more quickly.

He looked like he'd gone home and showered, changed into a T-shirt and plaid Bermuda shorts. His hair was wet, his cologne not quite dissipated enough yet. Was it cologne, or just his body wash? His smile when he saw her looked like someone had just plugged him in, despite being at the end of a long work day for both of them. She couldn't help but smile back, even though he was clearly not tempering his expectations one bit . . .

He was holding a paper grocery bag, now completely ignoring Gram, whom he'd been chatting with just moments before. Chase did not appear to have an ounce of guile in his entire body; he didn't have to look at her like she'd hung the moon. Of course it was gratifying, and it made her stupid heart beat out of her chest. But it also made her want to sweep the leg of anyone who so much as snorted at his earnestness, and that part felt dangerous since she did possess the appropriate skill set. Gram turned with a smile and grabbed her purse off the hook near the front door. Lizzie had asked her repeatedly to move her purse somewhere safer inside the house, since a potential home invader would be sure to spot it there through the stained glass window in the front door. But that wasn't her concern right now.

"Where are you going?" Lizzie asked, somewhat alarmed. Gram was always home in the evening unless the Mind Readers had something happening, and most of them didn't drive at night. Also, she'd conned Hattie into adding her to their group calendar, so she happened to know that she had nothing happening tonight.

Gram shrugged innocently. "Thought I might pop over to Barb's, see if she's run those eagles off yet. Do some last-minute planning for our trip."

"Why?" She'd had every detail of their France trip planned out for weeks. It was practically her full-time job.

Her grandmother chuckled a little. "You two have fun. I'll see you later. *Much* later."

Okay, so she was obviously leaving to let them be alone, but that was completely unnecessary. Despite his comment about activities that didn't require talking, Lizzie had no plans to do anything that required privacy tonight. And besides, she'd sort of planned on keeping Gram around as a conversation buffer. But now her buffer was walking out the front door, whistling on her way to her car. *Traitor*. Pancake's nails against the wood floor brought her back to reality; he was jumping on Chase again.

"Down," she commanded sternly, and he lay at Chase's feet, practically vibrating with excitement as his tail went nuts. She eyed him, sending a silent message to stay, then turned her attention to Chase.

"Hey," he greeted warmly, pulling her in for a one-armed hug, as the scent of him enveloped her. *Sage. Lemongrass. Such a hippy.* And yet, they reminded her of chicken soup and the fancy spa Lottie had taken her to once that had a waterfall inside the waiting area. It was where her love of pedicures had started.

"Hey," she greeted back, giving him a tentative squeeze. "What's in the bag?"

"Oh," he said, peeking into the bag like he hadn't packed it, "just snacks. I know we're just hanging out, but I'd like to spoil you if that's allowed." Lord, he was seriously going to have to turn down the charm. He was going to end her with the sheer force of her embarrassment. She kept the topic on point: snacks were her love language, after all.

"What kind of snacks?"

"Pretzels, trail mix, jerky . . ." Oh good. For a minute there, she'd half expected something overly romantic, like chocolate-dipped strawberries. "Gummy bears."

"Dibs," she said. She probably shouldn't; the sugar was just going to make her more wired. Yet here she was, peeking into the bag for them like she had the right. Her face flushed hot when he grinned at her. "Sorry, I shouldn't—"

"Please," he said, tipping the bag toward her, "help yourself. I told you, I brought these for you. Take whatever you want."

"I shouldn't," she repeated, grabbing them anyway. "They'll keep me up."

"I thought you said you usually stay up late."

"I do. But I probably shouldn't."

"Getting good sleep has been an unexpected side effect of my new routines and my anxiety being better controlled. I can't say I'm mad about it." He was digging around in the bag himself and came up with a bag of fancy potato chips. "As long as I don't drink coffee too late in the day. But you don't have that problem."

"No." *And you remembered.* Did he pore over her letters repeatedly like she did his?

His eyes flickered with curiosity. "What's your excuse then? Just a night owl?"

The stars. The moon. The quiet. The darkness around me like a blanket. She shrugged.

"Probably all of that TV light flashing in my eyes." She tried to pinch the middles of the bag and pull the top open, but it wouldn't go. He watched her struggle for a minute, then held out his hand for the bag. When she pulled out her multi-tool and snipped the top open instead, a slow, wide smile spread across his face. Good, he wasn't one of those guys who was irritated by her doing things her own way.

"How was your day?" he asked, running a hang through his damp hair.

She told him about breaking up another James and Levi argument—this time about James's car getting scratched in the parking lot—and serving a few court summonses, the least interesting part of her job. She stole a few of his French onion potato chips as she went on to tell him about the sword someone had found on River Road.

"A sword?" His eyes were comically wide. "Like, should I be watching out for ninjas?"

"It wouldn't hurt," she deadpanned, "but I believe it belongs to a group of theater kids at the high school who cosplay in the woods. I've had calls about them before." She flipped her hair over her shoulder as she leaned forward again for more food. "How was your day?"

That got a big sigh out of him. "Oh. You know."

Lizzie hesitated. *Honesty time. Ugh.* At least it was a small thing.

"I actually don't know what you do, except that you work for your dad at TFPP."

"Oh. Right. Uh, I'm in marketing. So I basically come up with the ad campaigns and partnerships that convince people to buy our products."

She felt her brow furrow. From what she knew about him, it wasn't a terrible fit for Chase; he was outgoing, friendly. He always seemed to put her at ease and imagined that the same was true of their customers. Still . . .

"It's more than just toilet paper, huh?"

He chuckled. "Honestly, it's mostly toilet paper. But they're trying to get into other products as well. Our new thing is low-waste cardboard packaging that's easier to reuse since people are ordering more and more things online. Of course, we also have the regular coated and uncoated papers, ranging from sixty-pound to eighty-pound . . ." Chase chuckled again as he tipped the end of the bag directly into his mouth. "You're glazing, Lizzie Lou."

She blushed, more embarrassed by the nickname than her lack of comprehension about his job. She pursed her lips, trying to figure out if she should reject it, but really, what was the harm? She was more surprised that he knew her middle name was Louise. Had she ever mentioned it in a letter? She knew his, too. She could use that against him.

"I'm not glazing, Chase Bobby . . ."

He stopped chewing and his eyebrows lifted. "What . . . what in the world?"

She pushed her shoulders back. "You called me Lizzie Lou. It's analogous."

"It's just alliterative, that's all. I was just being funny. Please don't call me Chase Bobby, that's . . . that's weird. Makes me sound like a Kennedy."

From anyone else, Lizzie might've felt embarrassed, but his face, contorted in such open disgust, had her laughing instead, their folded knees knocking together a little in a comfortable way that made her blush nonetheless. That launched them into a discussion about family names: Chase had gotten his middle name from his grandfather, Lizzie had gotten hers from her mom. From there, thankfully, it spiraled away from the topic of parents into a conversation about aunts and uncles and how kids can tell which ones like them and which ones are worried they're going to knock their turn-of-the-century Tiffany-style lamps off their antique end tables. Then holiday stories and swapping high school horror stories until Gram's keys in the front door startled both of them.

"Hey, you two. Mind if I turn on a light?" she asked, groping for the hook to hang up her purse.

"No, of course not," Lizzie said, wiping her hands on her pants. When had it gotten so dark? The light from the kitchen was still giving them some ambient light, and apparently, distracted as they were by each other, it had been enough that they didn't notice the dark. "What time is it?"

"Almost 9:30," Gram said, yawning.

"Oh man," Chase said, gathering up the now-empty bags, stuffing their wrappers into them. "I've gotta get going, I've got a meeting tomorrow at seven." *And sleep is important to him,* Lizzie thought. *I should respect that.*

"Oh, okay." It was stupid to feel disappointed, she told herself. Her heart informed her that it did not care. She didn't want this night to end; it had been sweet in a way that had nothing to do with the sugar. She hadn't even gotten to the awkward part yet. How was she going to learn to push through the awkward lapses in conversation if she didn't practice?

"Thanks for letting me come over to hang out." He was moving toward the front door now. Were they not going to plan another hangout? Is that something they'd do now or later? She kicked herself for not texting some of these questions to Lottie earlier in the day when she was just restlessly pacing in front of the front windows, but then again, Lottie hadn't spoken to her much since their blow-up over her engagement. As in, she hadn't spoken to her at all. Lizzie uncurled herself from the couch, following him out to the front porch. It was a beautiful night by any measure: warm and clear with a light breeze, birds singing from the red cedars down behind Mrs. Cooper's house. The porch light was off, but she could see his face clearly. He appeared to be struggling with how to end this night just as much as she'd been. He was watching her carefully, shifting his weight, scratching at his temple. *Does he want to kiss me? Do I want him to?* Then he pulled something out of his back pocket.

"Here."

She accepted the invitation-size white envelope. "What's this?"

"Just read it. Not now. After I'm gone."

She could still see the taillights of his car when she ripped into the letter he'd apparently pre-written.

Dear Lizzie,

I had a great time tonight. You might think that I couldn't have known that I would before our hang-out. But I did. I knew from your letters that we'd have loads to talk about. I didn't worry about that. The only thing I worry about is pushing you too fast for too much. But I like you, Lizzie. I like talking to you, I like just hanging out with you.

So do you want to come to my place next time? I didn't want to put you on the spot and ask you so soon after we'd been together, because I know you like to think things over sometimes. Just let me know. You can bring the snacks next time. I hope there's a next time, and I didn't screw things up too badly. But I guess if you're getting this note, then I must not have, because I could always just throw it away.

Anywho, I hope you had fun, too. Talk to you soon.

Sincerely,

Chase

What a nerd. Sweet, thoughtful nerd. Lizzie pulled out her phone, then debated. She didn't care about appearing eager; she was eager. She'd wanted him to stay longer tonight, so there was no way she was passing up another opportunity to hang out with him. But her own space appealed to her more, and she didn't want him tempted to use his phone while driving, as it was unsafe and also illegal. So she composed her text carefully, then set a timer for forty minutes to send it then. That should be enough time for him to get home.

> **Lizzie:** I had fun, too. Can we hang out here instead?
> **Chase:** Yup. Whatever you want.
> **Lizzie:** Thursday? Same time?
> **Chase:** Thursday it is.
> **Chase:** It'll be the highlight of my week.
> **Lizzie:** Seriously, dude. You. Expectations. Manage them.
> **Chase:** No need. You're an awesome hanger-outer, Elizabeth.

She snorted, then picked up her toothbrush. He hadn't used the word 'friend,' and she felt that was intentional . . . Chase wanted more. They were friends, certainly, but based on his comment behind Annie's, he didn't want to stay that way. It wasn't easy to get her teeth really clean when she was grinning that hard, even as her doubts held on like plaque.

CHAPTER EIGHTEEN:
Chase

"AND AS YOU CAN SEE, this one's got three bedrooms as well..."

Chase followed Tansy up the stairs of the blue Victorian, letting his hand trail over the curved, polished railing.

"Mm-hmm." He didn't really need to see the upstairs; this one wasn't right. It needed some serious repairs, and he didn't have the emotional energy for that. He liked the size, and the style reminded him of Hattie's house, which was a happy place. But renovations... months more of living at the estate... he shuddered. No. If he could avoid that, he would.

Just this morning, he'd been eating breakfast with his mom, his new ritual, when Christopher and his dad had come into the kitchen.

"Do you want a ride today?" Christopher had asked, sweaty and out of breath from his run, then chugged a large bottle of orange juice. Chase hadn't thought his twin had noticed that they seemed to mostly keep the same schedule.

"Uh, not today. I'm meeting a realtor after work, looking for a new place."

"Finally," his father had said, leaning against the quartz counters, waiting for Mrs. Sánchez to pour his coffee into a travel mug.

"Finally?" Chase had asked, trying to keep his tone light. "Could you explain what you mean?"

"You've been back from rehab, what, three weeks now?"

"Thereabout, yeah."

"So that's plenty of time for you to get yourself together and move on from this unfortunate chapter."

Chase had put down his spoon in his bowl without letting it clatter against the side. "Don't take this the wrong way, but I'm not sure you have reasonable expectations when it comes to my recovery."

Harrison had snorted. "Recovery? Recovery from what? You spent months out at that *rehab*"—he might as well have spit the word—"and this is what you've got to show for it? Where's the son who was top of his class at Duke? Where's the man who led his team to State senior year? The man I was hoping help me lead TFPP into the future? You used to be somebody, Chase." His father had shaken his head sadly.

"Now I'm somebody else," he'd quipped, feeling snappish, the words out before he could stop them. "But I'm still your son. Substance abuse disorder is a medical issue, and it's a recovery, just like any illness." Anxiety was tightening the screws inside him, and he hadn't trusted himself to say any more. Willow was fidgeting, looking between the two of them. Chase had put a hand on her arm and found that the action calmed him as well.

"I'm trying to give you a compliment, and all you can hear is insults," Harrison had grouched. "I'm saying you have potential, Chase. You're just wasting it."

"I don't think I'm wasting anything." *Except my breath in talking to you.* Out of the corner of his eye, he had seen Carter approaching the kitchen, his steps slowing as he'd seen how many people were already in there. It was one of those large, gourmet kitchens with a set of two islands and an eating area, but apparently, only four Carpenters and their housekeeper had filled it up. Carter had grabbed his coat and bag from the closet and given Chase a little nod on his way out with a look that expressed apology. That was unnecessary; if anything, Chase had thought he should've been apologizing to him for creating such a tense moment in the kitchen when Carter probably just wanted his morning bagel. He had considered ordering one to be delivered to Carter's work . . . *No. Carter can take care of himself. He chose not to come into the kitchen, he can find himself another breakfast. You are responsible for you, he is responsible for him.*

"Look at your brother," Harrison had said, throwing out an arm. "Same materials. Much different result. I have literal proof that you could be so much more."

"I am not less than Christopher," Chase had growled. "The same genetics don't mean anything. He doesn't have anxiety. I do."

"You don't have anxiety," Harrison had said, laughing. "You just don't want to work for success." That had done it. He wasn't going to sit there and be called lazy for caring about his own wellbeing.

"I'm done with this conversation," Chase had announced, getting to his feet. "I'm going to go shower." He had pivoted to Christopher, who was eating a bowl of Cheerios in the corner of the kitchen like he was afraid to sit down with either of them. "Thanks for offering a ride. Maybe tomorrow." Chris had given him a nod, but Harrison had scowled.

"I'm not. Sit down."

"No, thank you." Chase had set his dirty bowl in the sink, knowing Mrs. Sánchez would understand. Then he'd fled up the back stairs, shaking.

Now, following Tansy up a different set of steps, he had to roll his shoulders to try to shrug off the memory. Chase stopped her with a hand on her shoulder.

"You know what? I don't think this one's for me, so let's not waste time up here. Didn't we have one more to see?"

Tansy turned and shook her head, her gray curls bobbing around her face. "I'm afraid not. This was the last one. There was one more that looked interesting, but I haven't previewed it, and it's on the other side of town. I know you'd said you'd prefer to be closer to work."

And farther away from the estate.

"Yeah, I would."

"We'll keep looking," she said with a smile. "Don't worry. We'll find you something perfect. This is a good time of year to be looking; the closer we get to school letting out, the more things will be coming on the market."

Chase gave her a nod. "Sounds good." He turned and started back down the stairs.

"Did you and Elizabeth have a nice time together last night?" Much like her granddaughter, Tansy didn't beat around the bush, but strangely, it wasn't triggering his anxiety. It was game-playing and subtext that messed with his head the most, now that he thought about it.

As she locked up the front door again, he considered his answer. "Of course we did. Your granddaughter is lovely."

"Inside and out," Tansy agreed. "I'm glad you enjoyed yourselves." She paused as they arrived at their cars. "Would you like some advice about Lizzie?"

He studied her hazel eyes, hoping this wasn't a trick question somehow.

"Absolutely."

"When she was a girl, she spent a lot of time in her room. I wasn't sure how normal that was . . . at the time, people assured me it was just a phase, but . . ." She looked down at her keys, spinning the ring between her fingers, then smiled a little. "When we wanted her to come downstairs, we'd cook bacon. That girl's stomach is in league with her heart. Just feed her, don't push her, and she'll keep coming back."

Chase gave himself a mental pat on the back for all the snack food he'd brought. "I'll remember that. Thanks." He pulled out his phone. "When can we go out looking again?" The sooner he got out of his dad's house, the better.

"Unfortunately, it'll be a few weeks. I'm taking a trip to Europe."

"Hey, congratulations," Chase said. He wanted to hug her, but he thought that might not be a professional move, so he kept his hug to himself. He'd spring it on one of his relatives later; Martina seemed to mind them the least. "Are you celebrating something or just wanted to go?"

"Just always wanted to go, bien sûr," she said, and Chase laughed.

"Well, that's awesome. I'm glad you're going. Just give me a call when you're back in town, and I'll make time to go out again."

"If you're really desperate, I do have someone who's watching my business . . ." Having to wait was a disappointment, but the idea of having to express himself to someone else was worse.

"No, no. I'd like to work with you. Waiting is good. Waiting is better." He was not getting shuffled off to someone less competent and less . . . Lizzie-adjacent.

Tansy's gaze narrowed a little, perhaps shrewdly, and Chase felt his neck getting hot.

"Very well. I'll be in touch when I get back."

"Great. Thanks, Mrs. Draper."

He closed her car door for her and gave her a wave as she took off. That meant his date with Lizzie next week would be in an empty house . . . this week's had been, too, but they'd known she was going to come back. He was definitely going for a good night kiss at the very least this week . . . maybe even a good night makeout on her porch. She'd been giving him this look last night . . . her pupils were blown, even as her gaze had darted around his face, trying to read him as hard as he'd been trying to read her. Surely this time, it would be okay to start a little something physical with her . . .

"You gonna stand in a stranger's yard all day or what?"

Chase snapped out of his thoughts to see the town's unofficial mayor standing in front of him. "Oh. Hey, Hattie."

"Hey yourself. What are you doing on this side of town?" She leaned on her gnarled walking stick.

"I'm in the market for a new place."

Her eyebrows went high, disappearing under the brim of her hat. "Really? You're coming back to Timber Falls?"

"Yeah. It feels right."

Her bright smile seemed genuine. "Well, that's delightful news. I'll keep my ears open for you."

"I'd really appreciate that, thank you."

"I hear you came calling on our deputy."

Chase chuckled as he leaned on his car with one arm. "Word travels fast."

Hattie waved a hand at him. "I've got a group chat with her grandmother. You have book group approval, by the way. We wouldn't let just anyone date our Lizzie. She's a special one."

He stood there, staring down at the long grass in the yard, thinking about how he didn't feel like he deserved their acceptance, feeling grateful for it nonetheless, pondering how much he agreed with her about Lizzie for reasons he couldn't even really explain. It was just a gut feeling. Lizzie was just herself in the same way he was trying to be just himself; there was a purity to her, as confusing as she could sometimes be. He must've fallen quiet for too long because Hattie stepped closer.

"What are you thinking about so hard, young man?"

"Too many things," he muttered, but he gave her a wry grin. "Thank you for your blessing. That means a lot." His voice cracked embarrassingly on the last word, and he cleared his throat as he looked away.

"Chase," Hattie said firmly, and he made himself look back at her. "You hold your head up high. You are a Timberite. This is where you belong. Don't let anyone make you feel otherwise. And if they do, you text me their names and I'll take care of it."

"There's nothing . . . I mean, no one's . . ." He couldn't get the words out. How could he explain how it felt to come back here, where he'd messed up so badly and so publicly? How could she understand how it felt to know that people were whispering about you, how it felt to know that you were the screw-up of such a prominent family? Hattie engulfed him in a hug; her head only came up to his shoulder, and she knocked the hat off her head to hold him more ardently. She smelled like argan oil, and it reminded him of his grandmother. He held her back. Man, what would they do without Hattie? He cleared his throat again as she gave him a final squeeze and let him go.

"Are you going on the big trip to Europe?"

"I sure am," she said, refitting her hat. "It's gonna be a heck of a time. I can't wait. I'm gonna eat snails."

Chase laughed. "Well, have a great time." He paused; there was something he'd been thinking about lately, and if there was any chance of success, he'd need her support. "When you get back, I want to meet up and talk to you about an idea I had."

"Shoot."

"What, now?"

She watched him expectantly in the falling dusk. "Give me the elevator pitch now."

"Lizzie mentioned that you've had increased problems with opioids . . ."

"True. We're both troubled by it."

This next part was the tricky part; if he just came out and recommended needle exchange, the chances were high that she'd say no. "There are measures that a community can take to help reduce the harm done by opioids, but they're pretty progressive. I don't know if the council will go for it."

She tapped him on the arm with her stick. "Send me some case studies and articles. I'll read them on the plane and send you my thoughts."

"Mais oui."

"Merci," she said, giving him a wave over her shoulder as she continued her trek toward the river. "A bientôt!"

It was a good day. Unexpected, but good. Maybe he'd celebrate by taking himself out for dinner at Annie's; there was a pizza sub calling his name.

CHAPTER NINETEEN:
Lizzie

THE WEEKEND WAS SUCH a whirl of Gram's last-minute packing activity and double-checking that Lizzie knew how to do everything around the house that she spent most of it in her room trying to hide, watching TV on her laptop, just to get some peace. To make matters worse, on Monday, Mark wanted to tag along with her again . . . only this time, he wanted to drive. All their morning stops ended up being very routine; a few court documents were delivered, did a welfare check for an older member of the community, etc. They went back to the station for lunch, and Lizzie hoped she could shake him off for the afternoon, but he had caught her trying to sneak out to the cruiser.

"This is the place?" Mark asked, squinting through the windshield. "There's no house number."

"It's on the mailbox," Lizzie answered, wishing he would just park already. Gram was leaving on her big trip today, so there was a pair of slippers and a bowl of popcorn with her name on it at home in lieu of dinner. The thought of a completely empty house thrilled her. Mark pulled up to block in the red Oldsmobile in the driveway, then reached down for his notebook.

"Forrest Heidleberg, nine unpaid parking tickets. Forrest likes to run into the coffee shop 'just for a minute' while he parks in the fire zone, according to the deputy who wrote the tickets."

"Yes, I'm the deputy who wrote the tickets," Lizzie said, giving him a small smile. "I just didn't know he'd moved back in with his aunt. I think he's working at the self-storage."

"This says he was caught growing weed in the empty units a few years ago."

"Yup, that's right." The owner of the self-storage had called to complain about fraud from the electric company . . . that's the only reason she'd investigated at all. She'd never forget throwing open that sliding garage door and discovering all those grow lights. He probably wouldn't have gotten caught if he'd just grown it in the woods like everyone else.

They got out of the car, slamming the doors simultaneously, and started up the sidewalk of the single-level home. A flash of red through the window put Lizzie on high alert. "He's going out the back." She charged around the side of the house and heard Mark right behind her. There was no time to ponder why he hadn't gone around the *other* side of the house . . . the dying grass meant the ground was soft, and she struggled to gain traction as her parking ticket offender hopped the chain link fence in the back.

"Forrest! Stop!" she called, but her command went unheeded. She looked around; there was nothing back there but Mr. Powell's fields. Without thinking about it, she went up and over the fence, hitting the ground running. Forrest was not in the best shape of his life, because he was only about fifty feet ahead of her. Hopefully, he wouldn't let the sheep out; she did not want to spend all afternoon running down wandering livestock.

"Forrest Howard Heidleberg, you know I'm going to catch you," she panted. "Let's not do this." She made a point to know people's middle names; if her experience in her grandmother's household had taught her nothing else, it was that someone's middle name could be wielded as effectively as her service weapon when applied correctly. She was within ten feet, dodging some rusty piece of large metal farm equipment that had been there for a while based on the hip-high grass around it when she went down. Her foot caught in a hole of some kind, and when she went down, she felt the snap. Lizzie cried out at the pain and the surprise of her knee and shoulder biting into the rocky soil. She rolled to her back, clutching at her ankle, where the pain emanated like heat from a cattle brand. Her loud sobs could not be contained; it *hurt*. Worse than the time she broke her thumb on Gracie Taylor's trampoline when she landed wrong. Worse than taking a softball to the side of the head in P.E. in eighth grade. Worse than her sledding accident in second grade when the tree didn't get out of her way in time. When she opened her eyes, a trio of concerned faces was peering down at her in the long grass.

"Shit, Lizzie, are you okay?" Forrest had apparently come back when he realized she was in distress. At least that was something. She said nothing, rocking back and forth, trying to give the pain somewhere to go, but it was clamped to her leg like a cougar. Mark, Mr. Powell, and Forrest were discussing how to get her out of the field when Lizzie burst out.

"Mark! Arrest him first!"

"Seriously?"

"YES!" she cried, trying to pull out her phone to call 911 herself. Sheepishly, Mr. Powell pulled his out, and the ambulance from Santiam made good time and even brought a stretcher. After a quick examination to make sure she hadn't hurt her back, RJ and Vince lifted her onto the carrier. They got her into the ambulance and Vince hopped into the driver's seat. Mark, a handcuffed Forrest, and a concerned Mr. Powell were still staring at her through the back windows.

"Deep breaths, please," RJ said, smoothing the hair away from her face, and Lizzie tried to get her breathing under control, feeling her chest burning as she took deep, gulping breaths. "Who can I call to meet you at the hospital?"

"N-n-nobody," she blubbered.

"Take it easy, deputy," he murmured, sliding the IV into her vein so quickly and easily she almost missed it. "I've got some relief coming to you." He paused as he adjusted the drip of the IV. "There's gotta be someone," he pressed.

There must have been some kind of painkiller in the saline, because the pain throbbed a little less insistently, and she summoned the energy to shake her head.

"Gram's out of town. That's it." It didn't occur to her to even mention Lottie. They weren't speaking. She was in Eugene. Why would she come?

He covered her with a blanket, taking her temperature and heart rate as they bounced along until they got to Highway 22. Vince didn't use the lights and sirens, and she felt a little cheated. If she was going to be hurt, she at least wanted five-star treatment. RJ had his phone out, texting someone.

"If you wanted attention, Deputy Painter, all you had to do was ask," RJ teased, and it just made Lizzie cry harder. The look on his face said he hadn't meant to do that, and RJ held her hand, giving it a squeeze as they race down the highway. He and Vince carefully carried her out of the vehicle and into the lobby of the ER. Kyle Durand's concerned face came into view.

"Trivia teammate, what happened?" That made her laugh a little through her tears, and she wiped them away as RJ explained her situation. They didn't make her wait, just transferred her to a gurney and rolled her straight back into the hospital, past more concerned faces. They blurred as she tried to see them through her tears. The pain was a duller throb now, and she shivered on the unyielding gurney, feeling like a kid again, her head pressed against a cold window as the car flew down the freeway, the bright fluorescents going by like streetlights. At least that had felt safe . . . she knew Kyle would take good care of her, but . . . the tears came back as she thought back to RJ's question. She was so alone. And most of the time, she liked it that way . . . but sometimes . . . sometimes she resented it. Like now, when a group of young doctors were taking turns shining lights into her eyes, checking her for a concussion, trying to see if she was hurt anywhere else. He'd just finished herding his interns out to let her rest, when she heard the bellowing.

"Where is she?" Chase's voice was sharp enough to cut someone. A pacifying but firm voice answered him, but Lizzie couldn't make out her words.

"Listen, lady, my father donated all the money for this wing. You see the name on that plaque, 'Carpenter?' That's my name. You want to see my driver's license? Is that what it'll take?"

Flustered now, the woman responded again, but apparently, Chase was out of patience with her.

"Take me to Deputy Elizabeth Painter's room *now* or I'll be making a call to your administrator, and it will not go well for you after that."

Her door was opened by a red-faced nurse and Chase appeared, looking like he was ready to lose his shit until his gaze met hers. Then her normal friend was back.

"What the heck did you do to yourself, Lizzie Lou?" He took her left hand in both of his, being careful of her IV.

"What makes you so sure this is my fault?" she asked, trying to tip her chin up, even if the pillows behind her head made it difficult.

"Because you're clumsy like me," he said, looking her up and down, like he was cataloging her injuries. Ever so gently, he lifted her blanket to see her ankle and grimaced. "That looks awful."

"Sugar-coat it, why don't you?" she yawned. Then she glanced down; her ankle was swollen, black and blue. He wasn't wrong. "What happened out there in the hall?"

"What do you mean?"

"I mean you're 'Mr. Laid-Back, Go With the Flow Dude'. That was more 'Hard Sell, Throw My Weight Around Dude.'"

"No," he said, wiping his forehead with the back of his hand, "that was 'Anxious Chase Bullying the Nursing Staff', and I know it wasn't right."

"Then why did you do it?"

Chase stared at her, opened his mouth to say something, then snapped it shut again. When he turned toward the window, she figured he wouldn't mind a change of subject.

"How did you even know I was here?"

"Kyle texted Ainsley who called Martina who called me." He seemed completely unconcerned by how the phone tree worked out, and he rubbed little circles in the back of her hands with his thumbs. "I know your grandma is out of town, so I'm going to take you to my place when they release you."

Fear seized her; he lived with literally a million people. "What? No. I'll be fine, really."

"Lizzie, you've severely injured your right ankle, maybe even broken it . . ."

"Kyle said it's not broken. He said it wouldn't hurt so bad if it was broken."

"That's not the point," Chase pressed. "You can't even drive. How will that be fine? How are you going to get up and down the stairs, let alone cook your meals and take of care bodily needs?"

"I'll figure it out. I'm used to being on my own."

"Not when you're injured," he said gently. "Please. Let me take care of you." His blue eyes were pleading with her, and he wasn't making it easy to refuse him. But she managed it.

"No."

He sighed like he'd expected that answer. "Fine. I didn't want to bring this up, but . . ."

"But what?"

"It's not fair to Pancake." The thought of those big, hairy paws making contact with her chest when her balance was off was not a pleasant one. "And I hate to say it, but he's a wild thing and he's going to jump on you and probably knock you down unless there's someone there to help control him." She considered that as she looked over at the beige wall on the opposite side of the room. That was sort of true.

"That's exactly why I can't go to your place," she returned. "Who would take care of him? He'd feel totally abandoned!"

Chase stared at her for a minute, then nodded slowly. "You're right."

"I am?" This felt like a trap. She could practically feel the web he was weaving around her.

"Of course," he shrugged. "The obvious solution is for us both to move into your house."

Whatever fear she'd felt before at being trapped at Chase's house all day with virtual strangers was nothing compared to what she felt now. Chase in his pajamas (did he even wear pajamas?). Chase on the couch watching TV with her every night, warm at her side. Chase making her soup. Chase doing her laundry. It frightened her because she wanted it so bad, because it sounded so wonderful, she couldn't believe it was even possible. Her dream of the non-ending date was on the precipice of coming true.

"You'll be at work all day," she whispered. "How will that even help?"

"I can work from home for a while. No one will care."

Your dad might if he knows it's me you're taking care of. For obvious reasons, his dad was not her biggest fan, nor she his. Sometimes she wondered why Chase still worked there, beyond needing an income. It seemed like there were a handful of other things he was qualified for that would suit his temperament better.

"I care." That was true. She didn't want him to go to any trouble for her. It wasn't necessary. Someday soon, Gram would be gone for good, and then she'd have to figure all this out on her own anyway. Might as well prepare for the inevitable.

His voice went low, rumbly like a motorcycle. "Well, I care about you. And I want to do this."

"No, thank you."

His eyes flashed with irritation, and she noted their blue color had changed a little. "Does Hallway Chase need to come in here?"

"Hallway Chase has got nothing on Stubborn Lizzie, who's here 24/7," she retorted, and that earned her a smile.

"Fine," he said, sitting back, "I'll just make sure you get home okay, then."

"I don't need you to."

"I didn't say you did," Chase replied, cleaning his already-clean fingernails. "It's entirely for my peace of mind."

"Whatever," Lizzie grumbled. Chase sat with her while she waited for her x-ray. He chatted with her as they waited for the results. They were watching *Family Feud* when one of the interns came in, flanked by more interns.

"Ms. Painter, good news. You just have a sprained ankle, no surgery necessary." Her heart sank. She'd so been hoping for a simple injury . . . this meant she'd be out of the field for weeks. How was she supposed to earn her promotion when she was laid up inside, stuck on the couch? She felt tears gathering in the corners of her eyes, and she looked down at her lap, surprised to see that Chase was holding her hand. When did that happen? He was a very sneaky sort of friend. She should really make him leave. She would. Just as soon as they discharged her. The intern whose name she couldn't remember was still talking, explaining that she needed to ice it (ugh), rest it (makes sense), keep it wrapped (with what?), and keep it elevated (hard to do at a desk).

"And here's your prescription," he finished, ripping a paper off a pad and holding it out to her. Chase saw the name of the drug before she could even accept it.

"Vicodin?" he snarled. "Are you joking? What does she need Vicodin for?"

"Sir, this kind of injury can be very painful . . ." the doctor said, but he seemed far less sure of his opinion than he had a moment ago. Lizzie's gaze bounced between the two of them, and it didn't click for her why he was *so angry* . . . until she realized. *Vicodin. That's what he was hooked on.* Automatically, Lizzie put a hand on his arm; Chase kept staring at the man.

"I need some air," he muttered, pulling away from her. Halfway to the door, he turned and pointed at her. "Don't leave without me. I want to see you safely home."

She nodded once in agreement, and Chase shut the door behind him so hard the mini-blinds on the door started swinging.

"You were saying?" Lizzie calmly prompted, turning back to the red-faced doctor and his colleagues, all of whom were shifting their weight nervously.

"J-just that you can fill that i-if you need it," he went on, fiddling with his collar. "But no pressure."

"Thank you," she said, holding out her hand to shake his, and they all seemed relieved to be leaving her room . . . but perhaps not anxious to run into Chase again, based on the cautious way the intern looked both ways down the hall before exiting. She tucked the prescription into her purse with a sigh.

CHAPTER TWENTY: Lizzie

LIZZIE WAS STARTING to get antsy to leave when a male nurse came in pushing a wheelchair; she recognized him as Trevor, Diana and Patton Harper's youngest son. Chase hadn't come back yet, and she wondered how much air he could possibly need.

"Got a present for you," he grinned, holding up a pair of crutches, and she groaned.

"Do I really need those?"

"Do you really want to get around without making your injury worse?" Trevor quipped, and Lizzie rolled her eyes. "Don't worry, you get to take a chariot ride on your way out. Who's taking you home today?"

"Chase Carpenter."

"Ah yes, I think he blasted past me a few minutes ago."

Lizzie felt her heart squeeze with concern. "Did he leave?"

"I'm not sure," Trevor said, gathering up her care instructions. "Let's go see if we can find him." He stepped out to give her a minute to put her muddy clothes back on, then pushed her toward the reception desk.

"Oh, there he is," Lizzie said, pointing out the front doors.

"Convenient," he said, pulling up to the front desk. "I've got three things for you to sign before you go, and then I'll let Chase take it from here."

"Okay, sounds good." She watched him through the sliding glass doors, ignoring the people passing her by. When he exhaled, she realized he was smoking a cigarette, and Lizzie frowned. Was that a trigger for opioids? Was this a gateway back to that kind of lifestyle? He noticed her through the doors and immediately threw down the cigarette and stomped it out. Chase hurried into the lobby, still reeking of smoke.

"Sorry, I'm here. Are you ready to go?"

"No need to apologize," she said. "We were just about to come find you." Lizzie stared up at him, noting the way his always-scruffy cheek worked against the collar of his raincoat. He looked like a model for Ralph Lauren or something, his hair all askew. Well, maybe a little heavier than those models, but that certainly didn't matter. She'd always thought those men looked too skinny anyway.

"Good to go," Trevor confirmed, and the way his gaze lingered on Chase, Lizzie thought maybe he was having the same thoughts about that scruff and coat business. But the look was gone as quickly as it started, and then he was pushing her out the front doors and into the parking lot. "Where am I going?" he asked, and Chase pointed to his red SUV on the end.

"Sorry it's not better for getting a wheelchair patient into, it was the only spot left, and I didn't know what had happened, just that she was here."

"No worries," Trevor grunted. "I've got it." Lizzie was impressed with his skills as he carefully wheeled her between
the cars, opened the door and helped her inside. "We'll see
you for your follow-up in a week, Deputy."

She wasn't going to any follow-ups. She wouldn't need
them. With any luck, she'd be back at her desk on Monday.
A doctor who once froze a wart off the bottom of her foot
told her that she had a high pain threshold. With any luck,
that would translate to a speedy recovery.

Chase was quiet as they pulled out of the parking lot. He
stopped for a mom with a kid who wanted to cross the street,
and Lizzie summoned her courage.

"You said you needed some air."

"Yeah. Sorry about that. I just . . ." He seemed at a loss for
words, so Lizzie filled the silence.

"It's a bit ironic, I have to admit."

He hazarded a glance at her. "What is?"

"Well, it's just that you said you needed some air, and
then you filled your lungs with smoke."

Chase pursed his lips like he was thinking. "I'm sure
there's air mixed in."

"Smoking is super bad for you."

"Not as bad as punching a doctor."

"No, smoking is still super bad for you."

"Well, I'm trying to quit. But it helps me when I'm
tense."

"You didn't want me to take those pills . . ." Lizzie guessed, and Chase nodded.

"I really, really don't want you to take those pills. It's no reflection on you, Lizzie. I don't want anyone to take them. I don't want anyone to take the chance that they'll go through what I've gone through."

"I've taken them before," she said gently. "I had a really killer ear infection once."

"Still." He ran a hand through his hair. "It's not worth it."

"I hear you."

"I know I have no right to ask that of you; I'm sorry that I sort of lost my cool."

"It's okay."

"No, it's not okay. I know the pain might be bad, I just . . ."

"Chase." She put a hesitant hand over his on the gear shift, just long enough to squeeze it. "It's okay. Really."

He nodded, and she saw his throat move in a hard swallow. Lizzie turned and looked out the window. This was nuts. She'd had one date with this guy. Half the time, she could only communicate with him in writing. And now, he was trying to move in with her? Such a bad idea. A bad, bad, bad idea. She couldn't allow it. They were quiet the rest of the way to her house.

Lizzie's phone rang just as she got to the top of the porch steps. It was Gram, of course. She'd known she would hear through the grapevine eventually but it had happened even faster than she thought it would.

"Just a second," she said to Chase, who was currently trying to wrangle Pancake into the laundry room. Lizzie hobbled further down the porch with one crutch, balancing on the railing.

"Hi, Gram," Lizzie answered with as much enthusiasm as she could muster.

"I hear you had a little accident," said Gram, her voice crackly on the line. "I'm on my way home."

"Oh, Gram, no, don't. I'll be fine. Someone's looking after me."

"Oh?" Her skepticism was thicker than the cloud layer overhead.

"Yes, a friend came to the hospital. I'm home now. I think I have everything I need. I don't want you to cancel your trip. This is the chance of a lifetime for you." Lizzie's voice caught on the word lifetime, thinking of how this might be the last trip Gram would ever take. She couldn't be the one to take this away from her. She'd given up so much for Lizzie and Lottie when they were kids. She deserved a true vacation. She deserved to see the world.

"This friend," said Gram slowly, "is it anyone I know?"

"Um . . ." Lizzie stalled. At that moment, Chase came out onto the porch, his voice booming.

"Okay, I got him all put away. Let's get you inside now, Lizzie Lou."

Lizzie winced at the telling silence on the other end of the phone. But when Gram started talking again, she could hear a smile in her voice; a fact that did not exactly put her at ease. Lizzie didn't need her making too much of this.

"Well, if they can handle Pancake, they must be someone special."

"Turn around and go back to your gate," said Lizzie firmly, a little desperate now to both end this conversation and to be assured that Gram was not canceling her trip. "Do that for me. Please."

"Yes, I will," her grandmother answered. "But please check in with me tonight, okay? Even if I don't answer?"

"I will. Enjoy yourself. Don't worry about me."

"All right, Lizzie. Listen to Chase."

Her grandmother hung up before Lizzie could try to deny the identity of her caretaker. She was tired; she felt almost attacked by fatigue, blurring her thoughts.

"I need to sit down," she muttered, and Chase held the screen door open so she could go inside. She made her way to the couch; she'd just sleep here.

"You still want me to go?"

Even though she was starting to have second thoughts, Lizzie nodded. The rocky way she'd left things with Lottie didn't help; she hadn't even said goodbye when she and Jeremy left the morning after her party. It would be tough to call and beg for help now. Chase sighed.

"Okay. What can I get you before I go?"

"I don't know." She stretched out on the couch, trying to get the remote with her fingertips, which was just out of her reach. Chase nudged it closer for her, and she smiled at him gratefully. He stared at her for a long moment, then turned and went into her kitchen.

"Chase?" He didn't answer, but she heard him open the fridge. He came back a few minutes later with a peanut butter and jelly sandwich, potato chips, and an apple. Leaning over her, he perched it on the back of the couch.

"In case you get hungry," he muttered. "That way, the dog can't sneak a taste." He paused, watching her. "Can I come by in the morning and check on you?"

"I don't think that's necessary," she said, fluffing a blanket over her legs. It was thin. She glanced toward the hallway without thinking about it . . . getting up the stairs was going to be tricky.

"Can I get you anything else before I go? A drink? A quilt? A pillow? A change of clothes?"

Each of his suggestions sounded better than the last, and as her ankle and shoulder started to throb again, the temptation grew stronger to just let him stay. *No. I'm fine. I'll be fine.*

"A quilt and a pillow would be great."

"Pajamas?"

"Sure." She pointed to a laundry basket on the dining room table. "Might be some in there." He peered uncertainly at the stacks of clothes in the blue basket, and Lizzie snickered. "Nothing's going to bite you in there."

Chase gave her a playful glare and tentatively pulled out a lacy camisole. "This yours?"

"Gram's."

He carefully folded it and put it back in the same pile. "I recognize this . . ."

It was her NASA shirt, the one she'd worn to Trivia the first night, and she nodded. "Should be some blue shorts in there, too." Chase found them and brought them over, putting them carefully on the arm of the couch. He crossed his arms over his chest, then let them drop, pacing.

"You're sure I can't stay?" His agitation was making *her* stomach hurt. What was he going to do with all this nervous energy when he left? *Not your problem.*

"Yes." Her annoyance bled into her voice. She really did want to get out of these dirty clothes, and she couldn't do that with him here. "Can you let the dog out before you leave?"

"Do you want me to take him with me? I can take him with me if you don't want to have to worry about him. No, wait, maybe you want him for protection . . ."

She cocked her head at him. "Protection?"

"Yeah, you know. Protection. You're here by yourself. And you're a woman."

"A woman with guns," she said flatly. "Nobody's going to break in here."

"Right. Okay." Chase turned suddenly and went down the hall, and a moment later, Pancake came bounding into the living room, sniffing her all over. When Chase came back in, he brought the pillow and quilt he'd promised.

"Do I smell like sheep?" she asked her dog, and his tail wagged so hard, he knocked a magazine and a candle off the coffee table.

"Okay. I'm off," Chase said, pausing at the front door. She watched him as she scratched her dog behind the ears with both hands.

"Thank you," she said, and Chase nodded, then closed the door behind him. Lizzie listened for the sound of his car starting, but it didn't come. She waited until her show ended, then grabbed one crutch and stumped over to the front windows. He was still sitting in his red SUV, inside lights off, talking on the phone.

CHAPTER TWENTY-ONE:
Chase

SITTING IN THE DARK outside her house, Chase tried to pull himself together. He was being a bully, trying to make her see reason, and he hated the way he was acting. He was diving into this too fast. They'd been on one date, and now he was trying to move in with her? What had happened to his take-it-slow plan, the wooing phase? He shook his head at himself, baffled by his own behavior. It had all gone right out the window when he got that call from Martina. She'd had far too little information to offer him, and he'd panicked. *"Ainsley just said Lizzie's hurt and she's at the ER. That's all I know."* He'd texted Kellan immediately, and he'd reminded him that he was in the care of God. But that had been very hard to remember as he raced through the halls, searching for her, unassuageable despite the nursing staff's best efforts. He'd have to send that lady a nice bouquet. When it came to Lizzie, he clearly did not have the self-control he needed yet, and that was a problem. A big one.

"Hello?"

"Hey, it's me, Chase."

"How'd it go at the hospital?"

Chase blew out a long breath, and Kellan chuckled.

"That good, huh? What happened?"

"She's got a sprained ankle. Doctor tried to give her Vicodin and I flipped out."

"Does she have a problem with opioids?"

"Not that I know of . . ." Chase knew where this line of questioning was going. It was going exactly where he should've taken it himself when he was standing next to her in her hospital room. And he was kicking himself now.

"So why can't she have opioids?"

"She can, but she shouldn't. What if she gets addicted like I did? It'll ruin her life. And I've been reading a lot about this, doctors are prescribing this shit way too often. They don't understand what they're doing to people."

"Sounds to me like this isn't about Lizzie's health. This is about you and your fears."

He said nothing. He was not ready to admit that out loud. In the dark car, he let his head tip back against the headrest. But apparently, Kellan heard the truth in the silence.

"I know you want to go full 'white knight' for this woman, but for now, stay focused on yourself and your health. Instead of dictating what Lizzie shouldn't do, trying to save someone who doesn't want saving, I want you to acknowledge where you've gone wrong here."

"I shouldn't have yelled at the doctors and nurses."

"Agreed."

"I shouldn't have insisted she let me take her home."

"True." When Chase paused, Kellan went on. "Anything you did right?"

"I . . ." This part was almost harder. His anxiety didn't like hearing him acknowledge that he wasn't constantly blowing it, even if it was the truth. Chase swallowed. "I left when she asked me to."

"Good. It's hard to give up control—I'm glad you listened to her."

"It was *hard*." Hard didn't begin to explain it. He wanted this so much; he wanted to take care of Lizzie. But not at the expense of his sobriety. He needed to protect that like an egg, tucked safely beneath him in a nest of boundaries and hard-won advice from people who cared about him. It couldn't live on its own yet. Maybe it never would, exactly. It hurt to think that sobriety would never feel second nature. He swallowed hard.

"Of course it was. Part of what we fight is our need to be in control. We have to feel all our feelings now, and it doesn't all feel good. But listening to someone you care about is important. What else?"

"I—" His phone buzzed with a text, and he looked at it. "Hang on a second."

Lizzie: Go. Home. Chase.

Her silhouette gave him no hint of how mad she was, but her punctuation was not a good indicator, and guilt took a giant bite out of him.

Chase: I was just talking to my sponsor. Sorry. I'm going.

Lizzie: Okay. Sorry. I thought you were going to sleep out there or something.

How in the world could she have guessed that?

Chase: No, I understand. I'll finish up, then go.
Lizzie: Okay. Talk to you tomorrow.
Chase: Promise?
Lizzie: Yes.

"Chase?"

"Yeah, sorry. Lizzie was texting me, we had a misunderstanding. All good now."

"Okay. You gonna head home?"

Both of them? They both guessed what I was about to do? If there were two people who he needed to see right through him, it was these two.

"Yes."

"Because you'll sleep better in a bed . . ."

"I'm heading home." He'd told both of them. Now he had to do it.

Kellan chuckled a little, probably at Chase's barbed tone. "Okay, man. Take care of yourself tonight."

"I will. Thanks for the talk." Chase hung up and sat there for another minute before he pushed the button to start the car. It felt so wrong. It felt intolerable. His stomach was churning; it felt like a tidal wave of acid in there, just rolling around. He took a few deep breaths. *God grant me the Serenity to accept the things I cannot change, Courage to change the things I can, and Wisdom to know the difference.* He didn't close his eyes, he just let the words express his fervent wish that he not screw this up.

He took the back way home, avoiding the highway, crossing the river to wind through the shadowed woods. At the top of the hill, he stopped and shut off his car. He could hear the sound of the falls, water rushing headlong over the edge. *Her charger. I didn't bring her the phone charger. What if it dies in the night and she can't get a hold of me? What if she falls and cracks her head?* The thought made him want to curl up in a ball. He'd failed her. He'd failed to convince her to let him stay. He'd failed to give her the things she needed to be safe. *No,* he pushed back against his anxiety. *She didn't want me to stay. She said she had it handled. Success is not final, failure is not fatal: it is the courage to continue that counts.* That last part was Winston Churchill, not NA, but it helped a little nonetheless. All he could do was be there for her as much as she'd let him . . . even if it was a lot less than he'd like.

AROUND SIX A.M., CHASE startled awake, sloshing the cold chamomile tea he'd left sitting on his nightstand as he groped for his phone, which was ringing.

"Hello? Lizzie?" It was technically tomorrow, but much earlier than he'd expected to hear from her.

"Hi." Her voice was soft, tentative. "Were you asleep?" His impulse was to lie, and he squashed it down hard—enough of that lately. Too much.

"Yeah. How was your night? Are you okay?"

"My night was . . ." She hesitated. "Rough. You could come by today. If you wanted to."

He flopped onto his back, massaging his temples. "Change your mind?"

Her sigh was laden with frustration. "Pancake needs someone able-bodied to deal with him . . ."

He was not laughing at her, he was absolutely not . . . but it was a good thing they weren't on a video call so she couldn't see the glee he felt that she'd turned to him and not someone else.

"Well, Pancake's a great dog, so I'd be happy to help. Let me grab a shower and I'll be right over. I can bring breakfast."

"Do you think . . ." She trailed off uncertainly.

"What?"

"Nothing. See you in a bit." She hung up before he could begin to guess what she'd wanted to say. He took the world's fastest shower, not even waiting for the water to get warm, then texted Kellan from the line at the café that he was going back over to Lizzie's.

Kellan: If she wants you to stay, what are you going-ing to do?

Chase: I don't know.

Kellan: Chase, now's the time to think about that. Before it happens. Before you're more concerned with hurting her or upsetting her. Make a plan.

Plan? He didn't have a plan beyond making sure Lizzie was cared for. But if he didn't think beyond her needs to his own, he was asking for trouble.

Kellan: Do you have your program materials? The things you'd need to meditate, ground yourself after a rough day?

He didn't even have a change of underwear, let alone that other stuff.

Chase: Just my recovery app.

Kellan: Caregivers have their own support groups for a reason. I can see it's pointless to tell you not to do this, so if you're going to do it, at least give yourself the best shot at success.

You're screwing this up, his mind taunted. *Even your sponsor thinks so.*

Chase: Okay. I hear you. If she wants me to stay, I'll go home and grab the stuff I need.

Kellan: And you'll ask her if there's drugs in the house.

Chase winced at his blatant request. Out of the corner of his eye, he noticed Christopher, sitting with his laptop open at a corner table, staring off into space. He waved at him, and he snapped out of it, moving his attention back to the screen without acknowledging him. *Jerk.* And yet, it served as a reminder that Kellan actually cared, unlike his family. He'd be a fool to ignore his advice.

Chase: Yes, I will. And I'll be at the meeting on Monday.
Kellan: Good.

CHAPTER TWENTY-TWO:
Lizzie

TRUE TO HIS WORD, CHASE showed up an hour later with buttermilk pancakes from Riverside. She didn't want to need help, but at least for a while, she was going to, and the fear of that had made her heart palpitate. But he'd come back when she'd asked him to. He hadn't shamed her or made fun of her for changing her mind. They ate on the couch side by side, neither one speaking, neither bothering to get a plate. The compostable container was tough enough. *Just wish I was . . .* Once it seemed like he was almost done, she cleared her throat.

"I did some reading last night," she said.

Chase turned his head to see her. "Yeah?"

She nodded. "It seemed like my . . . situation really triggered you."

"Yeah, it did." He set down his food and tucked one leg under himself as he pivoted to see her better.

"I don't know . . ." She stopped. Lizzie felt helpless to express what she was thinking, and this wasn't a time to just blurt out her feelings—not that she was normally prone to

that. But her reading had been enlightening, and she wanted to confirm some things from the get-go. She cleared her
throat to try again.

"It felt like I drove you to smoke yesterday. I don't want
to make things worse for you, for your anxiety. It isn't good
if—"

Chase's eyes were wide, concerned. "Hey. No, that's
not—"

She held up a hand and noticed it was shaking a little.
"Let me finish, please."

He nodded, and she took another deep breath.

"I felt like I made things worse. That's one reason I didn't
want you to stay. But the articles said I should let you set
your own boundaries and depend on your sobriety supports,
rather than tiptoeing around you, trying not to set you off."

He nodded ardently, leaning forward, as if he needed to
affirm that as strongly as he could, but wasn't sure if he was
allowed to talk yet. It was a little bit funny, but she wasn't
ready to laugh about this yet.

"So thank you for giving me that space to kind of sort
through my own thoughts and feelings on everything that'd
happened. Were you okay last night?"

"Yes," he said emphatically. "Yes, I was okay, but yes to
everything else you said, too. I have to take responsibility for
how I act, and I acted horribly yesterday. I'm sorry I was so
pushy. I'm going to try to do better. And it's just like your accident—do you blame Forrest for your injury?"

Lizzie shrugged one shoulder. "I was the one who
stepped in the hole."

"Right. And if I make a mistake, that's on me, not you." That made some sense to her, but it just prompted more questions.

"Is smoking a mistake?"

Chase shook his head. "I'm allowed to smoke. But I can see why you thought that. I should've explained myself better."

"Oh, that's okay," Lizzie said, her cheeks pinking a little. She didn't expect people to explain themselves all the time. Lord knows she didn't want that kind of pressure aimed in her direction.

"Would you consider staying?" she asked, not bothering to mention her midnight trip to the bathroom that had left her crying on the ground, forced to crawl back to the couch, a situation she'd rather not repeat.

His nod was slow. "I would. But there's some things we'd have to get out of the way first."

Her mind spun like a game show wheel. *Payment of some kind? First dibs on the shower? No kissing? What does he want?*

"Like what?"

Chase rubbed at his nose. "So, this is an awkward question, but it must be asked. Are there any drugs in this house, illegal or otherwise?" The way it hurt his pride to ask was written on his face in the lines around his mouth, his grimace.

Lizzie tucked her hands under her thighs. "Not that I know of. Gram's pretty good about getting rid of stuff." She paused, not sure where to take the conversation next. "Would you like me to check?"

"No, I can do it. But can I flush whatever I find?"

She frowned. That wasn't a good idea. She wasn't going to hold back all the time. Once she started walking on eggshells around him, they might as well end this friendship . . . or whatever it was.

"It would be safer to take them to the hospital. That's the nearest DEA-approved disposal site."

"Legally, that's probably true," he said, licking the last of the syrup from his fork. "But not emotionally for Chase."

Lizzie drummed her fingers on her knee, which still really hurt. "Okay. But don't flush them. We'll lock them in my car and I'll keep the keys under my pillow. Does that work?"

"No, I'm not making you a gatekeeper, Lizzie. I can run them to the hospital."

"Or RJ might pick them up for you."

"RJ?"

She nodded. "He's a paramedic in town," she said, trying to give him a meaningful look . . . and was met with a blank stare. "He's the one . . . he was there when . . . when you . . . when I arrested you." It was still painful to think of Chase that way. She definitely did not want to go through that again. "You might not remember him; his parents moved here a few years ago, and he followed them later on."

"Oh." He was frowning a little. "I didn't make amends to him." He pulled out his phone and made a note, then shoved it back into his back pocket. Making amends; she'd read about that last night.

"Step . . . seven?"

"Eight," he corrected with a smile. Talking about the steps gave her another thought.

"What about your sponsor? Could he help?"

Chase rubbed at his chin thoughtfully. "Or Martina. She'd know what she was looking for." He turned to her more fully. "Would you feel less weird about her coming and combing through your stuff than a stranger?"

She thought for a minute. "Yeah, that'd be fine." She still thought her suggestions were better, but the look on his face and the way he hugged the throw pillow to his chest made her swallow down the words. "Okay. Do what you need to do."

"Your grandmother won't be mad?"

Lizzie snorted. "No. Gram doesn't really get mad."

"Ever?"

"I guess she did once . . . but that was when she was worried about someone else." Lottie had been out all night without calling. They'd both dozed, sitting up on the couch, waiting for her to come home, the two of them unable to rest properly without knowing the third member of their little band was safely home. It was one of the peculiar things about having such a small family; one member missing was a crisis. Mysteries were not allowed. Especially not past-midnight mysteries. Gram had railed at Lottie from the front porch when the boy dropped her off at four a.m., and Lottie had tucked tail and run upstairs, her face tear-stained and humiliated. But she didn't tell him that. She didn't want to talk about Lottie now.

Chase stood up. "Let me go call Martina and see if she can swing by today," he said, jingling the keys in his pocket. He went out to the front porch. Her uninjured knee was bouncing, her nervous tic in action. What if Martina couldn't come? Would she have to insist on looking with him, then going to Santiam together? Should she? She wasn't going to feel right sending him on his own . . . but those articles said partners should give the person in recovery space sometimes. Were they really partners? She suddenly regretted not making her desire for a kiss more obvious after their hangout; she wasn't even sure if he'd wanted to. She put her head in her hands, just for a minute, and without warning, a large pink tongue was lapping at her face.

"Ugh, dog, stop. That wasn't the kind of kiss I wanted." He gave her a slow wag, watching her expectantly. "And I don't know what you want." He dipped his head and stared pointedly at the chewed, woven rope he'd brought to her feet. "Right. Of course." She picked it up and tossed it, but he was going to be insufferable if he didn't get some serious daily exercise. Maybe she could pay Maggie Durand to walk him; she'd seen her around town doing odd jobs lately.

The sound of the front door opening had her looking up at Chase expectantly.

"Will she do it?"

He nodded his head slowly, but he had one hand behind his back . . . why did he have one hand behind his back? "We had a good talk. She'll be by in about an hour. And I think I found something that belongs to you."

Lizzie stared at him, confused. "Not too surprising, since this is my house . . ."

"When I was sat on the porch swing . . ." He whipped his hand out dramatically. "This fell off." A small glass bottle of wet *n* wild nail polish was poised between his fingers, a robin's egg blue color she happened to know was called

"Putting On Airs". She'd painted her toes outside last weekend and must've forgotten to bring it in.

Lizzie cocked an eyebrow at him as if to say, "So?"

"To whom does this belong, Elizabeth?"

"Why does that matter?"

"Because unless you're hiding a thirteen-year-old girl around here somewhere, I'm pretty sure no one else buys this brand anymore." That barbed a little. There was a reason she didn't show her affinity for nail polish on her fingers, and this was it.

"Hey." She pointed a finger at him. "When I find a brand I like, I stick with it."

"Loyalty," he smiled, and he tossed the bottle to her, which she caught easily. "I don't see it on your fingernails . . ." He sat down next to her on the couch.

"It doesn't fit my work persona," she sniffed. "I want to make sergeant this year. Sergeants don't wear blue nail polish." She did not mention that she painted her toenails in a different shade every Sunday; he'd just happened to find the color she used the most.

"Interesting," he said, shadowing her as she stumped across the room back to the couch. "There aren't any other female deputies, are there?"

"There are no other female officers of any rank."

"You're supposed to elevate."

She blinked at him. What, rise through the ranks? That was an odd way to put it. With a grin, he pointed to her ankle. Chase waited for her to lift her leg to the coffee table, and he slipped a pillow under her ankle carefully.

"So what made you want to get into law enforcement?"

"Captain Hansen. He was very helpful when my parents passed away. He . . ." *Wow, tears? Now? After all this time?* That was a real surprise; Lizzie hardly cried about anything. She cleared her throat as Chase sat back next to her. "He's kind of watched over me and Lottie and Gram. Whenever we need help, Gram calls and he shows up."

"So it's sort of the family business?" He put his own feet on the coffee table with a thunk, and she smiled.

"I guess. In a way." She turned on the TV, not caring what it landed on, missing her Europe-gallivanting chaperone, even though it was too easy to talk to Chase. They were still alone. It wasn't close to nighttime yet, but it would be eventually. Being alone with a guy in her dark house was still . . . uncertain.

"Interesting."

"It's kind of the same for you, isn't it? You work at the paper mill?"

He nodded. "I work in marketing at TFPP because of my dad. That was a path he . . . encouraged."

"Mandated."

"Yeah, that."

"What did you want to do, as a kid?"

He tipped his head to one side, and it happened to be the side Lizzie was on. Which is why he happened to tip over a little so that their elbows touched. "I don't know if I should tell you."

"Why not?"

"I'm pretty sure you'll make fun of me."

"Try me."

"I wanted to paint houses."

Lizzie covered her mouth with one hand and tried to nod sagely. But despite her best effort, she was not giving off the thinking vibe she was trying to project.

"You're laughing."

"I'm not," she said with a shrug, still covering her mouth.

"I see you," he said, peering closer at her. "Don't make me tickle you. You're injured."

Lizzie let her hand drop then, her shoulders shaking with the effort of holding in her giggles. "Dude, you went to *Duke*. Since your fancypants education doesn't match up with that line of work, why did you want to be a house painter?"

"I don't know," he said, his voice turning contemplative. "When I was eight or nine, we had our house painted inside and out, and I just thought they had a really fun job. It seemed peaceful. They just got to, like, listen to their radio and make our house look great. And sure, it was kind of messy, but they were so careful and precise and it was always pristine when they left. I just thought about what a sense of accomplishment they must have at the end of the day. Like, they did this amazing thing."

"No such satisfaction in marketing, huh?"

"Not so far, no." He rubbed at his face, and Lizzie could feel the fatigue coming off him as he let out a huge yawn.

"You should go home and take a nap," she said softly. "I'm fine. And you said you need good sleep." Truth be told, she wanted to know more about his job and what he wanted to do now, but he didn't seem like he was in any shape to chat right now. It had been a long twenty-four hours for both of them.

"Yeah, I promised my sponsor I'd go home and grab my program materials if I was going to stay. So I should . . . do that."

"Yeah. Definitely. And by then, Martina will be done."

He didn't move from the couch, so she muted the TV. When he still didn't get up, Lizzie leaned over and gave him a little push.

"Go."

"What's with the pushing?"

"It's not pushing, it's physical encouragement. Go."

"Fine," he laughed, getting to his feet.

"I'm going to run home. I'll be back to check on you in a few hours." Chase handed her the remote, but she didn't unmute the TV.

"Quesadilla."

"Hmm?"

"I'll take a quesadilla before you go. With sour cream, guac, and pico de gallo on the side."

He saluted her with a grin. "Coming right up." He burned it a little on the bottom since he 'wasn't used to electric burners,' but she didn't mind. Not one cheesy bit.

CHAPTER TWENTY-THREE: Chase

HE PUT PANCAKE IN THE laundry room before he left, in case she needed to get up while he was gone. The yellow lab scratched at the door, whining, and his heart felt the same. Separation felt wrong, wrong, wrong . . . but it was the right thing to do.

No one was home when he got there, unsurprisingly. Chase went up to his room and looked around. He still wanted to do this. He still thought he should. He sat down on the edge of his bed, letting his palms rest on his knees. A few deep breaths, and he let his eyes close as he fell into that dark, quiet place only meditation seemed to be able to take him. It was dark in a good way. It was as quiet as his mind ever got; he could let any negative thoughts float down the river away from him instead of feeling forced to wrestle with them. He slept for two hours and woke up feeling better. He took the quiet with him as he did some laundry, as he went down to the gym to walk on the treadmill. And at five o'clock, he texted his brother.

Chase: I think I'm going to crash with Lizzie.

Carter: Okay. Thanks for letting me know.

Chase: Any brotherly wisdom for me?

Carter: No? I mean . . . no, not really?

Chase: It'll be purely platonic.

Carter: I didn't think it wouldn't.

Chase: Her grandmother is out of town, so she's got no one to take care of her.

The phone rang in his hand, and the picture of him and Carter he'd taken during a rehab visit flashed up on the screen. The visit where he'd asked him to take over Martina's payments. And he'd done it. He'd been a good brother. He could be a good friend to Lizzie, too. He was reliable now. He could be that.

"Dude," Carter said without preamble. "Chill. If Lizzie wants you to stay with her, go stay with Lizzie."

"I just don't want to make a mistake." His own words to Lizzie came back to him, and he wanted to laugh at himself, but there was nothing funny here.

"Everyone makes mistakes."

"But my mistakes could land me back in rehab or addicted or . . ." *Dead.* He couldn't bring himself to say it, but it was true. He'd known friends from his past rehabs who were gone now; going onto social media had a new edge ever since he'd found a friend's name with the hashtag #gonetoosoon.

When they relapsed, the body was more sensitive, couldn't take the same kind of hit.

"Are you feeling tempted to use again?"

"Not really." And yet, the thought was always there, lingering, trespassing. It wasn't active, but it wasn't gone, either. It slept in his mind like a hibernating bear. He did not want it to wake up.

"All right." He heard Carter blow out a breath. "You wanted brotherly wisdom? Here it is. You can't avoid every mistake, but you can try to avoid the big ones. And if you need anything from me, I'm there. If you need me to take over and help with Lizzie, just ask. You're kinda getting in deep quick with her. If you feel the sharks circling, I'm here."

HE WENT BACK TO LIZZIE'S with pizza subs in hand, which were well-received. After that, he set up the futon in Tansy's office for himself, not wanting to be separated from Lizzie by a flight of narrow stairs. Lizzie assured him Tansy wouldn't mind, but he texted her just to make sure. It had been an emotional day, and it felt nice to just sink into the couch and talk and laugh. But he must have been more tired than he'd realized, because Chase woke to a whining sound and something licking his hand, jerking him from the comfortable, warm place he was in.

"What the . . ." He blinked awake to Pancake's plaintive face . . . and he suddenly remembered where he was; he'd fallen asleep next to Lizzie on the couch after dinner. "Do you need to go out, boy?" Pancake's slow wag and steady gaze served as a yes, and Chase carefully tried to extricate himself from Lizzie, who was hugging his arm in her sleep like he was her teddy bear. He carefully tipped her over onto the couch cushion where he'd just been, slipping a pillow under her head. She still didn't look very comfortable, now lying in an L shape, but maybe he could work on that once the poor dog's bladder had been relieved. He'd meant to let him out before he went to bed . . . but that clearly hadn't happened like he'd planned. *You're screwing this up, just like always,* his anxiety whispered. "Shove it," he whispered back as he quietly opened the front door, which he'd left unlocked, which just made the thought repeat itself more loudly. The dog quickly bounded down the front steps and into the grass, stopping to sniff the wind. He stood in the doorway, watching Pancake take his time.

"You're leaving?" Chase spun. Lizzie was sitting up, her plaid blanket pulled up to her chest.

"No. No, no. Just letting the dog out." Pancake must have heard Lizzie's voice because he came bounding back up the stairs and pressed his head right into her lap.

"Hey, get off, beast," she reprimanded, and Pancake begrudgingly retreated, but curled up under the tunnel her legs were creating between the sofa and the coffee table.

Chase decided not to address the perceived abandonment at that exact moment and instead came over to help her lie down flat. Part of him couldn't believe that he'd done that, just fallen asleep with her like it was the most natural thing in the world. Given his history of insomnia, it made no sense . . . but given the stressful events they'd been through lately, perhaps it did. Still, he'd promised himself that he was going to keep things friendly and PG, and sleeping together in any capacity was not going to support that agenda. The last thing he needed was an awkward encounter that led to her kicking him out. He'd stay with her for a few days, then see how things were going. Since it was Sunday, there would be a need to communicate with work soon about what was happening . . . and telling his boss meant telling his dad.

"Comfy?" he asked, and she nodded, but he noticed her wince as she tried to get comfortable. "Are you in pain?"

"Yeah."

He waited. Apparently, she wasn't going to elaborate, but based on the bruises she'd had blooming in the hospital, he couldn't imagine there wasn't more happening that he hadn't seen.

"Ibuprofen?"

"Yes, please."

Chase shuffled into the kitchen; it was three in the morning. No wonder he had a crick in his neck. He gave himself a little massage as he filled her water glass, still yawning like crazy. He brought her the glass, trying to figure out whether to say anything about her misapprehension earlier. He decided reassurance was the way to go as he shook out two pills into his hand and offered them to her.

"You can ask for anything you need."

"Not great at that," she muttered.

"Well, I'll be here all night. Just wake me up if you need anything until then, okay?"

She gave him a curt nod and knocked back the pills and water in one go. Her shaking hands were cause for concern, and he recognized the pain in her face, too. Had he been too hasty to get rid of that prescription? He couldn't be around that stuff. Couldn't. She'd said it was okay, but her grimace said it all: she was suffering.

"Do you need something stronger?"

"No. Go to bed." Late-night Lizzie was a grumpster. Tansy had texted him something to that effect: *Keep her fed, give her space, and don't wake her up. You'll both be fine.* He'd broken rules two and three.

"Do you want an ice pack?"

"No."

"A snack or something?"

"Chase!" she shouted, and the dog raised his head, looking anxiously between them. "For the love of Mike, go. to. bed."

"Fine," he said, holding up his hands, hoping to mollify her. "Sweet dreams." He shuffled back to the makeshift guest room he'd set up for himself. A light was shining in the window from the neighbor's security lights, probably triggered by Pancake a few minutes ago. It was the kind of blueish color that sometimes gave him a headache, but he lay down and fluffed the pillow a little, trying to get comfortable. Chase closed his eyes, listening to the tick of the kitchen clock. How on earth could she think he was leaving in the middle of the night? *She doesn't know me at all if she thinks I'd take off on her like that.* Maybe letters weren't enough. Maybe Lizzie was just that insecure . . . it had been a weird day, in her defense. With a sigh, he rolled to his back, and his eyes opened again. The light was still on. There were no curtains on the windows; he'd just wait until it went off. He folded his hands over his belly, looking up at the paneled walls and smooth ceiling. Whatever the challenges, he'd be even more stressed if he was relinquishing her care to someone else. Her grandmother had seemed relieved that someone would be with her, anyway.

Staring up at that smooth ceiling, he thought he'd like a house like this: a little bit worn, a little bit old. A house with history, that felt its age sometimes. Something he could tinker with . . . his childhood dreams of being a house painter came back to him along with Lizzie's amused reaction. He was rebuilding his life, wasn't he? It wouldn't be strange to consider a new profession, even at his age. He let his thoughts wander toward what that might look like . . . it felt almost sinful to imagine it. He saw himself working outside, bundled against the cold, enjoying the sun when it came out. Something that would let him work up a sweat sometimes, not be stuck behind a desk with the fluorescent lights buzzing overhead, surrounded by particleboard furniture, glass between him and fresh air. Maybe he could be a park ranger or something . . . Lizzie would know, she worked with the Fish and Wildlife people. Chase resisted the urge to pull out his phone and look it up now; it was just a dream, anyway. He was stuck at TFPP as long as he wanted a relationship with his dad. Harrison would never forgive him if he left. And he did want that. He'd finally put the notion that he needed to be forgiven for his drug problem to rest, but Chase wanted to heal the rift between them. He didn't even need his dad to be proud of him, though that would be nice—he just wanted to be able to have a civil conversation, a basic appreciation of who he was. That seemed like a reasonable thing to want . . . but it wasn't really within his control. And he knew where trying to control other people got you.

The light outside finally went off, and Chase's eyelids felt heavy. Turning onto his side on the firm futon mattress, he let them slide closed again with a sigh. They snapped open again a moment later when the light came back on. Chase sat up and peered out the window, letting the meager covers slide down. A young buck stared back at him, still munching on the neighbor's lawn. Chase flopped back down with a groan and covered his head with the pillow. That light would be going on and off all night if deer were hanging around . . . it was almost morning, anyway. Maybe he could tack a sheet up over the window in the morning . . . he couldn't very well sleep with Lizzie again.

"*Ouch.*" The hushed timbre of her voice told him she was trying to be quiet, but it pierced through his restless sleep. *Lizzie.* He sat up, threw off the covers, and got halfway through the door before he realized he wasn't wearing a shirt. It wasn't body consciousness that had him backtracking to find one . . . he didn't think Lizzie would be okay with him just hanging out bare-chested. The devil on his shoulder chuckled and whispered that he should do it just to get a rise out of her, but he mentally flicked it off. *You'd know how she feels about you if you did. You could read it in her gaze.* He shook his head as he pulled his soft, stonewashed blue cotton shirt over his torso. *Or you could screw it up permanently.* He didn't want to mess with her head, and her health was the priority right now, not whatever was happening between them. He wasn't going to make a move. He wasn't. Another bump and a soft curse drew his attention into the hallway again, and he ran a hand through his sleep-tousled hair as he went striding to find her. Through a crack in the door, he could see she'd made it into the bathroom and was attempting to brush her teeth while balancing on one foot. Annoyed, he pushed the door open.

"What do you have against the crutches, anyway?"

Startled, Lizzie's arms windmilled as she tried to regain her balance, and he reached out and wrapped her in his arms, pulling her into his side. She was still warm from being under the covers on the couch, her hair up in a sloppy bun, overflowing, and he had the sudden urge to pick her up, if only to be sure that she wouldn't fall. She stared up at him, a glob of white toothpaste dripping from the corner of her gaping mouth, and he couldn't help but think how adorable she was, how silly it was for her to keep telling him to temper his expectations.

"What do you have against privacy?" she snapped back, a fierce blush overtaking her neck as she came back to herself. "I'm in the *bathroom*, Chase."

"The door was open," he defended quietly, his voice going low and rumbly like it did when he first woke up sometimes. Lizzie's eyes widened again, and he thought maybe he didn't need to walk around shirtless to know what kind of effect he had on her, given that he was holding her in the tiny, under-the-stairs bathroom and she showed no discomfort whatsoever with the holding . . . just the location, apparently.

"Well, I . . ." she sputtered, spitting a bit of toothpaste onto his shirt as she tried to resume her morning ritual, and he let her go, keeping a hand on her other elbow to keep her stable. Lizzie pivoted back to the mirror, looking mildly discontented, and Chase had to keep his chuckle inside. He looked around the neat bathroom . . . toilet, white pedestal sink, pink roses on the wallpaper vining around the edge of the big, gold-edged mirror . . .

"There's no shower down here."

"Nope." Lizzie spit and stuck her head under the faucet to rinse her mouth, still balancing on one foot.

"So . . . how are we going to get you clean?" During their unintended embrace, he'd noticed a few smudges of mud on various parts of her arms. It wasn't too surprising he'd missed them last night; they'd both been exhausted.

"We?"

"Yes, Elizabeth, *we*. You're on a team now. Get used to it."

She smirked as she rinsed her toothbrush and put it down on the edge of the sink. "No uniform. No mascot. No registration. No equipment. No team."

He pressed his lips into a line and felt doubt for the first time that he should be here. "I might be able to get you up the stairs piggyback-style," he said, slipping a hand around her waist, a gesture she did not acknowledge, but also didn't reject. Yet.

"I don't think so."

"They're pretty narrow, though . . ." He'd been able to touch both walls as he'd gone up to look for drugs in her bathroom . . . and found that adorable blue polish. "What are our other options?"

"Again," she said, hobbling toward the door—*sans crutches again*—"Our options are only *my* options, and I'm going to grab my suit and hose off outside."

"I hardly think so," Chase said, trying not to picture her in a bikini. He failed. In his mind, it was yellow with white polka dots and made her skin look like milk. He wanted to drink her up. Chase cleared his throat. "You'll fall down." He glanced down at her ankle; it was considerably more swollen than last night. "And we need to ice that thing, pronto."

Lizzie glared at him as they slowly made their way to the kitchen table. "What do you suggest, then?"

"We could set you up in here. You'd have more room for a chair, we could fill the sink with water, you do your thing, but there's more room for me to help if needed. You can still wear your suit or whatever."

She sat down hard in the curved wooden chair. "I guess that'll work."

Chase turned to the fridge in search of milk, which just made him think of his bikini fantasy again. "What kind of cereal do you want?"

"I don't care."

He opened cabinets until he found the cereal, then pawed through the wide selection, unsure. She seemed to have a lot of food opinions . . . was this a test? To see what he'd pick? To see if they were compatible? *You're overthinking it. Just pick the first one.* As it happened, the first one was some kind of wheat flakes with raisins, and Lizzie wrinkled her nose when he held it up.

"Did I mention I failed mind-reading in college?"

One corner of her mouth curved up, a flash of a smile. "Had me fooled."

"Tell me what you want or you're getting Cardboard Flakes." Lack of sleep was catching up with him. *I should be more patient. I should be nicer. She's hurt, she's bummed to be off work . . .* but she didn't look bummed right then. She looked . . . flirty? Yes, that was definitely a sparkle.

"Loopy O's."

"That's not very healthy," he protested, getting the box down anyway. "I'm supposed to be taking care of you."

"You want to take care of me?" she asked, tipping forward to get her hands under her leg to prop it up on another chair. "Make me bacon and eggs."

I'll do whatever you need me to. I thought that was obvious by now. But the idea of making something more complicated did have his insides tensing up a little bit. Quesadillas were pretty straightforward; eggs were tricky. But he wasn't about to voice that.

"Now you're talking," he said, shoving the box back in the cupboard.

"I was just kidding," Lizzie said quickly, but Chase shook his head. That's what she really wanted; he was sure of it. And he was already salivating at the thought of salty, warm bacon on his tongue. It was awkward finding everything he needed, but after a moment, she began to direct him as to where things were, and that helped. He brought her ice once his coffee was brewing and the bacon was popping in the pan. He didn't sit down until she was nearly done: the woman ate like a vacuum cleaner. Chase took a sip of his black coffee to find her staring at him, but she glanced away.

"That was good," she said, looking out the window over the sink. "Thank you."

"It's no problem."

"It'd be a problem for me. I could never do . . ."—she gestured to him and his plate—"this." The eggs hadn't come out perfect, but he thought he'd done all right.

"You don't cook?"

"No, I mean, be in someone else's space, crashing on their futon, trying to take care of someone as . . ."

He waited for her to finish, his fork still speared through a bite of scrambled egg. He thought she might want him to finish her sentence for her, but he didn't want to. He just wanted to hear her. Her gaze came back to his, then dropped to her lap.

"Someone as stubborn as me," she finished. "I'm sorry for being a pain. I just hate this." She tossed her phone onto the table in a huff. "Captain Hansen's putting me on administrative duty for four weeks. He said he'll drop off some paperwork for me tomorrow." Ah, there was the frustration he'd expected before.

"Well, at least you won't be bored . . ." Chase said, shrugging one shoulder.

She gave him a quelling look. "I am never bored. Tired, yes. Lonely, often. But not bored."

"Lonely?" Chase repeated softly, scowling.

Her next words came in a rush. "I can't be on admin duty that long. I'll be so desperate to get out of this house, I may injure someone."

"I'll wear my helmet, then."

She speared him with her gaze. "You won't be here in four weeks."

He ignored her skepticism. "Let's do that bath. You'll feel better." Chase stood up and offered her his hand. Given how long she paused before taking it, you'd have thought he was asking her to marry him, not offering his help with basic hygiene. She got to her feet . . . or rather, to her foot, and Chase stabilized her on the way over to the sink. Better to do it now before he tried to figure out what to do with that bacon grease. Growing up with a housekeeper had its perks, but knowing his way around a kitchen wasn't one of them.

"Hmm." She looked at him. "Now what?"

"Now I . . . go get you a swimsuit, I guess? Unless you want to stand here in your underwear? Or naked?"

Lizzie blushed an adorable shade of petal pink. "I'll take the suit. Top drawer on the right."

He stretched back to the table and dragged a chair over to her to rest her knee on. "Check. Don't fall over."

"Check." He started up the narrow staircase, the stairs creaking under his weight, when she called after him. "And my shampoo and soap and a brush and a towel!"

"Yes, ma'am!" he called back, and he heard her laugh. He stopped at a linen closet at the top of the stairs and pulled out the necessary items. The shower was a little tougher; there were several bottles of shampoo, and he didn't know if some was her sister's or her grandmother's. Chase popped the top on the first one and sniffed. No, Lizzie wouldn't be caught dead using that flowery nonsense . . . and it didn't smell anything like her. *Lemons.* She smelled like lemons. He found the one that seemed the most likely to be citrus-scented and on impulse, grabbed a razor, too. But of course, he couldn't find a swimsuit in that drawer . . . pawing through her underwear was a bad idea, but he didn't have much of a choice. Chase didn't want to judge her choices, but it was all surprisingly practical. There was not a scrap of lace or silk in there. Not that it was mandatory, of course, but a lot of women liked it . . . and a lot of men liked to give it. His inner caveman was glad she hadn't had that kind of relationship with anyone else, yet he couldn't help wondering why. She was 28, for heaven's sake. His inner philosopher piped up then, reminding him that he had no business judging her relationship choices or clothing choices and that he should stop being creepy and go back downstairs. *There.* It was a one-piece, blue with waves across the chest. Chase snapped it up and slammed the drawer shut.

"Took you long enough," Lizzie grumbled, accepting the armload of supplies from him. "Now go into the living room. I'll call you if I need anything."

"I can't go into my room?" he gestured to the adjoining doorway.

"No. Now go." She was using her cop voice. *Ooh, someone feels vulnerable.* It was the same voice she'd used last night when she thought he was leaving.

"Why?" Chase laughed, leaning forward to chase her gaze as she busied herself setting up the supplies by the kitchen sink.

"Because."

"Because why?" he asked, straightening. "Are you afraid I'm going to peek? I'm not going to peek."

"Right. Because you'll be in the living room. Feel free to use the TV. I'll see you in a few minutes."

Chase rolled his eyes but ambled off, only glancing over his shoulder once. He wasn't an animal, he thought, even though he was stewing a little in self-pity at missing out on that swimsuit moment. He could control himself. He hated it when people acted like all men were just sex-seeking automatons whose circuits fried when they came across a lightly-dressed object of their affections. He shoved his hands into his pockets when he got into the living room, staring out the front windows. Pancake got off his bed, stretching, as if to say, "Oh, hello. Didn't know you were still here." Chase gave his head an affectionate ruffle, and the dog leaned harder into his leg. He pulled out his phone and opened his recovery reading app . . . he'd spend a little time getting his head right. TV would just drown out her distress if she needed him; something told him she probably wouldn't be vocal enough about expressing it. The water in the kitchen started to run into the metal sink, the sound softening as it deepened. Chase focused on his app, reading words he'd read plenty of times before. It was good to stay grounded. He lost himself in the familiarity, the cadence of the words, the metaphors about who he was and who he could be.

"Chase?"

"Mmm?" He was still deep in his thoughts, and he didn't look up from his phone. Pancake sighed like Lizzie had woken him up.

"Chase!"

"Oh, right! Yeah, I'm coming," he called, jumping up, startling the dog at his feet as he tossed his phone to the chair. "I'm here," he said, rounding the corner into the kitchen.

She was wrapped in the big, fluffy towel, swimsuit still on underneath. She looked annoyed, hair dripping into her face. "I can't wash my hair. I think I messed up my shoulder a little when I fell." Based on the bruising around the joint, it was more than a little, but he chose not to mention that.

"Oh. Okay. I can do that. Here," he said, turning the chair. "Sit here, and I'll, um . . ." He looked around for another towel. "Here, sit down and put your head on this."

Awkwardly, all knees and elbows bumping, they worked until Lizzie got herself positioned with a grunt, her hips at the edge of the chair, the back of her head resting on the edge of the counter, hanging into the sink a little. Chase ran the water in the sink, testing it, as she adjusted the big towel she still had wrapped around herself.

"What are you doing?"

"Warming up the water."

"Where do you come from, man?" Lizzie asked, grinning widely.

"Right here in Timber Falls, that's where. What's so weird about warming up the water?"

"It just wouldn't occur to me, that's all," she said, lacing her fingers over her stomach and closing her eyes. "I'm not an infant."

"Infants aren't the only ones who deserve consideration, you know. It's nice being nice."

"I'll take your word for it."

"You say that like you're not nice. You don't fool me."

They both fell silent as he carefully directed the sprayer toward the top of her head and watched her hair turn into a silky river of red. Chase ran his fingers through it, watching her for a reaction. All he got was the little wrinkle between her eyebrows falling away, her face smoothing into a peaceful expression. He cleared his throat.

"This was always the best part of Mrs. Durand's haircuts."

"Yeah." Lizzie opened one eye. "It feels nice. Thank you."

"Happy to help," he murmured, carefully removing a tangle as he combed his fingers through her tresses. It was going to be over too soon, as far as he was concerned; he pooled a quarter-size amount of shampoo in his hand and started to work it into her thick hair. It began to form great clouds of bubbles in her hair, and he liked the way his fingers disappeared in the thick mélange of white soap and red hair. Chase glanced at her face and immediately decided he could watch that expression on her face all day; the way her deep satisfaction seemed to travel through the air between them. The way the ambient light from the kitchen window lit her skin, making it glow, making each little freckle on her face stand out more, like they were inked there. She was still wearing that ring around her neck, and the small chip diamond winked at him; he couldn't help but wonder what it was and why she never took it off. The pink of her lips, the chickenpox divot right on her chin . . . it all made it hard to focus on actually getting her hair clean. He thought she might be asleep until a little shiver ran through her.

"Water too cold?"

"No, I'm just in a wet towel."

"Okay, I'm almost done, I think."

Lizzie smiled, but didn't open her eyes. "How will you know when you're done?"

"When you say, 'Chase, that's enough.'"

"Or maybe when the shampoo's all out."

"That'd work, too," he said, replacing the sprayer. "Okay, sit up." He opened up the towel she'd been resting her head on and tried to use it to squeeze out her hair.

The doorbell rang, and Lizzie leaned forward, trying to see down the hallway.

"Are you expecting someone?"

"No," she said, trying to wrap her hair in the towel and failing miserably. She huffed out a hurt sound and let her hands drop. "I can't answer the door like this anyway."

"I got it," he said, wiping his hands on his pants, jogging toward the front door. Chase peered through the watery stained glass before he opened it. A familiar hat and mustache were discernible, and he opened the door. "Good morning, Captain Hansen."

The man's expression went from warm to surprise to suspicion in the blink of an eye. "Good morning. I was hoping to talk to Lizzie?" He held a large, clear plastic box full of files.

"Oh," Chase said, gesturing over his shoulder with his thumb, "she's just getting cleaned up in the kitchen." Would she want him invited in? He couldn't imagine she wanted her boss to see her limping around in the kitchen in her swimwear and towel. "Hang on, I'll let her know you're here."

"Appreciated."

He jogged into the kitchen where Lizzie was busy freaking out, trying to wring the water out of her hair with the towel she'd had wrapped around her.

"He said Monday! This is not Monday!"

Chase was stunned stupid for a minute as he looked at her, beautifully half-naked and panicking, before he snapped out of it. "Here," he said, tossing her the clothes he'd brought down. "Just put them on over your suit. He'll never know. I'll stall."

You will? Oh, goody, Chase's anxiety snarked. *This should be entertaining.*

"Sorry about that," Chase said with a smile. "She'll be right out, she's just ..." *Getting dressed? Nope. This is basically her guardian. Getting changed? Is that bad? Does it make it sounds like we were fooling around or something?* "She'll be right out. Feel free to have a seat, sir."

The man set down the box onto the dining room table and crossed his arms, his muscles bulging against his T-shirt. "Chase, right?"

Captain Hansen's intimidating stance made him want to deny it. "That's right."

"I didn't know you were back in town." He said it mildly, but Chase's anxiety heard something else. *I didn't know you were back in* my *town.* Hattie's words came back to him, and Chase made himself relax. *It's my town, too.*

"Yeah, I just finished a great rehab program near Bend."

"Uh-huh. And you're staying here with Lizzie for a while?" Chase followed the man's gaze to his clothes; he was still in his pajamas.

"Oh, this is just temporary. Her grandmother's out of town, so Lizzie asked me to help out until she's back on her feet, so to speak."

The suspicion didn't drop from the captain's face, and he adjusted his hat. "I see. Well, that's nice of you."

Chase resisted the urge to downplay this situation any more, to try to explain it to the man. "Can I get you a cup of coffee or something?"

"I'm good, thanks. Just tell her I dropped this off, okay?"

"I'm here," Lizzie panted, breathlessly trying to crutch her way into the front room through the narrow hallway. "Sorry, sir. I'm here."

The relief on the man's face was instantaneous. He looked like he wanted to hug her but couldn't. Chase recognized the expression because he felt it so often, though hopefully, it was in a very different way. "How's the ankle feeling, Deputy?"

"Fine, sir. I'll be back to work in no time."

"Four weeks."

Her eyebrows snapped together. "Sir—"

"No. Four weeks. That's a minimum. You can count some of it as vacation if it makes you feel better. Lord knows you've got enough days stacked up."

"Captain—"

He held up a hand, and Lizzie fell into a tense silence. "Don't worry, there's plenty for you to do. Sue will be tickled to have help digitizing old records. You'll still be plenty useful."

Her shoulders slumped, but she nodded. "Right." An uncomfortable silence descended. Chase's palms felt itchy and wet at the same time. He wondered if he should leave. He wondered if he should make a joke. *Breathe, Carpenter.*

Captain Hansen smoothed his mustache. "All right, well, Sherri's waiting on me to take her into town, so I should get going."

Lizzie nodded again. "Say hi for me."

"I'll do that. She might stop by and check on you next week, she said something about dropping off her famous chicken soup . . ." He shuffled toward the door, gesturing toward the papers he'd left. "And let Sue know when you're done with those, there's lots more where that came from." Chase wasn't looking forward to his own work that he'd need to go pick up, but it was nothing like the absolute disdain with which Lizzie looked at that box as soon as the captain's back was turned. But she painted a forced smile on her face before her boss left.

"Thanks, Captain. I'll see you."

"Feel better, Deputy." Captain Hansen closed the door behind himself, and Chase turned to her.

"Well, that went fine."

Lizzie snorted. "Yeah, I guess. I'm gonna go put on a real bra."

That's a shame. He just barely stopped himself from saying it out loud, which was good, because it was absolutely not a respectful, friendly thing to say. He wasn't going to flirt with her while he was staying here. He'd figure out how to turn it off for a little while. Chase turned on the TV, more than ready for a little distraction.

CHAPTER TWENTY-FOUR:
Lizzie

LAST THING SHE KNEW, she and Chase had been crashed on the couch, making fun of infomercials. Now the sound of the lawn mower rumbled in from the front yard. Lizzie hobbled out to the porch and leaned up against the post. She folded her arms menacingly. Chase only noticed her when he stopped to wipe the sweat off his forehead. *He's outside working in the sun while I sleep? Terrible.* But the view wasn't terrible . . . not terrible at all, especially when he unbuttoned his cuffs and rolled up his sleeves slowly, staring at her the whole time. Surely he didn't know what she was thinking about his forearms . . . no, he couldn't. But his grin made her suspect that maybe she was wrong.

"Hello, Elizabeth." She would not be baited into flirting with him. Would. Not.

"I was going to do that."

"When?" he asked, sauntering over to the porch to stare up at her, hands in the pockets of his baggy cargo shorts.

"After my nap."

"Okay, next question. How?"

"I hadn't figured that out yet."

"Well, good news. Now you can go back to sleep."

"I don't want to go back to sleep," she said, scowling. "And I don't want you doing things like this for me."

"Why?"

"Because!"

He grinned again. "Because why?"

"Because it's too sweet, that's why! And I don't need it!" She crutched over to the top of the stairs to make sure he could see how mad she was. "You're already feeding me and bathing me . . ." She stuttered on the word 'bathing' as she remembered the heavenly feeling of his fingers in her hair, so carefully and thoroughly massaging her scalp. *I bet he's thorough at other things, too.*

"I'm a very sweet guy . . ." he smirked.

"I *know* that," she said, thumping her good foot against the porch for emphasis, but her attempt to punctuate her words resulted in a loss of balance. How he got up the stairs so fast, she'd never know. But suddenly a pair of strong arms were pulling her forward again, reversing her tipping instantly.

"Are you all right?" he asked, his eyes wide. He looked almost as perplexed as she felt. "Lizzie?"

"Yes," she forced out, but it came out breathy. *Yikes, Painter. Way to go full girl on him.* She cleared her throat and tried again. "Yes, I'm fine. Thank you for your help."

Chase didn't let her go. "So it's okay for me to catch you when you're actively falling, but not okay for me to prevent you from falling by doing your chores?"

"That's right," she said, giving him a hard look, but Chase just laughed.

"You should consider getting an electric lawnmower," he said, leading her back into the house with one arm around her waist and the other holding her hand, almost like they were dancing. "They're better for the environment." They stopped to get her crutches, and then she realized what he was doing.

"Don't distract me," she snapped. "You are not mowing this lawn, Chase Carpenter."

"Who's going to do it, then? Gram? Hattie? Mrs. Foster? Oh wait, that's right, they're all out of town."

"*I'm* going to do it."

"I say again: how? You can't even go six feet into the house without your crutches."

"I didn't say it wouldn't hurt; I said I'd do it."

"You're just going to make your injury worse. I told Tansy I would take care of you."

She crossed her arms, letting her hip lean against the kitchen table. It was a big heavy thing that had been a barn door her great grandfather salvaged. It could take it. "Since when are you two on a first-name basis? And when did you talk to Gram?"

He had the good sense to look uncomfortable. "When she texted me."

"Humph." She sat down in a kitchen chair. "I don't like being conspired against."

"Would it make you feel better if you paid me?" he asked, and she saw the teasing twinkle in his eye.

"You know, it actually would. Bring me my purse."

His eyes widened, then he frowned a little. "I was *joking*."

"Well, I wasn't. I think it's a fantastic idea. I was considering paying Maggie Durand to do it if I couldn't manage, but this solves the same problem."

"I don't want your money. That's not the way neighbors act," he complained.

Lizzie chuckled. "But we're not neighbors, are we? You live all the way on the other side of town. I mean, it's basically Stayton."

"It's not Stayton. My dad's house is in Timber Falls. I remember because he gerrymandered the city limits in order to make it so before he even broke ground."

Lizzie rolled her eyes so hard, it hurt. Of course he did. Harrison Carpenter got whatever he wanted. Even when it came to his son. It grated like a rash that Chase was still working for him, even after all his dad had put him through. And continued to put him through. But it wasn't her place to say anything about that.

"I saw that, Lizzie Lou," he said, pulling up a chair next to her. "We may not technically be neighbors, but we're in the same town, and we're friends, aren't we?"

"Of course we are."

"Well, friends help each other out."

"You're already doing too much for me," she grouched. "Even paying you wouldn't be enough."

"Lizzie," he sighed, raking a hand through his hair. She wasn't trying to exasperate him, but there had to be another solution. He scooted a little closer, and she could smell his cologne mixed with sweat. "Your gram warned me that you were going to be a tough nut to crack, but she didn't say that you were stubborn as a Missouri mule."

Staring into his expressive eyes, she softened a little. She didn't like that Gram had felt she needed to warn him about her; she shouldn't need to. "That's not a thing people say."

"Yes, it is. My roommate Jesse used to say it all the time, referring to me, mostly."

"You think you're a match for my stubbornness?"

He lowered his voice, and it entered that velvet zone she loved. "I think I'm a match for you in anything."

She held his gaze, unwilling to break their staring contest and stare out the window like she normally would. She was not backing down on this. It was bad enough that he'd up-ended his life to live here until Gram came back. She could find another way to get the lawn mowed. Just as soon as she stopped actively thinking about all the things she'd like to match up with him.

"We'll call Maggie about the lawn. End of story." Without thinking, she reached out and brushed her fingers over the grass stains on his pink shirt. Chase caught her fingers and brought them toward his lips like he was going to kiss them. Blinking fast, he suddenly let them drop and stood up.

"All right. I'll give her a call about next week. I'll just finish up today." He turned and bolted out the front door. She stared after him. Lizzie hobbled her way back to the living room; there would definitely be no going back to sleep after this perplexing conversation. Feeling tense, Lizzie put on the TV. She was still flipping through the channels idly when he came back inside and disappeared down the hall without a word. She had no idea what he would want to watch. She finally landed on an old episode of *Star Trek*, the original series. She'd only been watching a few minutes when Chase came back into the living room, still smelling of grass and sweat. With a raised eyebrow, he came over with a pillow and stood next to her. He looked pointedly at her ankle, which was not elevated in any way. Obediently, she lifted her foot over the coffee table, high enough that he could slide the pillow easily underneath. But he still gently cradled her ankle as he placed it just right.

Then he sat down on the other end of the couch, not as close as he usually did. *Probably just doesn't want to get me all sweaty.* He wasn't sulking, exactly, but it was obvious that he was put out that she wanted Maggie to mow the lawn. Lizzie willed herself to stop caring. Her house, her lawn, her rules. But after ten minutes of silence, he finally spoke, and Lizzie felt oddly relieved.

"Red shirt's gonna get it. Look out, expendable dude!" Chase called to the TV characters. "If they're not on the senior staff, away missions always spell disaster."

Lizzie glanced over at him, ready with a snide remark about him not looking like a *Star Trek* fan, when surprise silenced her. Was he . . . knitting? Chase tugged more mossy green yarn out of a cloth bag between his feet, creating a triangle between his pointer finger and thumb, weaving it intricately between the two sides, creating the first stitch on the long bamboo needle. Yeah, he was knitting, and his tongue slipped between his lips as he concentrated on his work. When he had thirty or so stitches on the needle, he noticed her staring.

"What?"

"Nothing." But she angled herself more toward him instead of the TV so she could continue to watch.

"It's good for my anxiety. It's very rhythmic."

"Makes sense." She couldn't stop staring, though. He was all hunched over as he turned it around, trying to see the tiny stitches. Finally, he sighed.

"You're a woman. What do you think I do with this long part?" He'd gotten back where he started, and there was indeed quite a tail hanging off.

"First off, assuming I know how to knit because I'm a woman is sexist. Second of all . . ." She reached one hand for her belt and opened the leather case where she kept her multitool, reaching out to him with the other hand. "Gimme."

He handed her the needle, and she snipped off the extra with the tiny scissors.

"There you go."

"Sweet. Thanks. And sorry, I didn't think . . ."

"It's fine. I've just never been into that stuff." She leaned forward to see better. "What are you trying to make?"

"A scarf." He stared down at the knitting somewhat dejectedly. "And at this rate, it'll be next year before I get to wear it."

"Your neck will probably be cold then, too."

"Good point," he said, turning to his work again, propping the ends of the needles against his thighs as he tried again. After a minute, he pulled out his phone, found a knitting help video, and watched it mumbling about pearls or something, moving the yarn this way and that, trying to get it in just the right place. Lizzie had to look away before she said something about how adorable he was. After about an hour, Chase stuffed it all back in the bag, got up, silently put on a floral apron, and got to work cooking dinner.

"You want something to drink?" he called from the kitchen.

"No, I'm fine."

He stuck his head into the room. "You sure? Dinner's almost ready."

"I'm sure." She stared at him. She didn't mean to, she just . . . when she was trying to figure someone out, sometimes she ended up staring. He gave her half a grin.

"What?" he asked.

"Nothing." She wrenched her gaze away toward the screen.

"It's the apron, isn't it?" He came into the room and gave a little spin like he was on a catwalk. "I knew you'd laugh." He did look kind of funny in Gram's pink and navy blue apron. She ran her fingertips mindlessly over the rubbery buttons of the remote.

"What else would you wear to protect your clothes?"

"I have one at home that says Kiss the Cook."

Lizzie snorted. "Why doesn't that surprise me?"

"It doesn't work, though. No one's ever kissed me when I wear it. Also, I don't wear it that often, really. I don't entertain much."

That had her daring another peek in his direction. She never talked to anyone who didn't have an active social life . . . partly because she didn't have an active social life, so it felt like everyone was going out and doing things without her. Also, she didn't talk to that many people.

"Why not?"

He shrugged one shoulder. "It kind of amps up my anxiety. I feel like people are judging me, even though I know they're probably not. Anxiety doesn't seem to respond to logic."

"I get that."

"Thought you might."

"Still surprises me, though, since you were Mr. Popularity in high school."

He snorted softly. "I'm sure it seemed that way. I actually didn't go to that many social events unless I had something to calm me down. Man, I hated that stuff. One-on-one, friends are good. But big groups of strangers? Other people I'm supposed to impress? It's amazing I didn't trash more of my room, back then. My anxiety was so bad. I'd get all sweaty and I never slept well, so I was just so on edge all the time, second-guessing myself. Trying to keep the people around me happy."

"You kept everyone happy except you," Lizzie murmured. She'd been guilty of that too when she was younger. She intended to value her own opinion more, to prize being herself over being a peacemaker. *Prickly. Stubborn. Hardheaded.* She was used to the words now. This lawn mowing thing was only the beginning. If she didn't start being herself now, she might never do it.

"That's right," he agreed, oblivious to her reflections. "And look where it got me. So even though I bet it looked like popularity, I just had a permissive dad and a big house with alcohol in it. You'd have been popular, too."

What Lizzie heard was *Even you could've been popular given those circumstances.* She looked back at the TV. "Unlikely."

"It's okay to be shy, you know."

"I know that." She took a deep breath. He must be getting to her because she didn't know that. Not at all. Everyone acted like she was at best eccentric and at worst a failure for keeping her own company. For loving the quiet of the night sky and a dark house. Lizzie felt his gaze boring into her, like he could see her thoughts and knew she didn't buy it. He was so intense; she was getting used to it, but usually she had him in smaller doses. She wanted to get used to him. She wanted to learn to sit with all his intensity, to be comfortable next to his musings and his probing questions and his overthinking. Her second deep breath brought her a whiff of something from the kitchen that made her nose wrinkle.

"I think dinner's burning."

Chase cursed softly and jogged for the kitchen. He returned a few minutes later and handed her a plate with crinkle-cut french fries, a big hamburger on a sesame seed bun, and a dill pickle. He set his plate on the coffee table, piled high with burned fries, while her own plate held golden, perfectly crinkled fries. That annoyed her; he seemed to feel he needed to overcompensate for his mistake. Quickly, she traded plates with him; they looked otherwise identical, except for a pickle, so she stole that, too. She was just taking her first bite of the pickle when he came back with a root beer and a tray of condiments.

"Hey!" Now he looked perturbed. "That one was mine."

Lizzie looked at him coolly. "Why?"

"Because I burned those fries."

"Maybe I like them that way."

"Do you?"

"No. But I bet you don't, either."

"We'll split them," he cajoled, sitting down next to her, reaching over to try to get the plate back.

She moved it to the other side of her body smoothly. "Hands to yourself, Carpenter."

"Fine," he muttered, flopping down next to her close enough to bump her elbow and disgruntedly picking up the other plate. She thought about it a lot later, and she never could decide whether he thought her keeping the fries was fine or whether keeping his hands to himself was.

CHAPTER TWENTY-FIVE:
Chase

CHASE WOKE WITH A START: someone had opened the front door. He reached for his phone, nestled under his pillow: 7:31. Whoever it was had been quiet about it, but the rattle of that loose pane had sent him to his feet so fast, he'd almost passed out. Why wasn't the dog reacting to this? Was Lizzie going somewhere? Why hadn't he brought his baseball bat? He probably didn't need a weapon, he told himself, as he swiped his heavy-duty metal flashlight off the desk anyway. Taking a deep breath, he stepped out into the hallway. A dark-haired woman with glasses was peering at Lizzie, and his shoulders dropped: it was just Lottie. She had a key. That's why she'd been so quiet. That's why Pancake hadn't barked.

"Psst," he whispered.

Lottie looked like she was going to jump out of her skin. She pressed her palm to her chest and rolled her eyes with relief. He motioned for her to come into the kitchen.

"Hey," she greeted softly. "So the rumors are true."

"Rumors?"

"Yeah, Gram said you two were shacking up together."

Chase recognized it as sarcasm, a form of love in this family, and gave her a smile as he started the coffee.

"I'm just caring for your sister while she's injured."

"How bad is it?"

He looked up sharply. "She didn't call you?"

Lottie crossed her arms over her stomach. "We're not really on speaking terms at the moment. Gram called me last night but said you had it handled. I guess I just needed to see for myself."

"That makes sense." Maybe Lottie was anxious, too, she just felt it differently. Handled it like an extrovert instead of tunneling inside herself like he and Lizzie did. "She's got a sprained ankle, but she's doing okay. She hasn't needed any heavy painkillers. I'm trying to get her to rest it as much as possible, which isn't easy."

Lottie snorted, and she sounded so exactly like Lizzie that Chase grinned. "You don't have to tell me. We stopped trying to tell Lizzie what to do ages ago. You're brave." She glanced over her shoulder toward the living room. "I'm surprised she's still asleep. Are you sure she's okay?"

"We were up late last night." At the slow smile that spread across Lottie's face, he quickly amended his statement. "I mean, she was up late. I just watched TV with her." *At least I didn't fall asleep on her shoulder this time.* This time, he'd stumbled to bed around midnight, even though she didn't show the slightest sign of being tired. If the security light had come on again, it hadn't broken through his heavy sleep.

"Of course," Lottie said, pouring herself a cup of coffee. "But if there was anything else you wanted to help her with, I certainly wouldn't be complaining." Lottie snapped a lid onto the travel mug, and it took Chase a minute to realize she was leaving.

"You're going? You don't even want to say hi to her?"

"Nope. It's better if she doesn't know I was here, and there's no reason for you to mention it to her."

He shook his head slowly as he poured his own cup, taking a moment to let the scent ground him. "I won't lie to her."

"Why not?"

"It's not who I am."

She was staring at him like he'd just told her he was starting a colony on Mars. The truth hit people that way sometimes. Despite having attended a school dance together that Chase had very little memory of, he realized that he and Lottie didn't know each other at all.

"Okay, well, you do what you have to do, then. I just wanted to check on her. Let me know if you guys need anything."

"Long drive to just turn around and go right back."

"It's only an hour."

He craned his neck to see behind her. "Just you today? She told me about the guy you were dating, what's his name . . ." *Germy*. "Jeremy?"

Lottie's expression shuttered. "We're not together anymore."

"Oh. I thought you were getting married."

"Yeah," Lottie scoffed, "so did I."

That sounded like a story he could listen to if needed. Chase pulled out a kitchen chair and gestured to it, a silent invitation. These two needed to talk things out, and Lizzie should know that her sister came to check on her. Lottie seemed to realize she was still standing around when she'd intended to leave.

"I have to get back, I've got laundry to do. You can tell her I stopped by if you want."

"Okay. Well, it was nice to see you again."

"Yeah," she smirked. "Thanks for taking care of her."

"Oh, it's my pleasure."

Lottie snorted again, shaking her head in apparent disbelief. "Boy, you've sure changed."

"No, I just dropped the stuff that wasn't me. But thanks for noticing." He gave her a genuine smile, and slowly, she smiled back.

"Start breakfast. That'll wake her up." Lottie cast one more affectionate glance at her sister from the front door. "Good luck."

She wasn't wrong; the minute he put the bacon in the pan, he heard her stirring on the couch. Pancake ran into the kitchen and gave him a meaningful look. It was like he was summoning him: *My pack leader is up. Please come help.* Chase winked at him, and the dog turned and ran back into the living room.

"Lizzie? You ready for the bathroom?"

The bacon sizzled, the kitchen clock ticked . . . but there was no answer. Pancake came back into the kitchen and barked at him. "Easy, boy," he said to the dog, but it was his own heart that was starting to pick up speed. Something was wrong.

"Hey," he called. "Can I come in there? Are you decent?"

"Just a second," she called back, but her voice was strained. Chase stood in the doorway of the hallway and peeked into the living room. Lizzie sat on the edge of the couch stiffly, holding her shoulder, half in and half out of her shirt, as if she'd been changing and needed to stop. He leaned back to preserve her privacy and somehow managed to hold himself back from charging in there . . . but his brain was screaming that it had been more than a second. A lot more.

"Lizzie?" He called again.

"Yeah, just . . . just hang on," she said, clearly annoyed. "Just give me a minute." Oh, she was going to be livid if he just walked into her space when she wasn't covered up, but a second peek told him that she wasn't going to be able to get that shirt back on by herself. That shoulder was bruised black and blue. She tried to lift her arm again, and the gasp she let out was perfectly audible even from six feet away. He hesitated for a moment before he made his decision.

"Okay," he said, stepping into the room, putting one hand over his eyes. "Will you please let me help you?"

"Chase! Get out."

"That shoulder is not right. Let me take you back to the hospital."

"Not going back to the hospital," she muttered, and he heard more clothing rustling before she let out a whimper of pain.

"You're killing me here, sweetheart, and even worse, we're letting the bacon burn. Do it for the bacon. Please." He waited with his hand still covering his eyes, splitting his fingers just a tiny bit to try to see her reaction. He could hear her sniffling like she was crying, and Chase shuffled forward carefully, bumping his shin on the coffee table nonetheless. "Ow." Lizzie laughed a little, and her watery tone confirmed the tears. "Can I open my eyes? I promise to keep my eyes mostly trained on your face."

"Mostly?" she asked, and he nodded somberly.

"I'm only human. Now let's get that shirt back on, eat some bacon, and we'll head back to see Kyle again. Won't that be fun?"

Lizzie groaned, but she muttered, "Fine." Chase let his hand drop. She was mostly covered, and as promised, he kept his gaze on her beautiful green eyes, still welled with tears.

"I hate this," she whispered.

"I know," he whispered back, pushing her hair out of her face briefly, before stretching the sleeve of her shirt out so she could gingerly put her arm through it. "But you've got to ask for help. You can't do this alone." He paused, letting his hands rest on her knees. "Is this why you haven't been using the crutches?"

"Hurts too much," Lizzie said softly.

"And you didn't say anything because . . .?" He let the question linger, unable to help himself from scolding her just a little.

"Because I can tough it out." She paused, looking away. "Or I thought I could. I don't know why it hurts so much more today."

Chase stood and held out his hands, helping her to her one good foot. Together, they hobbled into the kitchen, and he quickly turned the bacon, which by some miracle, was not actually burnt.

"I'm serious about the hospital, Lizzie Lou." She said nothing, but accepted the cup of orange juice he brought her. "I mean it. We're getting that checked out again today."

"Oh, goody," she said sarcastically, then she looked up suddenly. "Lottie was here?"

"Okay, how in the world did you know that?"

"She took her mug. Which is really my mug, the little thief." She carefully put her ankle up on the kitchen chair across from her unprompted . . . a worrying sign if he'd ever seen one.

"How's the ankle today?"

"Fine." When he shook his head sternly, she sighed. "Fine, it hurts just as much as yesterday. We'll do the hospital this afternoon."

"This morning," he corrected, putting down a plate of bacon and eggs in front of her, throwing in a banana for good measure. "Right after breakfast."

"What did Lottie want?" She asked, digging in, and he wasn't sure if that was assent to his demands or not.

"Just wanted to check on you. I asked her to stay, but she declined."

Lizzie snorted. "Yeah, I bet she did." She took a huge bite of food. "Did she mention that we're fighting?"

"She might have, yes." Should he tell her that she'd broken up with the source of the conflict? That didn't seem like his business. Gosh, he hated drama. Why couldn't people just talk to each other? Life would be so much simpler. "Where's your shoes?"

"What's the rush, dude?"

"The rush is," he said, knocking back the last of his coffee, "that I'm getting you in to see Kyle before the line stacks up. People are extra idiotic as the day goes on, I hear."

Lizzie cackled loudly at that, and the fear in his heart eased a little. She finished her breakfast, pocketing the banana. "Okay. My shoes are by the front door." He went and got them and knelt to put them on her, trying so hard not to jostle her ankle; they barely fit due to how swollen it was. She put a hand on his head, and he paused for a second, relishing her silent appreciation. Then he stood and picked her up.

"Chase!" She gasped. "What do you think you're doing?"

"You can't use the crutches. How were you planning to get down the stairs and into the car?"

Her arms came around his neck, and she pulled herself up a little higher on his body, wincing. "We shall never speak of this. And we're taking my truck."

"Fine by me." He managed to get the front door open, but Pancake squeezed by him. "Oh, come 'ere, boy."

"He's okay outside for a few hours," Lizzie said, glancing around the neighborhood, as if to see if anyone was noticing their strange arrangement. "Just check his water."

"Check." Chase got to the passenger side door of the truck. "Keys?"

"They're inside in my purse." Ugh. He did not want to carry her inside again; his back was barely holding on as it was.

He hesitated. "Can you stand here for a minute?"

"I could've limped here on my own, so . . . yes?" Her words were teasing, not angry, so he put her down by the truck and congratulated himself for not kissing her forehead when he did so. Maybe he should set up a reward system for only touching Lizzie when it was critical to her health; he'd almost kissed her fingers when she'd brushed the grass from his shirt. *Too many close calls with the kissing, Carpenter.* He went around the side of the house to check Pancake's bowl, which was empty, and he glanced up at his window. Which made him remember that he'd forgotten to take his anxiety meds when he was startled awake this morning. That could not happen. He took them immediately when he went inside to grab the keys, but . . . it was worrying. Chase set an alarm for tomorrow as he went inside, glancing up to see if she was still okay by the truck. She was. Of course she was. He looked around until he found her purse, tossed carelessly next to the couch. His phone buzzed.

Kellan: How are things going with Lizzie?

Chase: Okay. I have to take her back to the hospital.

Kellan: Oh wow. That sucks. But you're still coming to the meeting today, right?

Crap. He'd sort of lost track of the days, things had been so weird. Chase wanted to protest; there were other meetings. He could go on Wednesday. He didn't want to leave her alone if this was something serious, but getting a little break would be good, too. Chase motorboated his lips in frustration. He'd hedge.

> **Chase:** I'm planning on it, but we may not be done at the hospital yet.
> **Kellan:** Is there someone who could take over for you?
> **Chase:** I don't know. Maybe. I'll work on it.
> **Kellan:** Okay.
> **Chase:** If I need to, can I bring her with me?
> **Kellan:** Nope, it's a closed meeting, so no outsiders. Sorry.
> **Chase:** Okay.

There was a long enough pause that he thought the conversation was over, and he jogged back down the steps, pausing to lock the front door first. When Chase put his hand to the door of the driver's side, the phone in his hand buzzed again.

> **Kellan:** Growth is hard, Chase. I know. But you can do it.

Chase blew out a big sigh. He passed Lizzie her purse as she settled herself in the other seat.

"Everything okay?"

"Yep. But I have to do a meeting this afternoon, just so you know." He pulled out of the driveway onto the road.

"You're working today?"

"It's not . . ." The truth was more uncomfortable coming out of his mouth than it usually was. "It's an NA meeting. Well, it's an AA meeting, but it's the best we've got here. And my sponsor wants me there. He's right. I should go."

"Who's your sponsor?"

"I can't tell you that."

"Oh. I'm sorry, I didn't know."

Chase gave a nod, not sure if he should elucidate any more on recovery culture, so he stayed silent. *Elucidate. I bet that's worth at least twelve points in Scrabble.*

"Huh. Okay, well, that's fine. I'll be fine for a few hours." Her fingers were drumming on the console. "Is it every Monday?" Lizzie shook her head. "Sorry, that's invasive. Not my business."

He reached over and gave her fingers a gentle squeeze to stop their frenetic motion, then withdrew, so as not to seem like he was holding her hand, even though he wanted to.

"I don't mind. Yes, I have them every Monday."

"Okay." She was quiet the rest of the way to the hospital, and Chase's anxiety was messing with his head. *She's mad. She's judging. She doesn't think I can do this.* But when she hooked up her phone to the stereo with an aux cable, her face wasn't saying any of those things. *Stupid brain.* He pulled up into the drop-off area and threw the truck in park.

"I'm going to go get you a wheelchair. Hang tight."

"Over my dead body."

"You'd rather be carried again? That's fine . . ."

Lizzie cursed, and Chase grinned.

"As I said, I'm going to go get you a wheelchair. We don't need you becoming further injured." Some wheelchairs were sitting right by the front door, and Trevor noticed him grabbing one and came over to help.

"Just couldn't stay away, huh?" The nurse teased Lizzie as they helped her into the chair. She rolled her eyes.

"Her Majesty isn't speaking to us," Chase explained. "Her royal personhood did not wish to be transported back here."

"Aw, and here I thought we were close after I gave you that chariot ride last time." Sudden, fierce jealousy seized Chase, and his brain resented it.

"My stupid shoulder is just injured," she grumbled. "This is so unnecessary."

"I know," Trevor soothed, as he wheeled her toward the front doors. When they opened, he stopped and turned back to Chase. "You coming? I don't want to be stuck with Her Highness's bad mood all by my lonesome."

"Uh, I'll just go park the truck," Chase said, pointing to the parking lot, still trying to sort through his jumbled emotions.

Trevor gave him a thumbs-up, and Chase slammed the truck door with more force than necessary. Trevor was always flirting. It was nothing. It meant nothing. But . . . *but she's mine.* Chase argued back with his heart that that simply wasn't true as he maneuvered the wide truck into a space meant for a much smaller vehicle. But it seemed to be taking lessons from the object of his obvious affections because it ignored him. *Mine, mine, mine.*

He came through the hospital front doors and started scanning for her red hair.

"Hey man," a man in a paramedic uniform greeted him. "How's it going?"

"Yeah, it's going," Chase bluffed. He did look a little familiar, in a blurry way: dark curly hair, pale in the way most white Oregonians were, shorter than he was. "How are you?"

"Fine, thanks. You looking for Lizzie?" Okay, so this was not just polite social contact; this guy knew Chase. His anxiety immediately spiked; he hated being caught off-guard. But he might as well be honest.

"Yeah. You seen her?"

The man pointed down the hall. "Trevor took her straight back. Slow day."

"Okay, thanks, man. And hey, I can't remember your name."

"Oh, forgive me—I'm RJ Horowitz." *Oh. RJ, the paramedic who helped when I overdosed.*

Chase shook the man's hand but didn't bother introducing himself, since RJ clearly knew more about him than one would expect. *The Timber Falls rumor mill is as active as ever, I see.*

"Room 6."

"Thanks, RJ." And although he wanted to go find Lizzie in case they were giving vital information he'd need to combat her stubbornness later, this was a moment he needed to have. "And I just want to say thank you for your help with my medical problem a few years back."

"No worries, man." He looked like he meant it. "It's really good to see you healthy. Been sending you lots of good thoughts since then. I'm glad to see they're working."

That touched Chase. Maybe this could be a new friend; he didn't have many. "Thanks." He glanced down the hall. "I've gotta go catch up with her or I'm sure she'll find a way out of that wheelchair on her own."

RJ laughed. "Yeah, she looked none too happy to be back. Good luck, man."

Chase went down the cream-colored hallway until he found the room. When he opened the door, the smell of vomit overwhelmed him, and he had to step back into the hall.

"Whoa."

"Sorry," she said, wiping her shirt with a paper towel as Trevor washed his hands in the sink. "Someone in the lobby had a gnarly injury." She wasn't kidding about her gag reflex, then. Kyle came in a few minutes later, looking at her shoulder with a seeming lack of concern, and Chase nodded to both of them as he sat down across the room from her.

"It's possible it's a subluxation. It's like a dislocation, but not as severe. How was it jostled when you fell?"

Lizzie tried to show him, and Kyle's face stayed flat. "Have you dislocated it before?"

"Once. When I was twelve. Fell off a horse." *She rides?* Chase had been missing horses fiercely. That had been his go-to on a hard day at Gretta's. It'd be good to find another place to interact with them.

"The same shoulder, correct?"

"Yeah, the same one."

"When you dislocate it once, it becomes more susceptible to it happening again." He poked at it and adjusted it a little bit more until Lizzie's sharp intake of breath made him stop. "Okay, here's what I want to do. Let's give it a couple more days. Even if it's a subluxation, it may correct itself. I want you to ice it when it hurts, and I want you to use the wheelchair with someone's help. Will you do that?"

When Lizzie hesitated, Kyle's gaze narrowed. "I can admit you if I need to."

"No," she blurted out. "I'll do it."

"Any directions for me?" Chase asked, and Kyle blinked like he'd forgotten he was there.

"Oh. Will you be acting as her caregiver?"

"Yep, I'm the lucky one," he said sincerely, and he hazarded a glance at Lizzie. She was staring down at her lap, and Chase wondered if he'd said something wrong. She seemed to be taking this awfully hard.

"Oh. No, just the ice. No lifting. No crutches."

"Am I allowed to put her over my shoulder like a caveman to get her up the stairs?" Chase deadpanned.

"A piggyback ride would probably be more comfortable," Kyle replied, and if he was joking, Chase couldn't tell. "But you two work it out." He turned back to Lizzie. "Any other questions?"

"Would it help if I put it in a sling?" Her question was quiet, depressed, and Chase desperately wanted to hug her.

"Yes, probably," Kyle said, typing some notes into the computer, eyes trained on the screen. "If only because it reminds you not to use it." He typed another sentence, then turned to her. "That's hard for you, isn't it?"

"Yes." And that single word was laden with grief. Her lower lip trembled, and Chase couldn't stop himself from coming to stand by her and hold her hand. He rubbed the back of her hand with his thumb.

"Are you done?" He didn't mean to bark at Kyle, who seemed taken aback, but he *hated* seeing Lizzie in pain. It was unbearable. *Then why did you put yourself in this situation?* He knew why.

"Yes, we're done. Please set up a follow-up for next week or send me a message through the portal to let me know how things are going."

"Sure," Chase said, offering his hand in an effort to smooth things over. After a moment, Kyle took and shook . . . and then sanitized immediately on his way out the door. Chase chuckled a little about the overt rejection of the contact, but his amusement died quickly when he heard Lizzie stifle a sob.

"Whoa, whoa. What's happening?" He was holding her around the ribs in a flash, gently pinning her good shoulder to her side.

"I'm never going to get my promotion now!"

"Promotion? What promotion?" He rubbed her back in a way he hoped was soothing.

"C-C-Captain Hansen is l-l-leaving. M-M-Mark is going to be in ch-ch-charge, and he asked me out, but I didn't want to go so I said no, th-then he asked me again, and now I d-d-don't think he'd be very open to the p-promotion." She blew out a long breath, wiping the tears from her face with both hands. "So if I don't c-c-convince Captain Hansen, it's not going t-t-to happen."

"Wow. That sucks, Lizzie Lou." He squeezed her, letting his cheek rest against the top of her head until she started to get her breath back. Anger sprung up; she shouldn't be denied a promotion just because she'd turned her boss down. Maybe he could throw some of that Carpenter weight around on her behalf . . . *No. It's her problem. Let her solve it. You don't need to be in control.* When he looked down, she was covering her face.

"I'm sorry."

"For what?"

"For breaking down on you." She let her hands drop and looked up at him with those soulful green eyes. "You didn't know you were agreeing to watch an emotional wreck."

"Having big feelings about something you really want isn't the same as being a wreck . . ." He whispered into her hair. "You're still tough. I know that. And it sounds like this is really important to you."

"I need to be able to support myself. Stand on my own two feet."

He didn't think she meant it as a dig about his trust, so he let the comment slide.

"Come on," he said, giving her one last small squeeze, "let's get you home." She climbed into the wheelchair without prompting, much to his surprise, and he wheeled her back to the front desk of the ER. Trevor was still there, but he dropped his teasing smirk when he noticed Lizzie's red, swollen face. Trevor took her out to the car, while Chase made a follow-up appointment and finished signing stuff he hadn't read. *Good thing I'm not a lawyer.* That was the second time lately that he'd thought even obliquely about a career change. Maybe he should think about it more seriously. *You can't leave TFPP. Dad would be humiliated.* But that was becoming less important to Chase, and the thought made him sad. He loved his dad. They'd had some great times when he was younger . . . true, most of them were based on Chase excelling at something so Harrison could be proud of him, but still. He wanted to think that his dad would be proud of the person he'd become someday.

"Mr. Carpenter." He turned. It was the same nurse he'd bullied the other day, Amanda Franklin. She gazed at him steadily and showed no sign of being intimidated, which was a relief considering how he'd treated her. "Dr. Durand said to let you know that he put in another prescription for pain meds to the pharmacy if she needs it."

"Oh, thank you. And I want to apologize for the way I spoke to you the other day; I had no right to barge past you like that."

Amanda cocked her head, then gave him a nod. "You're forgiven. Fear makes us all do abnormal things sometimes." *Like throwing away a prescription my friend needs? Letting her be in pain because of my selfishness?*

"That's very understanding of you. Thank you."

"You're welcome, Mr. Carpenter." He gave her a grateful smile as he headed for the exit. Their drive home was quiet. He got Lizzie settled on the couch with two ice packs then made them both a sandwich before he went to his meeting.

"You're sure you don't mind?"

"Nope," she said around a bite. "I'll relish the quiet."

"Ouch." He pretending to pull a knife out of his back, and she laughed quietly.

This particular meeting was lightly attended, which made sense given that it was a Monday afternoon. He took one of the metal folding chairs in a semi-circle in the church basement. Chase took a seat toward the front and silenced his phone. Several people shook his hand, and a few hugged him, one even before he'd introduced himself. It made Chase feel at home. Today was a speaker meeting; Dean told his story, how he'd ended up stealing mail out of people's mailboxes and using their credit card offers just to keep himself afloat. His own story had never come to that, but he realized that was a form of grace that had little to do with him as a person. Dean talked about his mom, how she'd been a functional alcoholic for years, drinking in secret. It made Chase wonder about his own mom. Not Willow, but his biological mom, Carmen. He hadn't thought about her for a long time; she'd left when he was four, and she'd only visited sporadically after that. Kellan did one final reading to wrap it up, and to Chase's mild surprise, it was more focused on his kind of addiction.

"When at the end of the road we find that we can no longer function as a human being, either with or without drugs, we all face the same dilemma. What is there left to do? There seems to be this alternative: either go on as best we can to the bitter ends—jails, institutions, or death—or find a new way to live. In years gone by, very few addicts ever had this last choice. Those who are addicted today are more fortunate. For the first time in man's entire history, a simple way has been proving itself in the lives of many addicts. It is available to us all. This is a simple spiritual—not religious—program, known as Narcotics Anonymous."

A new way to live. That's why it was so hard, he was carving out a new path for himself, one many people had walked before him: Gretta, Kellan . . . and yet, it was still unique to him. His anxiety. His family history. His privilege. His temper. Instead of going straight back to Lizzie's, he turned west and got back on the highway. Codeine wasn't his drug of choice, he reasoned, and she might need it in the night. If he filled it in Salem, no one would have to know, and then it would be available to her. He'd leave it in the truck and give her back the keys. He wouldn't go into her purse. He would do this for her . . . chances were, she'd never even have to know.

CHAPTER TWENTY-SIX:
Lizzie

CHASE WAS QUIET WHEN he got back from his meeting on Monday. After he cooked them some kind of hamburger helper meal, he spent most of the evening trying to knit, and from what she could tell, he made about an inch of uneven progress on the scarf. She waited about an hour before she asked the question she was shy to ask.

"Can you go get me some nail polish from upstairs?" She hadn't had a chance to paint her nails yesterday.

"Sure. What color?"

Should she admit that she knew the names of all of them? And that there were a lot more of them than the one he'd found and teased her about?

"Any of them are fine."

"No, come on. What color? Don't make me choose, I don't know anything about nail polish."

She wanted the gold one called Ready to Propose, but she absolutely could not ask for that one. "I'll take Nuclear War. It's orange. Bottom drawer in the bathroom."

Chase gave her a thumbs up and jogged away, down the hall. Lizzie pulled off her socks and cursed. She'd forgotten to ask for the acetone and a cotton ball. Now he was going to have to run back up for them.

"I brought this down, too . . ." Chase said, voice trailing off uncertainly, holding out the remover. She wished she could help him worry less about his own choices. He knew just the right thing to do so much of the time.

"Perfect. Thanks." She tried to bend her knee to bring her foot closer to her face, but she squawked and let go. It must still be bruised from her fall.

"Need help?" Chase hadn't picked up his knitting yet.

"What? No. You don't want to touch my nasty feet."

"I touch them every day when I elevate your ankle because you don't seem to think it's important." Chase put a pillow on his lap and patted it. This was seriously going to mess with her tough girl image if anyone found out.

"Not a word to anyone," she said sternly, carefully putting her foot on the brown pillow. Chase made an 'x' over his heart and grinned at her.

"Your foot is freezing," he commented as he massaged her arch, and it felt way too good to be legal.

"Always is," she replied. "I have cold hands, too. I probably need to work on my circulation."

His hands were warm and the smooth way he dragged his thumbs over her muscles just made her sink deeper into the couch. She stayed there when he moved from cleaning off the blue to putting on the orange. It felt nice to be touched; Gram hugged her sometimes, but in general, it wasn't part of life. He kept one hand on her foot to steady it, focusing so hard, cursing softly under his breath when he dripped a little on the edges, wiping it precisely with a tissue. He was talking, as usual.

"I think I should paint your fingernails, too."

"Not a chance."

"Why not?"

"No one would take me seriously."

"But there's no one here except me. It's the perfect time to spoil yourself." This seemed to be part of the man's life philosophy, that any time was the perfect time to spoil yourself. She couldn't say that she hated it; in fact, she was getting very used to all his positivity and joy. But she also wasn't going to be influenced into making a fool of herself in front of the town.

"Hush now, it's *Jeopardy!* time."

"He's got pancreatic cancer," he said, carefully getting the excess off the tiny brush on the side of the bottle.

She turned to him. "Who?" Chase pointed to the host.

"Alex? Really? Oh." Well, that was sad. What would her evenings be without Alex Trebek? It was hard to even imagine. That lovable Canadian was such an integral part of her TV life. Her phone dinged.

Gram: How's it going, kiddo?

Lizzie: Fine.

Gram: That's all I get?

Lizzie: Yes.

Gram: You sure know how to make a grandmother grumpy. Can we do a video chat?

Lizzie: Not right now.

Gram: Is Chase still there?

Lizzie: Yes. He's taking very good care of me.

Lizzie: Did you know Alex Trebek has pancreatic cancer?

Gram: Yes.

She was just messing with her now, mimicking her one-word answers.

Lizzie: Miss you. Are you having fun?
Gram: Fun doesn't begin to cover it. Love you, kiddo. So glad you're okay.

When *Jeopardy!* was over, she chose a movie. Then another show. And another. When Chase was yawning so hard that he had to put his knitting down, Lizzie decided to have pity on him. She could stay up another two hours, but she knew he wouldn't go to bed until she did.

She gave a big stretch for show and watched Chase's gaze go to her chest, which just made her blush. "Bathroom then bed?"

"Sounds good," he muttered, tucking away his project, wiping at his eyes. "Human crutch, piggyback, or wheels?" It wasn't just that the wheelchair was hard to get through the narrow doorways of the old house. It wasn't that it was a continual reminder of her clumsiness. Secretly, she was starting to enjoy the closeness of having Chase carry her. But she couldn't say that.

"Human crutch." It was the respectable option, she informed her libido, which stuck out its tongue at her. Even though Dr. Durand hadn't mentioned that this option was okay, they'd figured out that afternoon that he could support her around the waist at a better angle without putting pressure on her shoulder, kind of like a three-legged race. They'd make an amazing team at the town's birthday this summer if they were together then. *Don't get ahead of yourself, Painter.* After all, there had been less flirting lately, no mention of another date, nothing. If they were dating, surely he would've kissed her by now? She didn't know what their relationship was, just that she didn't want it to end. Just that she'd be sad when it inevitably did.

Tuesday morning, she woke to a note on the coffee table with a breakfast sandwich and a glass of cranberry juice:

Dear Lizzie,

Ran to my mom's to get more clothes and to TFPP to pick up some files. Be back around lunchtime.

Sincerely,

Chase,

P.S. Use your wheelchair. I mean it.

He'd also moved her computer and her box of work closer to her. She pulled out her phone.

> **Lizzie:** Thanks for setting me up, but where's the chamber pot?
> **Chase:** the what?
> **Lizzie:** You know, the chamber pot. The thing people pee in.
> **Chase:** gross. I have limits.
> **Chase:** You gonna work this morning?
> **Lizzie:** I guess so.
> **Lizzie:** If I was a guy, do you think he'd be giving me administrative work?
> **Chase:** Don't know. Probably not.
> **Chase:** gotta focus on driving now.
> **Lizzie:** Do not text and drive! What is wrong with you!
> **Lizzie:** I should cite you.

He didn't say anything, so she hoped he was doing what he said. But she was still annoyed with him when he got home.

"Raspberry iced tea," he said, holding out the glass bottle to her. "Paige says hi."

Lizzie folded her arms, snubbing the drink. "Were you texting in the car?"

He grinned. "Technically, yes. But I was at a stoplight." He shook the drink a little, daring her to take it.

"Do not text and drive, Chase. I'm serious. Since 2014, we've had over 20,000 distracted driving incidents that resulted in an injury."

"In Timber Falls alone? That's, what, fifty infractions per person?" When his lips pulled to the side, she knew her glare was communicating how much she did not think he was funny. "But I wasn't driving," he protested, "I was just in my car, stopped."

Lizzie glared harder. "I *will* cite you."

He chuckled. "Okay, okay. I'm sorry, I won't do it again." She took the bottle from him and opened it. She should sip it so she didn't have to get up again to pee so soon; she'd already limped her way there once this morning and knocked her ankle against the doorway. Her loud cursing scared the dog, who then knocked her down in his ardent concern and slobbered her with kisses. She played it safe and crawled back, which hurt her shoulder, of course. She was going to have a nasty bruise on her hip. Hopefully, Chase wouldn't notice.

"How's your work going?"

She sighed. "Fine. But people in this town really need to learn to get along better."

"Don't we all?"

"Yes, that's what I'm saying," she deadpanned, and he laughed again. "Did you get what you needed?"

"Yup." He dropped his stuff on the dining room table but didn't get anything set up. He seemed to be hesitating. Lizzie chuckled internally. Anxiety was such a pain in the backside.

"Chase?"

"Yes?"

"Would you like to come work on the couch with me?"

"Yes!" He had the same look Pancake look outside when she picked up a tennis ball. "I was going to give you your space."

"A little late for that," she muttered, not really annoyed, and he grinned again. "The TV going to bother you?"

"Nah." He hauled his stuff over to the coffee table, propping his legs up next to hers. When he'd been working about twenty minutes, Lizzie couldn't hold back anymore.

"Why are you sighing?"

"Huh?"

She imitated one of the big, gusty sighs he'd been doing. "Sighing. You. Every two minutes."

"I don't know. This job has just kind of lost its allure, I guess."

"Gonna go paint houses?" she teased.

He shook his head. "I don't think I'd like the smell. Even VOC-free paint has a scent."

"What, then? Plumbing? That would have your 'end-of-day' satisfaction."

Chase shrugged. "I've thought about photography, but I'm not very artistic. I'd like to be outside, though. Marketing is largely an indoor activity."

"You don't say," Lizzie said, grabbing another file. "Maybe you should be a private investigator. You're nosy."

"Rude, Painter," he said, whacking her with the small throw pillow at his elbow. "Just because I'm taking care of a *friend* doesn't mean I want to stick my nose into strangers' business."

"You could be a caregiver, like for old people like Martina."

"I don't think I'm cut out for that much illness or injury. It'd make me so sad when the old people died."

"Same. And all those bodily processes make me throw up." She focused on her data input for a few minutes, sitting in companionable silence, the keys of both their laptops clicking away. Chase sighed again, and Lizzie burst out laughing.

"I can't help it! Why did I even like this?"

"Did you?"

His long stare toward his feet told her he was thinking. "No, not really. But I liked being the "go-to" guy, the guy people praised for a job well-done."

Pancake came over and dropped his rope at Chase's feet, and he picked it up and threw it.

"Okay, so an outside job, something with clear results . . . not counseling. Nothing with computers."

"It's pointless to talk about it," Chase said, and there was an edge of frustration to his voice. He rubbed the back of his neck so hard, it turned red. "I can't leave TFPP. My relationship with my dad would not survive."

"Really?" It wasn't such a surprise. Every time she'd interacted with Harrison, she liked him less. But she couldn't say that to his son.

"Not that it's so great now . . . I don't think he really . . . gets me."

Lizzie nodded. "Still, it doesn't hurt to dream, right?" She pulled the next file.

March 12, 2004

Second-degree manslaughter, vehicular. Deputies Hansen and Hillerman reported to the scene at 9:51 p.m. Two vehicles were involved, a maroon Ford Explorer and a teal green Toyota Tercel. There were no survivors. Toxicology reported no apparent impairment on the part of the other driver; the driver of the Tercel appeared to have crossed the median line and struck the other vehicle head-on. The drivers were identified as Penelope Louise Painter and Joss Franklin Zane; Barry Richard Painter was the passenger.

She closed the file quietly, trying to draw as little attention to her actions as possible. She got out a pad of sticky notes and wrote in careful script: "Not digitized. ELP." Sue would understand.

"I don't know if it hurts to dream, I—what's wrong?"

"Nothing," she said too quickly, jamming the file into the back of the file box.

"Seriously, though. You just went white. Are you in pain? Do you want ice? Meds?" Something about his comment clanged, but she brushed her suspicion aside for the moment.

"No, I'm fine."

Chase looked unconvinced, but he hesitantly went back to his work, glancing at her every few minutes until she finally lost patience. She pulled the file back out of the box and held it to her chest.

"I'm going to give you this. You're going to read it. But we're *not* going to talk about it. Do you understand?"

"Not really . . ."

Lizzie rolled her eyes and started to shove it back in.

"No, no, no," Chase said, clamoring for it, grabbing her arm. "Gimme."

"We're *not* going to talk about it," she said, holding the file aloft, even though it wasn't exactly out of his long reach. "Say it."

"We're not going to talk about it. Now hand it over."

"You're going to want to," she warned him, yanking it out of his grip when he lunged for it. "You're going to be desperate. But we're not going to."

"Fine. I can do that." This time, he managed to get it from her, and she tried to go back to her work as he opened the folder, grinning over his victory, so unprepared for what he was about to read. Out of the corner, she could see his hands on the papers. He stroked the glossy picture of her mangled car gently with one fingertip, as if he didn't want to hurt it any more. He read for another minute, then he closed the folder and held it out to her.

"Thank you." His voice was light, but not teasing.

She took the folder and put it back in the box, more carefully this time. Like it was precious. Lizzie slumped a little lower on the couch and went back to inputting data. After a moment, Chase scooted closer to her, matching their thighs and hips and elbows and shoulders. It wasn't all that comfortable, really. But she stayed where she was. Neither of them moved until her stomach rumbled, and then Chase was up off the couch in a flash, hurrying to make her a sandwich.

"Or pasta or egg salad or whatever you want. Just tell me what you want, okay?" Her options were getting more and more complicated, and she suspected it was sympathy pasta.

"A peanut butter sandwich is fine."

"Jam?" he called from the kitchen.

"Strawberry, please."

There was some clanging and muttering from the kitchen, and then the noise stopped. Lizzie paused her typing. Chase came out, shoes on, digging in his pocket for his keys.

"Forget something at work?"

"Uh, no." He opened the door. "I'll be right back."

This didn't smell right, and Lizzie commanded, "Stop." Chase froze in the doorway, his back still to her. "Tell me where you're going."

"Corner Stop." That was the little grocery store up on Highway 22.

"Why?"

"Because we're out of strawberry. I'm just going to get some." It was very convenient having a boyfriend who didn't believe in lying. *A boyfriend? Yeah, a boyfriend,* her mind accused. *Anyone who snuggles with me while I work in an attempt to comfort me over my dead parents is more than a friend.* This was all getting out of hand.

"No. Just give me grape."

"No one likes grape! I don't know why you even have it!" He erupted playfully, throwing up his hands, sending his keys inadvertently flying across the living room, which startled the dog from his nap.

"Chase. Grape. I don't need you to waste the gas on me. Just add it to the list."

He closed the door and stomped over to his keys, snatching them off the floor. "Fine. Be that way. Eat an inferior sandwich."

"It's not worth making a trip just for that."

"It would be to me!" he pronounced, then marched back into the kitchen. Lizzie laughed. It was kind of him to want to spoil her, but entirely unnecessary. He obviously didn't know how much sweeter he made her life just by being there.

They put their laptops aside as they ate, then both went back to work. Sometimes, she pointed out something funny on the TV just to make him laugh. Pancake made himself comfortable under the tent of their legs. Chase went into his room to do an online NA meeting and a work call, and she missed him. He was gone for *two hours*. It was profoundly annoying.

The rest of the day and the next passed like that—mostly together, except when they were on the phone, in the bathroom, or asleep. She worked from the kitchen table to keep him company while he cooked. In truth, she didn't do much work. Watching his lips move as he read directions on frozen pot stickers and boxes of instant rice, digging around in the fridge trying to find the soy sauce, tied up in that stupid apron, glaring at her stove when "it" burned things . . . it was the best entertainment. *So handsome. So bad at making food.*

So she was all ready to head into the kitchen on Wednesday night when he came back from his conference call with his coat and shoes on.

"Ready to go?"

She just stared at him.

"To Trivia Night?"

Lizzie cursed. "I totally forgot. I haven't eaten yet." She was tired of being home, and she knew Chase would take her home as soon as it was over. He didn't usually seem to hang around either.

"I'll buy you dinner at the bar. Come on." *No, you won't. Not without defining what the heck this is first.* She looked down at her OMSI Planetarium shirt, which was covered in cheese dust and a drop of Italian dressing from an anomalous salad she'd ingested in an attempt to appear healthy.

"Yeah, you're right," he said, nodding, as if she'd spoken her thoughts. "I'll get you a clean one." He was only gone a few minutes before he came barreling down the stairs, feet thundering against the wooden steps.

"I like this one," he said, holding up a black sleeveless polyester blouse Gram had given her a few years ago. "The flowers would go with your hair. And the lace edge dresses it up a bit. But I know you're opinionated, so I also brought this." He held up a plain light green T-shirt with two fingers.

She pointed to the first one. "I can't wear that with jeans and running shoes."

"Oh, sure you can," he said, looking at it again, as if to confirm his own opinion. "It'll be dark. No one will care."

"This from a guy I've never seen not in cargo shorts and a sweatshirt."

His eyebrows went high, and he had that sparkle, that thinking look again. "You want me to dress up too, Lizzie Lou?"

Yes. She wanted him to comb his hair for once, instead of it falling his eyes all sexy-like. And shave that beautiful scruffy beard. With a grin, he threw the black one at her.

"Fine. It's got buttons, so I thought you could get it on yourself. I'll go change."

"Wait," she tried to call, but her voice came out soft. Mostly because she didn't mean it at all, like when people ask if anyone cares if they take the last roll. *No, don't go change just to appease me. Don't put on something fancy because of my whims. Don't indulge me.*

She carefully removed her dirty T-shirt; her shoulder was feeling a little better since they'd been icing it, but she still had to be gentle with it. Gentle was not her best thing. She pulled it off over her head with her good arm and looked down. Dang. She was wearing her electric blue lace bra. It didn't usually matter what color it was, but this might peek out the top a little bit if she leaned forward to get something at the table. She was just buttoning the top button and trying to look down to see whether it was showing at all when he came back in. Lizzie's jaw dropped. He'd styled his hair back away from his face and just trimmed the beard to a short, smoldering blond fuzz on his face. His dark blue trousers hugged his hips where his crisp white dress shirt was tucked in, sleeves rolled to his elbows. But he was still obviously Chase, because he was wearing brown leather flip-flops. Were there angels singing? There should be.

"See? You look great! Let me get your shoes for you," he said, looking around, apparently oblivious to the potent rush of hormones she felt at seeing him all dolled up like that. *Dolled* was the right word; he reminded her of a Malibu Ken doll she'd had as a child. Her heart was beating out of her chest; all she could do was stare at him.

"Lizzie? Come on, we're gonna be late! Carter hates it when I'm late." He held out a hand, and she accepted his help in getting to her feet, self-consciously running a hand through her loose hair.

"I like it when you wear it down like that," he said quietly. Chase moved into place to help her to the door, and oh no, was he wearing cologne? She was done for. She was never going to make it through this night without blurting out something highly inappropriate. It was a Lizzie Painter Guarantee. Keeping her mouth shut: that was her only hope. Tight-lipped, she smiled and nodded.

"You okay?"

"Yep."

"Was it the hair comment? Because I didn't mean—"

"It's fine. Let's go."

He sniffled like she'd hurt his feelings as they descended the front steps. "And here I dressed up for you and everything. See if I go to that effort again."

Lizzie giggled, unable to help herself. When he shut her door, he lingered there a beat too long, just smiling at her through the window. Yep. She was completely done for.

CHAPTER TWENTY-SEVEN: Chase

IN THE DARK, NOISY room, Chase glanced over his shoulder at Lizzie for the hundredth time since he'd come to the bar. Ever since he'd come out of his room in these silly clothes, this vestige of his past, she'd been quiet. If she was in pain, he could fix it; the answer was right in the glovebox outside. If he'd said something wrong, he wished she'd just tell him what it was. She'd hardly spoken to any of them; he blamed Ainsley's wolf-whistle at their outfits when they'd walked in. She'd insisted on paying for her own dinner, which was fine, but she didn't even finish her fries. A sure sign that something was wrong.

"Hey." Carter was at his elbow.

"Hey, bro. How's your week going?"

"Fine. But I thought the drama quotient would go down when you went to stay with Lizzie."

Chase furrowed his brow a little as Annie slid him his ginger ale. "Did it not?"

"Oh no. No, no. Last night, I woke up to a screaming matching in the hall between Chris and Dad."

That was concerning. They usually did their fighting in low, snarly, sarcastic tones. "Over what?"

"You, actually." Carter ordered a Coke, then turned back to him. "Dad wanted to know where you were. Chris said he didn't know. Dad called BS, said you were always thicker than thieves and you wouldn't leave without telling him why. Chris said that wasn't true anymore and it was Dad's fault. Dad said it was Mom's fault, and it devolved from there until I came out and broke it up before they woke Mom up."

"Wow. I didn't think to let them know. I didn't think they'd care." Chase sipped his drink while he thought. *Mom's fault? Why would it be her fault?* "Did you tell them where I was?"

"They didn't ask me, actually," Carter chuckled. "They still think of me as a useless kid."

"That's the real BS, bro. You're amazing, the way you take care of Mom."

"Speaking of caretaking, how's it going with Lizzie?"

"Pretty good. I think. Well, it was, up until we left to come to Trivia."

"Yeah, she seems quiet tonight. More quiet than usual. She looks cute, though."

"That's what I said!" Chase said, exasperated. "We both changed our clothes and I said she looked cute, and I liked her hair like that, and then . . ."

"And then she shut up?"

"Yeah," said Chase, spinning his glass. "You think I embarrassed her? She said that wasn't it. I asked if I said something wrong, and she said no. Maybe I should've said hot? or sexy? Was cute too friend-zone?"

"Maybe she's just trying to avoid giving you fire eyes."

Chase snickered and barely caught his drink before it came spewing out his nose. "What are fire eyes?"

Carter leaned closer and lowered his eyes. "That's what I call it when Martina's giving me the 'I want you but can't have you' look. Fire eyes." He took two fingers and gestured toward his own eyes meaningfully.

"You think Lizzie's got fire eyes?"

"You *don't*?" Carter snorted. "For someone who stares at her so much, you sure don't see what's happening sometimes. And you have your sleeves rolled up. Ladies love that."

"They do?" Chase took another long drink.

"Oh yeah, for sure."

Chase put a brotherly arm around Carter and gave him a squeeze. "So not useless. You're the best, man." His phone buzzed as they made their way back to the table for the second half. Chase was in the middle of patting himself on the back for not going out for a smoke when he noticed who'd sent the text.

Dad: Where are you?

Chase: At Annie's

Dad: What time will you be home tonight?

Chase: I'm staying with a friend right now.

Dad: You'll come here tonight. I need to speak with you.

Chase: About what? Is Mom okay?

Dad: Be here by ten.

Chase: No, I'm not coming home tonight. I told you that.

"Everything okay? You're frowning." Lizzie was leaning over to talk into his ear, and he could see down her shirt a little. He noted that her affinity for electric blue extended to more than her toenails, then looked away like a gentleman.

"Yeah. Wait, no. My dad wants me to come by tonight."

"Oh." Now she was frowning. "Well, Martina would probably run me home. I'd be fine for a while by myself."

"You sure?"

"Sure I'm sure. I'll probably go right to bed, I'm tired." The phone in his hand buzzed again.

Dad: Make time in your "busy" life. 10:00.

Now it would seem like he was caving to his father's demands. He hated that.

Chase: I'll be there when I can.

They finished the round, but Chase's mind was elsewhere. It had to be, because if he started fixating on what his dad might want to yell at him about, he'd get even more anxious. He scrolled through his notes app for some of the affirmations he'd collected: *I've decided that I am enough. It's not their job to like me, it's mine. I am worthy of respect. I can be known for my kindness and strength. I embrace my individuality.* It helped, but he still wished he had his cigarettes for afterward. When it was time to go, he automatically went to help Lizzie, leading her out into the parking lot.

"Um. Chase?"

"Yeah?"

"Martina's car is . . ." She pointed in the other direction. "That way."

"Oh, right."

"You sure you don't just want me to come with you? I don't mind . . ."

He let out a big sigh. "That's tempting, thank you for the offer. But no. I don't know what he wants, so . . . no reason to drag you into the drama."

"Okay." She paused. "But you do remember that dealing with tense family drama is a big part of my job, right?"

"I do, yes. Same answer."

"Okay." They'd finally made it to Martina's little black car. The passenger side door was open, and Martina was kissing Carter good night. Check that—they were making out. Chase glanced at Lizzie as he helped her into the car, and her pink cheeks told him she was embarrassed. But there it was: fire eyes. Maybe she was regretting their chaste goodbye situation, too. Chase cleared his throat loudly, and the couple parted, Martina giggling.

"Sorry. Let's go, L-train."

"My given nickname will be fine, thank you," Lizzie said, folding her hands in her lap. Chase felt his body tense up as he considered putting Lizzie into the car with someone else, and Martina gave him a look as she slid into the driver's seat.

"Relax, bud. Say goodbye to your housemate, we're outta here."

Chase leaned with his hands braced on the open car window. "Bye, housemate."

"Bye, housemate," Lizzie echoed, her voice quiet.

"Call me if you need anything and I'll come right home."

"Okay."

"You won't be bothering me."

"All right."

"Especially if you fall. I can make it in twenty. I—"

"Chase?" Martina interrupted sweetly.

"Yeah?"

"I say this with love: let go of my car."

Begrudgingly, he pushed off the car and stepped back, watching them go.

CARTER WAS WAITING for him out front when Chase pulled up in front of the mansion.

"I'll be in the kitchen if you need me," he said, shadowing him up the stairs, and Chase gave him a grateful pat on the back. Most of the lights in the house were off; his father would be in his study, still working. *Always working.* Chase approached slowly, trying to ground himself by using his senses: listening to the slap of his shoes, feeling the cushion of their comfortable soles, inhaling the scent of lemon wood oil that had recently been used on the mahogany paneling of the walls. But his anxiety was still shouting for him to turn around and leave. Chase pushed the door open and knocked at the same time.

Harrison gestured him inside. "Have a seat."

Chase chose a maroon leather chair in front of the desk. He took a deep breath and sat down.

"I see you're decently dressed for once. Too bad you smell like smoke."

"I was at a bar with friends."

"Is that why you haven't been to work all week?"

Chase bristled. "I've been working from home."

"On whose authority?"

"Victor said it would be fine. My friend hurt herself. I'm helping out while her grandmother is out of town."

His father straightened. "Not that uppity little deputy?"

Chase grimaced at the characterization. "I don't know what's so little about her. In fact, I've been carrying her around, and I can tell you, there's some weight to the woman . . ."

"You know what I meant," Harrison snapped. "She's the one who arrested you."

"Yes, Lizzie arrested me."

"And now you're living with her? What the hell is—"

"Hey," Chase warned. "I'm willing to hear your concerns, but please stay calm."

"My concern," Harrison snarled, "is that you're blowing off work for the sake of a woman who ruined your life."

"I'm not blowing off work, and Lizzie didn't ruin my life. I did."

Harrison put down his pen and steepled his fingers. "How much have you spent on her? How much has she gotten out of your trust already?"

"Nothing," Chase said, rubbing his sweaty palms on his pants, his stomach feeling like an ocean of acid. Technically a lie, but he wasn't going to mention that prescription now;

it would just validate his dad's lack of confidence in his decision-making. "I'm just helping her recover."

"Is she paying you?"

"What?" Deep offense rattled his calm. "No. Not everything's about money, Dad. She's a friend. She'd do the same for me." Technically, she'd admitted that she didn't think she could do the same for him, but she would do something of equal necessity, he felt sure.

"Did you connect with Kroger about their concerns about the merger?" His department was preparing to release the new logo in a few weeks, and Kroger was one of their biggest clients.

"Yes, we had a long meeting on Tuesday. They seemed to feel fine about it by the end; we're going to try to keep the marketing strong with Pacific Northwest symbols, even if our name isn't first. People want to associate paper with Oregon over New York anyway, according to the focus groups we did." He'd called in remotely to listen in. It was somehow less nerve-wracking that way.

"Are you sleeping with her?"

Chase stood up. "Have a great evening." He turned to go when his dad called his name. Chase turned back in the doorway, waiting, thumbs hooked in his belt loops. "What?"

Harrison looked at him over the top of his glasses. "Don't disappoint me."

Chase felt his throat closing like he was allergic to the pressure, the lack of genuine love. "Dad, I love you, but I don't think that's possible, not the way you mean. The good news is that I'm proud of myself, even if you can't be." This time, when he turned to go, his father didn't call him back.

His hands were still shaking as he got in the car; he'd never stood up to his dad like that before. It made him want to throw up and buy himself a medal at the same time.

When he got back to Lizzie's, she was still awake.

"So?"

"Will it sound weird if I say I need a hug?"

Lizzie pushed the blanket from her lap and stood up, wobbly, tugging down her white pajama tank top. Then she opened her arms. Chase went to her, and when she held him tight around his ribs, rubbing his back, he felt some of the pain of the evening dull.

"He's never going to be proud of me," he said into her shoulder, hoping it wasn't the hurt one.

"Forget him. You're awesome."

Chase huffed out a laugh, trying not to cry.

"I mean it, Chase. I know you won't ghost him, even though you should, but don't let his opinion carry one bit of weight. You hear me?" It was her cop voice, and it made him feel safe and cared for and a little bit scared of her intensity, as usual. "A jackass like him doesn't deserve anything from you. You let him live in your head rent-free and you'll end up paying, one way or another."

"That sounds true."

"It is true," she said, leaning back without letting go entirely, and he stared into her eyes, wishing so badly that he could kiss her. *Not yet. Hang in there, Carpenter. Hang in.*

He cleared his throat. "You ready to brush teeth?"

"Martina helped me. And she got me ice and meds." She sat gingerly back down on the couch.

"Okay," he said, gesturing over his shoulder. "I should probably let you get to bed, then." It was sort of an excuse; after Trivia, it seemed like she was usually tired, ready for some alone time, even if she wasn't ready to sleep. He thought she was going for the remote to turn off the TV when Lizzie reached down for his knitting bag and held it out to him. She wasn't looking at him, still focused on the quiet TV. He hesitated, wanting to sit next to her and just be for a few minutes. But without eye contact, he didn't know if this was "go to your room and knit away your anxiety, weirdo" or "come sit by me and knit away your anxiety, weirdo." Then she picked up the blanket and moved it from his usual spot, tossing it onto the floor. She still sat in the middle of the couch, and if he sat there, they'd be pressed up against each other. He could soothe away this troubled evening in the glow of the TV and the rhythm of the needles and the sound of Lizzie's quiet laughter. Chase slipped off his shoes in the middle of the floor, and Pancake immediately trotted over and claimed the left one, taking it to his bed.

"Hey!" Chase snatched it back. "Sorry, dude." He tucked them into the bench by the front door, then joined her on the couch . . . as soon as he'd put a pillow under her ankle.

"He needs a good, long run," Lizzie yawned, snuggling in next to Chase unabashedly. When he looked over a few minutes later, she was asleep.

CHAPTER TWENTY-EIGHT: Lizzie

BY EIGHT O'CLOCK ON Friday night, Chase was back at his knitting again, this time with some kind of new technique to master. It was now a nightly ritual, one she was enjoying immensely, even if the hobby seemed to frustrate him to no end.

"It's called purling?"

He nodded, squinting at his work. "It's kind of like backward knitting."

She peered at it. "It looks to me like you're going in the same direction."

Chase frowned. "Maybe I'm not doing it right. And now I've got a snarl in my yarn . . ." He held up a large tangle of green, and Lizzie reached for her multi-tool.

"Is that your solution to everything?" Chase asked, holding it away from her. "You'll ruin it, I don't know how to start a new string!"

Lizzie laughed out loud. "Here, give it."

"Give me the knife first."

Shaking her head, Lizzie handed over her tool, and he traded her for the mess of yarn he was holding. There was a moment when they touched; they'd been finding lots of those moments over the last two days, and the chemistry between them felt like a beaker about to boil over. She didn't know how to turn down the heat, and frankly, she didn't want to. It was a rush. She pulled up her feet and stuck her cold toes under his legs as she detangled; her ankle was starting to feel better enough that she could put a little pressure on it.

"What are we even watching?" he asked, looking at the screen for the first time all night.

"I don't know. It's some kind of historical something. I usually like that, but this one's weird."

Chase quirked an eyebrow at the couple on the TV awkwardly embracing. "Those people kiss like someone's making them."

"Someone *is* making them," she replied, drawing out a long length of green yarn.

"But I assume they're paying them to make it believable. They look horribly uncomfortable."

"All kissing looks uncomfortable to me." If it was possible to regret something faster than the speed of sound, Lizzie did. Before the words were even out of her mouth. She felt Chase turn toward her.

"You can't mean that."

"Why can't I?" she asked, continuing to pull at loops in the yarn. "Sloppy. Germy. Weird."

"You just can't! Kissing is great, kissing is one of my absolute favorite things to do! Doesn't movie kissing make you think of your top ten?"

"My top ten . . . what?"

"Kisses, Lizzie Lou. Your top ten kisses." He'd reclaimed part of the yarn snarl, and he was trying to detangle it, too.

"I've never been kissed."

Chase let his hands drop. Lizzie pretended not to notice. "Huh."

"What's that mean, *huh*?"

"Just . . . wow."

She put down the project and reached for her popcorn bowl, but her stomach was suddenly too tight for any more food. "I think I'll go to sleep."

"But the movie's not—"

"The movie's awful. And I'm tired."

The way his forehead wrinkled reminded her of Captain Hansen any time the arrest numbers were up, but he didn't fight her. "Do you want help going to the bathroom before bed?"

"I have my crutches." *Somewhere. And then there'll be no one to make me feel bad for never finding someone to lock lips with me.*

"All right," he said, slowly getting to his feet, taking his bowl with him. "Call me if you need anything."

"Will do."

Chase was gazing at her, some strange mix of hope and frustration and something else she couldn't name, and Lizzie found herself gazing back, all the little lines of his face more interesting than any constellation. Then he sat back down slowly, and Lizzie didn't like where this was going. Chase looked like he was overthinking again, and so far, nothing good had come of that.

"There's no shame in knowing who you are and what you want," he said, his voice sincere, his voice pitched low. "And getting kissed? That'll happen when the time is right. It shouldn't be a rite of passage, it should mean . . ." He swallowed hard. "Mean something." Then suddenly, he stood up and grabbed the quilt from the back of the couch. She rearranged herself so she was lying down, and he spread it over her, tucking it in around her. "Good night, Lizzie Lou."

She watched him turn and disappear down the hallway to the studio. She rolled carefully onto her side to turn off the TV, but ended up leaving it on. The couple was kissing again, but it was just as awkward as before.

Chase should date women who were like him: Rich. Corporate. Suit-wearing. She never dressed up unless someone was making her. Then again, he seemed to be a pretty different person than he'd been the first time they met. She didn't think that guy would be sleeping on a futon to make sure she was okay. It was honestly very perplexing. She stared at the flashing screen, thinking, until her stomach rumbled, apparently recovered from its earlier stress. She glared down at her middle, as if she could censure it for not being satisfied with the huge meal Chase had cooked them (even if he had burned the pizza crust a little). With a sigh, she threw off the quilt and sat up, ignoring the stupid crutches. Lizzie hopped her way into the kitchen on one foot, bracing herself against the wall and the fridge. The oven clock said 1:29 a.m. Her candy stash was in the cupboard above the fridge where most people kept their booze. She didn't know why; it wasn't like she needed to fool anyone and hide it. She had, however, underestimated how hard it was going to be to go up on her toes on only one foot. She looked around for something to stand on, but the footstool was so far away, and she didn't want to hop too close to Chase's room, lest she wake him.

"What're you doing?" His sleepy voice made her wince, and she pivoted to see him standing in the doorway of the kitchen. He was wearing basketball shorts and a white T-shirt.

"Getting a snack."

"You're supposed to use your crutches, and you're supposed to ask for help if you need it . . ." he muttered, putting a hand on her hip as he reached over her to grab the bag of peanut M&M'S.

"You were asleep."

"That doesn't matter." He passed them down to her, yawning. He was already turning to help her back to the living room, when she stopped him, her hand on his arm, her heart in her throat.

"Did you mean what you said earlier?" He blinked rapidly, then rubbed at his face.

"About kissing happening when the time is right?"

"Yeah."

"Of course I meant it."

"You should kiss me, then." The kitchen was dark, and she couldn't see his face clearly, but he moved a little closer so they were standing right together.

"You sure?"

"Why not?"

His chuckle was throaty. "I can think of a lot of reasons why not. Haven't you ever watched a rom-com?"

"Once or twice."

"So once the friends kiss, nothing is ever the same."

That's what I'm hoping, she thought. *I wouldn't mind it with you. Maybe I can trick you into falling in love with me.*

"That's a risk I'm willing to take. Are you?"

He lifted a hand to her cheek. His fingers were warm and gentle against her skin, and she suddenly felt aware of her hair standing on end in various, illogical parts of her body. "Yeah," he muttered, "I'll risk it. Put down the chocolate."

"Why?" She kind of wanted to hold the chocolate. It kept something between them. It made the whole thing safer somehow with snacks pressed to her chest.

"Because you only get one first kiss," he said, smiling, gently pulling the bag from her hands to put it on the counter.

"Now I don't know what to do with my hands," she complained, but the words died on her tongue when Chase pulled her good arm around the back of his neck. With her tailbone balanced against the kitchen counter, she felt perfectly stable on one foot and completely off-kilter in every other sense. In the dark, her other senses came alive; she could hear the tick of the pig clock above the microwave, his slow breathing. She took a deep breath and a faint lemongrass and sea salt scent clouded her thinking. And the man himself? He was so close to her, head to toe. Chase nuzzled his nose against hers, his arms banded around her, holding her against him, his warm breath tickling her skin.

"You know the good thing about kissing?" he asked quietly.

She shook her head. *Would we be here if I did?*

"There's really no wrong way to do it."

"Except the way those actors were doing it."

"Right, but that was wrong because there was no feeling in it." She wanted to look into his eyes, but it was too dark, so she closed her eyes and whispered her worst fear instead.

"Is there any feeling in this?"

Despite him being so close to her, his lips against hers startled her momentarily. But then she leaned into the kiss; it was less wild than she'd imagined. She probably did watch too many late-night movies. This was a fairytale kiss, not a TV kiss. She felt she wasn't even doing anything but reveling in his closeness, the softness of him, but she could hardly breathe for how overwhelming it was. She felt relieved and frightened and happy all at once, and she hoped to God he wouldn't use his tongue; she'd probably die if he did that. He pulled back and began giving her tiny kisses, painting her lips with kisses so sweet and slow, she felt all her thoughts vaporizing until she was just one big feeling from head to toe. She tried to mimic what he did, and she could've sworn she felt him smiling against her lips as they danced slowly back and forth into each other's space. Her pulse was so strong, it must have been visible in her neck from ten feet away. She wondered if her heart's normal action even counted as beating compared to this.

He pulled away and she could tell he was looking at her, but she couldn't see what he was feeling in the low light. In the split second she had available, she decided to play it safe.

"Thanks."

Chase's eyebrows snapped together. "*Thanks*?"

"Yes. Thanks. Now I'm not some pathetic loser who hasn't ever—"

"Lizzie." The word was hot, angry, a wasp's nest. Then, a warning: "Don't."

"Don't what?" she muttered, even though she knew exactly what he meant.

"Don't pretend this was some form of pity. And don't pretend you don't want me."

Lizzie's mouth fell open at his blunt words, and Chase took the opportunity to kiss her again, harder this time, slipping between her lips, his tongue caressing hers. Lizzie whimpered. She couldn't help it. It felt so good, so right, to be wrapped up in Chase. She wanted to push him down and explore his sweet mouth as much as she wanted, for as long as she wanted, right there on the kitchen floor. How had he known, when she'd hardly known herself? Lizzie felt wholly outclassed, the naïve one yet again. She pushed Chase away by his shoulders and he stumbled backward, eyes wide.

"I didn't say I didn't want you," she snapped, wiping her wet mouth with the back of her hand. She wobbled, and Chase stepped forward to steady her, a warm hand against her elbow, his body close to hers again now.

"'Thanks?' Come on. You were trying to play this off as something it's not. I know you."

"No, you don't. You know what I've let you see, what I've told you. That's all." His face hardened, but he didn't bother arguing with her. They both knew it wasn't true.

"Lizzie. I like you. I'm asking you not to push me away just because you're scared. I'm scared, too."

"I'm not scared," she whispered, but the lie tasted like apple cider vinegar on her tongue, sweet in the feeling of infatuation and sour in that she'd denied it. "I'm not *that* scared," she amended.

"Lizzie. Do you want me or not? Because I don't want to play games."

Lord, how did people talk about this? Just blurt out their most private feelings for everyone to hear? This was exactly what she'd been afraid of. This was exactly what she'd known would happen, that her shyness would dominate her good intentions and her affections and confine them inside her. She reached a hand behind his neck and tried to pull him down to her lips, to get back to that good place where there was no talking necessary and her tangled tongue was no problem at all when it was twisted around his. But Chase tipped his head up, just far enough to be out of her reach.

"Say it," he whispered. "Say it, and I'll kiss you again. I'll kiss you until the sun comes up if that's what you want."

"Fine," she huffed out.

"Fine what?" he pressed, moving a fraction of an inch closer. *Not close enough. Not by half.* Letting the truth out was the only way through this.

"Fine. I want you, Chase Carpenter."

"And this wasn't a pity kiss."

"No."

"And we're not going to let it rom-com us out of happiness in the morning. We're going to talk about it."

"Never mind," she said, releasing his neck and turning toward the kitchen sink. "You taste like burnt crust and toothpaste anyway."

"Shut up, Lizzie," he laughed, gently turning her face back to him. His kiss was exultant somehow, victorious—was it possible to kiss smugly?—and she found she didn't mind losing to him. Not if this was the consolation prize.

It was nearly three when he helped her back to the couch, tucking her in tight again and pressing one more kiss to her lips.

"Sweet dreams," he whispered, and Lizzie fell asleep with her fingers pressed to her lips, as if that would keep his kisses there a little longer.

CHAPTER TWENTY-NINE:
Chase

CHASE HAD BEEN UP FOR an hour when he heard Lizzie stirring. *Finally.* He should've started that bacon as soon as he got up. In his nervousness, the coffee he'd made was already cold . . . and she didn't even drink coffee. He heard Pancake's nails dancing against the wood floor as he went over to greet Lizzie; he'd also forgotten to let him out. *Calm down. It'll be fine. Maybe a little weird for a while, but fine.* Had he been too aggressive with her? When she'd tried to play it off as a favor, he'd lost his cool. It was just insulting. But he hadn't had to push her like that . . . would she be mad this morning?

"Chase?"

"Yeah?" He went hustling into the living room. She was already standing next to the couch on both feet, and he forgot about everything he'd been worried about all morning.

"Hey! Look at you! How does it feel?"

She rocked a flat hand back and forth, as if to say "so-so," then flipped her tangled red hair away from her face. He needed to wash it for her again; it'd been a few days. The days were starting to warm up, now that spring was starting to show itself in earnest.

"You want to try to get to the bathroom on your own?"

"Will you walk next to me?"

"Of course," he said, slotting in next to her on her weak side, one arm around her waist, careful not to jostle that ankle. They'd done this dozens of times by now, but now that he knew what it was like to hold her in his arms, it felt different. He stared down at her ankle, trying to tell if it was less swollen.

"Chase."

"Hmm?" He looked up and she kissed him softly, sending his blood rushing away from his brain. When he made a startled grunt, she quickly pulled back, her cheeks pink like the dogwood blossoms out front, her eyes guarded, hand covering her lips.

"Sorry," she whispered, but Chase pulled her hand away and kissed her again, teasing the line of her lips apart. He had to show her that she hadn't offended him, just surprised him. Pleasantly so. The kind of "on your toes" feeling he had around Lizzie was the kind he didn't mind.

"Don't be," he murmured, grinning. "That's a great way to say good morning."

Lizzie looked at him sternly, but he saw the way her mouth quirked. "It's not sloppy, germy, and weird?"

"Not at all. Even with unbrushed teeth. Can I make you some breakfast, girlfriend?"

"Oh, is that what I am now?"

"Yeah, it was in the fine print last night when you admitted you wanted me."

She shook her head a little as she began to gingerly move forward. "I don't think I said *that*."

"You didn't?"

"No, that doesn't sound like me."

"Who was that redhead I made out with, then?"

"Maybe it was a dream," she deadpanned, and Chase stopped them in the narrow hallway, tipping her back until her back met the plaster.

"It definitely was," he said with a smile, giving her plenty of warning as he leaned in slowly to kiss her again. It was heady, getting to touch her like this, getting to hold her for more than practical reasons. And based on how her pulse was racing in her neck as he kissed his way down, Lizzie was feeling it too, even if she wouldn't admit it in the bright light of a Saturday morning.

"Seriously, though. Let's hold off on the labels. And I'll take pancakes," she said, giving his hair an affectionate rub, and he adored the way that felt. More than anything, he wanted her to feel comfortable with him. The dog came sliding in from the kitchen, where he'd been curled up in the corner by the oven.

"Not you," Lizzie laughed, wincing when he stepped on her foot.

"Sit, pup," Chase commanded, and the dog obeyed, tail still thumping the wood floor.

"I swear he listens to you better than me," Lizzie grumbled, then she turned and went into the bathroom, closing the door behind her. Chase stared after her for a minute, just grinning, until Pancake whined.

"You're right, let's get those pancakes started for her. You can have the ones I burn," Chase promised him.

"Then there'll be none left for us!" Lizzie shouted through the door, and Chase threw back his head and laughed. He made them from scratch since he couldn't find the mix. Mixes weren't good enough for her, anyway. He added some frozen blueberries he found in the freezer, too, and both Lizzie and Pancake seemed to approve. The bacon might've helped, too. They lingered at the table, her drinking her cranberry juice, him sipping the coffee that he desperately needed already, just chatting. He was just collecting the plates to do dishes when there was a knock at the front door.

"I got it," she said, getting up carefully, limping her way to the front door. He heard an unknown female voice, and he peeked down the hall. Maggie Durand stood in the doorway, nodding politely at something Lizzie was saying. *So she did call her. Stubborn beauty.* It made even less sense to have Maggie do it now that they were together, but whatever. If this was making Lizzie feel empowered, what did it matter?

"Hey, Maggie, how's it going?" Chase said, striding over to shake her hand, even though he kind of wanted a hug. He appreciated her helping them out. She seemed like a good kid.

"Hey, Mr. Carpenter."

Chase blinked. *What the . . .*

"Maggie, I'm the same age as your brother. You can call me Chase."

She gave him a shrug, and he laughed. "So mow the lawn on Saturdays, $20. Anything else?"

Lizzie stared at her blankly.

"On the phone, you mentioned some sort of delivery, I think?"

"Oh!" Lizzie limped over to the dining room table, where they both had stacks of paper piling up. "Here you go. You're eighteen, right?"

"Yes, I just turned eighteen," she confirmed.

"How much do you charge?"

"Is this a one-time thing, or would you like ongoing service?"

The question impressed Chase. She was just about to graduate high school, but she was already talking like a businesswoman. Lizzie seemed impressed, too. She eased herself into a dining room chair. "Well, that depends on a few factors. 1. How busy we are at the station. 2. How often you're able to work. 3. Whether you enjoy the work. 4. Whether I think you're doing a timely job of accurately delivering the paperwork. Shall I go on?"

Maggie shook her head, turning over the envelope. "Seems like it'd be easier to just mail it."

"Letters like this have to be hand-delivered. The court wants to make sure they received it. It's important, but if they won't take it, you can just leave it on their doorstep. There shouldn't be any confrontation involved with the person who's receiving it."

"I see." Maggie blew out a breath that fluffed the hair she wore over one eye. "How does $20 sound?"

"That'd be fine," Lizzie agreed. "Can you send me an invoice?"

"Yeah, I can do that through PayPal."

"Great, what's your email address?"

Was she blushing? That seemed like an innocuous enough question to Chase, and Maggie didn't have the same pale coloring that Lizzie did to turn beet red at the drop of a hat.

"Um, it's MargaretDurandArt@gmail.com," she said, keeping her voice low, as if she didn't want to be overheard. Even though it was just the three of them.

"Are you an artist, Maggie? I didn't know that . . ." Chase said. "I'd love to see your work sometime."

The young woman shifted her weight and muttered something about failed ventures. "Do I need to be licensed or anything?"

Lizzie shook her head. "I looked into it, and you only need insurance if you're delivering a Writ of Garnishment. The only qualification is that you be a disinterested person of the court."

Maggie's smirk made Chase grin back. "I'm known for being disinterested, so it sounds like a perfect fit . . ." She put the envelope carefully into her messenger bag. "Thanks, Deputy."

"My pleasure. Thanks for stepping up."

"Are you going to Trivia Night again this week? You're on my brother's team, right?"

"Yes, I'll be there," Lizzie said, much to his surprise and delight.

"You guys did great," she grinned. "We might do better this week if Frankie would quit cracking everybody up."

"Francesca Lopez?" Lizzie asked. Did she literally know everybody in town?

"That's her," Maggie said, adjusting her bag. "She's kind of my partner in crime. So to speak." So that's why Kyle and Martina had both kept glancing over there; they had siblings on that team. There was nothing illegal about it since the Trivia Night had been declared a non-alcoholic event, but it was sweet to see both their family dynamics.

"I'm sure it's nothing of consequence," Lizzie said, putting on her friendly (but not too friendly) cop persona. "I'm glad you were able to come." She glanced at Chase. "You want to take Pancake to the m-e-a-d-o-w?"

"Why are you spelling 'meadow'?" The minute the word was out of his mouth, the dog came over and jumped on him, barking madly.

"That's why!" she said, wincing at the noise.

"Your dog knows the word meadow?" he asked, and Lizzie nodded, snapping her fingers for Pancake to get down. He did, but he ran over to the front door, doing his ping-pong stare between them and the wooden torture device that separated him from his beloved meadow.

"Can you grab his leash and the flinger thing? It's the long orange thing with a ball attached. Oh, and get a second ball."

"Yup." Chase moved to obey her request.

Maggie gestured toward the front yard. "I'll just be outside."

"The lawnmower's in the shed in the back," Lizzie called after her, and Maggie waved.

Once they were both changed, Lizzie led the way out the front to the wrought iron gate. They didn't need the leash, since Pancake was wholly focused on the tennis ball in the flinger. Chase moved it right and left, as if he was hypnotizing the creature, and Lizzie elbowed him. He took her hand, and that earned him a smile. They were moving slowly, and he wasn't too happy when she took them off the end of the sidewalk at the end of the street; the ground here would be uneven and make her prone to reinjury . . . but it wasn't his call. The receding sound of the lawn mower reminded him that he wanted to tease her.

"So you called Maggie." Chase shook his head in mock disappointment. "And here I was looking forward to being covered in grass clippings today."

"I told you I was going to."

"I still don't exactly understand why it was necessary . . ." He was only half joking. It felt wholly reasonable that he take over all the household chores she needed done. His help was free, and he wanted to do it. He wasn't sure what it was going to take to convince her that she wasn't a burden. But apparently, this was not the moment for this conversation.

"Chase. Don't."

"Fine," he said, raising the hand with the flinger in it, delighting in the way it sent Pancake's gaze shooting skyward to follow the ball. "Boy, he really goes for this thing."

"I usually take him a couple of times a week, plus a daily run."

Chase frowned. "I could've done that."

"But I didn't ask you to. He was fine. Don't worry about it."

"Telling someone with anxiety not to worry is like telling a fish not to swim," he muttered, and she squeezed his hand. "Maggie's gonna work for the station, huh?"

Lizzie nodded. "I've been doing all the subpoenas myself, but they take a long time, and I can't now that I'm out for a while. Besides, it's been on my list for a while to find someone, and when I found out all the odd jobs she does, it just made sense."

"What kind of odds jobs?"

"Oh, she's watching pets and houseplants for the Mind Readers while they're gone. I'm not sure all the details. But I'm always glad to see young people kept busy by positive activities."

"Like Trivia?"

"Better than starting fires somewhere or hanging around up at Foster's Point."

Chase felt a little incensed at that. He'd spent some fun dates up there. "What've you got against Foster's Point?"

Lizzie stopped and took the flinger from him, hanging on to his arm for balance with her other hand. She chucked the ball into the knee-high grass and Pancake went tearing off after it. "I don't have anything against it, but it's public land and teenagers shouldn't be up there hanging out."

"*Making* out." That blush. It was just too easy and too fun. All that kissing was bringing out his wicked side.

"I know what they're doing, I'm the one who has to shine my flashlight through the foggy windows, all right?"

Pancake came back, panting, the ball still in his mouth.

"Drop it," Lizzie said, but Pancake just lay down in the field, gnawing on it. Her voice turned schoolmistress-stern. "Pancake. Drop it." The animal ignored her. Chase couldn't help but think that he'd do pretty much whatever she wanted if she used that tone with him. Gladly.

Lizzie sighed. "Do you have that second ball?" He pulled it out of his back pocket, and the animal's eyes lit. Pancake scrambled to get to his feet, the first ball forgotten.

"Load me." She held out the end of the flinger, and he popped the ball in. With a flick of her wrist, Pancake was off again, and Chase laughed.

"That's all it takes? A second ball? That's genius."

"Just trial and error," she said, but she was smiling. Why had he been worrying earlier? Half the time, he couldn't remember. It seldom made sense when he looked back, and he wished he could apply that insight to the future, but it didn't work that way. *Little things comfort us because little things distress us.* It was a quote by Blaise Pascal, one of Gretta's favorites. And now, they did seem small. But not her smile. That seemed massive.

"Are you nervous about work tomorrow?"

Chase nodded. "I think I'll go in, just for the morning."

"I'll be fine alone. I can always call you. Captain Hansen's going to come by in the morning and drop off more work."

"Are you going to ask him about your promotion?"

Lizzie twisted her lips to one side. "Do you think I should?"

"Seems like a good opportunity. He'll be focused on you, not distracted by other people and their needs. You don't know what he'll say until you ask. Being injured shouldn't disqualify you; you'll be back to full health in a few weeks."

She gave a single nod, then picked up the abandoned ball and had it shooting through the air before Pancake dropped the one he had.

"I think I can get upstairs to the shower, but will you wash my hair when we get back? Because of my shoulder?"

"Definitely." He couldn't think of a better way to pass the morning.

CHAPTER THIRTY: Lizzie

THE TV WENT ON THE moment her anxious boyfriend left. She was warming up to the word . . . it seemed more apt than anything else she could come up with. With her pile of paperwork taken care of, channel surfing would have to do for entertainment. She wanted to text Gram, but they were eight hours ahead in Paris. Some quick time-zone math in her head told her they were probably eating dinner, probably snails or some other gross thing she wouldn't want to try. Also, Gram would probably ask a lot of questions she didn't want to answer right now. That was reason enough to put it off. The house felt almost eerily quiet without Chase humming, banging around in the kitchen, playing with the dog. Said dog was currently curled up at her feet, and she rubbed his soft belly with her good foot. He needed a bath, but it wasn't quite warm enough yet to do it outside. When Captain Hansen pulled up, they both scrambled up; it took her a while to get to the front door.

He was scowling. "You didn't have to get up."

"I'm fine," she said, forcing a smile. "Come in, Captain."

"Must be feeling a little better," he said, observing her walk to the dining room. He put the box down on the table, trading it for the other one.

"Yes, sir. I'm feeling better every day. We even took Pancake to the meadow yesterday."

"We?"

She ignored how her face heated at the admission. "Yes, Chase Carpenter is still staying with me. He's been really helpful."

"Seems like it. Not many people would put their lives on hold like that to help a friend."

"You did. And you didn't even know us." She hadn't meant to bring up the accident, but it was true.

"Well, that was different," he said, his voice growing gruff as he took off his hat and reseated it tightly on his head. Lizzie smiled. She wouldn't bother arguing with him.

"Have you and Sherri decided where you're going first?"

"Hawaii's looking good to us. Kauai's got some great hiking."

"Sounds like fun," she agreed. She'd never even left the West Coast. Everything she needed was here. She cleared her throat, gathering her courage. "So speaking of your departure..."

"Yes? Here, sit down." She did. But only because she was already shaking a little.

"I'd like you to promote me to sergeant."

Captain Hansen's salt-and-pepper eyebrows both went high. "Huh. Not corporal?"

"No, sir. I think my exceptional record deserves sergeant." It was asking a lot. She knew that. But she wanted this. She wanted it so bad. And Mark wasn't going to give it to her.

"Lizzie," he started gently, and her stomach sank. *He always calls me deputy . . . probably trying not to rub it in.* "You're a great deputy. I love having you on staff, I do. But I can't promote you unless I can send you out to car crashes without worrying that you're going to come apart." She wouldn't have wanted him to sugarcoat it, but the truth felt like a punch to the sternum. And she'd know, because she'd taken an elbow there recently, breaking up a fight at Annie's at 1:00 a.m. between James Miller and Levi Zane. Those idiots just wouldn't let their feud go.

"You're amazing with the Timberites," he went on. "There's no one I'd rather send out to deal with them. But as I told Mark, you're just not ready for a promotion until you can handle the more intense stuff." Lizzie felt numb. They'd already decided without her. This person she'd trusted, who'd been there at their accident, found their car. Come to her house, taken them both to his house until her grandmother, a woman she barely knew, could drive up from California. In the coming months, he'd taken her and Lottie out for ice cream and mini-golf and bike rides. In a very real way, he'd sheltered her, but in her opinion, his hesitance was more about his own trauma than hers.

He sat forward, his gaze concerned and fatherly. "I one hundred percent understand why you can't. I know you've always had kind of a weak stomach, anyway . . ." His voice trailed off. He didn't need to say more. Even before the accident, she'd had a gag reflex with a hair-trigger; if she looked at a plate of Jello the wrong way, it could set her off. So bodily fluids were something she avoided at all costs . . . and that usually wasn't possible with car accidents.

He cleared his throat, and it didn't disguise the pain in his voice. "That crash was one of the most difficult scenes I ever worked, Painter. Period. Even being obliquely involved would deeply affect anyone. There's no weakness in that."

Lizzie couldn't sit there any longer. She stood up, brushing off her jeans. "I want a promotion, sir. If that's what it takes, I'll do it."

His face was etched in discomfort. "I'm not suggesting you should."

"I want to go out to the next crash. I can handle it, sir."

He rose from his chair unsteadily. "Well, we'll see how your ankle's doing."

"With all due respect, I don't need a functioning leg to investigate a car accident. I should be getting an air cast soon."

The captain stared at her hard, as if trying to see inside her head. Then he sighed. "All right, Deputy. Keep me posted on the ankle. Enjoy your digitizing."

"Thank you, sir." She didn't bother walking him to the door. She sat back in the chair, unwanted tears stinging her eyes. Pancake pushed his way between her legs, nosing her hands, and she caved and petted him, pressing their heads together until she felt a little better. Chase texted an hour later.

Chase: How'd it go?
Lizzie: Bad. He said no.
Chase: Bummer.

Lizzie scoffed. Of course that would be his reaction. Mr. Laid Back Trust Fund Guy. How could he understand? He barely tolerated his job; this was her life's calling. She was made to be in law enforcement. He was still looking for his life's purpose, and that was fine, but she'd found hers, and she wanted to pursue it as far as she could.

> **Lizzie:** Yeah.
> **Chase:** Did he say why?
> **Lizzie:** It's complicated. But not health-related.

She stopped herself from adding *unless you counted mental health*, mostly because Chase probably did consider mental health as important as physical health. He read those books from NA every day.

> **Chase:** I'm sorry. Can I bring you a consolation sandwich for lunch? My treat.

> **Lizzie:** No. I have leftovers.

> **Chase:** Okay. I'm sorry.

She tossed her phone to the other side of the couch with a sigh, then pulled the new box of work closer to her.

CHAPTER THIRTY-ONE:
Chase

CHASE'S STOMACH HAD been in knots all morning, and he didn't think it was the three cups of coffee he'd had. Well, maybe it was, but it was also Lizzie's meeting with the captain and the prospect of speaking to his dad. There was no reason to think he'd see him today; they often went days without passing each other in the halls at TFPP . . . but something told Chase this wasn't one of those days. Something told him that the conversation they'd had last week hadn't been the end of it. Something told him his dad was just biding his time, waiting to bring up Lizzie and his work-from-home situation again, and the tension was boiling inside him. It was a good thing those pills he'd left in Lizzie's truck were inaccessible. He texted Kellan that he was having a hard day, and he texted back, thanking Chase for letting him know. That felt a little better, even though their exchange was brief. Sometimes it just felt good to admit his weaknesses out loud. He'd spent too much of his life pretending they didn't exist.

Sure enough, around 9:30, he was summoned to his father's office via his secretary.

"Nice of you to come in today," Harrison said. "Shut the door."

Chase said nothing. His mom had always told him that if he didn't have something nice to say, he didn't need to say anything. Though even that was imperfect, since it encouraged silence in the face of mistreatment, and mistreatment seemed to be normal with Dad.

"I've been thinking—"

"So have I," interrupted Chase. "Where's my mother?" Carter's relayed conversation in the bar the other day had been bothering him, scratching at the back of his mind.

"Your mother's at home, as far as I know, with that little nurse you employ."

"No, not that mom. My biological mom. Where's Carmen?"

He'd never seen his dad look so startled; he went momentarily white, then his face turned purple as the rage hit. "What does *she* have to do with anything?"

"You tell me. Carter said you were yelling about her the other day." It was a bluff, of course; he didn't know for sure, but it didn't seem likely that he'd meant Willow. She couldn't possibly be to blame for his condition.

"I suppose you'll want to go find her, now that you're exploring your life's true purpose, or whatever it is you're doing."

"I wouldn't mind seeing her, but—"

"She's dead."

The noise in Chase's head went momentarily quiet as he tried to process this information. He'd imagined her living in Colorado: she used to talk about wanting to go to this ceramics ranch there as they pinched and sculpted playdough together. When she didn't come back, his small brain had told him that's where she went. Dead? No. Dead didn't make sense.

"How do you know?"

"Her lawyer sent me a letter. She willed her belongings to you and your brothers. I sold them and added it to your trusts." *I could've had a piece of her. Something precious to her*, he thought, his heart fracturing slowly like a windshield that met a piece of gravel at high speed. The trauma was but a moment, but the cracks were slow.

"And you're telling me this now? At work?"

Harrison shrugged. "You asked. And if any of you boys deserves to know, it's you."

The pang of fear that hit Chase was so strong, it had him tasting metal in his mouth. *Did I bite my tongue? Is that blood?*

"Why?" he whispered. He didn't want to know. Whatever the reason was, it couldn't be good. He wanted to leave, to jump up and knock the chair over and run for the door before he could hear the truth. Before he could hear something that would break his heart.

"Liver failure. Probably got Hep C from a dirty needle."

Chase closed his eyes. It just made the dizziness worse. He put his elbows on his knees and his head in his hands. He felt locked in that dark place, putting pressure on his eyes, blocking out all the light coming in the corner office windows, trying to remember how to breathe.

"Now you understand, don't you? Why I've been so hard on you. Why I tried to lead you down a different path than she took. You were supposed to be stronger than her."

I am stronger than temptation. That was the affirmation he'd struggled with the most. Because on his own? He wasn't. Without a community, without support, without his meds, he'd fail. He knew that as surely as he knew the sky was blue. But the thing was, he did get it. He could see what his father was trying to do. He must have been terrified, watching his son go down the same road his wife had. But he still hadn't handled it right, not by a long shot. That was the trouble with believing that a medical problem was a moral failure, that Chase could've chosen differently. He couldn't have. He'd tried.

Chase slowly raised his head, letting his vision clear. "What did you want to talk to me about, before I brought up Carmen?"

"Your cop friend."

"What about her?"

"If you need to come to our house to get high, I won't say anything."

"Dad, I'm not—"

"I know, I know, you're a 'changed man.' But we all need to take the edge off sometimes. If she catches you, they're going to throw the book at you this time. I won't be able to save you again. It'll be jail time." For a split second, Chase felt so stupid. It was so stupid to let this man, who didn't believe he was sober or that sobriety was even possible for him, who tried to help in the most misguided, horrible ways, continue to be in his life. And then he remembered that he wasn't stupid. And he was in control of his life now.

Chase stood up. "I'm going to find a new job. I can't be around you."

Harrison chuckled. "I beg your pardon?"

"Did you really not hear me? That's okay, I'll write it down. You'll have my two weeks' notice by the end of the day."

"What—you can't be—" his father sputtered. "Who do you think is going to hire an addict?"

Chase shrugged, shoving his hands deep into his pockets. "I don't know. But whoever does, it'll be better than working for someone who's just waiting for me to relapse." He turned and walked out, closing the door quietly behind him, smiling at his father's secretary. The feeling in his chest was hard to describe; relief was all twisted up with guilt and shame, fear that his dad was right. Right about how he was like Carmen. Right about how he wouldn't find another job. When he got back to his office, he shut the door and sent two texts: one to Kellan, asking to meet, and one to Lizzie, asking about her meeting with her boss. Lizzie responded first: it sounded like hers hadn't gone any better than his, though she was hopefully still employed.

He had a bigger problem, though, which he realized as he tried to comfort her. When she didn't need his help anymore, he had to either move back to the estate or move into Carter's condo in Salem. Either way, he'd just created a seriously difficult situation for himself. Without really seeing the words, Chase wrote his letter, gathered up some work, and left. Kellan had texted while he was driving and said they could meet after dinner tonight. That felt far away, and Chase said so, texting back at a stoplight. Kellen promised to try to move around some commitments so he could meet earlier. Lizzie wasn't surprised to see him, since he'd said he was only going to work the morning from the office. But his next proposal did seem to catch her off-guard.

"Let's go pet horses." He sat down on the couch, putting his head on her good shoulder.

"What?" She tore her gaze away from her work. "Where?"

He shrugged. "Wherever. Wherever you went riding as a kid."

Lizzie stared at him for a long moment. "Hattie's got horses. They're probably lonely without her, actually. She spoils them."

"We'll jump the fence."

"Chase, that's breaking and entering. And I've got a key." Lizzie put her hand over his. "Are you okay?"

"Not really. I quit my job today."

"What?!" She turned to him so fast, his head fell off her shoulder. "What happened?"

"My dad was on his usual BS about how I'm going to relapse. And he dropped a truth bomb about my mom."

"What about her?" Her green eyes seemed so concerned, his heart felt a little patched.

"Not Willow, my first mom. Carmen. Apparently, she struggled with addiction, too. And my dad thinks she died from Hepatitis C. You get it from sharing needles; that's why I suggested to Hattie that we do needle exchange, even before I knew all this. But especially now, it's important. It's a way to keep people from getting even more complications, even if they're not ready to get help for their addiction or can't afford it. It might've saved her life."

"That's really sad." She squeezed him tight, so tight he couldn't get a full breath. His phone buzzed, and he pulled it out, hoping it was Kellan, able to get away from his commitments sooner. It wasn't.

> **Christopher:** I heard you quit. WTF.
> **Chase:** Shouldn't be a surprise, you both treated me like crap.
> **Christopher:** don't quit. don't be an idiot.

This wasn't helping. He shut off his phone.

"I don't think I can . . ." Chase paused. This was all screwed up, he couldn't get his head around it. "I don't know if I can feel all my feelings yet. But I think horses would help."

"Horses it is," she said softly. "Just let me find my shoes, and we'll go. These files aren't going anywhere."

He squeezed her back, unable to get out the 'thank you' that was inside him, but suspecting she felt it anyway.

CHAPTER THIRTY-TWO:
Lizzie

THE NEXT TWO WEEKS went by fast. They went back to the doctor, and he gave her an air cast, which delighted her. Chase met with Kellan almost every day; he explained it was just to stay grounded in a time of transition, and that sounded wise to Lizzie. Mornings, they got up late and worked from home, always pausing to have lunch together. Evenings, they watched TV on the couch, Chase knitted until he got frustrated, and then they made out until bedtime. But the longer time went on, the more nervous she could tell Chase was that he didn't have another job yet. There honestly weren't a lot of options in town, and the thought of him moving to Salem was a bad one. That's where he'd fallen in with his old friends, and Lizzie wanted him as close as possible for purely selfish reasons. Between working sessions, they went for slow walks and visited Hattie's horses, Sir Patrick Stewart and Dame Maggie Smith. The guy who'd been supposed to take care of them had been slacking: their stalls hadn't been mucked out, so they fixed that and filled up their water. When she texted Hattie about it, Nick showed up the next day, shamefaced and sullen.

"I could do a better job than that guy," Chase muttered as he drove them home on Sunday.

"So why don't you?"

"I'm not a vet or anything." He gripped the steering wheel tight for a minute, then relaxed.

"Neither is Nick. He's just a college kid who needed money. I think people would like having someone they could trust."

Chase's face went soft. "And you think I'm trustworthy?"

"Of course I do. Look, Maggie's running herself ragged trying to take care of all the Mind Readers' pets and stuff. Maybe you could offer housesitting and pet sitting. It wouldn't take a lot of start-up capital; you've already got a car. I've seen how you are with my dog. Maybe later on, you could offer training or something. I'd sign up."

"Pancake's not that bad, he's just young." He paused, and she could see his wheels turning. "It's got some of the qualities I wanted. Meaningful work. Tangible."

"And you'd be outside a lot, walking people's dogs."

"Yeah." He sounded hopeful for the first time in two weeks, and Lizzie couldn't help but grin. "What?"

"Did you just start a business, Chase Carpenter?"

"I think maybe," he said, grinning back. "I'll give Maggie a call and see if she can give me some references."

"No. First, you need a name."

"Carpenter Pet Services is probably throwing my family name in people's faces a little bit."

Her mind started cranking out ideas, but most of them were no good. She was no writer; the closest she ever got to creativity was sandwich toppings. They kept talking all the way home but still didn't have a name.

"Let's see, it's for people who are leaving, right? So maybe something about freedom?"

"Furry starts with an F, can we work with that somehow?"

"'Furry Freedom' sounds like something else," he joked, but Lizzie just felt confused. She shrugged it off. "Home-Care?"

"That sounds like you do what Martina does." She flopped down on the couch; her ankle was sore, so she automatically put it up on the table. Her toenails were purple this week, expertly painted by Chase again. "What about Petocity? Petacular?"

"It goes beyond that, though. I want to do home services, too. Making sure people's plants don't die and stuff."

"Guardian Home Services?"

"That sounds like a security company. What about Anywhere Home Services? Like, go anywhere you want, your house and your pets will be fine while you're gone."

"I like that. Go with that one." She picked up her computer again. "Ooh." It was an email from Captain Hansen, which she read aloud to Chase; she'd petitioned him to come back to work, now that she had her air cast. He'd approved.

"Hey, this calls for a celebration!" Chase whooped. "I'm going to bake something!" Oh, Lord. His baking was even worse than his usual food. Oh well, even burnt chocolate was better than no chocolate. Maybe she'd luck out and he'd use a mix.

EVERYONE APPLAUDED the next day when she walked back into the station, and Lizzie waved them away, embarrassed. Waved them away with light pink fingernails that she'd done herself. She'd also French braided her hair. These weeks at home, she'd gotten comfortable looking how she wanted to, and she wasn't ready to give that up. Maybe she'd work her way up to the wild colors like she had on her toes. But if anyone said anything about her new look, she was going to smack them. Surprisingly, no one did. Most of them were husbands and fathers (or grandfathers), so maybe they'd learned not to say anything about a woman's appearance changes.

"Welcome back, Elizabeth!" Mark shook her hand heartily, and Lizzie smiled. "We've been trying to take care of Timber Falls, but we are all extremely glad to have you back."

"Glad to be back," she affirmed, and it was true. Did Mark know she was taken now? She and Chase hadn't exactly been subtle about being together . . . but whenever he ran in to get coffee at Riverside, she waited in the car. And they'd mostly kept their own company. Hopefully, he wasn't glad to have her back for *that* reason.

"Although it's amazing how much less trouble we've had without the Mind Readers in town," Captain Hansen chuckled, and Lizzie laughed, too. He gave her a friendly clap on the shoulder, then went back into his office. Before she could even sit down, Sue came over with a note.

"There's been a car accident in downtown Timber Falls. You want this one?" Then she hesitated. "No, wait. No accidents. I'll give it to someone else."

"No." She snatched the yellow paper from her fingers, scanning the details. Ranger Zane had called it in; not her favorite person, but she'd dealt with him at last year's Fall Festival just fine. "I've got it. I'll be back." She got out to her truck so quickly, Sergeant Hillerman was running to catch up with her.

"You move pretty good in that thing," he huffed. "Wait up for an old guy, will you?"

"What are you doing?"

He claimed the front seat with a gentle smile under his gray mustache. "Captain Hansen asked me to back you up."

"Not necessary." Yes, she said it hotly. She had a right to be annoyed.

"Well, nevertheless, here I am." He pointed to the parking lot exit, and Lizzie clenched her jaw as she pulled out. They made it to town in less than ten minutes. Ranger was in the parking lot of the library; she could smell the antifreeze when she got out. The grill of Ranger's shiny black Ford 350 sat scrunched against the back of a silver Tahoe, and she knew whose. There were no paramedics to be seen; they must've left already or weren't needed. Lizzie groaned. Not only was she going to have to deal with two people she didn't like, but this barely qualified as an accident. Lizzie chided herself; she shouldn't want anyone to be hurt. And she didn't, but . . . but if they were hurt already, then she could prove her mettle.

"Is that Charlie Miller?" the sergeant asked.

"Yes." Both of these men were obsessed with their cars. This was going to be ugly . . . but as awful as it sounded, it wasn't the kind of ugly that she needed to prove her point and get her promotion. She put it in park and reached over to open the glovebox and get out her ticket book, but winced when her shoulder tweaked.

"I got it," Hillerman said, digging through the napkins, random papers, and first aid supplies to find her ticket book. Then he paused. "You hurtin' much, Lizzie?"

"No, why?" she asked, opening the door to get out.

"Never mind." She straightened her uniform, trying not to hide her fingernails. "Morning, gentlemen."

"Morning, Deputy," Charlie spoke up, straightening from where he'd been leaning against Ranger's truck. "Just a little fender bender."

"A little—" Ranger choked out in rage. "You backed into me, jackass."

"If you hadn't been flying through the parking lot, maybe I could've seen you better . . ."

Lizzie held up her hands for quiet. "Mr. Miller, you know the person pulling out has the responsibility to avoid collisions." He wasn't as bad as his dad, but he was close. These families just hated each other; she never had been able to figure out why. It probably didn't hurt that the Millers were rich and the Zanes weren't. She turned to Ranger. "And Mr. Zane, you know that the speed limit is five miles an hour in the parking lot. This isn't the first time I've had to warn you to reduce your speed in public areas."

"Well, I guess it's nobody's fault," Charlie said, shrugging, and he opened the door to his car. It would be easy for him to get his car fixed; his brother Jason would do it for free, she was sure, since they owned the dealership in Aumsville together. Ranger stiffened as Charlie started to get inside.

"Deputy, he's leaving the scene! He's leaving the scene of the accident," he shouted, storming toward the other man, pointing his finger like it was going to prevent Charlie from doing God knows what.

"I see that," Lizzie said, holding up her hands for calm. "Charlie, let's get this settled first. Were there any witnesses?"

Grumbling, he got back out, slamming his door. "No, there's no witnesses. I need to get to work, I was just here to talk to my wife."

"Thought she was your ex-wife," Ranger drawled, and Charlie flinched. He wrenched off his suit coat.

"You want to fight, Zane? I'll fight with you."

"No, no, no," Hillerman said, getting between them, pressing a hand to Charlie's chest. "No one's fighting. We'll ticket both of you. Ranger, yours is for speeding, and Charlie, yours is for a traffic collision with Zane's vehicle. Now both of you cool your heels, or we can add assault charges to that."

They continued to argue, and Hillerman tossed Lizzie the ticket book so he could stay between them. Good thing he'd come along; her shoulder couldn't have taken that kind of stress, trying to keep them apart. She used the hood of

Charlie's car to fill out the paperwork, then took statements and photographed the cars.

"You can pay at the station. Now both of you, go somewhere else and let people check out books in peace," Hillerman commanded, and grudgingly, both men obeyed. Lizzie breathed a sigh of relief.

"Welcome back, Deputy!" Hillerman joked, and Lizzie smiled, shaking her head.

"Yeah, right."

CHAPTER
THIRTY-THREE:
Chase

TODAY WAS THE DAY. Tansy and the other Mind Readers were coming back. They'd talked it over and decided that Chase should go back to his house. Gram did use her office, and even though he could sleep in Lottie's room, it felt like it was time. Kellan had encouraged him to try to make peace with his dad and his brother, both of whom he'd been ignoring for a while now. It would just be temporary: hopefully, he'd be in his own place soon. There was a place with some acreage that he'd found online and wanted Tansy to show him. But he was going to miss hanging around with Lizzie all the time.

"I'll miss you," he whispered, bumping her nose with his as he came in for a kiss.

Lizzie smiled. "You'll see me tomorrow." But he could see in her eyes that she felt sad, too. This had been an amazing few weeks. Things were going to change. *God, give me the Serenity to accept the things I cannot change . . .* it was inevitable. They'd weather it. He was almost sure.

"I'm taking you to Foster's Point. Be prepared."

Lizzie paled. "What? No."

"Yes. It'll be fun."

She sneered. "Not interested."

Chase shuffled closer, putting his fingertips on her elbows to draw her near. "I like kissing you on your couch," he said, "but I'd like to kiss you other places, too."

"Not. Interested," she repeated, even though her breath was speeding up. "Illegal."

"What if I find somewhere legal?"

She was just about to answer when the front door flew open.

"Lizzie Lou! I'm home!" Tansy called unnecessarily, and Pancake started barking his happy bark, the same one he gave the ball flinger. They hurried into the living room, and Lizzie held out her arms for a big hug. Chase's heart warmed as they both teared up at seeing each other again. He heard his girlfriend mutter something about 'not such a long trip next time,' and Tansy muttered something back about 'not breaking body parts next time.' They appeared to have forgotten all about him, which was great. His stuff was already in the car, and he'd already washed all his linens and their dishes, even though Lizzie had argued that he didn't have to. Chase tried to quietly open the front door, but Pancake's attention shift toward him, and both women turned.

"Where do you think you're going, young man?" Tansy asked, wiping her face, turning to open her arms to him. "I haven't even begun to thank you properly." Before he could protest, Chase found himself engulfed in Tansy's ardent embrace, rocking side to side as she hugged him. "You're our hero, you know that? An absolute hero. Thank you so much for taking care of my girl. You'll never know—" Her voice caught, but she swallowed the tears down. "You'll never know how much it meant to know that someone cared enough to come be with her. I thought I was going to have to turn around, to hand off my planning notebook to Hattie and bow out. You made it so I didn't. Thank you." Kellan's words about playing the white knight came back to him, and he felt troubled that they saw him that way and that it evoked such strong feelings in him.

Chase couldn't talk, so he just nodded and shrugged. *I love your granddaughter.* Yes, she'd been prickly and hard to handle sometimes . . . but love. It made it easier. He didn't think Lizzie was ready to hear that, even if it was true.

"I expect to see you here often; I have lots of gratitude treats to share with you from Europe." Chase did like the sound of that.

"Thank you, Tansy."

"Oh, please. Call me Gram."

That caused another surge of emotion; everything seemed to remind him of Carmen these days, even though he hadn't missed her or thought about her in so long. It didn't seem to matter. Something about being gathered into Lizzie's family had him teary, wishing things had been different in his own family. Wishing they were different now.

"And I'm going to take you out to see some houses this week, I've got some appointments already set up, including that one you sent me. It's a little older than you were thinking originally, but it may still be a good fit."

"Okay, that sounds great. I'll give you a call."

"If you don't have anywhere to be, I'd love it if you'd stay for dinner," Tansy said, her face sincere. "I haven't cooked in weeks."

"Oh, no," Lizzie said, "he's got a meeting with Hattie. But he'll be over tomorrow."

"Very well," Tansy said, looking mildly displeased. "But I'll hold you to that."

Chase laughed, then gave them both one more hug. Lizzie also got a kiss. And as he backed out, he saw Pancake watching him from the front windows, his paws up on the ledge. How had he gotten so tangled up with this little family? Glancing in his rearview mirror, he saw Lizzie's truck and suddenly remembered that prescription in the glovebox. He hadn't gotten rid of it. He'd planned to do it after she was asleep one night . . . but he'd been admittedly distracted most nights by those sweet lips. How the hell was he going to get it back now?

"I APOLOGIZE FOR MY low stocks," Hattie said, pouring Chase a cup of jasmine green tea. "But as you're well aware, I've been traveling."

"How was the trip?"

"No words, Chase," she said, sitting down in the wooden kitchen chair. All her furniture seemed to be handmade, and he loved the squirrels on the back of these chairs. It made sense that a woman who owned a paper company would love wood in all forms. "There are no words for the wonders that we saw. Things I've been wanting to see my whole life."

"That's awesome."

"I did get a chance to read the literature you sent me on the plane on the way home—it's an awfully long flight, you know—and the research is very interesting. I think we'll be up against some old thinking . . . if we did some community education before you propose the needle exchange, I think it may be better received. And it wouldn't hurt to have Lizzie present the law enforcement perspective as well, and perhaps the Horowitz boy could talk about the medical implications. I'll block you all off some time at the next town meeting." Despite not being on the town council, her attitude implied that wouldn't be a hardship.

"That would be great, Hattie. Thank you so much. I think this could be a great move for the community."

"I was curious about the other drug they mentioned, Nah . . . Nah . . ." She groped around for her glasses as she searched for a paper with the other hand.

"Naloxone?"

She snapped her fingers. "That's the one."

"They used that when I overdosed. Lizzie administered it." How she could claim she hadn't saved his life still baffled him. His current theory was that she just hated praise.

Hattie nodded slowly, still scanning the page. "I'd like to see more people trained in how to use that."

"Training is really important. There are some harmful myths surrounding that drug, in particular that it makes its recipient violent. If they use too much, it can lead to some aggressive tendencies, but it's very safe to use."

She looked him in the eye. "You're doing a good thing here, Chase. An important thing. I'm so glad you're bringing this to the town's attention. It'll mean more coming from you. I bet either of the Durand brothers would be interested in helping you out with that. Or even Evan. He might have more time for special projects." He squirmed a little in his seat; apparently, Lizzie was not the only one who hated praise.

"Kyle's on my Trivia team. I'll talk to him."

"Good. Be ready for some pointed questions." She looked at him over her glasses. "Some folks may not be as open-minded as I am."

"Okay. Right."

"Just get your research in order, and you'll be fine." She patted his hand. "The meeting's on Friday."

"I'll be there." He sipped the tea and enjoyed the way it warmed him all the way down. "And now I want to hear about the Louvre . . ."

"Ah, mon ami," she sighed, laughing. "Très belle."

CHAPTER THIRTY-FOUR:
Lizzie

CHASE'S THREAT TO TAKE her up to Foster's Point seemed to have come to nothing, because he just came over for dinner the next night and the night after. She had Monday off, so they agreed to meet at Riverside around ten, which was usually not a busy time during the week. It was a nice sunny morning, so she decided to walk. She wasn't back up to full strength, so she left Pancake at home, but she was getting closer to normal. She spied him sitting on the back deck, sunglasses on, hair nicely coiffed, dressed up like he was going to the office. *Well, it's nice that he put in effort for our date.*

"There you are," Lizzie grinned, plopping down in his lap. "You got a haircut." Before he could answer, she grabbed his face and pulled his lips against hers. It felt way too long since she'd kissed him, and she felt a sense of contentment at being close to him again . . . and yet. He tasted . . . weird? Sort of minty and ashy . . . was he smoking again? Lizzie felt him gently resisting her, putting his hands on her wrists, so she released him, confused. He pulled away from her, laughing a little.

"Christopher!"

Lizzie's head snapped toward the café's back door, and heat raced across her chest at what she saw. Chase stood in the doorway wearing his Duke hoodie and flip-flops and shorts, holding two cups, chest heaving, his eyes livid. *Christopher?* She scrambled off the strange man's lap, shaking, and Chase crossed the distance in two strides to gather her into his arms.

"She started it, I swear," the man who'd just had his tongue in her mouth smirked. "But I see why you'd blame me. I am the evil twin, after all." The minute he took off his sunglasses, she could see how different they looked, despite being identical. Chris's face was sharper, his skin better cared for, his hair shorter.

"Are you okay?" Chase asked her, his gaze searching, rubbing her back soothingly.

"I'm sorry," she whispered. "I didn't realize he wasn't . . . I thought he was . . ."

"Do not apologize, it's not your fault," he assured her, squeezing her tighter, and she breathed in the scent of Chase: bright lemongrass, chamomile, and sea salt.

"Yes, my resemblance to this clown is unfortunate," Christopher drawled, getting up out of the white Adirondack chair.

"This is *not* funny," Chase growled. "You should've corrected her right away, Chris."

"Hey, I did correct her. You never minded sharing before," he replied, his grin lascivious, and Chase's face turned bright red.

"That was then. I'm not the same person I was. It wasn't right to trick them like that. And if you ever touch Lizzie like that again, I'll—"

"You'll what?" Christopher asked, arms folded, leaning toward them. "Will you do an interpretative dance about how immoral I am? Or maybe you'll read me a condemnatory poem . . . maybe even one with a four-letter word? Nah, you don't talk like that anymore."

Fire flashed in Chase's gaze, but just as quickly, it died.

"I don't care what you think. I really don't. Be unhappy if you want to. But since you obviously care what *I* think, I'll just say this: I don't think you're a bad person, Chris. And I wish you'd stop letting my new lifestyle come between us. It's no condemnation. It's just that this lifestyle makes me feel like I don't have a bowling ball on my chest for the first time in years." He turned to Lizzie, and when she gazed into his blue eyes, so warm and tender, she didn't know how she'd ever mistaken one brother for the other, twins or not. "And Lizzie makes me happy. She's all mine. Go find your own happy, man."

"What I want," Christopher said slowly, pulling a pack of cigarettes out of his inside pocket, "is to not be here. Not even your magic girlfriend will able to help me with that." Christopher sheltered his cigarette as he lit it, and Lizzie could see the indecision on Chase's face as he watched the smoke curl around them.

"Shouldn't you be at work?" Chase asked.

"I'm meeting a client here, since this is what passes for a nice restaurant around here." He strolled back inside and went straight out the front door, leaving it open behind him. He didn't even bother to put out his cigarette, she noticed, and she was tempted to cite him.

"I'm sorry about him," Chase said, still staring after his twin. "He's . . ." He sighed. "I don't know what his deal is, actually. I used to. But since I got sober, he seems to feel like I'm judging him or something."

Lizzie didn't know what to say, so she just slipped an arm around his waist and rested her head against his shoulder. Seeing his hurt at being pushed away, however, felt like an indictment of her own behavior. Lottie's intentions in getting engaged had been good; she thought she was in love. It was wrong for Lizzie to go on ignoring her. Childish. And more than that, Lottie avoiding her meant she was also avoiding Gram by default. That wasn't fair. She needed to heal the rift between them.

"You should go find out."

Chase turned to see her face. "Really?"

"Yes. Quit letting him get away with stuff like that, storming off and being a jerk. Go find out what's eating at him."

Her boyfriend nodded slowly, his shoulders straightening. "Okay. You'll wait for me?"

"No, I've decided to run away with Trevor, my flirty nurse from the hospital. It's better this way."

Chase grinned and planted a kiss on her cheek. "You're the best, Lizzie Lou." As he trotted back inside, Lizzie pulled out her phone.

Lizzie: You coming up this weekend?

Lottie: Can't.

Lizzie: I want to talk to you.

Lottie: Well, this is a first . . .

Lizzie: Ignoring that. I was wrong to be judgy about your engagement.

Lottie: Engagement's off.

Really? That was a surprise. The whole thing had been a surprise, but she'd made such a huge deal about it.

Lizzie: I'm sorry.

Lottie: Let's not pretend.

Lizzie: Well, I am sorry that I hurt your feelings, and I'm sorry because I know this is what you wanted.

She paused just for a moment to think about what it would feel like to lose Chase, and it hurt to take in a breath even at the thought. *But we're in love. Germy had just been convenient.* Still, now she knew what it was like to have someone you wanted around. It wasn't better than being alone, but it was addictive. Lottie was probably lonely.

Lottie: Okay. I hear that.

Lizzie: Okay. And come home any time.

Lottie: Wouldn't want to interrupt your sleep-over with Chase . . .

Lizzie: He's back at his mom's now. He's looking for his own place.

Lottie: Oh, nice. Will you stay there?

Lizzie: No, I'm happy where I'm at. We're good. We both like our space sometimes.

It was something she'd been worried about in the back of her mind. What would it be like to live with Chase for real? Sharing grocery costs, negotiating who would take out the trash . . . all the daily things they hadn't had to do when he'd been there to serve her. It wasn't on the table, of course, but . . . the possibility was there, and it loomed. Then again, it hadn't been hard having him around when her ankle was busted. *Not hard at all . . .*

Lottie: I would've come. When you got hurt. If you'd called me, I would've dropped everything.

Lizzie: Yeah, I should've. I will next time.

Lottie: Next time? ::big emoji eyes::

Lizzie: You know what I meant.

Lottie: Yeah, I do. I gotta go. Thanks for the chat.

Lizzie: Okay. Love you.

Lottie: I love you, too.

It wasn't like her sister never said it, but it wasn't often. They were such different people . . . Gram said Lottie was more like their mom and she took after her dad. But they were family. Lizzie was getting a better handle on what that meant the longer she knew Chase, even if it meant cutting into their date time.

CHAPTER THIRTY-FIVE:
Chase

IT DIDN'T TAKE HIM long to catch up with his brother, who was walking back to his car.

"Hey!" He wanted to say worse, but other people were walking by, some of whom were still staring. *The price of being Timber Falls royalty.*

"All right, what is your problem?" Chase spit the words, and to his surprise, Christopher stopped. He stood motionless, back still turned to him.

"Yes, I should've told you myself about quitting, and I'm sorry for that. You shouldn't have found out through the grapevine, but come on, man. You've been ghosting me for months now. Every time I turn around, you're finding new and fun ways to express how much you don't care about me. So yeah, I didn't bother telling you."

Chris turned around. "Can you take this diatribe elsewhere, please? My client will be here any moment."

Chase shook his head slowly. "Your client can order himself a drink while we finish our conversation, especially since he's late." He crossed his arms, then let them drop again.

Don't get defensive. Just be honest. "I'm sorry if I let you down, but can't we get past this, this, whatever this is? Whatever I did, just tell me, and I'll try to make it right."

Christopher snorted then, looking away, and Chase stepped closer. Was he going to have to guess? *Fine, we can play that game.*

"Did I steal a girlfriend? Break something? Miss your birthday, what?" Twin jokes usually had Chris busting a gut. No reaction this time.

"It wasn't what you did," Christopher said, his voice low, and Chase strained to hear him over the passing traffic. "It's what I didn't do."

Hurt. It was laced in every word his twin said.

"What didn't you do?"

Christopher was looking past him toward the coffee shop windows; he turned to follow his brother's gaze, but caught just a flash of blonde hair as someone turned away from the window, so he knew it wasn't Lizzie. *Who was that?* Chris had lots of girls in Timber Falls and elsewhere, but none of them were serious. Or so he thought.

"I didn't stop you. I'd hear you pacing on the other side of the door at night, hear you outside at that stupid basketball hoop at all hours. The meds, it seemed like they were helping you calm down, helping you sleep. I thought they were okay, I didn't realize how hooked you were until . . ."

Chase wasn't a masochist. If he knew what moment Chris was thinking of, he wouldn't make him recount it, wouldn't make himself listen to the moment he'd broken his brother. He hadn't been there when he was arrested; what other moment could he mean?

"Until when?"

His gaze turned hard, skeptical, blue eyes flashing. "You really don't remember?"

Chase shook his head. "I'm sorry."

"I guess I shouldn't be surprised. You were high, really high. Kept telling me about all your plans for TFPP. You were still at the office at 2:00 a.m. I told you to go to bed and you just laughed. I've never felt so . . ." He swallowed hard. "I should've been here for you, I shouldn't have let Dad send me to New York. I should've stopped you before it got bad. But I didn't want you to write me off. I knew that if I told you the truth, you'd choose the drugs over me. I didn't know how to get you back, the real you. And now you *are* the real you, and I don't know you at all. I *lost* you, and I just let it happen."

Chase was squeezing the stuffing out of his brother before he could stop himself, right there on the sidewalk, probably wrinkling his brother's expensive suit. After an awkward moment, Chris's arms came around him, squeezing him back just as tight.

"You didn't lose me. I'm right here. You'll get to know me again, okay? You didn't do anything wrong."

"I did." Hearing Chris choke up almost made Chase cry, too. There was no shame in it, but he had more to say, and he didn't want tears to garble his words and make him unintelligible.

"No, you didn't, bro. I promise. I was sick. You're no doctor. You hear me? Not your fault. Probably wouldn't have listened to you anyway. Don't let this weigh on your conscience. I'm getting better now. And Carter was there for me.

So quit blaming yourself because I want my brother back, too."

Chris gave him a nod, and Chase gave him one more cobra squeeze before he let him go, wiping his eyes. Then, as easily as he'd dropped his guard, it was back up.

"My client's here. I'll see you at home."

"Yep." Chase waited until Christopher was inside with his client before he went around the back to rejoin Lizzie on the deck.

"How'd it go?" She'd claimed her iced tea, and he sat next to her on the long bench, where he could hold her hand.

"Not bad, actually. Marvelous by Carpenter standards." He lowered his voice to a whisper. "There were almost tears."

"Wow." She snuggled closer to him and watched the hummingbirds at the many feeders along the deck. "Do you want to look through my telescope?"

Chase gaped at her. "I'm sorry—your what?"

"My telescope. I thought maybe you'd want to look through it. With me."

He couldn't help but smile. "Is that a come-on, Elizabeth?"

She scowled. "What? No. Never mind." When she turned, it was obvious she was displeased; he tried hard to solemnize his face.

"Lizzie, I would love to . . ." Oh, it was hard. Even looking at her angry face. So hard. Maybe if he got it out fast. "Iwouldlovetolookthroughyour—" He started laughing again, and Lizzie huffed.

"I would love to look through your telescope," he whispered. "Thank you for inviting me."

"Offer rescinded."

"Noooo," he howled, tipping his head back like he was appealing to the heavens.

"You have a dirty mind, Chase Carpenter," she chided. But at least she wasn't frowning now.

"Please, Lizzie? Please? I'm sorry I made fun of you . . . but come on. You can hear how that sounded, right?"

"I suppose it did sound a little funny," she admitted. Chase's phone rang.

"It's Gram," he said, looking at Lizzie curiously.

She shrugged as she lifted her drink to her lips again. "Answer it."

"Hello?"

"Where are you? Are you busy? It's perfect, Chase. I mean, I don't want to tell you what to do, but it's everything you said you wanted, and it just went on the market today, and I think it's going to go quick. Can you come and see it now? I'll text you the address." Gram hung up.

Chase chuckled as he turned to Lizzie. "How do you feel about going to see a house?" When her eyes lit up, they hurried to his car. On the way over, Lizzie regaled him with fond memories of hanging around open houses with her grandmother on Sundays, and he listened and let himself be distracted from the worries that were crowding the joy of the moment. *What if it's perfect and I don't get it? What if I take too long to decide? What if I love it and Lizzie doesn't?*

But when he pulled up in front of the butter-yellow farmhouse, Lizzie's face was as excited as his. Good fencing all the way around the property, four bedrooms (one for an office, two for kids, one for them, Gram explained, getting way ahead of herself in ways Chase didn't even bother articulating). The kitchen was a little small, but it was cozy. The plumbing had been updated, and he liked the copper fixtures. And then he stepped out on the back porch, and what he saw took his breath away for a moment. Fifty feet from the house was an old barn, unfinished wood, but it had electricity to it.

"They've been using it as a woodshop," she said, pulling the sliding doors open, "but I saw . . ."

"Stables."

"Exactly. If in the future, you wanted to board animals, this would be an ideal space." He walked clear through to the other side and slid that door open to reveal a large pond behind the barn, apple and pear trees dotting the hillside, next to a pasture where horses could graze.

"How much?"

"It's at the top of your range, but it's doable. I can waive my fee."

Chase shook his head at her. "You will not. I'm paying you."

"That's fine," Gram said, nodding sagely, "then I'll just pay you for the home health services you rendered to my granddaughter on my behalf. One month, full-time."

Chase rolled his eyes. "Not at all the same, Gram." Lizzie came up next to him and squeezed his hand. "What do you think?"

"I love it," she confessed. "I can see you happy here. It's a happy place." *Just me, or you too?* His anxiety wouldn't let him ask, and he could see how much she loved it.

"Yeah." He leaned down and kissed her. "I'm gonna do it."

Lizzie squealed—actually squealed—and Chase cracked up.

CHAPTER THIRTY-SIX:
Chase

THEY ALL WENT BACK to Tansy and Lizzie's house, and he spent a while with Gram going over the paperwork. After dinner, they watched *Jeopardy!*. Chase didn't know any of the answers, but he didn't care. Then at 10:00, when he thought Lizzie was going to shoo him home, she disappeared upstairs and came down with a shiny red telescope.

"It's finally clear enough to use this. Come on. Grab that stuff."

When they got to the end of the street, Pancake took off into the meadow.

"It's above the horizon," she said, breathless from the reckless way they were barreling through the grass, long now with summer.

"What is?" Chase asked, trying to keep up.

"Hang on." Getting out her phone, she directed the lens exactly where she wanted it. "Look." She pointed to the eyepiece. "Just look."

Chase bent obediently and looked. A sense of awe filled him; his soul got quiet. He stared through the telescope at what looked like a giant flashlight in the sky. "Lizzie, what is that?"

"That's a comet," she said, her voice filled with as much awe as he felt. "It was unexpected, we didn't know it was coming. But it won't pass this way again for a long time."

He stood up, trying to find it in the night sky.

She pointed. "It's just there, below Ursa Major."

"Below what?"

"The big dipper," she said impatiently, as if the Latin names of constellations were common knowledge. It sat nestled just above the tree line like it was trying to gently touch the hill, and he squinted at it for another moment before going back to the telescope. The idea that he was looking at a huge chunk of rock and ice careening through the galaxy thrilled him. Wait, what were comets made of, anyway? Maybe he should get a book or something. Stream a documentary. This was obviously important to her.

"I remember seeing a comet go by as a kid," he said, still looking through the telescope. "Is this the same one?"

"No, that was probably Hale-Bopp . . ."

"Yes!" He cried, snapping upward. "It *was* Hale-Bopp, and I remember because every time my brothers said that name, we'd punch each other in the arm."

Lizzie wove her arm through his, pulling their sides together. "Boys are weird."

"You know it. I want to say I'd never let my kids act like that, but . . . they'd probably just do it when I wasn't looking, wouldn't they?"

"I don't know." She was quiet for a minute, and then she let her head tip over to rest on his shoulder, and Chase's heart swelled. The kind of peace that settled over him when she was around was so hard to describe. He tried to turn his head to see her better, and she looked up. "You're not looking at the stars."

"Neither are you." She was giving him her full green gaze, that vivid sage that he'd never get tired of looking at. He just let himself look at her in the dark. Chase turned to face her more fully, putting his hands on her hips, unsure of what they were doing, just knowing that he wanted more of her. Out of the corner of his eye, he could see Pancake still sniffing around in the grass closer to the river.

"If you come back tomorrow, you can see the ISS," Lizzie whispered, and he leaned forward instinctively. Every time she showed how intelligent she was, he just wanted to kiss the heck out of her. He just stared at her instead, nodding slowly.

"I can do that." He paused. "What's the ISS?"

Her smile was forgiving. "The International Space Station."

He shuffled closer to her. "Would I get to look through your telescope again?"

She caught the teasing this time and rolled her eyes. "No," she whispered, "you can see it with the naked eye."

"Lizzie," he said, and he didn't even know what he was trying to ask. He just felt like a burning ball of forces more powerful than any star, a tumultuous need to kiss her overtaking his senses, slowly wrecking the inside of him. But he needed to say this more.

"Yes?" she asked, her eyes wide.

"I love you."

Her answering smile had him feeling like he too was glittering in the dark, something marvelous that any passerby would stop to stare at.

"I love you, too."

"You do?"

"Of course, goofball."

"Well," he said, trying to get a hold of himself, "that's good. I'll definitely be back to see that USS thing."

"ISS," she corrected, grinning, still staring up at him.

"Do you work tomorrow?" He just didn't want to keep her up too late.

"I don't want to talk about work," she whispered.

"Show me more stars," he whispered. "Where's the north star?"

"It's in the little dipper," she said, pivoting to point to it for him. "Do you want it through the telescope again?" His plan hadn't been as smart as he thought; he'd redirected her to the sky because 1. It was fascinating. 2. She thought it was fascinating. But it was distracting her from "I love you, too" kissing, and he wanted that.

"Here," he said, unfolding the fluffy quilt with interlocking circles. "I'm getting a crick in my neck." Chase plopped himself down, spreading his long legs into the grass, patting the spot next to him. She sat down next to him, but she glanced around before she did it. The grass was tall enough that no one could see them . . . what was she worried about? Appearances? Proximity? They were shoulder to shoulder now, and she scooted close enough that his arm was right up against her.

"It's more private than Foster's Point," he teased, and she elbowed him in the belly. "Where's the little dipper?" Chase looked back up at the sky, but he put his fingers over hers on the quilt.

She put her head close to his and pointed so he could follow her finger with his gaze. "There. The north star is called Polaris."

"Mmm." A breeze ruffled the grass, and Chase felt his soul stir with it. His body felt heavy against the ground, and he wanted to lie down. He felt pulled toward the earth by a force greater than gravity. *Distraction.* "Does the little dipper have a real name, too? Like Ursula Major? Is that what the villain in *The Little Mermaid* is named for?"

Lizzie snorted. "Believe it or not, it isn't. *Ursa,* not Ursula. Ursa means 'bear.' And the little dipper is called Ursa Minor. It was first cataloged by Ptolemy in the second century."

"Wow," he whispered, putting a hand behind his head to scratch his head in wonder, "that makes me feel small."

He gave in to the force of the moment, flopping onto his back and propping his arm under his head. Apparently, she thought the move was an invitation, because she followed suit and let her head rest on his shoulder. Chase blinked down at her. She hadn't tangled their legs. She wasn't stroking his chest. The innocence of her touched him; she didn't seem to have an agenda beyond being closer. He settled his arm around her shoulder, combing his fingers through her hair for a moment to test her reaction. She snuggled in deeper, letting her arm fall across his belly with a deep sigh that seemed to spread to the farthest tip of her body as he felt her wholly relax against him. *Snugglebug. A snuggle-bug who loves me, too.*

"It doesn't make me feel small," she said softly, and he tried to remember what they'd been talking about. *Oh, right. Taller-Me.* "It just makes me feel like I'm part of something. Think how many people have looked up at these stars for thousands of years."

"Longer maybe."

"It connects me to them," she said, her conviction almost tangible. "It makes me feel less alone."

"You're not alone."

"Not anymore," she agreed, squeezing him. They kissed quietly, him caressing her arms, the early summer evening singing around them, insects buzzing, and Chase drank in the peace of the moment. Just as his lips were actually starting to get tired, she pulled back and put her head on his shoulder again, yawning.

"You awake?"

"Mmm-hmm," she said. "See if you can find Venus. It's bright tonight."

He squinted up at the sky above them, but it was so full of stars, it was hard to even find the constellations he knew. The deep dark felt calming, pinpricked with beautiful light. It made him want to write about it. "Where's Orion? That's that hunter guy, right?"

"Wrong season," Lizzie murmured. "Wrong hemisphere."

"Oh. That's not him?" he said, pointing up to their left. "Lizzie?"

She was asleep. He felt it without being able to see her face; the even breathing of her, the light snore that was more adorable than annoying, the heaviness of how her curves fell against him, molding to him. Chase curled his other arm around her and held her, pressing a light kiss to the top of her copper-colored hair, just treasuring her trust for a moment. *Maybe that's why I liked those copper bathroom fixtures so much.* He'd wake her up in a few minutes . . . as soon as he'd gotten his fill of snuggles under a summer sky. The moon was just a tiny sliver, hanging there in the infinite black like a nightlight. He stared at it, his eyelids heavy. He'd get her safely to bed soon. Really soon.

CHAPTER THIRTY-SEVEN:
Lizzie

WHEN LIZZIE WOKE UP the next morning, she was lying on top of Chase and under a second quilt. She tried to gently push away from him, but even still asleep, his arms tightened around her. *Well, this is quite the pickle.* And how in the world had he gotten them a blanket when she was crushing him? Maybe she'd rolled to her back, and he'd gotten it then? How they'd gotten covered up was not her most pressing issue at the moment; that issue was her bladder, and undoubtedly, her dog's growling stomach. Where was Pancake, anyway? She tried to gently extricate herself, but Chase's subconscious would have none of it. His arms tightened around her, and he muttered, "No, stay . . ."

"Chase," she whispered. "You have to let go." He smacked his lips and rolled, taking her with him, trapping her even more firmly under him.

She stared up at his face; he needed a shave. She liked all the various shades of blond and brown in his light beard. It reminded her of when she'd arrested him; she'd watched him so carefully that day, trying to make sure he was okay.

So worried. Terrified that she hadn't administered the naloxone correctly; she should've waited for RJ, but she'd panicked. His pupils had been so tiny, his skin so clammy and his breathing shallow. Today, he looked like a different man; he'd gained weight, for one thing. If she was honest with herself, she thought the pudge around his middle was pretty cute. He was so soft and squeezable, so cozy. Lizzie tried to rub his back, to wake him up gently, but it was no use. Desperate measures were going to be necessary.

"Chase," she said at a normal volume this time, and he startled awake. His gray-blue gaze landed on her. For a moment, he just kept holding her, staring at her, as if he was trying to figure out how they got here. Then he smiled that grin she loved, the one that was pure delight at just seeing her face. The one that looked like he hadn't seen her for days or weeks instead of hours.

"Hi."

"Hi," she said, happiness flooding her like adrenaline. "I have to get up."

"Oh, right," he said, giving her one more squeeze before he let go, and she missed the warmth of him immediately, now that she could feel the morning dew in the air. But Chase was still smiling at her, propped on one elbow, and she couldn't bring herself to care how she looked. She got to her feet, trying to dust off the strangeness of the night as she brushed her hands over her damp clothes. She wanted to flop right back down next to him, but duty called. Instead, her shoulder now fully healed, she offered him a hand up, and he gratefully accepted it, clearing his throat and ruffling his hair so it flopped into his eyes. And those eyes were turning unhappy . . . she didn't know if it was anxiety over the fact that he'd kept her out all night or that he'd have to go home now with this mild awkwardness hanging in the air. Her stomach growled, having been deprived of its late-night snacks the previous evening.

"Where's the dog?"

"He must've gone home and gotten Gram, who then covered us with a quilt."

"A regular Lassie, that one. Breakfast?"

"Yes. And I'll cook."

"That's not necessary," she said, gathering up the quilts. "You're not here to take care of me anymore."

"See, that's where you're wrong," he whispered, leaning close to give her a scratchy peck on the cheek. "Eggs and bacon, coming up." He took a quilt from her, lacing their hands together as he led the way back toward the house. "Watch for gopher holes."

"I will."

"Because if you break your other ankle, I can't move in with you this time. Gram has first dibs on the home health care duties." Lizzie shuddered, and Chase laughed. "I thought you might feel that way."

WORKING WEEKENDS AT the station was a crapshoot as far as activity; it was either too much or not enough. Today was a "not enough" day, and Lizzie breathed in the scent of stale coffee, grease, and the strong-smelling gun cleaner as she took apart her service weapon on the cloth, then sighed. The phone rang.

"Linn County Sheriff's office, Sue speak—okay. Yes. We will get someone out there right now." Sue was gesturing frantically at Lizzie, and she quickly reassembled her firearm and holstered it. She wrote down *Highway 22, near Fisherman's Bend Recreation Area.* That was close by.

"What is it?" Lizzie mouthed, and Sue covered the phone receiver.

"Car accident." Just that one word had her gut sinking. Everyone else was out. It was just her. Sue turned back to the caller. "Yes, we'll send EMS. Please stay on the line." She covered the receiver again. "Do you want me to call in the captain? Or Lieutenant Wright?" Did she want either of those men to know that she couldn't handle it? Absolutely not.

She shook her head no, then grabbed her keys from her desk and headed out to the truck. She could see the smoke from down 22, and it just added to the mild panic she was holding at bay. A fire at this time of year could spark the whole forest. Lizzie cranked down the window to try to get some fresh air; she felt like her breath was already coming too quickly. It blew wild strands of red out of her bun, streaking across her face, irritating her more. The drive felt long; this far out from Timber Falls, there wasn't a lot of traffic, which meant she didn't need her lights and siren. When she pulled up, RJ and Vince already had one person out of their vehicle on a stretcher, shining a light into her eyes. Blood. It was on her temple, in her blonde hair, and her eyes were closed. There was someone else still in the vehicle, just a dark shadow from that distance. He wasn't moving.

"Lizzie?" RJ frowned. "They just sent you?" Were her deficiencies that well-known? She turned away from the scene. *Focus. Let the paramedics work. Create a space.* Lizzie went back to the truck, hands shaking. She opened the passenger door, hit her four-way flashers, and reaches under the seat for her road flares. But she came up empty. Frustrated, she opened the glove box. An orange pill bottle tumbled forward, and she caught it in her hand. A pill bottle with her name on it. Her eyes widened as she realized the only person who could've filled this prescription. She cursed. She cursed the innocent pharmacist who'd filled it for him. She cursed Kyle for writing it. And most of all, she cursed herself for not realizing he'd been lying to her all this time. At that moment, it was the only explanation her mind would accept.

Did she know him at all? Had it just been a ruse? That frightened her, the idea that all their sweet moments and long talks and shared meals had just been a fabrication. That she'd been an easy mark in a scheme to get revenge or get high. And yet . . . her heart knew that wasn't true. It couldn't be. It had felt too real. He couldn't have known she'd hurt herself when he started writing to her. She needed to talk to him.

> **Lizzie:** I'm sending you a location. Get down here.
> **Chase:** I'm having dinner with my brothers in Salem.
> **Lizzie:** Now.

Chase: Is something wrong?
Lizzie: Yes.

Salem. That's where he'd filled it, too, undoubtedly so he wouldn't get caught by the pharmacist at Santiam, who would know better than to put codeine in his hands. She put her phone down on the seat and pressed her hands into the old tan vinyl, arms shaking. Then she whirled and stumbled to the bushes. It didn't take long to empty her stomach, and once she did, it was easier to focus on the task at hand. *Set a perimeter. Take pictures before it gets dark.* She didn't start crying until they pulled out the passenger.

"They're going to be okay, Lizzie," RJ said, watching her with concern.

"Okay," she said numbly, wrapping her arms around herself, rocking without meaning to. She sat down on the shoulder and buried her head in her arms, unable to watch anymore. Lizzie wanted to stop thinking about that pill bottle, about Chase, about what it all meant, but she couldn't. This was a clear violation of his deal with the judge. Even from an NA standpoint, buying it never should've happened. She told herself that she'd asked him to come here just to talk, but she knew it wasn't true. Even given this somewhat circumstantial evidence, she had to arrest him. If Captain Hansen found out she hadn't investigated, she'd be fired.

"We've got this in hand, Deputy," Vince said, putting a gloved hand on her back, and she shied away from his touch. "You can go home." The gravel was jabbing into her backside. The cold wrapped its arms around her as the sun went down.

The tow truck came and took one of the cars away. Finally, Chase arrived.

Eyes wide, he climbed out of his SUV, running over to her, Carter right behind him.

"Are you all right? What happened?" He knelt next to her, wiping the tears from her undoubtedly dirty face. "Lizzie, are you hurt? Answer me, please."

She shook her head.

"Put your hands on the hood of the truck," she said, her voice wavering. Chase and Carter shared a confused look.

He looked back at her.

"What?"

She turned him toward the truck by his elbow as she took out her handcuffs. "Do it."

Watching her warily over his shoulder, Chase did as he was told. "What's this about?"

"Chase Carpenter, you are under arrest for possession of a controlled substance in violation of your parole." Lizzie wished she'd looked away from his face so she didn't have to witness the moment when he knew he was caught. When it clicked into place for him he'd screwed up so badly and thoroughly that there might not be any coming back from it where her trust was concerned, just as the handcuffs clicked shut. She spread his legs with her knee, being careful not to hurt him. There was enough hurt happening right now as it was. Carter stood back and said nothing.

"This is a *mistake*," he said, his voice pitched lower. "A misunderstanding."

"You have the right to remain silent," she went on, her voice shaking. "Anything you say can and will be held against you in a court of law . . ." She cursed internally. *I cannot do this. I cannot.* But if he was using again, it was better that he get caught. Sweeping it under the rug wasn't doing him any favors. At least there were no bystanders to this tragedy besides his brother, no one inclined to whisper about the shattering of her heart and the damage to his reputation.

"Yes, I filled your prescription, but it was for you. I didn't touch it, I swear I didn't. This isn't what it looks like . . ."

"Yeah," she muttered, ignoring the new tears that dropped onto her cheek, "it never is." She was used to people's protests by now, the constant excuses no matter what the evidence against them. Everyone in jail was innocent.

"Deputy, you can arrest me, but you're gonna have to listen to me eventually. Because if I only get one phone call, it's you, babe."

"You have the right to an attorney," she said, her volume rising, trying to force the words out. "If you cannot afford one, one will be appointed to you." She wiped frantically at her face; the tears kept coming. And she resented every one, because she'd trusted him so completely, believed him when he said he was sober. If he wasn't, what did that mean for them? And what if she was wrong? Would he still want her after this? Because she was hurting him now, too. She had no choice.

"Lizzie." She knew that tone. He wanted to hold her. He wanted to make it better. It took her from a broken thing to something recast in iron in a split second. Because if she leaned into that tender tone, she'd fall apart entirely.

"Save your sympathy for yourself," she snapped. "Because if you've been doing drugs in my town again, you're gonna need it all." She knelt to pat down his legs for weapons, and it wasn't difficult to keep it professional.

"I haven't," he whispered. "I swear it, Elizabeth. Give me a drug test. Let me prove it to you."

"Stop talking!" she shouted. "Just stop talking."

"Lizzie," he pleaded, and she shot him a withering look that finally silenced him. She turned to his brother, who had one hand in his hair, his eyes glassy and sad. There was too much happening there for her to process, so she turned back to Chase. "You'll submit to a voluntary drug test?"

"Yes." His voice was meek, and she hated it. But she still couldn't hate him, and that was the worst part.

"Fine. Let's go to Santiam and do it now."

"Can I come, too?" Carter asked quietly, and Lizzie nodded.

"You want to ride with us?"

"No, I'll follow in his car." Lizzie would've appreciated having him there as a buffer, but it would be better to have his car somewhere safe rather than out here in the middle of nowhere.

She helped Chase into the back seat, leaning over his lap to buckle his seatbelt for him.

"Will you do one thing for me?" His question was humble, broken. It was dangerous, being this close to him, and she felt her lower lip start to tremble again. He looked rough; his eyes were red-rimmed, pleading and scared, and she couldn't tell him to be quiet again.

"What?"

"Will you count the pills? They're all there. Just count them."

"Fine."

She shut his door with a definitive slam. He didn't try to talk to her again after that. If she were in his place, she wouldn't try to push her luck, either. She was clearly a hot mess; one glance at her own eyes in the rearview mirror, bloodshot and smudged, confirmed that. She touched her mom's ring on the delicate chain around her neck as she drove; the sad was sinking down into her soul. Whether he'd used them or not, he'd filled them. He'd crossed a line.

CHAPTER THIRTY-EIGHT:
Chase

THE THREE OF THEM SAT together in the waiting room at the hospital for the lab technician to call his name. Chase slowly massaged the skin on the inside of his wrists where the cold handcuffs had touched him, trying to think his way out of this. It was nice of her to take them off before they came inside; he was clinging to that shred of hope with every scrap of dignity he had. The test would be negative, he knew that. But on either side of him were two of only a handful of people he loved in the world, and neither of them had the same confidence. Even he had to admit, it looked bad. It was bad. Based on their stoic faces on the verge of crying, these two didn't want to talk to him, so he pulled out his phone.

Chase: I messed up.

Gretta: How bad?

Chase: Pretty bad.

Gretta: Details, Chase.

Chase: I bought codeine. But I didn't use it.

Gretta: That's a big one, all right. Legally?

Chase: It was my girlfriend's prescription. I bought it for her.

Chase: She'd sprained her ankle.

Chase: I don't know what to do now.

Gretta: You in jail?

Chase: Not yet. My girlfriend arrested me.

Gretta: You're dating the cop AND you used her prescription?

Gretta: This is a new one.

Chase: I am so stupid.

Gretta: Hang on now. Don't go there.

Gretta: You did some things right, as mistakes go.

Gretta: 1. You didn't buy it on the street.

Gretta: 2. You didn't use it.

Gretta: 3. You're reaching out for help now.

Gretta: So no more "stupid" talk. We can repair this.

Gretta: Are they doing a test?

Chase: Waiting for it now.

Gretta: Okay, good. When it comes back negative, you're in the clear legally.

Gretta: Fixing the trust in your relationship will be tougher, but I have faith in you.

Gretta: You're a goodhearted person, Chase.

Chase: Thank you, Gretta.

Gretta: Text your sponsor. He may have some advice, too.

Gretta: I'm headed to bed. Update me tomorrow?

Chase: Yes, I will.

If by 'advice' she meant lots of angry words, Chase had no doubt that would be true.

"Chase Carpenter?" The lady with the clipboard smiled at him despite the late hour. "Come on back." He shuffled after her, still feeling chained inside.

"How's your day going?" the woman asked brightly.

"Bad. Really, really bad. How about you?"

She looked taken aback. "I'm sorry to hear that. My day's going well, thanks." She handed him the plastic cup and explained how to pee in it. It was pretty straightforward. He completed the assignment and put the half-full cup on the paper towel in the bathroom. "It'll be about twenty-four hours," she said, and he nodded his thanks. When Chase came back to the waiting room, both Carter and Lizzie had lost their battle with tears, their faces red and blotchy. He opened his arms, and they both came in for a group hug. He held them, knowing that they cried because they loved him, feeling so damn sorry for what he'd put them through. The guilt hung around his neck like a millstone.

"You scared the hell out of me," Lizzie whispered, and Carter nodded in what Chase could only assume was agreement.

"Did you count them?"

"Yes."

"And were they all there?"

"Yes, and that's the only reason you're not sleeping in the holding cell at the station tonight." Lizzie let go and stepped back, wiping under her eyes. "Go home." Then she turned and walked out, not looking back.

"Carter . . ." Chase started hesitantly, but his brother held up a hand. He walked out, too, and since it was his car they'd taken, Chase figured it was okay to follow him. But even then, he wasn't sure. He felt like he was picking his way through broken glass, unsure which move was going to cut him next. He stayed silent until they got into the car. Then he turned to him. He opened his arms just in time for another hug, and Carter sobbed into his shoulder. When he calmed down a little, Carter smacked him in the arm.

"What the hell were you thinking?"

"I don't know."

"I can't watch you go through that again."

"I know. You won't."

"Sure didn't seem like it tonight. Seemed like I was right there all over again, watching you get loaded into the sheriff's cruiser."

"I'm sorry."

Carter cursed as he swiped at his face. "Can we please go home?"

"Sure. Right. Sorry. It seemed like we were having a moment."

Carter chuckled a little, but it was obvious he resented it. "You better start figuring out your groveling. She is pissed. Martina, too."

"Pretty sure I'll have all night to work on it." As tired as he was, he thought the likelihood of sleep was low.

THE NEXT MORNING, HE got a text from Lizzie.

Lizzie: Drug test was negative.

Lizzie: But that only proves you didn't use within the last two days.

Chase: I haven't used. I promise.

Lizzie: Why did you even have them? I didn't need them.

Chase: Kyle gave me the option when your shoulder was hurting. I wanted them nearby in case you needed them in the night.

Lizzie: And why didn't you get rid of them later on?

Chase: I couldn't figure out how without admitting what I'd done.

Lizzie: I'm so mad at you, I can hardly type.

Chase: I deserve that.

Lizzie: Stop saying the nice things! I'm going to be mad for a long time. Loooonnnggg time.

Chase: That's fair.

Lizzie: UGH.

He didn't get anything else from her that day. Or the day after. On Monday, he sent her flowers—roses, and not the cheap grocery store kind. Red. Long-stemmed. From a florist. Nothing. On Tuesday, he bought her favorite snacks and left them on her doorstep while she was at work. Pancake nearly gave himself an aneurysm, barking at him frantically through the window, trying to figure out how to get through the horrid glass that was keeping him from his third-favorite person. Nothing. On Wednesday, he got smart and sent her a letter.

> *Dear Lizzie,*
>
> *I really thought I was doing it for you. I wasn't trying to lie to you or trick you. I promise I wasn't. I know it looked that way, though. I get that. I'm sure it was a shock to find that in your truck. All I can say is I'm sorry.*
>
> *I hope you can forgive me.*
>
> *Love,*
>
> *Chase*
>
> *P.S. Are you still coming to the town meeting on Friday to speak with me? Even if you're mad at me, this is more important. Please.*

Wednesday night, he got a text.

Lizzie: Will probably forgive you eventually, but I'm not there yet.
Lizzie: I will be there on Friday.
Chase: Thanks, babe.

THE MEETING WAS ABOUT average attendance. Kyle and his wife Ainsley were there, as were Hattie and all the Mind Readers. Carter and Martina came, too, though Martina made it clear that he was not out of the doghouse with her yet. Doghouse or not, he'd close on his new house tomorrow. And he had two housesitting clients, much to Maggie's relief. RJ and Vince came and sat with him in the front row, and he gave them a firm handshake with his profuse thanks. They'd speak after Lizzie, but before him. He was last. It was the worst thing for his anxiety, but the best thing for the emotional punch of the presentation.

She sat on the other side of the aisle from him, also in the front row, but she hadn't so much as glanced at him since she walked in. *I guess what they say about a woman scorned is true.* And it couldn't have been easy to find those pills right at the moment she was trying to save her promotion and failing miserably. When she got up to speak, though, he noticed she was wearing the blue nail polish on her fingernails, and she'd braided her hair again. Chairman Park was introducing her, everyone was clapping, and all he could see was her fingernails.

"I'm Deputy Lizzie Painter, as you all know." She touched her forehead, rubbing it with two fingers. "I guess he already said that." Man, was she nervous. He gave her a little thumbs up and a wink. She straightened, taking a deep breath. "I've been watching this community fail to stem the opioid crisis for years now. And I'm tired of doing nothing but sitting and watching." He couldn't tell if anyone was nodding along, but whatever she saw behind him seemed to encourage her, and by the end, she spoke with such impassioned dignity, he wanted to jump up and applaud. But he didn't. But maybe later he would, in private. Once she wasn't mad at him.

His part went fine; he didn't share the gory details of his substance use disorder, and he was sure there were a few disappointed listeners. But he did share how it affected the people who loved him, and the people he loved.

"I found out recently that my biological mother passed away from substance abuse related causes; some of you knew Carmen." Heads bobbed somberly. "There are things this community could do to prevent those deaths. There are things we can do to help people like me who are struggling with a medical problem that's not allowing us to find peace in this world. I hope you'll join me in advocating for those things." Light applause. Well, that was good. He hadn't expected a standing ovation. But it was something.

He caught Lizzie in the parking lot, just as she was getting into her truck. "Thanks for coming tonight."

Lizzie said nothing, her hand still on the handle of the driver's side door.

"Still giving me the cold shoulder, I see."

She spun to face him. "Believe it or not, yes, I am still pissed at you. I'm pissed that you would endanger your recovery for me. I don't want or need that. I could've called Maggie or Martina or someone else to pick up my prescription if I needed it. If you're going to be a damn fool, leave me out of it, and don't you dare lie to yourself and claim that this was for my benefit."

"It's not a lie. It *was* for you. It was destroying me to see you in pain like that."

"Pain's part of life, Chase! If I wanted relief, that's a problem that I could solve for myself."

"If you weren't so damn proud, I might actually believe that. But as it is, you leave me guessing about what you need, because you're terrified to depend on anyone!" *Not better. You are not making this better. Shut up, shut up, shut up.*

Lizzie shoved him with both hands, and he went stumbling backward before he caught himself. "Don't you dare make this about me! *You* got those pills. *You* hid them from me. *You*—"

He paced forward again. "First of all, please stay calm and do not shove me. I was not hiding them, I was—"

"Don't interrupt me!" Lizzie bellowed, fists balled at her sides, face red. Chase winced. "You deliberately made the worst decision possible."

"I could've handled it. I *did* handle it. And if anyone had asked me about it, I would've told them the truth."

"That's not the point. The point is that you can't love me more than you love yourself. Not right now. Not at this stage in your recovery. And the very fact that you'd put yourself in that position for my sake—"

"I was trying to take care of you!" He pointed at her. "And you're the one who arrested me, when you could've just listened to my explanation. What do you think that does to people's perception of my recovery? You think I haven't been an object of pity since the moment those cuffs went on?"

"I was doing my job!"

"Which one—preventing Chase's inevitable relapse, or the one you get paid for?"

She flinched like he'd slapped her. Her chest was heaving with anger, but her voice was low.

"I never treated you like a relapse was inevitable, Chase Robert Carpenter, and you know it."

That was the hardest part; he did know it. She'd believed in him so hard, worked so hard to help him, been willing to suffer for him. He just hadn't been willing to let her. Into his silence, she spoke.

"I think we should take a break."

Chase ran a hand through his hair. "You're right, let's go for a walk. We don't have to talk about this right—"

"No, Chase. A break from us. This isn't healthy for you."

It should have been the biggest compliment she could've paid him. She was pushing him away because she valued his recovery more than her own happiness. He hadn't wanted her to be in pain; well, her pain right now was blinding, splintering, heart-shattering. And he'd caused it.

"Okay." His voice cracked, and tears were burning behind his eyes. It didn't help when she approached him slowly, putting her arms around his neck, drawing him close to her, her lips at his ear.

"Figure out what happened. Then come back. I love you." She kissed his cheek tenderly. He couldn't squeeze his eyes tight enough to keep the tears in, and he crushed her into a hug.

"I love you, too," he choked out, burying his face in her shoulder. "I love you, Lizzie."

"Write to me," she whispered, and he nodded. "Real letters, not emails. I need a piece of you while you're gone."

"I will. I promise."

"You'd better."

"I will."

She released him then, wiping her face, and he shuffled back, trying not to count the lasts he'd just had with her: last time to hold her, the last time he'd feel her soft lips against his cheek, the last time he'd breathe in her lemon scent. *Not forever. Just for a while. Just a break,* he told himself sternly, but his anxiety and his heart were having none of it. They were breaking lamps, throwing books, going full tantrum at being separated from her indefinitely, and he couldn't do anything to stop them.

"I'll see you," he said, more as an act of hope than an actual fact.

"Yup." She was still crying, silent tears flowing down her speckled cheeks. He turned toward his car without saying goodbye. Goodbye would feel like an end. And he was determined to make this . . . this *detour* as temporary as possible.

CHAPTER THIRTY-NINE:
Chase

CHASE DROVE TO THE church early the next morning. Kellan wanted to meet at his office. He'd been out of town when everything went down, but now he was back. He never wanted to meet at his office. Was he going to yell? Did he just not want to expose Chase to any more public scrutiny? Was he about to lose his sponsor? Where would he find another one? The questions in his head were coming too rapidly to even consider the horror of each one individually; it was just a giant lump of collective fear. He tried not to throw up as he pulled into the parking lot.

The receptionist wasn't in yet, but the front doors were open, so Chase let himself in. Kellan's office was down a long hall, and Chase felt worse and worse with every step he took. Words like *worthless* and *screw-up* and *addict* bobbed around in his head like ducks, taking turns diving into his soul to nip at him. The door was open, and Kellan was bent over a leather notebook, writing. Chase hesitated. Should he knock? Come back? They had an appointment, but he looked busy, maybe he'd just try again la—

"You coming in or are you going to talk from the doorway?" Kellan asked without lifting his head. Rescheduling, it seemed, was not an option.

Chase slinked into the office and tried to sit on the couch as unobtrusively as possible for someone his size. *What am I doing? There's nowhere to hide.*

His sponsor cleared his throat, and Chase jumped. He was sweating.

"Are you going to try to bullshit me? Because I really hate that."

"No." Chase swallowed hard, squeezing his fingers. "I screwed up."

"You can say that again." Kellan's gaze was hard, but his voice was quiet. He sat back in his rolling chair, arms folded over his chest, just staring. Chase knew he wasn't trying to make him uncomfortable, but maybe the yelling would've been better than this silent disappointment.

Chase opened his mouth and the whole story poured out: Lizzie's shoulder was messed up, she was in pain, he wanted to be prepared to help her. He'd lied to himself about the codeine being necessary, even though he hadn't used it. He'd lied to Kellan and Lizzie and the whole NA group by not confessing what he'd done. It had felt so impossible then; knowing they were going to be so mad at him and so upset and so hurt and so concerned, he just . . . couldn't come clean. His anxiety had forbidden it. He'd been so sure he could just fix it, get rid of it, and they'd never have to know.

Kellan was quiet through the telling, and Chase was afraid to look at him. Afraid he'd lost his friendship and his trust, afraid he'd see scorn and disdain on the face of this man he respected so much.

"What's the third step?"

"We made a decision to turn our will and our lives over to the care of God as we understood Him," Chase quoted from memory.

"Only you didn't, did you? You took matters into your own hands." He heard the chair squeak as Kellan leaned forward. "That's the problem here. Not that you cared about your girlfriend, but that you didn't trust God or anyone else to take care of her."

Chase looked out the window. He hadn't thought of it like that, but it was kind of true.

"You cannot put yourself in that position again, Chase. It might not end so well. And worst of all, it's sliding back into the old control issues that got you here in the first place; that's the real danger here."

"I know." If his head hung any lower, his chin was going to touch his chest. His lower lip was trembling uncontrollably. "I know it's useless now, but I really am sorry. And it's all for nothing because I might have lost her anyway. . ."

"You two broke up?"

"I don't know. She said we should take a break until I'm back on track."

"Huh."

Chase hazarded a look at his sponsor. "What's that mean?"

"I just didn't expect that. It's good, actually." *Good?* He had the audacity to label this burning pain in his chest as *good?*

"It hurts like hell," Chase blurted out angrily. "I need her. Nothing feels right without her. She's the only person I want to be with."

"I'll try not to take that personally," Kellan quipped, but Chase couldn't laugh. "You don't resent her for arresting you?"

Chase shifted uncomfortably. "She was just doing her job."

"Not what I asked." He tapped his journal with the pen still in his hand. "Do an inventory. Tonight. Because if someone who I thought trusted me had arrested me, even quietly, I'd have some things to say about it."

"Okay."

"And since you seem to have some big feelings about this relationship break, let's meet every day again."

A tear slipped down Chase's cheek before he could stop it. "Are you sure? I can find another sponsor if you want me to."

Kellan laughed. "Oh, that's big of you, but you're not getting off the hook so easy. No, you're gonna sit here on my couch and face the music. Nice try, though."

"Okay," Chase said sheepishly. "Thanks, man." He looked up then, wiping his face, and he found nothing but humor in the man's expression. "I appreciate it."

"You're welcome, Chase. And good news—you'll get to see her when you're making amends."

Chase made a face, which just made Kellan laugh again. He wasn't ready to laugh along, but the powerful relief of knowing where they stood had him feeling almost shaky. He took that moment of distraction to pack away the unkind words his anxiety had been throwing at him. He seized hope. Because Kellan was right—it was a good sign, even if it was ripping him apart. The very fact that she'd had the sense to step back instead of diving into "fix it" mode, trying to help, to coddle him, to explain away what he'd done proved that she was the right partner for him. And he was going to do whatever it took to get her back.

CHAPTER
FORTY: Letters

DEAR LIZZIE,

My sponsor says I can write to you, so I wanted to say I'm sorry. Addicts say that a lot, so often that it loses meaning after a while; just ask my brothers. But I don't think I've said that enough yet. I am sorry. I let my fear that I wasn't taking good care of you overtake my good sense. Maybe it was too early for us to get into a relationship, I don't know. But I've never felt about anyone the way I feel about you, and I didn't want to lose that. I didn't want to lose you.

Eventually, we will need to meet so I can make amends. Just throwing that out there. It can be brief; coffee, a walk. But it's important to me.

Love,

Chase

P.S. Hattie hired me to take care of Sir Patrick Stewart and Dame Maggie Smith, and I miss your help. They're a lot of work.

DEAR CHASE,

I accept your apology, but it's not like there was any chance of anyone else scooping me up in the interim, goofball. And I'm not going to see anyone else until we figure out if there's a future for us. So focus on you for a while. Get your feet under you again. Then we'll see.

I'm sorry, too. I let my fears drive me toward conclusions that weren't valid, and I felt pressure to do my job without appearing to favor you just because we're together. We can do the amends when you're ready.

Did you see that final Jeopardy! the other night? How the heck did he know it was Hesiod? I'd never even heard of the guy. And that's saying something.

Love,

Lizzie

P.S. Pancake misses you almost as much as I do. We are both being pathetic and whiny. On the upside, Gram has bought me a LOT of cookies, so . . .

⚬

DEAR LIZZIE,

There are a lot of cookies happening on this side of town, too. Mrs. Sánchez is spoiling the crap out of me every time I come over. But I've started exercising again. I took the dogs for a long walk last night (six miles!), and it felt good. Give Pancake a good tummy rub for me. I also called a counselor; I think it'd be good to talk to somebody about my mom.

*Yeah, seriously—Hesiod? Never heard of him. Jeopardy! is not as good without you. Nothing is. And I would like to point out that Mark *tried* to scoop, but you turned him down. So* *don't act like it's impossible. Thank you for bearing with me right now.*

    Love,

Chase

P.S. Still pissed?

DEAR CHASE,

    I need a hug. When you hold me, I feel like all is right with the world—or if not right, then faceable. I miss your hippy green tea scent. I miss your casual sense of style. I had to paint my own toes today: this week's color is Do Pass Go, and it's a bright, happy green that reminds me of the grass in the meadow when we watched the stars together.

    Can I call you? How'd the counseling go?

    Love,

Lizzie

P.S. Not so much. But still a little.

DEAR LIZZIE,

    Probably better that you don't call; I'd never get any sleep, staying up on the phone with you all night. Not that I'm sleeping so great at the moment. It's hard not to worry about you. I know you're a badass but when I wake up in the middle of the night, my anxiety whispers about how you're doing, what you're doing, whether you're okay. And since your last letter was all about needing hugs, I'm guessing you're doing about like I am. I've got you beat on pathetic, though: I let all the cats come into the house to snuggle with me the other night. Don't tell anyone;

the other animals will be jealous. Tore up my couch a little bit, too. Need to get some scratching posts if I'm going to keep that up.

Counseling went okay. We didn't get much into Mom, just that I haven't really seen a healthy relationship modeled for me. I've been thinking about that a lot. You're right; we need to have some boundaries, especially around my recovery. I know I violated your trust and my own best interest. I'm just struggling because it felt so right at the time. It felt like an act of love.

Maybe we could plan for lunch next week?

Love,

Chase

P.S. Still pissed?

DEAR CHASE,

As much as it pains me to say it, I think we should give it more time. I'm not avoiding you, I just want to make sure we're not falling into an unhealthy thing, you know? Maybe your counselor can help you figure out why putting yourself in danger felt like love. I love you and want you to be healthy. And if that means giving you time, I want to do that. There's no rush.

But please don't take anyone else to Martina and Carter's wedding, as it will actually kill me.

Love,

Lizzie

P.S. Not pissed, just missing you.

DEAR LIZZIE,

I'd sooner cut my heart out of my chest than take anyone else on a date; it belongs to you. Aren't you still coming to the wedding? Don't stay away because of me, please. She's your friend. You should be here. I promise I won't act relationship-y. I won't even talk to you if you don't want me to. Please tell me you'll come.

Love,

Chase

P.S. I mean it.

———— ⌖ ————

DEAR CHASE,

I had a good talk with Lottie today. (Yes, we're talking again regularly, and I think she has a crush on my boss, because she keeps 'dropping by' work on Fridays. I'm trying not to freak out about it.) She thinks we're being stupid, but she was polite about saying so. She says that everyone needs people to support them through difficult times, which I agree with. She doesn't think that isolating you from the people who care about you is healthy, either. The longer we're apart, the more I hate this. I don't know the right thing to do. How will we know when we're ready to try a relationship again? What do you think?

I don't like going to weddings alone. I don't have an appropriate dress. There's so many people invited, no one will notice whether I'm there or not. So it's not just about you . . . but maybe a little bit about you.

Love,

Lizzie

P.S. I love you.

DEAR LIZZIE,

I talked over your question with my counselor and with Gretta and Kellan. They all agreed that with some firm safeguards regarding drug availability, we should keep trying. That the benefits of being in a stable relationship outweigh the risks. But they also felt that if I started compromising my own boundaries again (skipping meetings, making excuses for having drugs around, not taking my anxiety meds, etc.), I'm probably not ready to be in a relationship yet. But they thought it would be good to make amends, at least.

I'd notice if you weren't there. I don't like going to stuff alone, either. So let's go together. It doesn't have to be a date, we'll just stick together, as friends. Might be good a first step for us. What do you think?

Love,

Chase

CHAPTER FORTY-ONE:
Lizzie

LATE. OF COURSE HE'S late. Lizzie's knee was bouncing like crazy under the metal table outside at Riverside. Every time someone walked in, she craned her neck shamelessly to see if it was him. She'd already drained her iced tea down to the last drop, and Paige had been over twice to check and see if she wanted anything else.

Yes. Chase. I want Chase. I want him back in my arms. I want him healthy. I want him safe. But more than anything, I just want to see him. But her boyfriend was not on the menu, so she politely told Paige that she was fine. It was far from true, of course; she could only think of one or two other times in her life she'd been farther from fine. If she didn't burst into tears the moment she saw him, it would be an act of God. Her thoughts had distracted her sufficiently that she looked up and saw him jogging toward her.

"I'm so sorry," he panted, hurrying over to the table, and she stood up quickly. He was still coming directly toward her, and she suddenly panicked. Was he going to kiss her? If so, would it be a friendly on-the-cheek kind of kiss or a more-than-friendly peck? Or a heart-and-soul, makes-you-want-to-melt kind of kiss that told her exactly how much he'd missed her? She knew which one she was hoping for.

But Chase stopped short, just out of reach, looking uncertain.

"Are we . . . Can I . . .?"

"I don't know," she said. "But I need to touch you." His worried face dissolved into complete longing. Chase opened his arms and she launched herself into them. *Oops, here come the tears.* He must have heard her sniffles, because he spoke softly into her ear, stroking her hair, whispering to her about how good it was to hold her, how much he'd missed her. That tenderness was her undoing, and the tears morphed into sobs. It was too public for this kind of thing, but as long as she kept her face buried in the darkness of Chase's shoulder, blocking out the world, she could pretend they were alone, and she could let go of all the pain of being apart. Finally, the tears ebbed, and she tried to take some deep breaths, hiccupping, wiping her eyes as she pulled back to look at him.

His sympathy was obvious in his gaze, but he was smiling.

"Well, I guess I don't have to wonder if you really missed me." He wiped his own eyes, and she noticed his tears for the first time. She hugged him again, rubbing her cheek against his scratchy jaw; she couldn't help it.

"Don't tease me. I'm fragile." She said it like a joke, even though it wasn't. How had she bonded with him so quickly? These last few weeks had been awful.

Chase kissed her temple and let her go. She sat down and tried to collect herself.

"How are you?"

Chase shrugged. "I'm sober. I'm working my steps. Still kind of a mess without you, but I'm hanging in there. What about you?"

Lizzie considered the question. "Miserable," she announced sincerely, and Chase smiled sympathetically.

"I'm sorry." He ran a hand through his hair and it stood on end. "I really am."

"It's not just your fault, it's my fault, too." She paused. "I know we came here for you to make amends, but I think I need to, too. I put a lot of pressure on you. And I'm sorry that I couldn't believe you that night. I was completely terrified, and I thought you'd been using me, and I . . . overreacted. I'm sorry I hurt you."

Chase was listening quietly, then nodded. "I understand why you couldn't take chances. I won't lie, it did hurt. But I also knew that you were just worried about my safety. I just wish you'd listened to me a little quicker."

"Or a lot quicker." She gave a shaky sigh. "I wanted to. I wanted to think I knew you better than that, but I never thought I'd find a prescription you'd filled in my car, so that just threw everything into question."

"Being in recovery means I don't get the benefit of the doubt." He said it so matter-of-factly that Lizzie's heart ached.

"I wish that wasn't true, but I think it might be. I'm still sorry. Will you forgive me?"

Chase reached out and put his hand over hers. "I will. And I'm sorry I put you in that position. I've thought a lot about how to make it up to you, but I don't know what's appropriate. If you wanted me to talk to your boss or make some kind of announcement at a town meeting, I could do that." The thought of him suffering any more embarrassment because of her made her feel a bit queasy, but she had to give him something . . .

"I will accept payment in foot rubs and toenail painting," she deadpanned, and Chase chuckled.

"It's a deal." He was staring at her, sort of softly, like he thought he might be imagining her.

"Can I buy you lunch?" he asked. When she hesitated, he grinned. "Come on, I know you're hungry. You're always hungry."

"I can't." It broke her heart to say it, and from the way his face fell, he felt the same. "It's not that I don't want to," she rushed on, "I just have another appointment and you were late, so . . ."

"I'm sorry I was late; I really wanted to be here, but Frank was supposed to pick up his dog, and his flight was de-layed."

"It's okay." She stood up. "Did your sponsor say anything about us being able to spend more time together again?"

"Oh!" His face brightened. "Yes, he said we could go to the wedding as a couple, and then we could talk more. See how it goes."

She nodded, relieved. It was a strange necessity, having someone else dictate the pace of their relationship, but she had faith that it *was* a necessity.

"Good. I really didn't want to go by myself. It'll be good to have you there," she said.

"Yeah, it'll be weird to be around so many family friends; they haven't really met me yet. It's not really about me, it's about Carter, but still."

"You're allowed to have feelings about it." And if he thought she wouldn't be taking note of who snubbed him, he thought wrong.

"Yeah. Exactly." He swallowed so hard, she could see his Adam's apple bob. "And I'm working on making amends to my dad, too."

Lizzie's mouth dropped open and her temper flared into flame, like sesame oil in a too-hot pan.

"What does he need amends for?"

"Well, he had to pay a temp all those months I was gone. Plus, I was still getting paid by TFPP. Not to mention the way I stole money from him to feed my habit."

She hated that he was right, but she swallowed her complaints.

"Okay, I guess that makes sense. Keep doing your steps and going to meetings, okay?"

Chase stood up and pulled her close. "I will. And you keep writing me letters and pick out a dress."

"I will." Crap, she was going to start crying again. Her dentist was going to think she was a total weirdo.

"I love you, Chase," she whispered. "We can get through this. We will." Then she pulled back and walked out before she could change her mind.

CHAPTER FORTY-TWO:
Chase

"DO YOU HAVE THE RINGS?"

"Hmm?"

"The rings, Chase. Do you have them?"

"Oh, yeah." He pulled out the velvet box out of his inside coat pocket and handed them to Carter, who rolled his eyes.

"Yeah, I didn't want them yet. But sure, I'll hold onto them."

"What? Oh, sorry, Carter. I'm sorry. Here . . ." He took the box back, but put them in a different pocket and knew he was going to have to search for them when they were up at the altar. His poor brother had enough stress as it was, dealing with a mid-August rainstorm ruining his outdoor wedding. Carter gave him a shove.

"Go direct flower placement, please. Just get them to the right room, they'll take it from there."

"Okay. Yes, I will." His heart whined that he wouldn't be able to see the front door when Lizzie got there, but his brain firmly insisted that this was Carter's day and he should focus up and fly right. In the ballroom, he'd gotten all the many person-sized vases placed more or less attractively, and he still had twenty minutes to go.

"Pastor's not here yet?" Francesca, Martina's sister, asked, and Chase shook his head.

"Not that I know of. Should he be?"

"Well, we're seating people starting in five minutes, so I should hope so. I wonder how fast I could get ordained on the internet."

Chase grinned; Maggie was right, Frankie was funny. "I'll text him."

Chase: You coming to this wedding or what?

The last few weeks had given Chase and Kellan a closeness that allowed for teasing. He'd drunk a lot of lemonade on the pastor's patio, talking things over, hearing more of his story. It was remarkably similar to his own, but instead of taking care of animals, he'd turned to taking care of souls.

Kellan: I got a flat.
Chase: Where are you?
Kellan: River Road, about two miles from the turnoff.
Chase: I'm coming.

"I'm going to go get the pastor; can you let Carter know?" Chase called to Frankie, and he got two thumbs up in answer.

It didn't take him long to find Kellan's hatchback . . . but he hadn't taken him for someone who'd have flares with him. The man was usually much more focused on people's hearts than things like roadside essentials. When Kellan stepped back, he saw who was kneeling in front of him, fitting the iron on the left rear tire, her sparkly purple dress dragging on the ground behind her.

"See, you tried to do the jack first, but it'll never work that way." She pushed a lock of her hair out of her face. "You've gotta loosen the lug . . ." Lizzie trailed off when she met his gaze. He was grinning like an idiot, he knew. He did not care. She was sizing him up in his tuxedo, and he could tell she liked what she saw.

"Can we use a multi-tool for this?" Chase asked.

Even though she was grinning, she looked like she might cry, too. She stood up and wiped her hands on a rag, moving closer to him. "Not for this, no," she whispered. "I missed you so much."

"I missed you, too." He wasn't sure what the touching rules were, so he stuck his hands in his pockets. But when she launched herself at him, he figured it would be okay to kiss her back.

"So these lugnuts . . ." Kellan started.

"Yeah, just keep turning that," Lizzie directed distractedly, as she continued to kiss Chase.

"We have to get to the wedding," Chase said gently, stepping forward to help his mechanically-inept friend.

"Okay, yes," Lizzie agreed, and she went to the back and somehow hauled out the spare without dirtying her dress.

"Sorry to ruin your reunion," Kellan said apologetically, "but they can't start without us."

"No, no, it's fine," Chase said. "It's the nail's fault, not yours."

"Nail?"

He tipped the old tire to show him where the nail had embedded itself in the rubber, and Kellan nodded. Lizzie dusted off her hands as she finished tightening the lugnuts again.

"Okay, you're good to go."

"Great!" Kellan jumped in and gave them a wave as he peeled out. Chase and Lizzie watched him go, then turned to each other and laughed.

"That was an enthusiastic greeting."

She blushed. "I got a little carried away."

"I've never been happier about that." He took her hands in his. "Have you forgiven me?"

She nodded. "But if you ever try to compromise your sobriety for me again, I will arrest you."

"I believe you." He squeezed her hands. "What did Captain Hansen say?"

"He said I was welcome to try again on car accidents when I was ready."

"Very gracious."

"It was. And he felt I made the right choice with not putting you in the holding cell, given the circumstances. He suggested that I take some investigation classes. He thinks I may be cut out for detective work more than accidents or other things."

Chase nodded. "I like that idea."

"They don't need us to start the ceremony, though, do they?" she said, giving him a coy smile, and he leaned forward to kiss her again until his memory slapped him.

"Oh crap! Yes, they do, I have the rings. We've gotta go." When Lizzie climbed into the front seat of his car, he gave her a quizzical look. "Do you have a flat, too?"

"Nope. I just need a little more time with you before I have to share you with everyone."

"We'll come back for it."

"Yeah." She squeezed his hand. "We'll figure it out."

CHAPTER FORTY-THREE:
Lizzie

IT WAS THE FRIDAY AFTER Thanksgiving, and they were at Chase's, recharging their emotional batteries. It had been a good celebration, but enduring it with both families was overly social for both of them and not without its potential pitfalls. Her sister had come home and surprised everyone by bringing a nervous Mark as her date. Lizzie had found it easier to be herself with Chase by her side, his frequent touch keeping her insecurities at bay. And Chase said his dad and Chris had both been polite, asking about his business, which was booming with everyone's upcoming holiday travel.

"Is there anything you won't eat?" He tossed himself a peanut, catching it in his mouth.

Lizzie munched her pickle contemplatively, flexing her feet against Chase's leg. "Not that I can think of. What about you?"

"Oh yeah. There's lots of stuff I won't touch. Unlike you."

"Shut up," she said, throwing a carrot at him. It bounced off his chest and rolled to the floor. The Millers' dog, Champ, ran over, sliding in his haste to see what treats had been dropped, only to sniff at the carrot and lie down in a huff. "What stuff won't you touch?"

"Dill pickles. Martina's freaky ferments. Cocktail onions. Black olives. Mushrooms."

"Oh, I don't like mushrooms. I know everything grows in the dirt, but mushrooms *really* grow in the dirt."

"They *taste* like dirt."

"Exactly. You get it. What else don't you eat?"

"I'm not crazy about curry."

"Red or green?"

"It comes in colors?" If it was possible to sound wide-eyed, Chase did.

Lizzie choked on her baby carrot as she laughed, and Chase patted her on the back until she got her breath back. "I'm going to make you Christmas curry," she gasped, still wiping the tears away. "And I'll make both. It'll be so festive."

Chase pantomimed laughter, then shoved gently at her shoulder. This thing, this comfortable way they had; she'd never had it with anyone before—not so wide as this. It was like the sun in a western movie, dominating the horizon of her internal narrative, it was everywhere she looked. Everything reminded her of something she wanted to tell Chase. Everything made her remember something funny or interesting or thought-provoking he'd told her. Everything. She couldn't imagine being without him. Well, that wasn't true; she had been without him, and it had been terrible. Lizzie was openly staring at him, and she wasn't embarrassed. That was the best part of it all; even times when she regretted something she'd said or done, he never made her feel ashamed of who she was. She watched him toss back another peanut.

"I'd like you to be my husband."

"What?" he asked, showing no outward reaction to the content of her message, just that he'd vaguely registered her voice, too quiet to be understood under the sound of the TV. She watched him, trying to decide. She could hide. She could lie. She could pretend that silly thought hadn't left her head, pretend that she hadn't just so un-romantically proposed to her incredible boyfriend. Or . . .

Lizzie sat up. "Pause."

Chase pulled his attention away from the TV and groped around in the couch cushions until he found the remote. He turned and gave her his full attention. Should she get down on one knee? She didn't have a ring or anything . . . she took a deep breath and took his hand in hers, bumping her thumb gently over his knuckles.

"I'd like you to be my husband." Lizzie kept her gaze trained on those knuckles . . . dusted lightly with blond hair, a little dry, a tiny freckle near his pointer finger. She was going to look up in a minute. She was giving him a minute . . . it wasn't because she was a ridiculous coward who just dove headfirst in a proposal completely unprepared. *I should have at least waited until we were done snacking. Waited for a sunset or something; I should've let the stars help me.* Then she felt warm fingers on her face, caressing her cheek, gently tipping her up to look at him. Based on his soul-melting smile, she hadn't needed help from the heavens after all. He moved in for his kiss slowly, much slower than she would've liked, but he made up for it when his hands came to her shoulders and he guided her back down against the couch.

"This is very unfair," he murmured, kissing his way toward her ear along her jaw. "You beat me to it by mere minutes."

"You heard me the first time, didn't you?" she grinned, and Chase pushed himself up to see her better.

"Yes, I did. I gave you the perfect out. I was totally going to do it tonight, I wasn't going to chicken out again this time, and then you come waltzing in—" his elbow collapsed, putting his weight against her again, and he kissed her hard— "cool as anything, all 'I'd like you to be my husband,'" he said, imitating her in a high falsetto. "And that's completely unfair, and I want a do-over."

"Okay," she said, brushing her fingers over his nape. "You can have a do-over. On one condition."

Chase nuzzled her neck affectionately. "Anything."

"I want a pickle, black olive, and mushroom cake at our wedding."

"Shut up," he laughed, tickling her with his scruff and his breath.

"They can be sweet pickles," she went on. "They don't have to be dill. Love is about compromise."

"You know, I'm so proud that you asked for what you wanted, I'll agree to the cake."

"Forget the cake. I want *you*."

"I sensed that," he said, slipping in kisses wherever he could between his thoughts. "It was kind of a dead giveaway when you said, 'I want you to be my husband.'"

"I'm sorry it wasn't more romantic."

"I'm not. It was perfectly you; direct, firm, yet polite. It's sexy as anything."

She felt the heat travel from her face clear down to her chest, and Chase propped himself back up on his elbows, grinning. "You're blushing, but you didn't tell me to shut up."

"No, you can keep talking."

"Careful what you wish for, Ms. Painter . . ."

"Mrs. Carpenter."

"Not yet. Soon."

"Yeah," she sighed happily, tipping her head back, pressing her hips up into him. "Soon. I don't want to wait."

"Let's have the wedding in the meadow or at Pine Mountain Observatory. At night, under the stars. Just a handful of our family and friends." She hadn't even thought that far ahead to all the grief of having a big wedding, but her stress melted at his suggestion. She didn't want the big church thing, and the fact that he knew that just confirmed why this would work. It would work. She turned over his words again and scowled.

"And your dad?"

He nodded. "Even him."

"Fine. But I reserve the right to eject him if he's being a jackass."

"He behaved himself yesterday and at Carter's wedding. Let's give him the benefit of the doubt . . . but agreed. No, I'll give you one better—I'll do it myself."

"That is better," she agreed. "Did you know I'm proud of you?"

"I could hear it again."

"I'm proud of you."

Don't miss a moment of Timber Falls fun!

Could Be Something Good (Daniel and Winnie)
Must be a Mistake (Kyle and Ainsley)
Right Back Where We Started (Martina and Crash)
More Than We Bargained For (Starla and Sawyer)
Just Getting Started (Lizzie and Chase)
Don't Push Your Luck (Christopher and Paige)

Also by Fiona West

Rocky Royal Romance (sweet fantasy romance)
Chasing Down Her Highness: a chronically-ill princess who fled from her responsibilities is forced to face the fiancé she abandoned and journey across a magically-unpredictable continent. Can she keep the life she's given up everything to build?

Breaking Up the Royals: a king caught between love and legality...can Abbie and Edward's relationship survive engagement and the opposition who wants to tear them apart again?

Serving Side by Side: a security professional finds herself paired with a shy, sensory-sensitive man on the night watch. Can their friendship blossom into something more?

Bringing Down the King: a single mother gets her dream job as a journalist, only to find herself caught in royal scandal, opposing her son's new mentor. When forced to choose between love and her career, can she still come out a winner?

Winning Back the Duke: a doctor takes an expedition with her brother's best friend that has life-changing results. Can she resist the underlying attraction that's been there for years?

Acknowledgments

TO MY EDITORIAL TEAM at Salt and Sage: you all rock. I can't say it enough: your professionalism, straight-up knowledge of your genres, and kindness make this so much easier. Mandy and Sachiko, thank you both for your expertise.

To my critique partners, Angela Boord, Rebecca, Ruth and Jen: you are both so good at picking out the little discontinuities, the little moments that could be amped up, pulling out what's good, but could be better. I'm so blessed that you enjoy reading my work.

To my expert readers, Elle, Bjørn, and Kathleen: thank you for helping me make this book as close to reality as I can! I so appreciate your time and your insights.

To my copy editor, Kristin Houlihan: I'm so glad to call you a colleague *and* a friend. Your courage inspires me and your professional skills take my work to the next level.

To my proofreader, Liz Schandorff: I keep waiting for you to tell me you're tired of doing this. Are you sure I can't pay you?

To my cover artist, Seth Smith: Do you know how many fangirls are gushing over this cover? It is not an insignificant number. You did that. 100% your fault. Thank you.

To everyone who's helped promote the book: Tressa at Prism Book Tours. Everyone who read an ARC: Melanie, Sarah, Karla, Smita, Nitya, Jenny, Andree, Paula, Meghan, Desi, Shay, Pragati, Marianne, Heather, Sara, Lisa, Sahana, Elyse, Laura, Tina, Melena, and Michelle. You ladies rock!

Thanks for helping me spread the word about my work. Couldn't do it without you.

Gratitude also to Ryan Hampton for his book *American Fix* and Judith Grisel for her book *Never Enough* for giving me a glimpse into the real lives of people in recovery. I am indebted to you.

And last, but certainly not least, thank you to my CFO, Mr. West. You're the salsa and guac to my nachos, babe. I love you so much.

Connect with Fiona!

Thanks so much for taking the time to sample my work. I hope you enjoyed reading it even more than I enjoyed writing it, though I doubt that's possible. Being an author is a dream come true, and getting to share my books with delightful, thoughtful readers like you just adds to the sweetness. Drop me a line and let me know what you thought or leave a review on Goodreads[1]!

Sign up for my bi-monthly newsletter, The West Wind, for freebies, deleted scenes, book reviews, and insight into my writing process at https://www.subscribepage.com/timberfalls.

On Twitter as @FionaWestAuthor[2]

On Facebook as @authorfionawest[3]

On Instagram as fionawestauthor[4]

On Goodreads as Fiona West[5]

Or email me at fiona@fionawest.net.

I love talking to fans!

---

1. https://www.goodreads.com/book/show/53491348-must-be-a-mistake

2. https://twitter.com/FionaWestAuthor

3. https://web.facebook.com/authorfionawest/

4. https://www.instagram.com/fionawestauthor/

5. https://www.goodreads.com/author/show/18433825.Fiona_West

www.ingramcontent.com/pod-product-compliance
Lightning Source LLC
Chambersburg PA
CBHW061349190726

48288CB00005B/1662